HOUSE FOR SALE SOLDIER INCLUDED

By Cora Seton

Author's Note

House for Sale Soldier Included is the second volume in the Elliotts of Chance Creek series, set in the fictional town of Chance Creek, Montana. To find out more about Lincoln, Charlotte, Carter, Amanda, Hudson, Nate, Gage and the other inhabitants of Elliott Ridge, look for the rest of the books in the series, including:

House for Sale Navy SEAL Included
House for Sale Airman Included
House for Sale Marine Included
House for Sale Ranger Included

Visit Cora's website at www.coraseton.com

Find Cora on Facebook at facebook.com/CoraSeton

CHAPTER 1

"**W**ELL?" LINCOLN ELLIOTT asked his mother. "I can tell you've got something you want to ask me. What is it?"

His entire family was gathered on the back deck of his parents' house overlooking Elliott Lake, as if they'd never left it. As if the whole town of Elliott Ridge hadn't emptied out twelve years ago and remained uninhabited until he and his brothers returned at the beginning of April. Now it was June and his parents had arrived last weekend in time to celebrate his youngest brother's wedding. Carter had exchanged vows with his bride, and his folks had enjoyed visiting their old stomping grounds, but soon they would need to return to South Carolina.

His father leaned against the railing close by dressed in jeans and a forest green shirt, focused on the boathouse that stood at the edge of the beach, probably calculating how much longer the roof would last before it needed a repair. His brothers sat clustered in a circle of deck chairs, in bathing suits or shorts, beach towels

1

draped around, chatting about everything and nothing. It was as if they'd all traveled back in time to their teenage years, before the problems that had forced their family, and everyone else, to leave the Ridge for so many years.

Lincoln's mother lifted an eyebrow. "You're right; I do have a question. When are *you* going to find a wife?" Celia Elliott stood only as tall as his shoulder, but she was a strong woman who never took any nonsense from him or his brothers. She wore white capris, a light blue top and sandals, and she looked younger than her sixty-something years.

Hudson must have been listening, because he sat up in his deck chair, slapped his thigh and crowed, "You owe me twenty bucks!" *Told you*, he signed to Lincoln surreptitiously. Lincoln glanced around to see if anyone else had noticed. He had four brothers, and Nate, the second oldest, had developed a secret sign language for them when they were kids, inspired by the characters in his favorite science fiction novel. What Nate, Carter and Gage, his oldest brother, didn't know was that he and Hudson had developed another sign language of their own. It was a twin thing.

Or it used to be. He couldn't remember the last time either of them had used it. They'd rarely been in the same place at the same time during the years they'd been away. All five of the brothers had enlisted in the military when they'd left their home, but none of them had served together.

The rest of his brothers focused on the new conversation. "Twenty bucks? For what?" Carter asked. He had the brown hair and eyes all of them shared, but his hair was a shade lighter than Lincoln's. He'd grown up during his years in the Navy, and his features were harder than they used to be, but his expression softened every time he looked at his bride.

"Lincoln bet me Mom would ask him when he was going to get married," Hudson said.

Lincoln nodded. Looking at his twin was like looking at a slightly inaccurate mirror. They were identical, but there were differences, too. They had the same dark brown hair and eyes, but Hudson preferred a scruff of beard to Lincoln's clean-shaven jaw. He had a tiny scar over his right eyebrow from where he'd fallen against the dining room table during a bout of roughhousing when they were eight. Hudson had always been the daredevil, choosing to fly fighter jets in the Air Force, while Lincoln had signed up with the Army and mostly kept his feet on the ground with the Special Forces.

"And you took that bet? You had to know she'd ask us all the same thing sooner or later," Nate said. He was the shortest of the brothers, although still over six feet, and his hair was a shade lighter than the others'. He was stockier than the rest of them, too. He'd spent the past twelve years in the Marines.

Lincoln's oldest brother, Gage, seemed lost in his own thoughts, but Lincoln wasn't fooled. Gage kept tabs on everything that happened around him. He had the same dark hair as Lincoln and Hudson, but his features were sharper and his eyes more deeply set. He'd served with the Rangers.

"I'm surprised Mom made it this far," Lincoln said. "Figured I'd win that money the moment she got off the plane."

His father let out a loud *humph*, which told Lincoln he'd been following the conversation and saw the humor in it. Amanda, Carter's bride, handed around glasses of lemonade and exchanged an amused glance with him.

"Don't tell me you're not ready to settle down," his mother said. "You're fresh home from a twelve-year stint in the Army. What are you waiting for?"

"Your mother's right. Time to get a move on," his father said. He shifted, and Lincoln wondered if his hip was giving him trouble. He was due to have it operated on in just a couple of days.

His parents had a point, he supposed. He had returned to Elliott Ridge to help his brothers make the family's lumber mill profitable again so they could resurrect the town the Elliotts had owned for generations. Under any other circumstances, it would make sense for him to look for a partner.

Unfortunately, he had a debt to pay before he could do so.

A big one.

"Well?" His mother took a drink of the lemonade Amanda gave her.

"Soon. I promise." He wasn't about to bring up the debt with everyone listening. It was his responsibility, and he would pay it.

"You didn't bring a plus one to the wedding," his mother said.

"No, he didn't." Amanda agreed. "Why didn't you bring a plus one, Lincoln?" She was clearly enjoying teasing him.

"I didn't have one to bring. No one else brought one, either." He gestured to his brothers, hoping to deflect his mother's scrutiny. He'd be happy to find a woman to spend his life with. These days Carter strode around brimming with energy and enthusiasm for the future. It had been a long time since Lincoln had felt like that—and it was his own damn fault.

"What happened to Katie?" his mother persisted.

"Who's Katie?" Amanda asked, moving to perch on the arm of Carter's deck chair.

Lincoln sighed. "She dumped me during my last deployment." He wasn't broken up about it, either, which showed she wasn't the one.

"What about the women around here?" his father grumbled. "None of them good enough for you?"

Lincoln glanced at him. He and his dad hadn't spoken much during his parents' time here. While his father was happy that Carter had gotten married, he hadn't approved of much else Lincoln and his brothers had accomplished so far. He seemed to think they were moving far too slowly.

"I've been here only a couple of months, Dad."

"So you keep saying."

"I'm doing the best I can. We all are." They weren't talking about him finding a girlfriend anymore. They were talking about how long it was taking to get the mill running at its former capacity. The lumber business had been the backbone of the community ever since the silver mine ran out during the 1930s. There wouldn't be an Elliott Ridge if they couldn't make a success out of it.

"I saw Hudson flirting with someone in town the other day," Amanda said, bringing them back to the topic at hand.

"I'm always flirting," Hudson said. "It doesn't mean anything."

Lincoln bit back all the cheap shots he'd normally throw at his brother if his parents weren't around. Hudson never lacked for female attention. He was boisterous and fun and never took anything too serious-ly. When they were teenagers, Lincoln used to wonder if people even noticed him once Hudson showed up. Identical twins ought to have the same luck with women, but Hudson played in a league of his own. More than once Lincoln had taken a shine to a girl only to have Hudson beat him to the punch.

"Stop comparing yourself to him, Lincoln," his mother said as if she'd read his mind. "Hudson likes to flirt. You're looking for that one special person."

There was no way to answer a pronouncement like that. "Sure thing, Mom."

His mother waved a hand at him. "Scoff all you want. It's true. Remember, Elliott men know when they meet *the one*. Right?" She turned to face her husband.

"That's right. Moment I saw you, I knew how it would all turn out," his father said complacently.

"Same thing happened to me," Carter said. "I spotted Amanda, and boom! Game over."

"Game just beginning," Amanda corrected him and leaned down to give him a peck on the cheek.

He kissed her back happily, and in a moment the two were lost in a mutual admiration that made Lincoln jealous. When would he meet a woman who looked at him like that?

He didn't buy the family legend, no matter what his father and Carter said. Love at first sight wasn't real. Besides, marriage was too important to take that lightly. He wanted what his parents had—a partnership that lasted through thick and thin. They'd seen boom times and bust times. They'd had to admit defeat and leave their home twelve years ago, then create a whole new life in a brand-new place. His father had health issues, was taking medicine for his heart and was scheduled for a hip replacement this week. Still, they treated each other with respect and care. Were genuinely happy to spend time together. Seeing them dance at Carter's wedding had eased his fears that their time in South Carolina might have put a strain on their relationship.

Lincoln's mother turned to face the house, and as her gaze traveled over its white clapboard exterior, a wistful expression came into her eyes. Lincoln knew his parents were waiting for the day they could move back. His mother had been reminiscing all week about the good old days when the town had been a going concern. Once, he thought he'd seen his father close to tears. They'd been down at the beach by the old barbecue pits where his dad used to hold court at family gatherings and community picnics. His dad had always loved to see all his people around him, knowing he provided jobs and homes for everyone who lived on the Ridge. It must be breaking his heart to know its inhabitants had scattered to the four winds.

"You boys have made a good start here," his mother said. "I have no doubt Elliott Ridge will be back on its feet in no time."

His father humphed again. "We'll see. Hate to think of Blake Warrington taking over the place."

Warrington was their neighbor of sorts. He owned a large property on the back side of the Ridge, and he'd made a bid to buy their land, too. The town of Elliott Ridge might have belonged to the Elliott family for over a hundred years, but Warrington wasn't much for tradition. He wanted to raze the place to the ground so he could double the size of the golf community he was building.

"We'll never let that happen," Lincoln assured his father, although concern tightened his gut. It was his fault his parents had even entertained such an offer when Warrington had made it last year. Instead of taking the cash, his parents had given him and his brothers a year to pay off the family's debts and bring their town back to life, but Warrington was doing his best to thwart them. He knew that if Lincoln and his brothers failed, his parents would have to sell.

"I hope you're right."

"Meanwhile, find yourself a wife," his mother said.

"I'll do my best," he told her, but he knew he was going to be so busy working to pay those debts for the next eleven months there was no chance of that.

"ARE YOU READY to go home? The game's going to be on soon."

Charlotte Holmes glanced up in shock at Ivan Gasparyn, the stocky man who stood beside her. He wore a dark, finely tailored suit that fitted the somber occasion, but his bored expression made it all too clear how little he cared to be here with her.

"No, I'm not ready to leave," she said, speaking more sharply to him than she'd dared in months. "This is my grandmother's funeral, and I'm going to stay as long as I like."

"Keep your voice down," he snapped, looking around to see if anyone had heard. The parish hall of St. John's Anglican church was full of people who had come to Iris Holmes's celebration of life. Charlotte's parents were long dead, and so was her grandfather, but her grandmother had participated wholeheartedly in the community and was well beloved.

"I will not," Charlotte hissed. "I barely saw her this year because of you."

"If you're going to act like a child, I'll go somewhere else." He stalked off, followed closely by several men in only slightly less expensive suits. Ivan liked to think of them as his entourage, but none of them spent time with him because of his wit or charm. They were his paid bodyguards, nothing more, nothing less. She'd grown accustomed to one or two of them tailing her every time she left Ivan's mansion, as well. She thought of them as her jailors and prayed every night she'd find a way to escape them.

Charlotte swallowed revulsion and grief. She couldn't believe her life had come to this. Trapped by her own stupidity and Ivan's iron control. Her grandmother gone. Two years ago, she'd thought all her dreams were coming true, but now she was living a nightmare.

If only all these people crowding around, carrying plates of finger food, chatting and reminiscing with each other about Iris's life knew what was happening in hers. What would they say if she simply shouted it out—that Ivan watched her constantly. That his thoroughbreds won races because he doped them. That he kept dangerous company—and carried a gun.

The knowledge that he—and his bodyguards—were armed even now kept her quiet. Ivan had made it very clear that anyone who helped her leave would pay.

The packed room was becoming overwarm, but Charlotte couldn't bear to leave the reception. With her grandmother gone, she had no one else. She'd lost her friends soon after she'd begun to date Ivan. He was good at making people feel unwelcome.

Someone bumped into her in the crush of people. "Charlotte?" he murmured in her ear.

Startled, Charlotte turned to find an older man in a rumpled suit standing closer to her than was strictly necessary. "Yes?" Who was this? Another of Ivan's lackeys come to round her up and force her home?

No, she decided. He wasn't dressed well enough for that.

"I'm Steven Prescott. Your grandmother's lawyer. She asked me to get in touch with you."

"Now?" Charlotte was incredulous all over again. First Ivan wanted to go watch a *game*, and now this stranger wanted to conduct business—at a funeral reception?

Steven kept his gaze averted, as if he was studying the nearby refreshment table rather than having a discussion with her. "You're hard to find alone. Your grandmother made me promise not to let Ivan hear a word of what I have to say."

"She did?" A tiny ray of hope pierced Charlotte's anguish, and she copied his body language, turning slightly away from him and surveying the room as if looking for someone else. If Ivan noticed her speaking for more than a few seconds to anyone, he'd come insinuate himself into the conversation.

"You know you need to leave him," Steven said.

"I've tried." Charlotte's voice cracked. She'd done everything you were supposed to do when you left a difficult relationship. Found a new job without telling Ivan. Leased an apartment she could afford on her own. Packed her things surreptitiously. Somehow Ivan had found out.

Steven winced. "I know."

"You know?" How could he know? She hadn't told her grandmother any of her plans—or what Ivan had done when he'd discovered them. Had tried to shield Iris from finding out how many mistakes she'd made.

"I've been watching you," Steven said with a shrug. "I was thrilled to report to your grandmother you were making moves to leave Ivan—and I was sorry when it didn't… work out."

Charlotte barely caught herself before she turned to gape at him. He knew she'd tried to get away—and the disastrous results? "Who are you?"

"A lawyer," he repeated. "A good one."

She didn't know what to say to that.

"I had hoped to extract you from your relationship with Ivan before your grandmother passed away." Steven frowned, as if he'd let himself down more than anyone else. "Her health deteriorated much more rapidly than I expected, however. I promised her I would help you as much as I could. So here I am. Helping."

She felt a tug at the pocket of the cropped black jacket she wore over her matching black sheath—the only outfit she owned remotely appropriate for a funeral.

"What are you doing?"

"Give me your phone," Steven said. He glanced over her shoulder. "We have only a minute or two, so if you want to get free from Ivan, don't ask questions. Just do as I say."

She hesitated only a moment. She wanted to get free of Ivan more than anything in the world. Charlotte passed her phone to Steven, and he handed it to another man who just happened to be walking by. The man kept going.

"He'll head in the opposite direction you're going to take," Steven said. "You do realize Ivan's been tracing you through that phone. Reading all your texts and emails. Listening to your calls?"

Shock pierced her. He could do that?

Steven shook his head. He must think her a fool, she thought.

"That's a burner phone in your pocket. My number is in it. Don't call me for at least a week. Go to the airport and get on a plane. And then get on another one and another one. Keep going for as long as you can stand it and then pick a place to lie low." He shoved a thick envelope into her hand. "Tuck that in your purse. You'll find prepaid credit cards, cash and your passport. Now, I want you to think of the very last place Ivan would look for you. Don't tell me," he hurried to add. "Don't tell anyone. Not even your best friend."

Charlotte swallowed the sob that rose in her throat. She didn't have one of those.

"Think," Steven told her.

She thought. Where was the last place Ivan would look for her? He liked to take her to flashy cities like Vegas, New York, Monaco, Rome. She'd loved those trips once.

What was the opposite of Vegas?

Montana, she thought. It was full of ranches and mountains and trees—but few people.

"Got it?" Steven asked.

She nodded.

"That's where you go last, when you can't stand flying anymore. You get off the plane, find a cheap place that no one would ever look at twice and lie low. Don't talk about yourself or your past. Don't call attention to yourself. Don't get in touch with the people you left behind." Steven looked at her intently. "Get lost, in the truest sense of the word, okay? This part of your life is over. Start again somewhere new. Can you do that?"

She nodded again, but her eyes filled. "I'm sorry," she said. "I wish I'd gotten to see Iris again. To tell her how much I loved her and what she meant to me."

"Your grandmother knew all that," Steven said firmly. "She loved you very much, and she wished she had more to give you. I'm the executor of her estate. I'll sell her house and possessions, and when I'm done, you'll get a small inheritance. I hope it helps. The important part is not to second-guess yourself when life gets hard. Don't sugarcoat your memories and reach out to Ivan once you're gone."

"There's no chance of that," Charlotte said. "I'm done with him. I'm done with men altogether."

"Don't say that." Steven touched her arm for just a moment. "You're too young to give up on love." He held up his hand so she could see his wedding ring. "Twenty-four years this August, and I would do it all over again in a heartbeat."

"I don't trust myself when it comes to men anymore," Charlotte said.

"Just because your first try turned out badly doesn't

mean the next one will. Learn from your mistakes, figure out what you want in a partner, then get out there and find him. That's what your grandmother would tell you. She had a happy marriage, too."

Charlotte's tears spilled over, and she hastily wiped a hand across her face. "I know what I want. Someone kind and honorable. Someone who cares about the people—and animals—around him. Someone who protects the ones he loves instead of bullying them into following his orders. Do men like that even exist?"

"Yes, they do. I'm one of them. Your father and grandfather were two more. Don't give up." He scanned the room, then turned to look at her. "Ready?" he asked. "When you walk out that door, you can't ever come back."

Was Steven right? Were there caring, loving men in the world? If she left now, could she have another chance to create the life she really wanted?

Every fiber of body ached for that to be true.

She took a shaky breath. Why not at least try? "I'm ready."

"Let's go."

"I HOPE YOUR trip home goes smoothly," Lincoln told his parents as they walked up to the departures counter of the Chance Creek Regional Airport a few days after their gathering on the deck. Amanda had asked to come along to see them off, needing to stop at the grocery store for a few things on the way home.

"I'm sure it'll be fine," his mother said. "You take

care of yourself. Take care of your brothers, too—and Amanda. Don't let Hudson get into trouble."

"I won't." It was a familiar admonition, as if he was his brother's keeper. Since when had he been able to stop Hudson from doing anything?

"You kids are getting old and slow. I didn't see Hudson up a tree once this whole week," his father said. "No logging going on, either. Guess he thinks he's got all the time in the world."

"Hudson has been helping with the mill. We needed all hands on deck to get it up and running first."

"Wait until you run out of logs. You'll wish you'd done things differently then."

"Oh hush," his mother said to his father. "They're doing what they can."

"Plenty of timber left in the High Ridge parcel," his father said. "Someone should get busy harvesting it."

"I'll bring that up with Hudson when I get home," Lincoln told him. Leave it to his dad to grow talkative at the last minute.

"Should have seen me back in the day. I could climb a tree faster than Hudson ever did."

"No, you couldn't," Lincoln's mother said. "No one is faster than Hudson."

"I could, too."

They were still arguing about it when they said their goodbyes. Lincoln's father shook his hand before they parted. His mother gave him a bear hug. They both embraced Amanda.

"Come for another visit soon," Lincoln told them.

"Got my surgery in two days. Won't be going any-where for a while," his father said.

"Take all the time you need to recover."

"It'll be fine." His father turned away, but his mother hung back and gave Amanda another hug.

"I'm so glad you're part of our family now."

"Me, too," Amanda said.

Lincoln's mother faced him. "Find a wife," she said again, hugging him, too. "Bring us back for another wedding."

"I'll see what I can do," he promised her and watched them go, cataloging the changes in them since they'd left the Ridge. He'd been twenty then. Now he was thirty-two. His parents were in their sixties. There were more lines on their faces. His father wasn't as certain in his gait anymore. Lincoln had a feeling his heart problems had undermined his confidence, alt-hough he'd never admit that. He'd lost weight, too. Once as muscular as any of his sons, his arms were thinner now, his face more angular. His dad had been nonchalant about his upcoming hip replacement through the whole visit, but Lincoln could tell he was worried.

"Ready to go?" Amanda asked softly when his folks were out of sight.

He nodded, but it was hard to turn toward the door to the parking lot. Memories washed over him of the good old days. Swimming with his brothers in the lake. Playing baseball with the other kids in the Circle. Riding horses on the trails. The Fourth of July beach barbecues.

It had been an idyllic childhood until hard times overwhelmed them. Hard times brought about by his own dumb ideas. He'd gotten too big for his britches, and his mistakes had taken his whole family—hell, the whole town—down with him.

Lincoln shook off his dark thoughts as he followed Amanda to the door. He was older now. Wiser. He wouldn't screw up this time. He'd right everything he'd done wrong in the past. Bring his parents home.

He scanned his surroundings automatically as he and Amanda walked outside, a habit he'd picked up in the military. A couple to his left were in a heated discussion, showing each other the screens of their phones while their little girl bent over a rigid plastic pet carrier, murmuring to the animal inside. Just past them stood a knot of men in business suits, something you didn't see often at the Chance Creek airport. They walked off in a group toward the parking lot. To his right, a pretty brunette in yoga pants, a gray T-shirt and black runners was looking through her oversized purse.

Lincoln focused on her, curious who she was. She looked a few years younger than him, but he hadn't seen her before. She hadn't gone to Chance Creek High, like he and every other kid in the county had. He'd have to ask around about her.

No, he told himself firmly. He wouldn't do anything like that. Not until he'd paid the debts his family had taken on because of his dumb ideas. He had eleven months to raise enough cash, and he couldn't waste a minute pursuing pretty women.

"Thanks for bringing me to town," Amanda said, distracting him. "Don't worry—I'm not doing a full shop for the week or anything. I just need a couple of things."

"No problem," Lincoln said. Amanda was in charge of meals for everyone who currently lived on the Ridge, so he understood what she meant. When she did her weekly shop for the whole crew, it took an hour or two. He was relieved this would only be a quick trip.

"Mr. Fluffy!"

The shriek from the little girl with the cat carrier made Lincoln stop short. A cat streaked past him, headed for the parking lot. The pretty brunette with the oversized purse looked up, and their gazes met—for an instant. She had expressive blue eyes framed by dark lashes, a full mouth, fine features and thick, wavy hair pulled back in a long ponytail.

Something pure and hot shot through Lincoln like a bullet from a gun.

She was the one. She was the woman he was going to marry.

"Stop! Mr. Fluffy!" The little girl raced past.

Lincoln's attention snapped to her, and he launched into a run. Girl and cat were heading straight for the stream of traffic leaving the airport.

Could he reach them in time?

He scooped up the girl in two strides, but the cat was faster. Lincoln kept going, hoping against hope he wasn't too late.

"GOTCHA!"

Charlotte closed her eyes and breathed a thank-you to the universe, her heart pounding. She'd watched in horror as first the cat and then its owner—a little girl no more than four or five years old—had raced toward the parking lot, but shock had frozen her in place. Thank goodness the dark-haired stranger had better reflexes. He'd lunged past her like a thoroughbred eating up the final meters of a track and had managed to snatch up first the girl and then the animal just in time.

She was almost afraid to open her eyes and risk the possibility of meeting his gaze once more, however. The first time had left her shocked and tingling all over. It was as if someone had raided her daydreams to create her perfect man. He was so handsome, his expression so open and alert, and he'd focused on her with... interest. Charlotte told herself it was exhaustion and fear leaving her so shaken by the experience. She'd been traveling for days, sleeping only an hour here or there in cramped plane seats. The stranger had caught her attention the instant she saw him. Then the cat and girl had raced past.

"Audrey, how many times did I tell you not to let Mr. Fluffy out?" the little girl's father cried as both parents rushed after her.

"She's okay," the breathtaking stranger assured them, gently cradling girl and cat as he strode back to meet them. "So is Mr. Fluffy." He was dressed in jeans and cowboy boots, a clean T-shirt stretching across his muscled chest. His dark hair was short, his bearing upright and confident. Charlotte remembered the description she'd given Steven of her dream man. Someone kind and honorable. Someone who cared about the people—and animals—around him. Someone who would protect the ones he loved instead of bullying them into following his orders.

Check, check and check. Maybe Steven was right— maybe there were good guys left in the world. A ridiculous hope fluttered in her chest. Could a handsome, kind, *normal* man like this one be part of her new life?

"No, he isn't all right! Mr. Fluffy's hurt! I let him out because he's bleeding!" Tears streamed down Audrey's round cheeks. She struggled in the man's arms, and he handed her carefully to her mother.

"Bleeding?" Audrey's father took the cat, who writhed and hissed. Sure enough, its paw was streaked with red.

"Oh, Lincoln, the cat *is* hurt." Another woman joined the group, a pretty blonde with long, straight hair caught up in a clip who put a hand on the handsome man's arm. If he was a thoroughbred, she was a dainty filly. Her wedding ring glinted in the sun, and disappointment washed over Charlotte like a frigid wave, shocking her all over again.

He was married. And she was a fool.

A single fool who'd stay single for the rest of her life if she knew what was good for her.

The problem was, she didn't want to stay single, despite her disastrous experience with Ivan. She wanted a husband and a family. True love. A home. Was that too much to ask for?

Probably.

Charlotte fought back her tiredness, lifted her chin and stepped forward with purpose to join the group surrounding Audrey and Mr. Fluffy. At least she could do something useful.

"Can I help? I'm a veterinarian." No time like the present to start making a place for herself in this new town if she planned to settle down here. Steven had told her to pick somewhere Ivan would never look for her. Waiting to board her first flight—to Santa Fe, New Mexico—she'd searched an online map of Montana for small, forgettable towns and found this one. Chance Creek. Now she needed somewhere to hole up and hide until Ivan forgot about her.

"If you hold him steady, I'll just take a look at that paw," she said to Audrey's father, projecting a confidence she hadn't felt in months.

"Thank you." He held Mr. Fluffy in a firm grip, while Audrey whimpered in her mother's arms.

Charlotte bent to look, finding herself blinking back the sting of unshed tears. She was exhausted and overwhelmed, that was all, she told herself. She wasn't sad that a handsome stranger was married. Lincoln could be as bad as Ivan, for all she knew. Anyone could fool you for a while.

Ivan had.

He'd flirted with her shamelessly from the first time she'd served him at the restaurant where she'd worked during veterinary school. Located near the Saratoga racetrack, it was fashionable among the track's patrons and Ivan casually let it drop that his horses often featured in the races there. Wealthy and sophisticated, and quite a bit older than her, Ivan had her thoroughly outclassed. When he'd found out her major, he'd made it a point to quiz her on the finer points of equine anatomy, and each time he came back, he requested a table in her section, and asked her more and more complicated questions. Each time she answered a question correctly, she could tell his opinion of her went up. At the end of his third visit, when she'd set his bill on the table, he'd placed his hand over hers. "Double or nothing?"

"What do you mean?"

"I'll ask one more question. Get it right, and I'll double your tip. Get it wrong…" He'd shrugged. "All this hard work for nothing. What do you say?" His gray eyes had challenged her, and she couldn't resist. She knew her stuff.

"All right."

The question concerned a finer point about the latissimus dorsi muscle. Charlotte answered it easily, and triumph had shot through her when he nodded.

"I'm Ivan," he'd said as he released her and took the bill. "Ivan Gasparyn. I think we'll be getting to know each other better." Of course, she'd seen his name on his credit card several times, but this was a formal introduction and she understood the significance of it.

When he'd got up to leave, Ivan had pressed a wad of bills into her hands. "Buy yourself something pretty," he'd whispered in her ear. "My little veterinarian."

He'd given her five hundred dollars that night and she'd had trouble speaking, excited by the boost to her bank account—and the knowledge he'd ask her out soon. Her hunch was correct. The following Friday he was back. He claimed a table for hours and when she finally left the restaurant, exhausted from her shift, she'd found him waiting for her outside, leaning against a very expensive sports car. He'd taken her out for a night-cap—and then took her home, as if their relationship was a foregone conclusion.

She supposed it was. He swept her off her feet with expensive meals, exotic weekend getaways, flowers and gifts. She'd never known a man like him.

Soon she thought she was in love.

She'd thought he loved her.

She couldn't have been more wrong.

Charlotte shook away the unhappy memories, stiffened her spine and straightened to face the little crowd. Ivan was well over a thousand miles away. He would never find her here—and she'd never let another man treat her like he had.

"Mr. Fluffy will be just fine," she assured Audrey. "Looks like he broke a nail. Don't worry; it will grow back. When you get home, clean the area and put a little antiseptic cream on it."

She stepped back as the family thanked her. Audrey's father carefully returned the cat to its carrier.

"Let's get Mr. Fluffy home," he said to his daughter. "He'll be happier there, and we can get him all fixed up.

Okay?"

Audrey nodded.

"Thank you. Both of you," her mother said to Charlotte and Lincoln. "I don't know what I'd have done if Audrey had been hurt."

"No problem at all," Lincoln said. He waved at the little girl, who buried her face in her mother's neck.

"That was quick thinking," Lincoln's wife said to him when they were gone. "By the time I pulled myself together, you'd already saved the day."

"I know," Charlotte said. "I didn't realize what was happening until it was all over. You reacted so fast!"

"I'm just glad I got there in time," Lincoln said. "Do you have a practice around here?" he asked Charlotte. "I've only been back in Chance Creek for a couple of months, and I haven't had a reason to call a veterinarian yet." He studied her, his dark gaze taking her in, reminding her of the way Ivan had looked at her in those early days. Lincoln's expression was open and friendly, however, rather than calculating, and Charlotte wondered how she appeared to him. She wore a pair of yoga pants and a T-shirt with the logo of a national park on it, both of which she'd managed to find in an airport gift shop. She'd acquired an oversize, black quilted purse, into which she'd stuffed everything she'd bought so far—snacks, bottles of water, another shirt and pair of pants. She'd pulled her hair back in a ponytail and wasn't wearing any makeup—she hadn't bought any yet.

Not her best look.

Still, she didn't get the sense Lincoln was judging

her the way Ivan would have. Ivan thought women were ornaments for men and should make an effort.

"Just got here myself," she said evasively.

"And that's all your luggage? You pack light. I'm Amanda, by the way," Lincoln's wife said.

Heat flushed her cheeks as Charlotte looked down at her oversize shoulder bag, embarrassed Amanda had noticed it was all she had. She hoped Amanda hadn't caught her reaction to her husband, as well.

"Are you staying at the Evergreen Motel?" Amanda went on, saving her from having to answer. "Doesn't look like anyone came to pick you up," she added when Charlotte raised an eyebrow. "The Evergreen is the only motel in town, but there are several guest houses. Maybe you're staying in one of them?"

Charlotte shook her head. "You were right the first time. I am booked at the Evergreen tonight, but I'm hoping to find a long-term rental." She meant to stay here for a while. Maybe forever. Like Steven had said, she couldn't go home.

Lincoln looked her over again with interest. Was he noticing her disheveled clothing and the smudges under her eyes? He must not have minded them, because he stuck out his hand.

"I'm Lincoln Elliott."

After a moment, she shook it. "I'm Charlotte."

"I'm still Amanda." Lincoln's wife smiled and shook Charlotte's hand, too. "What kind of a place are you looking for? Something in town or out in the country?"

"In the country," Charlotte said firmly. "Somewhere

quiet, where I'll be left alone." Where Ivan couldn't find her.

"Are you on vacation?" Amanda asked.

"Not exactly. More like I'm making a clean break and starting over."

"You're in luck, then. We know the perfect place where you can do that, don't we, Lincoln?" Amanda smiled at her husband and bumped his shoulder with her own. "It's remote, though. Forty-five minutes from town."

"Is it an apartment?" Charlotte asked doubtfully. Forty-five minutes was a long drive.

"A house," Amanda said. "In a ghost town," she added dramatically.

"A ghost town?"

"It's not a ghost town," Lincoln said. "It's just... empty. Everyone left twelve years ago. My brothers and I are trying to resurrect the place."

"It's been in Lincoln's family for over a hundred years," Amanda said.

"That's right," Lincoln said, nodding.

God, he was handsome. Charlotte was having trouble not staring at him and making a fool of herself. His shoulders were broad, his arms muscular. His eyes were to die for, she decided. A deep, warm brown.

And he was married.

"There are twenty-nine houses for sale and a bunch more for rent," Amanda said. "They're all really cute. There's a swimming lake and a big town hall. We even have a library. I'm in charge of that."

Not only was Lincoln married, but his wife was beautiful and seemingly without a care in the world. Her smile was contagious enough that despite herself, Charlotte smiled back. She couldn't even be jealous of this happy woman. "Sounds wonderful. I love to swim."

"We're looking for people who don't mind pitching in now and then. Folks who want to build a real community. There's a lot to do," Amanda warned her. "All the houses need work, for starters, but there are other opportunities for people who are motivated. We've got a small hotel and restaurant that aren't being used right now. There's even a chapel."

"Amanda likes to slip in there now and then and get away from us men," Lincoln put in. When his wife looked up at him in surprise, he shrugged. "I've seen you."

"He's right, I have kind of made it my personal sanctuary, but I don't mind sharing," Amanda said.

"I'd be happy to help out where I could, but I'd want my privacy, too," Charlotte said. She was adamant about that.

"Of course," Amanda said. "You can pick and choose when to join in. Right, Lincoln?"

"Right." He was still watching Charlotte, and she wondered if he had reservations about inviting a stranger to their community. There was a military air about him she recognized. Something in his posture. The way his gaze flicked up to scan their surroundings now and then.

"How many people live in the town now?" she

asked.

"My four brothers and a bunch of temporary workers," Lincoln said. "Dennis, the caretaker, and Carolyn Snyder, who lived there when we were kids. She moved back last month," he explained. "The town was a thriving concern until we had to shut down the lumber mill twelve years ago and everyone left. Now we've got it going again. Soon we'll get our logging operation running, too. We'd be happy to welcome a veterinarian to town."

"What kind of vet are you?" Amanda asked.

"I specialize in horses," Charlotte hedged. She didn't mention thoroughbreds, determined not to leave a trail of crumbs Ivan could trace to follow her here. She didn't know Lincoln and Amanda yet. Maybe they were the kind who posted their every thought on social media.

"Lincoln has horses. Two of them."

An odd way to phrase it, Charlotte thought. If Amanda's husband had horses, didn't they belong to her, too?

Maybe she didn't like riding.

"Nate has one as well, and I'm sure there will be plenty more on the Ridge soon. We've got large stables and paddocks," Lincoln said. "Besides, Chance Creek is teeming with them. There's always a need for a veterinarian in a cattle town."

That was one reason why she'd picked the place. "It sounds interesting." Was it too good to be true, though? More to the point, was their community obscure enough to escape Ivan's notice?

Maybe it was foolish, but she hoped Ivan would lose interest in her if she eluded him long enough. She'd never return to Saratoga, but if she kept her distance, surely he would move on.

Lincoln must have noticed her hesitation. His gaze sharpened. "Something wrong?"

"No. It's just…" What could she say? "I… don't know anyone here." That was true enough.

"You do now." His slow smile did something to her insides, and Charlotte tried in vain to steel herself against it. Her throat was dry when she tried to swallow. Was Lincoln always so… captivating? How did his wife stand it?

Amanda leaned closer to him, as if to stake her claim. "Is the newcomer deal still on?" she asked her husband.

Charlotte fought for control of her emotions. She was not falling for a married man. That broke all her rules, and she'd violated enough of them already.

"Newcomer deal?" she heard herself repeating, mesmerized despite herself by Lincoln's smile. "What's that?"

CHAPTER 2

I T TOOK LINCOLN a moment to realize what Amanda meant, but in a rush, he understood the opening she'd given him. When Carter came home to Elliott Ridge two months ago, he'd bought one of the town's long-empty houses for himself at market rate, but when he spotted Amanda for the first time, he'd decided then and there he was going to marry her someday. To lure her to the Ridge and keep her there long enough to start a relationship, he'd made up the newcomer deal and offered to sell her his house for a dollar. Of course, at the time, she hadn't known it was *his* house...

It had worked. Amanda had moved to the Ridge, accepted Carter's help with her new house's renovations, and they'd fallen in love. Now it was *their* house.

Was Amanda urging him to try the same trick with Charlotte? He sure wouldn't mind spending time with her to see where things went. Awareness of her prickled over every inch of his skin, and his fingers itched to touch her. The sweet curve of her cheek, her long, dark lashes and full lips all called to him.

Still, he held back. There were several reasons why offering Charlotte the newcomer deal wasn't an option. For one thing, he hadn't bought one of the houses in Lucy's Corner, the part of the town they'd received permission to subdivide.

For another, he'd planned to use all his savings to help cover the debts his family owed when their loans came due next spring.

For a third—

Charlotte reached up absently and tugged on her ponytail, elongating the curl at the end and letting it go so it bounced up and down a couple of times.

His throat went dry, and his pulse kicked up.

He'd like to wrap that ponytail around his hand and pull her in for a kiss. Feel her body against his. Get her alone and—

Hell.

Wait. What had he been thinking about?

"I think Charlotte would fit right in on Elliott Ridge," Amanda said brightly. "Maybe she should come and look at the houses at the very least."

"What is the newcomer deal?" Charlotte was focused on Amanda, and Lincoln hoped she hadn't tracked where his thoughts had gone. He didn't know what was the matter with him. He had a plan—a good one. And there wasn't room for a woman in it.

Even if she was *the one.*

He looked Charlotte over again, thinking it had to be raw lust interfering with his reason. He hadn't been with anyone for a while, and he was overdue for some fun. Unfortunately, it was going to be a long time until fun—or love, or marriage, for that matter—came into the picture. He had work to do.

The one. What a joke. You couldn't know seconds after seeing a woman that you wanted to spend your life with her. Guilt pricked his conscience, however, as he thought back to what his father and Carter had said on the deck several days ago. Family lore insisted you could. Even Lincoln's grandfather, when he was alive, had claimed he'd fallen for Lincoln's grandmother at first sight. Supposedly, it had been the same for Elliott men for generations.

"We're offering some of the homes at a discount. House 37 is particularly nice," Amanda said.

Lincoln turned to her sharply. He'd had his eye on number 37 ever since Carter claimed number 23. Had Amanda guessed that somehow, or was it just a coincidence?

"It's a great starter home for a family," Amanda went on. "Do you plan to have kids, Charlotte?"

Charlotte's brows rose, and Lincoln couldn't blame her. What kind of question was that?

"I'm curious because I want *my* kids—when I have some—to have friends who live close by," Amanda clarified.

"Oh. I… don't know." Charlotte's gaze flicked to Lincoln again. "I guess… someday?"

Kids? Lincoln swallowed hard. He wanted kids if he was honest with himself. He didn't want to wait a whole lot longer, either. Still, paying those debts came first.

"If you move to Elliott Ridge, you'll have to hurry up and start your family," Amanda was saying. "Or your children won't be the same age as mine."

"Amanda." Lincoln shot her a look. She was going to scare Charlotte off if she kept going like that, and he didn't want to scare her off, whether or not she was *the one*. He wanted…

Lincoln wasn't ready to admit what he wanted.

"Lincoln told you about his brothers. Three of them are single," Amanda said with a mischievous grin.

"Amanda!" Lincoln turned back to Charlotte. "She's got matchmaking on the brain," he said apologetically. He didn't like the idea of Charlotte considering any of his brothers as a possible father to her future children.

Charlotte shrugged after a moment. "I guess there are worse things to be obsessed with." The furrow between her brows was back, though.

Amanda must have noticed it, too. "I'm just kidding, Charlotte. Forget Lincoln and his brothers. When you're ready to meet someone, there's a whole town full of men in Chance Creek. No one's going to bother you if you don't want to be bothered. Except maybe Hudson," she added with an impish smile. "But you can handle him."

"Hudson?"

"Lincoln's twin. Same face, different personality." Amanda's smile broadened. "He flirts a lot, but he's a good guy. They all are."

Charlotte's gaze flicked Lincoln's way again. "There are two of you?" The idea must have struck her as funny because she smiled—for a moment. Lincoln's whole body woke up as if lightning had struck him.

"I'm the better version." Hell, there he went again, flirting with her, which he shouldn't do since he didn't have time for women.

Charlotte's smile faded. "I don't want trouble from any men."

Lincoln sobered quickly. He could tell there was a story behind that statement, one that involved Charlotte being hurt. His hands balled into fists, and he forced them open again. He didn't know anything about her past, and she hadn't asked him to avenge it, either.

He wanted to be the man she'd ask if she had anything to avenge, Lincoln decided. He wanted—

"Had enough trouble from men already?" Amanda asked Charlotte gently.

After a moment, Charlotte nodded. "That's all behind me now, though. I'm looking to make a new life of my own. Do you think I can do that on the Ridge?"

"Absolutely," Amanda said. "It's paradise there. You'll see. The perfect place to start over."

Lincoln was glad Amanda was there to answer, because he was stuck on the idea that Charlotte had experienced trouble from men. Now his protective instinct really kicked in, leaving him itching to get closer to her. He'd never thought of himself as a possessive type, but he had the feeling he could be that way about Charlotte. He wanted to step between her and any trouble she might encounter. Wanted to tell other men to back off.

Then he wanted to get to know her a whole lot better. What made this woman tick? When she was among friends, was she outgoing? Reserved? What were her hobbies?

What did she think of men like him?

He supposed he'd better offer her the newcomer deal if he wanted to find out. He could make sure she had all the peace and time to herself she needed to heal from whatever happened in her past. Meanwhile, he could work hard and make a success of the mill so his family could pay off its debt. Maybe when he'd done his bit and was ready to welcome a woman into his life, Charlotte would be ready to welcome a man.

Was she the one?

Yes, something told him. Some inner certainty it was hard to ignore. He almost took a step closer to her when he remembered he'd just met this woman. He didn't want to scare her off.

"Amanda's right," he said, with more conviction than he had any right to. "The Ridge is just the place for a person looking to start over."

"And we need more women. Please say you'll come and check it out. Carolyn Snyder is great, but she's busy all the time, and I need a friend my own age," Amanda said.

For a long moment, Lincoln was afraid Charlotte would say no. She bit her lip as she considered the plan, making his blood heat again. He wanted to kiss that mouth of hers someday—but he needed to be patient.

"Please?" Amanda reiterated.

Charlotte twirled the end of her ponytail around her fingers, driving Lincoln wild. "Okay," she said finally. "I'll come and look. No promises."

Relief rocked Lincoln to the core, and he realized he didn't know what he would have done if she'd said no. Kept going, he supposed, but all his joy in returning to the Ridge would have been gone.

He was putting too much weight on this chance meeting. Lincoln didn't like the way his emotions had been hijacked and his life script was careening out of control. For all he knew, Charlotte had a million irritating habits, and he'd hate her in a week.

No, that interior voice said. *You won't. She's the one.*

"No promises," Amanda agreed, bouncing on the balls of her feet. "But you're going to love it there. I swear. Do you have a car?"

Charlotte shook her head. "Not yet."

"No problem. You can ride with us."

As Amanda led the way to the row where he'd parked his truck, Lincoln gave up fighting the situation. Charlotte was coming to check out the Ridge. If she stayed, he was going to pursue a relationship with her—someday.

"You don't mind a quick stop at the grocery store, do you?" Amanda asked Charlotte. "I'm the head chef, and I need a few things for dinner tonight."

"Head chef, huh?"

"Town manager, librarian and postmistress, too," Amanda told her happily.

"I don't know what we'd do without her," Lincoln

said. He hoped neither woman noticed the huskiness of his voice. Had the last five minutes changed the course of his entire life? Somehow, he knew they had.

Charlotte ignored him. "I don't mind waiting while you run your errand," she said to Amanda.

"Great," Amanda said.

Satisfaction filled Lincoln. He was going to marry Charlotte. It was only a matter of time.

LINCOLN'S TRUCK WAS dusty but solid-looking, a workhorse of a vehicle meant to be used, not shown off—a little like its owner, Charlotte thought.

"You sure you didn't leave any luggage in the airport?" Lincoln asked as he opened the door for her.

Charlotte shook her head, finding it hard to talk directly to Amanda's husband, still way too attracted to him for comfort. She'd have to work on that if she was going to live near him.

"Leave her alone, Lincoln," Amanda said, settling into the passenger seat. "Charlotte doesn't owe us any explanations. Charlotte, if you're looking for a new life, you've come to the right place. When I got here a few months ago, I thought mine was over. Now I'm married and the happiest I've ever been."

"A few months?" Charlotte couldn't hide her surprise. Amanda had married Lincoln that quickly after she'd met him?

Amanda laughed. "The Elliott men work fast."

"That we do." Lincoln shut the door, walked around the vehicle and got in on the driver's side. "We've been back in Chance Creek only a few months ourselves."

"Where were you before?" Charlotte asked, trying to imagine a whirlwind romance like that.

"Scattered to the winds with the military," Lincoln said. "I was in the Army."

"Oh." So she'd been right.

"It's only ten minutes to town," Amanda said brightly. She pointed out landmarks on the short drive, and when they pulled into the grocery store parking lot, she said, "Do you want anything?"

"I can come in and give you a hand," Charlotte said.

"Only if you need to buy something, too. Otherwise it'll be quicker if I go on my own." Amanda got out of the truck. "Keep Charlotte company, Lincoln."

"Will do."

"Don't you want to go with your wife?" Charlotte asked him, panicking a little at the idea of being alone with a married man she found so damn attractive. With her luck, she'd stutter and blush when he spoke to her.

Amanda laughed, one hand on the door. "I'm not married to Lincoln. I'm married to his brother—Carter. Be right back."

Having dropped that bombshell, she shut the door and walked away. Suddenly the truck's cab felt far smaller than it had a minute ago.

"Carter is the youngest in the family," Lincoln explained. "Strange that he was the first to marry, but as soon as he met Amanda, they got on like a house on fire. That's why we were at the airport just now. My folks came out for the wedding last Saturday and spent the week with us. We were seeing them off."

"Got it. So you're…"

"Single," he affirmed, as if reading her mind. He held up his left hand and wiggled his fingers.

No ring.

He smiled, and she swallowed, desire curling deep inside her.

He was single.

Available.

If she was smart, she'd get out of his truck right now.

CHARLOTTE WAS ABOUT to bolt.

Despite the hungry way she'd looked at him a moment ago, her interest had turned to panic, and now she was reaching for the door. If she clutched her purse any tighter, she was going to snap its straps.

"Don't worry; I won't bite."

Her eyes grew larger, and Lincoln cursed himself inwardly. Wrong thing to say. "I have way too much on my plate to think about women," he added, not sure if he was making things better or worse. "How about you? Is there an angry husband combing Montana for you?"

She pulled back. "No. I've never been married."

"You're not running from the law, are you?" he joked.

"What? No. Nothing like that!"

"Lincoln! Good to see you!"

Lincoln sighed in relief when Megan Lawrence rushed up to the open passenger-side window and leaned her arms on the door. He was making a mess of things and a distraction was just what they both needed. "Megan. Good to see you, too. Just dropped my folks at the airport."

"You must have been sorry to see them go. It was so nice to meet them again at Carter's wedding after all these years. I wasn't sure if they remembered me."

"Of course they did."

"I was a teenager when you all left," she pointed out. She barely looked older than that now, with her cheeks flushed and her curly hair a little wild. She must be having a busy day.

"True." Plus she lived in Chance Creek, not on Elliott Ridge, so she wasn't around a whole lot. "I'm pretty sure they knew who you are, though. Megan, meet Charlotte. Charlotte, this is Megan Lawrence. She's our real estate agent and a good friend." For a little while he'd thought she and Gage might become a couple. They'd clicked at a mutual friend's wedding after he and his brothers had returned to town, but nothing seemed to come of it.

"Hi. Nice to meet you," Charlotte said from the back seat of the extended cab. Megan leaned farther in.

"Nice to meet you, too. How do you know Lincoln?"

"We just met," Charlotte said.

"At the airport," Lincoln said. "Charlotte's looking for a house, and we're going to show her some." Too late, he realized his mistake.

"On the Ridge?" Megan asked in surprise. "To buy

or to rent?"

"I… offered her the newcomer deal," Lincoln said, bracing himself. Megan knew all about the newcomer deal from the time Carter had employed it, and she wasn't going to like it that Lincoln was doing the same thing.

A series of emotions crossed Megan's pretty face. Shock. Disbelief. Anger. "Really?" Her voice was thick with all the things she didn't say. He and his brothers had offered her the commissions for any house sales she made in Lucy's Corner, once they'd fixed up those houses a bit in preparation to sell. If he and his brothers kept giving them away before they were even on the market, she wasn't going to earn a dime. He'd have to buy one at full price before selling it to Charlotte for a dollar, but they didn't pay commissions to Megan for houses they bought from themselves.

"Don't worry—we're working hard to clean out the rest of them. We'll have a bunch ready to sell soon." He caught Megan's eye and lifted his brows meaningfully.

"Oh. Sure thing."

Lincoln could tell she didn't believe him.

"I mean it," he said firmly. "It's a priority to get you those listings."

Megan accepted that with a sigh. "Good to hear."

"Is there something wrong?" Charlotte asked, looking from one to the other.

Megan straightened a little, suddenly all business. "Not at all," she assured her. "Lucy's Corner is a part of Elliott Ridge that only recently received permission to be subdivided, and Lincoln and his brothers are cleaning all the empty houses there so I can sell them." She smiled at him sweetly, letting him know she was going to hold him to his promise soon. Did that mean he'd have to rush to finish cleaning them out?

Pursuing Charlotte was becoming complicated.

Lincoln decided he didn't care one bit. He'd simply work at the mill all day and clean those houses at night, giving him two ways to earn money to add to his family's coffers. The faster they paid off those debts, the sooner he could move on with his life.

"Where are you from, Charlotte?" Megan asked.

"Saratoga," she said. "In New York." Lincoln was happy to see she wasn't clutching the door handle anymore.

An East Coast girl, he thought. "Isn't there a race-track there?" he asked.

"That's right."

"Never been to one," he admitted.

"Me, neither," Megan said.

"You aren't missing much," Charlotte said.

"Any family back there?" Megan asked.

"Not anymore. I lost my grandmother recently. She was all the family I had. My father died shortly after I was born, and my mother passed away when I was eleven. Health issues."

Megan's face creased in concern. "I'm so sorry to hear that. What a hard time you've had."

"Thank you. I miss them all," she admitted.

No wonder she felt she needed a fresh start, Lincoln

thought. He understood grief. When he'd left Elliott Ridge at twenty, he'd thought it might kill him, and it had taken years to think of the past without his breath hitching in his lungs. He was so lucky to be given a second chance. Maybe he could give Charlotte one, as well. He and his brothers—and Megan and everyone else on the Ridge—could become her new family.

"I lost my folks not too long ago, and I'm… having a hard time, too," Megan said. She looked surprised by her own admission, and guilt squeezed Lincoln's chest. It wasn't just Gage who'd taken Megan for granted. They all had.

"You should come up to the Ridge more often," he told her. "Charlotte is going to need friends."

Both women looked a little startled by his statement, but Charlotte nodded. "He's right. I will—if I stay."

"I hope you do stay. Let me get your number, and I'll call you in a few days. I can show you around Chance Creek after you settle in a bit," Megan said. "You'll want to come down off the Ridge sometimes." The women exchanged numbers, and Lincoln put Charlotte's number in his phone, too, liking the feeling of having it there.

"I have to get back to work. Talk soon!" Megan loped off with a bounce in her step, and Lincoln thought he'd done a good thing by promoting a friendship between the women.

"There's Amanda," Charlotte said.

CHARLOTTE SAT BACK and watched the scenery go by as

Lincoln drove, more comfortable with the situation after talking to Megan. If two normal, well-adjusted women were so at ease with Lincoln, he couldn't be a bad guy.

Just as he'd told her, the trip took about forty-five minutes, winding first through town and then out of it, heading through ranch land and up into the hills.

Amanda pointed out landmarks of interest, telling her who owned the ranches and how long their families had been in the area. Lincoln corrected her when she got the information wrong, and Charlotte could tell Amanda was trying hard to belong here the way Lincoln and his family did. When they began to drive through the forested hills, Lincoln gestured at the landscape outside his window.

"My family owns a large parcel of forest out that way on High Ridge. We'll start logging it again soon." He told her how his family had tried to balance harvesting trees with planting new ones. How important it had been to his father that they treat their property as a resource for countless generations of Elliotts, not just for the personal gain of the current one. She liked listening to him. Ivan had never talked about things like legacy. He had no interest in children or building something to pass on. The horses he bought to fill Gasparyn Stables were for his own financial benefit, not for a future generation's. Long before she'd left him, Charlotte had wondered why one man needed so much. "It's hard to get the balance right," Lincoln finished. "You can't plant a forest and have it turn out the way nature does it. I wish we could."

"It sounds like you feel a real connection to your family's property and business," she said.

"I do." He glanced her way in the rearview mirror. "Don't you feel connected to Saratoga?"

"No," she said. "Maybe I used to, but not anymore. My family never owned much property, anyway."

"Got it."

"What made you want to be a vet?" Amanda asked. "Did you have pets when you were a kid?"

"No. Grandma did offer to get me a kitten once, but I wanted a horse. Needless to say that was out of the question."

"You wanted to learn to ride?"

"I wanted to be a jockey." Charlotte pressed her lips together. She hadn't meant to tell them that. "Unfortunately, my dad was six-four. My mom was five-seven. By the time I hit sixth grade, it was clear I wasn't jockey material. I figured the next best thing was to buy a racehorse. Then my grandmother told me how much one cost." She shook her head. "That's when I hit on veterinary school."

"That's expensive, too," Amanda said. "Did she help with it?"

"As much as she could." This was treading on dangerous territory. Despite her scholarships and her grandmother's assistance, she'd had student loans when she'd met Ivan, which is part of how he'd gotten control of her so quickly.

"So you do like the races," Lincoln said.

"I used to."

Not anymore.

Lincoln nodded. "Welcome to Elliott Ridge," he said a moment later, dropping the topic. He turned onto a road marked Elliott Way, which wound uphill, then made a large circle around a grassy area. The settlement spread out around them. To her right, a rambling, white clapboard house overlooked a lake. Ahead of her were several larger buildings. To her left, more houses marched in curving rows, some clustered on flat ground, others in tiers up the side of the ridge that must give the little community its name. It all looked tidy, except for several piles of broken-down appliances in the grassy circle. Those were eyesores, but she figured they were there for a reason. Given the clean interior of Lincoln's truck, she doubted he was a man who let trash pile up.

She clutched her oversize purse and took in her surroundings as Lincoln parked in front of the white house. The lake was sparkling in the sunshine, riffled by a light breeze. The forested Ridge was pretty enough now in high summer but might cast a shadow over the houses during the long Montana winter. The small, unassuming homes suited the little community.

Across the Circle, a road cut through the houses and disappeared into the forest.

"The mill is down that way," Lincoln told her, then pointed to another road that edged along the lake. "That one eventually leads to the old silver mine."

"Whose house is this?" She gestured to the white one they'd parked in front of.

"My parents'. I grew up here. They live in South Carolina now, but we hope they'll move back when the town fills up again. Carter and Amanda live in number 23 on Second Street, but the rest of us are still camping out in our old bedrooms." He pointed at the road that led to the mill. "That part of town to the left of Center Street is called Lucy's Corner. Those are the homes we have for sale."

Charlotte nodded. From what she could see, the houses in Lucy's Corner were on the small side but big enough for her purposes. All she wanted to do was disappear for as long as it took for Ivan to forget she'd ever existed.

However long that was.

"Who's that?" she asked, catching sight of an old man heading their way. His stride had a hell of a hitch, like an old mule that had seen some hard living. Someone ought to have worked on that leg long ago. Would have saved him a lot of pain.

Charlotte stopped herself. She had a bad habit of seeing every living creature through the lens of her veterinary practice, judging their gait and working out the parameters of care needed to fix it. She wasn't in charge of fixing men, she told herself. She wasn't even in charge of fixing horses anymore.

"That's Dennis. Don't mind him," Amanda said. "He's gruff, but he's an old softy once you get to know him. He's been caretaker around this place his whole life. He kept it together during the twelve years everyone was gone." She opened the door to the truck and got out, and Charlotte followed suit. Lincoln joined them by the truck bed.

The caretaker looked to be in his seventies, with a heavy paunch, a halo of thinning white hair and a deep frown. Dressed in work-worn pants and a torn flannel shirt over a grubby undershirt, he wouldn't have been tolerated around Gasparyn stables, but Charlotte knew that looks could be deceiving. Anyone who moved that fast with that painful gait had to be a hard worker.

"More trouble, huh?" the man said to Lincoln as he shambled up to them.

Lincoln frowned. "No trouble here."

"That's what your brother said when he brought *her* back here." He jabbed a thumb toward Amanda. "I told him he'd regret it, and I was right!"

Lincoln faced him. "You know very well Carter doesn't regret bringing Amanda here one bit. You walked her down the aisle at her wedding last week! Stop being such a drama queen. Charlotte, this is Dennis. Dennis, meet Charlotte. She's come to look at the houses we have for sale, and if you don't scare her away, she might buy one."

Dennis harrumphed. "Her coming here settles it. It's another Calamity Year, just like I told you. Where are you from?" he demanded, turning to Charlotte.

"New York, originally," she told him. Calamity Year? She supposed that summed up her life pretty well right now, but she didn't know how he could guess it.

"New York?" Dennis made it sound like she'd said the moon. "Who comes from New York?"

"About twenty million people."

Dennis narrowed his eyes, but she thought she might have scored a point. "What're you doing here?"

"Charlotte is a veterinarian," Lincoln said. "I figure there's lots of work for a vet around here. Hell, we have some horses of our own, and we'll probably have a lot more of them by the time we're done." He turned to Amanda. "Would you mind if we take Charlotte to your place first? She can freshen up and check out your renovation before we look at the other houses. That way she'll know what's possible. See you around, Dennis."

"I'm happy to have met you, Dennis," Charlotte said. She was. Good workers were valuable, and this man obviously cared about Elliott Ridge. She bet he knew everything there was to know about the place.

Dennis grumbled but walked away.

"He should really get that looked at," Charlotte said, watching him go.

"What do you mean?" Lincoln asked.

"That limp."

"That's an old injury." Lincoln brushed it off. "He's walked like that all my life. He wouldn't appreciate us interfering, either." He retrieved the bag of groceries. "Let's go."

Charlotte put the problem out of her mind and followed Lincoln and Amanda across the Circle, down Center Street and left onto Second Avenue, where they turned in the driveway of a pretty, cabin-like house with a nice front porch. Amanda took the lead, but Charlotte's gaze kept slipping back to Lincoln. His gait was strong and true. He wasn't a thoroughbred, but his lines were pleasing, and he was obviously healthy. In his prime.

Stop it, she told herself. Good gait or not, Lincoln should be off limits until she'd learned to stand on her own two feet. When she had a home and a job, could easily pay her bills and was saving for her future each month, then she could think about dating again. This time, she'd make sure at least five friends approved before she allowed a man near her. Five new friends, since she'd lost all her old ones.

Charlotte squared her shoulders and followed Amanda and Lincoln to Amanda's house. Things were different now. She would never let a man isolate her like that again. She wouldn't let one get close to her until she was sure she could hold her own in a relationship.

But when Lincoln offered her his hand as they walked up the steps, she took it.

Which didn't make any sense at all.

CHAPTER 3

"LET ME STOW away these groceries, and I'll get us some drinks," Amanda said as she opened the door. "I've got pop, seltzer and juice. What do you want?"

"I'll have a seltzer," Charlotte said.

"Pop for me," Lincoln said. He led Charlotte to a couch, sat down with her and reluctantly let go of her hand as Amanda bustled into the kitchen. He gestured to the room around them. "What do you think? Carter and Amanda did a good job, didn't they?"

While the house was small, it was bright and cozy, the floor plan as open as it could be. Charlotte liked the way the rooms flowed one into the other and all the large windows let in plenty of sunshine.

"It's a wonderful house. I love the kitchen." Most of it was visible from where they sat, with a large island separating the two rooms.

Amanda beamed at her as she returned with their drinks. "I do, too. Of course, we eat most of our meals at the town hall with everyone else right now, but I still get to use it when I whip up a snack for just us two. Carter was renovating this house when I moved here. We ended up finishing it together, but he's the one who designed it and chose most of the materials."

"He did a terrific job. Both of you did."

"I never dreamed I could have it so good before I got here." Amanda sat down in an easy chair across the room.

"Where did you live before?" Charlotte asked.

"LA." She exchanged a look with Lincoln that he understood. Her story wasn't a happy one. "I like it much better here."

"Despite it being a Calamity Year?"

Uh oh, Lincoln thought. He'd hoped Charlotte would ignore Dennis's ramblings. He hurried to smooth the waters. "Don't pay attention to Dennis. He's been on a kick about the Calamity Year all spring. It's just some story he made up." He was afraid she'd think Elliott Ridge was dangerous. "We're perfectly safe up here."

"Apparently there was a strange year back in 1933 when the mine ran out of silver, before the Elliotts turned their hand to lumber," Amanda added. "According to Dennis, women kept drifting into town, each one in more trouble than the last."

"But it's just a story," Lincoln said again.

"It's not like someone is trying to kill you, right?" Amanda joked.

Lincoln sent her an exasperated look, but he knew why she'd asked the question. Amanda's father had almost managed to do her in when she first came to Elliott Ridge, which is why Dennis was so sure he was right.

Charlotte choked on the sip she'd just taken of her drink. "I sure hope not."

"Then there's probably nothing to worry about," Amanda said.

Lincoln was grateful for the distraction when the front door swung open, but his mood dimmed at seeing Hudson walk in. His brother never passed up the opportunity to hit on a pretty face. What if he scared off Charlotte?

What if he won her over?

Hudson had a history of doing that. The two of them had been inseparable when they were young, but after puberty hit, their companionship had turned into relentless competition. Lincoln was never sure if they had the same taste in women or if Hudson had an uncanny way of guessing which ones he liked—and asking them out first. It happened so often, Lincoln had started to date girls he wasn't attracted to, hoping against hope Hudson would steer clear. Things came to a head their senior year in high school when Hudson took the competition too far. Now they tolerated each other, but that was about the extent of it.

They'd rarely been in the same place at the same time during the past twelve years, and the separation had smoothed over some of the bad blood between them, but tension tightened in a band around his chest at the thought of Hudson making a play for Charlotte.

He wouldn't step back and play second fiddle to his twin this time.

"Who's got something to worry about?" Hudson asked. "Are you talking about Dad? Did something happen?"

Charlotte straightened and looked from Lincoln to his brother. He knew she was taking in their similarities. His brother's tone surprised Lincoln, though. He wasn't usually one to jump to conclusions like that.

"Nothing's wrong with Dad," Lincoln said. "When I dropped him and Mom at the airport, they were both fine."

"Good." Hudson nodded. Then he caught sight of Charlotte. "Who's this?"

Lincoln reluctantly made the introductions, the tightness back in his chest. "Charlotte, this is Hudson, my brother. Hudson, this is Charlotte. Why aren't you at the mill?" he added, wishing Hudson was anywhere but here.

"Needed to clear my head, so I took a walk. Noticed the lot of you entering Amanda's house and came to see what was going on."

"We met Charlotte at the airport," Amanda said. "She's looking for a house."

"Really? That's good news. We could use more women around here." Hudson came to shake hands with her. Lincoln noticed he held on a little longer than was necessary, and irritation began to simmer inside him.

"I haven't seen much of the town yet." Charlotte

pulled her hand away.

"I'll give you a tour in a minute," Lincoln assured her.

"Or I could," Hudson offered. "You should get to the mill, Lincoln. You're the boss, right? Need to set a good example for the workers."

"I'm off until after lunch," Lincoln reminded him. "You're the one who's supposed to be running things this morning. Get back to work."

"Charlotte? What do you think?" Hudson asked her. Lincoln's irritation increased. Just like he thought; his brother was back to his old tricks.

"Sounds like you have a job to do," Charlotte said pertly. "Lincoln, I'm ready any time you want to go." She stood up. "Amanda, do you mind if I use your powder room?"

Lincoln would have laughed at Hudson's expression if he didn't think it would start a fistfight, something that didn't seem appropriate in Amanda's living room. Hudson wasn't used to that kind of rebuff.

"Let me show you where it is." Amanda got to her feet and led the way. Hudson watched their progress. Lincoln could almost see the gears turning in his brain. Nothing moved Hudson from casual interest to real obsession quicker than a woman blowing him off. His twin was halfway smitten with Charlotte now, but Lincoln knew he'd won this round.

"Back off," he told his brother when the women were gone.

"Hell, no," Hudson said cheerfully. "Charlotte can

choose for herself who she wants to be with."

"She might not want to be with anyone."

"We'll see about that."

"YOU'VE GOT TWO Elliotts interested in you now," Amanda said in a low voice when she'd led Charlotte to the back of the house.

"I'm not here to make trouble between brothers," Charlotte said. She didn't want any more drama, period. Ivan had provided enough of that.

"Those two compete about everything," Amanda said. "At least, that's what Carter says." She pointed to a door. "Powder room is in there." She smiled. "I hope you decide to stay. Hudson is right; we do need more women around here."

"I'm looking forward to seeing the rest of the town." Charlotte slipped into the little room and shut the door, glad to be alone for the moment. Hudson's arrival had thrown her off balance. His charm offensive reminded her too much of Ivan. The first day she'd met him, Ivan had touched her like that, almost caressing her fingers before he let them go. At the time it had excited her. Now the memory made her shudder.

She faced the mirror and smoothed an errant tendril into her ponytail, wishing for all the makeup and products she'd left behind in Saratoga. Soon she'd find a place to live and start replacing them, but for now her bare face left her looking younger and more vulnerable just when she wanted to project strength and competence.

She supposed she shouldn't be too hard on Hudson. He was cocky, but he didn't have the slick edge that Ivan had. She'd gotten good at spotting creeps lately, and she didn't think Hudson fit that profile. It was interesting to compare the brothers, though. Where Lincoln was clean-shaven, Hudson sported several days' growth of beard. Where Lincoln walked with purpose, Hudson moved with a kind of swagger. If the two of them were horses, Hudson would be faster out of the gate, but Lincoln would beat him every time through sheer commitment to purpose. Ivan, on the other hand, was the kind of vicious stallion that would bite out the throat of a rival and win the race covered in blood.

Ivan isn't here, she reminded herself. There was no reason to think he'd be able to track her down, either.

She'd make it clear to Hudson she wasn't interested… and she'd keep Lincoln at arm's length, too, despite her attraction to him. If she had to choose between the brothers, she'd choose Lincoln, but right now she needed to put herself first. Find a home, find a job, create safety and security so she'd never be at the mercy of a man's cruelty again.

She shivered a little at the thought of how much worse it all could have been. What if she'd married Ivan? There'd been a time she would have happily done so.

She freshened up and returned to the living room in time to see Hudson leaving. He paused, halfway out the door. "See you later, Charlotte. You'll stick around for lunch, right?"

"We'll see," she said firmly. She felt it best to show Hudson, and any other man who came along, that she was a woman who made her own decisions in her own time.

He hesitated a moment longer, then nodded and shut the door behind him.

"Ready for that tour?" Lincoln asked.

"Sure am." She was determined not to let her worries about Ivan stop her from moving on with her life.

"I'm going to the town hall," Amanda said. "Come over for lunch when you're done. We eat together, and the mill workers join us for lunch and dinner," she explained to Charlotte. "The guys take turns serving breakfast to the family. I handle the other meals."

"Sounds like you handle everything around here."

Amanda laughed. "Not really, but I do keep busy. When I get tired of one job, I just move on to the next one. We'll talk more at lunch. I look forward to hearing which houses you like."

They parted outside, Amanda walking back toward the Circle, while Charlotte and Lincoln stood at the end of the driveway.

"There are twenty-nine empty houses in Lucy's Corner," he said. "We can walk through all of them if you like, but if you know what you're looking for, we could narrow it down a bit."

Now they were alone again, she was aware of Lincoln in a visceral way, despite all her determination not to be. To her surprise, she didn't feel a trace of fear around him. During the first few days after she'd left

New York, she'd often found herself looking over her shoulder, afraid Ivan would pursue her, and she'd thought that feeling would color her reaction to any new man she met, but that wasn't the case with Lincoln.

She liked the shape of his jaw and his intelligent gaze. She didn't get the feeling he was calculating his return on investment the way Ivan had with every social transaction. She liked the way he watched her, as if interested in everything she had to say. It was going to be hard to keep her head straight around him, but she'd find a way.

As she hesitated, she heard the mill in the distance, the whine of saws transforming logs into lumber. The town was situated in a forest, sunlight coming through high branches. The day was warm, and the air smelled fresh, with a tang of newly cut lumber. Despite her worries, Charlotte relaxed, her shoulders lowering for the first time since she'd left New York.

She knew she should tell Lincoln she couldn't afford to buy a home yet. Steven had given her enough cash to last a month or two if she watched her pennies, and she would get herself a veterinarian job just as soon as she could, but even with the small inheritance she would receive, she doubted she could get a mortgage until she was more established in the community.

She opened her mouth to ask to see some of the rental houses, then closed it again. She was curious about these empty houses for sale. A girl could dream, couldn't she? After they toured a couple, she could let Lincoln know a rental was probably a better fit.

What *did* she want in a house?

"Front porch or no front porch?" Lincoln prompted.

"Definitely a front porch." As long as she was dreaming, why not ask for the best? Ivan had owned a mansion in Saratoga, but rather than choosing one of the town's wonderful old Victorians, he'd had a new monstrosity built for himself. She'd never felt at home in it.

"One story or two?"

"Two, I think." There was something mesmerizing about having this man's attention focused on her. Lincoln's eyes were the most stunning shade of brown. He stood with feet planted wide, his hands on his hips. They were large and square, and dwarfed hers, making her feel dainty.

She didn't often feel that way. Working with horses day in, day out left her fit and sure on her feet. She had always been sporty and couldn't remember anyone ever describing her as delicate. Ivan, only an inch or two taller than her, had dominated her with his will, his anger and his wallet. If Lincoln tried to dominate anyone, it would be through his size and calm self-assurance, but she didn't think he'd ever try that with a woman. Amanda was far too relaxed around him for Lincoln to be that kind of man.

"Okay. What about inside? Anything special you want?" he asked.

"Um... a good bathtub? Something I can soak in?" It was one of her little luxuries. She loved to light candles, put on some music, pour a glass of wine and relax at the end of a trying day. "And a lot of windows. I like to feel I can see outside."

"I know a couple of places that fit that bill." He held out his hand, and Charlotte found herself taking it again. His large fingers wrapped around hers reassured her and brought to life a longing inside her she'd told herself she'd long ago left behind. Boundaries, she reminded herself. She needed to set boundaries with Lincoln.

And she would—later.

For now, she allowed her hand to remain in his, telling herself it was the last time she'd do so. She liked walking beside him, matching her stride to his, aware of Lincoln as a man, not just as a person. She'd forgotten how delicious raw attraction could be. These last few months she'd thought she'd never feel desire again.

Lincoln led the way to a little blue house with a sharp roofline. It had a generous front porch and a solid wooden door that creaked when he opened it. Inside, it was a little musty from being shut up a long time, but the kitchen had been gutted and the walls prepped with primer.

"I like this one because the living room is so big," Lincoln said. "It's got decent bathrooms, too." He took her inside and showed her around. "The windows probably need to be replaced, but it's a good space, right?"

Charlotte nodded.

Behind the living room was a small room he said

had been used as an office but could also be a bedroom. On the other side of the house, he showed her a sunny kitchen, a laundry room and a good-size bathroom. Upstairs they found two bedrooms and a bathroom that was nearly as large. It had a serviceable, but not terribly exciting, bathtub in it.

"We could swap out this tub for something better. Add a separate shower stall."

She nodded slowly. "That might work." She was caught up in the possibilities, but she was mindful that owning a house like this was only a daydream for now.

"Let me show you the backyard." It was fenced, with a small outbuilding that might originally have been a shed but had been spiffed up. "I think you'd call this a she-shed these days," Lincoln told her, "but when we were kids, it was Emma Crawley's studio. She was a painter. A passably good one."

"It's a nice space. Not sure what I'd use it for."

"Could be anything you want. Maybe a home office?"

"I guess." She thought that over and discarded the notion. She didn't like taking work home with her. "I like this house…"

"But…?" Lincoln prompted. "It's missing something?"

"A screened-in porch. I've always loved them." She knew she was wasting Lincoln's time, but she couldn't bring herself to suggest they look at a rental yet.

One more house, she thought. *Just for fun.*

He chuckled. "Amanda's right. You probably would

like number 37. Let's take a look at it."

Let go of his hand, Charlotte told herself when he turned to head back inside. *Let. Go. Of. His. Hand.*

Her fingers refused to comply. Instead, her imagination conjured up images of renovating one of these houses with Lincoln. Working hard and getting a little sweaty. Their hands touching when they maneuvered a board into place. Getting backed into a tight corner. Lincoln tossing away his hammer and bending close to give her a kiss.

Stop it, she told herself. Had she learned nothing during her time with Ivan?

Charlotte gave herself a talking to as she and Lincoln cut through the house and out to the street, then wandered over a block or so to another house. She was midtirade about responsibility, learning from your mistakes and cultivating patience when Lincoln stopped in front of a stately gray house. It wasn't large, but it knew its place in the world, Charlotte thought, a structure that held its head up high. Her heart gave a little throb. She already knew she wanted this house.

As she looked it over, Lincoln stood close, holding her hand firmly but lightly, his shoulder barely an inch from hers. An outsider might think they were a couple already, and Charlotte had to stop herself from leaning against him. Somehow it didn't seem like it would be strange to do so. It was as if they'd already known each other a long time, like they'd been friends growing up and now were turning into more.

What would it be like if Lincoln was her man? Was

he fun and playful? Serious and romantic? She already knew she wanted him.

Stop. It.

Charlotte would be mortified if Lincoln could hear the argument raging inside her head, but he seemed oblivious to it. Maybe he held everyone's hand when he showed them the houses.

She forced herself to focus. It was time to tell Lincoln she couldn't afford a house like this. Not yet, anyway. Before she could open her mouth, Lincoln tugged her up the seven steps to the porch, which ran the length of number 37. The door was painted black and had three small windows cut into it. Lincoln ushered her inside. She missed his hand encasing hers, but the press of his fingers at the small of her back was some consolation.

"This isn't one of the homes I cleaned out," he told her. "This one is in Hudson's section. It's got a good tub, though."

Charlotte liked it immediately. The stately living room to her right had large windows up front and two leaded ones high in the side wall that gave the room charm. Toward the back of the house, built-in corner display cabinets and a low-hanging light fixture suggested the dining table was meant to be positioned there. A door led to a large, screened-in porch at the side of the house, perfectly positioned to catch the breeze if she wasn't mistaken. Around the corner from the dining room was an open-plan kitchen with tons of cabinets and a large peninsula workspace.

An archway led from the kitchen to a family room on the other side of the house.

"These floors are real hardwood," Lincoln said. "We could easily sand and refinish them."

Charlotte could see the possibilities. She would have to price everything and make sensible decisions if she ever bought a place like this.

First she needed to find a job.

"Let's go upstairs," Lincoln said.

Her blood leaped in her veins at the suggestion, but she quickly realized he only wanted to show her the rest of the house. She gave herself another stern lecture as they climbed to the second story.

"Three bedrooms," Lincoln announced when they reached the top. "And two bathrooms." The one off the hall had a tub-shower combination, sink and toilet. The second was en suite to the largest of the bedrooms.

Charlotte peeked in. "Oh, look at that!" Past a dated vanity and toilet, an enormous old claw-foot tub reigned supreme next to the far wall. She and Lincoln crowded into the small room together.

"Hudson should have pulled out that linoleum." Lincoln gestured to the floor. "We can refinish the tub if it needs it. You don't mind taking on a project, do you? This house could be something special if we fixed it up."

"We?" she repeated. She hoped he hadn't somehow intuited her fantasies about renovating a house with him. She really needed to come clean about her financial situation.

"I'll help—after work and on weekends," he said. "That's part of the deal."

"It is?"

He nodded. "Like I said, we need more women in town, so I'll do what it takes to get you to settle here."

"Including home renovations?" That seemed drastic.

"Among other things." Lincoln paused, shook his head and rubbed a hand over his face as if to wipe off the smile tugging at the corners of his mouth. "Hell. That didn't come out right. Sounded downright creepy."

"It kind of did," she admitted with a laugh.

"Won't happen again."

She nodded, but he didn't have to worry. She'd already decided he was the furthest thing from a creep, which made him far more dangerous in a different way. He could steal her heart if he wanted to.

"Do you know much about renovations?" Charlotte asked, buying more time before she burst the bubble of the rosy scenario he'd been outlining for her.

"I'm a pretty capable guy."

"I can believe it."

His smile grew wider, and Charlotte gave up pretending she wasn't flirting with him. It was too late. She was hooked.

"How much is the house?" she asked, wanting to know if she could ever afford a place like this here on the Ridge.

He thought a moment, nodded as if he'd come to a decision and held her gaze with his. A shiver traced down her spine at the feral interest she saw there. Someday soon he was going to kiss her, and it was going to feel good.

"You remember Amanda mentioned we have a newcomer deal going on right now?"

"Um-hmm." Would he be willing to hold the house for her for a few months until her inheritance came through? It might be just enough for a down payment. If she could quickly find work, maybe she could convince a bank to take a chance on her after all.

"We're not advertising this for obvious reasons, but we're selling houses for a dollar to the first few takers. Just to get our community going."

"A dollar?" Surely she hadn't heard him right. The absurdity of it took her breath away.

She could afford a dollar.

"Plus the cost of renovations, but it's up to you how much you take on and how fast you get to them. We're starting from scratch," he added with a shrug. "Not many people want to take a chance and move to an empty town, and I don't blame them. If a community can't reach a certain population, it stagnates. We don't have any guarantees that we're going to succeed in resurrecting it, but you can be sure I'll do my best. We all will."

She supposed that made sense. Kind of. "What's the catch?"

"No catch, other than the cost of those renovations," he said. "We're looking for people who are ready to settle down in Elliott Ridge, so if you're thinking about turning around and selling out for a profit, I'd rather you told me right now."

"That's not my intention," she said truthfully.

"Good. This place was special when I was growing up, and I believe it can be that way again."

"I'm interested." She cut off his next words. He didn't have to sell her on Elliott Ridge, because she was already sold on this empty little town in its sweet-smelling pine forest. She was interested in Amanda's enthusiasm, Dennis's doomsaying and the Elliott brothers' ambitions. She was damn interested in Lincoln and the chance to have a normal, healthy relationship with a normal, healthy man. "I'd like to take the newcomer deal," she clarified. "But I don't understand how you can afford to offer it to me."

"It's more like we can't afford not to," Lincoln said. "We need to prime the pump. Get a few people like you to buy in and populate the town, so it doesn't seem so empty when other people come looking to purchase houses here. Do you have enough money to fix up a house?"

"Yes," Charlotte said slowly. "But not all at once." Her inheritance would help her get started, but she didn't have a job yet. If she couldn't find one, she'd be in trouble.

"That's all right. We can do it a bit at a time." He thought it over. "We serve meals in the town hall, so you won't have to do the kitchen right away, and this house's plumbing and wiring is sound—all of it was upgraded in the nineties. We'll tackle the bathrooms first, then refinish your floors and paint the walls throughout. You can do the kitchen at the end. Should work out just fine. Like I said, I'll help with labor."

"I'll do as much as I can myself." She was used to working hard, after all. She hadn't done much carpentry, but she was sure she could learn. She was sure she'd be able to find work, too, sooner or later.

He leaned against the tiled bathroom counter and looked down for a moment. When he looked up again, his expression was serious.

"There's just one thing," he said, and she sucked in a breath, bracing herself for what he'd say next. Of course there was a gotcha. This whole scenario was too good to be true.

"What's that?"

"I need to be honest with you. I think I owe you that."

"Okay. Now you're scaring me," she admitted.

He smiled again, but it was wistful this time, and Charlotte stilled at the way her heart sped up.

"You're my type," Lincoln said. "I'm having some feelings for you I probably shouldn't be having for a woman I met only a couple of hours ago. I want you to stay, but it's only fair to warn you that if you do, I'll likely make a play for you sooner or later." He shook his head. "I didn't have meeting you in my plans for this year, but that can't be helped. I think I'm going to have to rearrange those plans a little now you're here."

His admission both disarmed her and sent a thrill through her veins. She was beginning to think she might have to rearrange a few plans of her own. She didn't say that out loud, though.

"What if I shoot you down?" That was a far more sensible response.

Lincoln winced. "I'll survive. But, woman, I swear if you fall for Hudson, I'll be more than a little twisted up."

Charlotte laughed despite all the feelings swirling inside her. "Hudson's not my style," she reassured him.

"Then you'd be a first." His smile reached his eyes, and she found it hard to breathe. Lincoln was her type. How could she ever have thought Ivan was?

"I won't fall for him," she promised Lincoln truthfully.

"Good."

"DO YOU WANT to see any more houses?" Lincoln asked Charlotte when things began to feel a little awkward. He was suddenly aware of how quiet it was in this empty house. He wanted to take her hand again, anything to keep the connection going between them, but he figured he'd pressed his luck enough for one day.

He told himself it didn't matter that he was taking such a wild leap with his heart—and with his pocket-book. He'd intended to pass his savings over to the family coffers anyway, as part of his contribution to paying off their debts. By purchasing number 37 for market value, he'd still be handing his savings over to the family—he'd just get a house in return for his trouble. Which he'd then sell to Charlotte for a dollar.

He knew someday, if things worked out between them, he would have to set Charlotte straight about how the newcomer deal actually worked. After all, Carter had confessed to Amanda before they'd married that he'd tricked her and paid for her house himself. If a miracle happened and he married Charlotte someday, he'd do the same. If things didn't pan out, it didn't really matter. One way or another he was going to give that money to his family.

He *was* going to marry her, though.

He couldn't explain how he knew it. He just did, which admittedly made little sense. He'd met pretty women before. Smart ones, too. Ambitious ones. Hardworking ones. Sweet ones.

If someone asked what made him certain about Charlotte, what could he say? *She tugged on her ponytail, and I knew she was the one?* It was too—dumb.

"I guess I could see more houses," Charlotte said, interrupting his train of thought. "It's going to be hard to top this one, though."

"Let's check out a few more just so you're sure."

"Okay." She turned to go but crouched down suddenly and reached behind the open bathroom door. When she stood again, she held a tiny pewter horse figurine in her palm. "Looks like the house's former owners left this behind by accident. Do you know who they were?"

"The Petersons. I think they moved to Memphis. They never owned this house, though, only rented it. Elliott Ridge was always a company town, which means the Elliotts owned the houses, and the workers rented them from us."

"Got it. You should track them down and see if they want this back. Someone might have loved it."

"I guess I can do that." He put the horse in his pocket and gestured for her to go ahead of him down the stairs. Outside, they walked from house to house until they'd toured about ten of them that met Charlotte's basic criteria.

"Want to see any more?" he asked after they toured a yellow house with four bedrooms.

She shook her head. "I really like the gray one. Number 37."

"I like that one, too." He checked his phone. "It's time for lunch, but afterward, we can make a list of renovations and start assigning costs to them, so you can choose what order to do them in."

"What about paperwork? I have to buy the house first, don't I?"

Only then did Lincoln realize he'd glossed over a detail or two about their situation he really needed to clarify. "Let's go eat and talk things over with my brothers. We'll get it all worked out."

"What about my reservation at the Evergreen Motel? Do you think I should cancel it?"

He nodded. "We'll set you up with a bed in your new place for now. No need to spend a fortune on a motel room when you have a house of your own."

"A house of my own," Charlotte repeated. "I like the sound of that." She took out her phone. "I'm not getting service here."

"Use mine." Lincoln pulled out his own, tapped in his code and gave it to her. Charlotte quickly made the call and gave it back.

As they strolled to the town hall, Lincoln's fingers itched to reach out and take her hand again, but he restrained himself. All in good time. Once she'd settled in, he'd start small. Help her with some renovations. Drive her into town to do some errands. Help her find a vehicle of her own when she was ready. Then ask her out for a real date.

Inside, lunch smelled good, but before taking her into the cafeteria, he opened a door to the left.

"Here's the library Amanda was telling you about. She cleaned it up and rearranged it. It's still a work in progress, but it's a lot better than it was when we got here." Tall windows allowed light to stream into the large room. Rows of shelves held books, magazines, DVDs and anything else that had been left here over the years. There was even a collection of records.

"Those windows are amazing." Charlotte brightened and stepped into the large room to get a better look. "And there are window seats, too. You'll never get me to leave once I curl up on one of them with a good book."

She joined him in the entryway again, and Lincoln shut the door behind them. "It was Mom's pet project. People had been leaving books here for decades in an informal way, but she was the one who brought in the shelves, organized the books and set up a system to track them. Our mailboxes are over there. We'll get you assigned one." He pointed to a wall of them. "Here's where we eat." He led the way into a large cafeteria. A half-dozen tables had been set up near a pass-through window to an industrial kitchen. His brothers and most of the mill workers sat around them. As soon as the men noticed Charlotte, they turned to look with interest.

"Hey, everyone," Lincoln called out. "This is Charlotte. She's looking to settle here at Elliott Ridge, so be nice to her."

There was a chorus of greetings, and Charlotte gave a little wave. Lincoln brought her to the table where his brothers had gathered. He caught some of the mill workers checking out Charlotte and moved closer to her, gesturing to a seat by Carter. He wasn't too worried that anyone would make a move on her, though. Most of these men would be here for only another week or so. He and his brothers were in the process of hiring permanent employees now they'd proved to themselves they could get contracts for their lumber.

Carter greeted her with a smile. "Nice to meet you, Charlotte. Amanda has been telling me about you. I'm Carter Elliott."

"Nice to meet you, too," Charlotte said.

"You've already met Hudson," Lincoln said, taking up the introductions. "This is Nate, and that's Gage."

"Hi," Charlotte said.

"Food is ready," Amanda called from the kitchen. The men surged to their feet and moved to form a ragged line near the pass-through window. Lincoln and

Charlotte followed them. Amanda served people one by one, and they carried their trays back to their seats.

"We have industrial dishwashers back there that make cleanup relatively easy," Lincoln told Charlotte. "Eating all together like this has been a good system so far. This current crop of mill workers are temporary, and they're staying in barracks by the mill. The kitchens there are rudimentary."

Charlotte nodded as they sat down.

"Charlotte would like to buy number 37. The old Peterson place," Lincoln announced when his brothers had taken their seats and begun to eat. He waited until they looked his way, then casually splayed the fingers of his right hand on the table and brought them together again.

His brothers straightened. They knew that sign and its implications. It was part of the secret language Nate had developed when they were kids. This particular gesture meant *shut up and listen—and go along with whatever I say*. It had played an important part in their childhood when they'd all been apt to get into trouble and frequently needed each other to back up their alibis.

Luckily Charlotte missed the gesture.

"Charlotte's going to take advantage of the new-comer deal," he said clearly. Understanding dawned in his brothers' eyes. After all, Carter had pulled this same maneuver not too long ago. "I hope that's okay with all of you."

Carter looked down to hide a smile. Hudson considered him with a narrow-eyed gaze. Nate shrugged, but Gage shook his head and sat back in his chair. Lincoln knew he still wasn't convinced they could really make their town successful again.

"You explained all the rules?" Nate asked.

"Not yet," Lincoln admitted. "Do you want to take a stab at it?"

"If you want me to." He turned to Charlotte. "The main thing is that we're all here on sufferance."

"What does that mean?" she asked, her fork poised over her salad.

"Our parents still own Elliott Ridge," Carter said.

"And there's an offer on the table should they decide to sell the property." Gage spoke up from the head of the table. Lincoln squashed an urge to interrupt him. Charlotte ought to know everything about the situation, including that Gage was here reluctantly.

"Hey, I'm the one who's supposed to be explaining," Nate said. He waited for the others to go back to their meals. "Carter is right—our parents still own the Ridge. Gage is right, too—they've received an offer for the entire property. A good one. None of us wants to sell, but we're carrying some old debts, including a balloon payment due next June that's going to be a big stretch for us to make. We just got permission to subdivide part of the property, which is why you're able to buy house number 37. We'll use the proceeds from the sale of the houses and the money we make from our lumber and logging operations to keep up with the monthly debt payments and to cover the balloon payment next June. If we don't manage to pay it off, my parents will need to sell the whole town. If that happens, you could find yourself living beside a luxury golf course."

"Huh," Charlotte said. She put her fork down, salad untouched.

"But you'd be out only a dollar—plus the cost of your renovations," Lincoln reminded her. "And if the worst happens, you'll almost certainly be able to sell your property to the buyer for a very tidy profit. Blake Warrington has made it clear he wants to own the entire Ridge. Besides, you don't have to worry about that scenario. We're going to pay those debts and then the five of us will inherit the town. The place should be bustling by then."

"Cheers to that." Nate lifted his drink, and the others did, too, although Hudson still seemed peeved and Gage reluctant. They clinked their glasses together.

"To Elliott Ridge," Carter said.

"To Elliott Ridge."

COULD SHE REALLY buy a house for a dollar and settle here?

Charlotte couldn't believe how quickly her life had changed in one short week. Nor could she believe she was considering buying into a community she hadn't even heard of until a few hours ago.

She finished her salad and tackled her enchilada, which was surprisingly good, letting the flow of the conversation swirl around her. Lincoln and his brothers chatted about meeting an upcoming deadline for a lumber delivery. Amanda, done serving for the moment, came to sit with them. She jotted down menu ideas while she ate. The mill workers at the other tables were a boisterous bunch. Charlotte was aware she was receiving attention from some of them, but she kept her gaze on her plate.

Where would she go if she didn't settle here? That was a better question.

Charlotte couldn't imagine finding a house for a dollar anywhere else, and so far, Lincoln's family seemed like reasonable people. Amanda's presence on the Ridge reassured her. She hadn't seen anyone resembling Lincoln's description of Carolyn Snyder, but when she asked, he told her Carolyn often volunteered in Chance Creek and was gone most of the day.

But to buy a house—even for a dollar? That meant making a commitment, which was terrifying after the disaster her last one turned out to be.

She glanced up to find Lincoln watching her.

"What do you think?" he asked her.

"So far, so good," she managed to answer him. "I'd like to look around more after lunch, though, to get a better idea of what it would be like to live here."

"I'll give you the grand tour."

"I hope those are good walking shoes." Amanda leaned around Carter to talk to her. "It really is a grand tour if you want to see the whole place."

"I've walked miles in these," Charlotte assured her. She'd kept busy at the stables. When she'd first met Ivan, Peter Illych had been his on-site veterinarian. It had stunned Charlotte to realize someone could be so wealthy that he could keep staff like that on retainer, but Ivan had grooms, jockeys and more in his employ at the stables and a whole army of people to run his home and many businesses.

Hudson set down his fork and glared at Lincoln. "You blew off work this morning, and now you're going to take the afternoon off, as well? What kind of a foreman are you?"

"The kind who's got a potential customer to show around," Lincoln said. "I'll be only an hour or two."

"I can entertain myself this afternoon," Charlotte hurried to say to him. "You can show me around after work." She wrinkled her nose. "But it's the weekend. Why are you working at all?"

"For the moment, we're working every day," Hudson said. "Got bills to pay. Right, Lincoln?"

Gage looked up. Took in the tension between his brothers. "Grow up, Hudson. Any of us can run the mill for the afternoon. Of course Lincoln needs to show Charlotte around."

"I could show her."

"Seems like Lincoln's got things in hand," Gage said mildly.

Amanda leaned forward again, caught Charlotte's eye and smiled, cutting a glance toward Lincoln and raising her brows suggestively. Charlotte realized Amanda hadn't offered to take her around, even though she was the only one who didn't work at the mill. Was she deliberately trying to throw the two of them together?

Charlotte bit back a smile of her own, suddenly seeing the humor in the situation. Hudson was trying to start trouble because she'd turned him down earlier, but Gage had saved the day for Lincoln.

She was glad of that. She was looking forward to spending part of the afternoon with him.

"I appreciate you taking the time," she told Lincoln.

"My pleasure." Lincoln sat back and smiled at her.

Across from him, Hudson tapped his finger on the table a few times, clearly irritated.

"Language!" Amanda snapped, then bit her lip, sinking down in her seat as everyone else at the table turned to her. "Whoops."

Charlotte didn't know what she'd missed. No one had said anything remotely offensive.

"Are you serious?" Hudson asked Carter. "You taught her—"

"Time to get back to work." Gage stood up, scraping his chair over the floor. After a second's hesitation, Nate and Hudson stood up, too. They took their plates to the kitchen. Charlotte still didn't know what was going on.

"Sorry," Amanda said to Carter as she gathered her dishes.

"Don't worry about it," Carter said, giving his wife a hug before following the others.

Charlotte took her last bite of enchilada, pushed her plate away and turned over the sequence of events in her mind. What had just happened? Had she missed something significant?

"You ready?" Lincoln asked.

"I guess." She was still mulling things over when they took their dishes to the counter and left the cafeteria.

"What was that all about?" she asked as they made their way outside. She wasn't going to pretend something strange hadn't happened.

"We're brothers. We have a way of making each other understand what we're thinking," Lincoln said. "Hudson was pissed you didn't pick him to be your tour guide. I knew he was cussing me out silently. Guess Amanda has been around long enough to know it, too."

"You think Amanda read his mind?"

Lincoln shrugged. "Not too hard once you know the guy."

Charlotte let it go as they made their way toward a paddock that contained three fine specimens of horse-flesh—none of them bred for racing. All of them looked healthy, though. No work for a veterinarian at the present.

"Those two are mine." Lincoln pointed out a chestnut stallion and a bay mare, both American quarter horses. "Colonel and Thorn. The other one is Nate's." He pointed to a dun gelding she suspected was an Appaloosa. "His name is Eagle. We'll be acquiring more of them soon. We all like to ride." He cocked his head. "You said you always wanted your own horse. There's plenty of room in the stables if you still want one."

"I'll think about that." Though she'd taken riding

lessons for years, she'd never had a horse of her own, even after she'd left school and become a veterinarian. The horses in Ivan's extensive stables were of the highest quality, but they weren't all thoroughbreds. He maintained a social schedule worthy of a man of his wealth and provided mounts for any of his guests who desired one, including her—at least at first. Later, he made sure she didn't have time to ride. Keeping her working day and night was another way he controlled her.

Charlotte patted Colonel's neck. He was inquisitive, whereas Thorn held back. When Eagle pushed his muzzle close, she stroked him, too.

"Want to ride?" He nodded toward the horses.

"I'd love to."

Lincoln saddled the horses, and Charlotte was thrilled to mount Thorn and take the reins in hand. They followed the road that curved first along the lake before turning inland and swooping in switchbacks up the steep slope. The air smelled good here, and she couldn't think of where she'd rather be. Certainly not back at Gasparyn Stables.

Charlotte felt a pang for all the horses she'd left behind there, though. She wished she was wealthy enough to buy them and let them loose on a ranch where they could run at will rather than at the direction of a man whose sole concern was the money they could earn him. It pained her now to think how naive she'd been when she'd loved the races. Back then all she'd seen was the horses' pluck and the jockeys' daring. She hadn't realized the price both paid for the audience's enter-tainment and the owners' pocketbooks.

Three-quarters of the way up the Ridge, the road opened into a clearing.

"That's the entrance to the mine." Lincoln pointed it out. "Stay away from it. It's blocked, but it's still not a place to mess around in. Those buildings, too." He shook his head as he pointed to three outbuildings slumping beside the mine. "They're in bad shape. As soon as we can, we'll take them down. They're a men-ace."

"I'll keep clear of them," Charlotte assured him.

"Let's go to the mill next." He urged his horse to-ward a narrow path that cut straight back down the Ridge. Charlotte was grateful for her horse's careful steps a time or two as they made their way down the steep terrain. Eventually, they found themselves passing between houses, coming out onto pavement again. "My parents' house—number 1—was the first house built on the Ridge, but these cabins are the next oldest," Lincoln said, gesturing to the nearest buildings. "They housed the first workers who came to mine the silver."

Charlotte surveyed the row of log cabins, small, square homes that could contain only a room or two.

"Bachelor quarters," Lincoln said. "They're pretty rough."

Next came timber-frame homes that were only slightly bigger. Soon Charlotte spotted the back of the town hall, where they'd eaten lunch. When they reached the Circle, they followed it to Center Street, turned and walked past Lucy's Corner, deeper into the woods.

A quarter mile away, the road widened, and the sound of machinery and men's voices filled the air. A large, rectangular building dominated the scene, surrounded by tall piles of logs. Several enormous trucks were parked nearby, ready to haul them but empty for now.

"This is the sorting yard," Lincoln said, bringing his horse to a halt. "The actual work goes on inside that building. You'll want to mostly stay away from here, too," he added, "but the mill is the lifeblood of our community."

"It's impressive," Charlotte said.

"There's a lot of room for improvement in our systems. We modernized most of our equipment just before the shutdown, but I wish we'd done the whole line. We've got a couple of pieces that are about to fall apart." Lincoln shoved his hands in his pockets and stared at the mill like it was a puzzle to be solved, and she wished she could help him. If you already owed money, the last thing you wanted to do was spend more, but Lincoln struck her as the kind of man who wanted to solve problems immediately. It must be killing him to have to wait.

"You're the boss?"

"For now. Dad should be in charge, but he's having hip replacement surgery in two days. Not sure how long it'll take before he's on his feet again."

"A couple of months. My grandmother went through it some years back," she explained when he raised an eyebrow. She wished she could smooth away the worry in his face, but she didn't know him well enough to touch him like that.

"Before the crash, when my dad started struggling with health issues, Gage stepped in to run the mill because he was the oldest. Then the foreman of the logging operation took another job and moved away. I think he saw the writing on the wall before the rest of us did. Gage switched over to that job. That's when I took charge of the mill."

"That's a lot of responsibility for someone so young."

"We all did what we had to do." Lincoln's shoulders were tense, as if the conversation was bringing up unhappy memories.

"Gage doesn't want to run the mill this time around? Or is he in charge of the logging operation again?"

Lincoln shifted his stance. "He doesn't want to be in charge of either. He wasn't as excited as the rest of us to come back here."

"He wanted to settle somewhere else?" Charlotte shoved her hands in her pockets, too, then noticed she'd mimicked Lincoln and pulled them out.

"It's not that. He loves it here just as much as the rest of us do, I think. It's more like—once burned, twice shy. Know what I mean? He took it hard when we had to leave. He's worried we can't make a go of it." Lincoln seemed to remember he was supposed to be selling her on the place. "He's wrong, though. We'll get it up and running again. The crash was a fluke."

"Workers are happiest when they know who the boss is." She thought of the way Ivan had constantly ignored her advice and treatment plans for his horses, and how everyone who worked at the stables quickly followed his lead. She'd been hard-pressed to make anyone take her seriously. "Hudson is right; you shouldn't stay away from the mill too long." She pressed her lips together. Who was she to give career advice to anyone?

"I won't."

They gave the men working in the lumberyard a large berth as Lincoln led the way around the building to the back. "This is the graveyard."

"Graveyard?" As far as Charlotte could tell it was a dumping ground for broken machinery.

"Looks like an eyesore," Lincoln said, "but it's actually more like a storehouse. I'm good at fixing things. My dad used to go to auctions and buy machinery that bigger companies were getting rid of. He'd bring it home for me to fix and then we'd get years more use out of them. Couldn't afford the brand-new versions. This is storage for spare parts."

"Ah. That makes sense." She supposed it was good to reuse things that way, although she was grateful this wasn't the view from her new house.

"Someday I'll show you what I mean," he said. "You might find it more interesting than you think."

"I'll look forward to it." She wasn't teasing him, although she had a feeling he thought she was. She looked forward to learning all there was to know about Elliott Ridge—and Lincoln. Would this town prove to be a friendly community? Or did its peaceful surface hide depths of treachery, like Gasparyn Stables did in the end? She shouldn't get too attached to the place until she knew for sure. She could always walk away from a dollar investment, but once she'd started the renovations, it would be harder to leave.

She glanced at Lincoln. She had a feeling it would be hard to leave him, too.

CHAPTER 4

A WOMAN'S SHRIEK startled Lincoln awake just as he was finally dropping off to sleep sometime around midnight. He was on his feet and over to the window in a heartbeat, pushing up the sash. He'd decided to spend the night next door to number 37 in house number 35, just in case Charlotte needed anything. Earlier in the evening, he and Nate had lugged over the mattress from Lincoln's childhood bed as well as some bedding from his parents' linen closet so she could spend a comfortable night in her potential new home. Luckily, the electricity and water had already been turned on to the houses in Lucy's Corner because he and his brothers had been cleaning them in preparation for selling them. Lincoln had done his best to arrange the bed nicely for Charlotte and had run back for a bedside lamp, some towels and washcloths and anything else he could think of that would make the house more comfortable. Later, he'd found a sleeping bag and foam mat from his camping days and set up Spartan quarters for himself next door.

"Charlotte? You okay?" he called across the distance between their houses. He'd noticed earlier that she'd left her bedroom windows open and hoped she could hear him inside her room.

He held his breath, his heart racing, until her answer came. "Yes. Stubbed my toe on the way back from the bathroom."

"Turn on your light."

A moment later, the light came on and Charlotte appeared at her window. He made a motion for her to open it wider, and she did.

"I can't believe you heard me from over there," she said.

"It's a warm night. My window was open, too. Is your toe okay?"

"Yes. I didn't hit it that hard. I'll be fine." She sighed. "I can't sleep, though. I was exhausted when I went to bed, but as soon as I turned out the light, I became wide awake. It's being in a new place." She craned her head as if to look in his window. "I thought you told me you lived in the house where you grew up. What are you doing over there?"

"I thought I ought to stay close by—just in case."

"In case of what?"

"In case you got scared in the middle of the night. Thought it might be a little spooky with so many uninhabited houses around."

"I don't get scared that easy."

"Glad to hear it." He'd enjoyed his day with Charlotte. After their tour, he'd gone to the mill for a couple of hours of work, and Charlotte had explored on her own until dinnertime, when they'd met up again and eaten with the others.

At dinner Nate presented Charlotte with the paperwork for her house. She'd read it over while she ate, agreed to the terms and then fished out a dollar from her purse. They'd need to finalize the paperwork with a notary in town, but they'd broken out a couple of six-packs, and everyone had toasted Charlotte, then taken turns coming up with ideas for how she could renovate her new house. All too soon, Charlotte had gently let them know she was tired and ready to be on her own.

"I'm not sleepy either," he said to Charlotte now and thought a moment. "We could take a walk if you want. Go down to the beach for a few minutes and look at the stars. See if the night air tires us out so we can get some shut-eye later."

Charlotte considered that idea. "That sounds… nice," she said slowly. "You're not an ax murderer, are you?"

"Nope."

"The problem is if you were an ax murderer, that's what you'd say."

"Guess you're going to have to trust me. Or you could call Amanda and ask her," Lincoln said.

"It's pretty late for that. Besides, she already told me you were harmless."

Lincoln laughed. "Not sure if harmless is the word for me, but I'll take it. Meet you in five minutes?"

"Okay."

When Charlotte withdrew from the window, Lincoln hurried to pull on jeans and a T-shirt, gathered up a couple of blankets and the mini cooler of beer and snacks he'd brought over from his parents' house. Outside a few minutes later, he crossed to her porch and waited until she opened the door. She'd slipped on jeans and a shirt, as well, and had braided her hair.

"I feel like I'm sneaking out and I'm going to get in trouble if my grandmother catches me," she said.

Lincoln knew what she meant. He had gotten in trouble plenty of times for escapades like that when he was a kid.

"Gage, Nate and Hudson are staying in number 1, so we'll have to be quiet as we pass by on the way to the beach," he warned her.

She nodded. Starlight filtering through the trees gave them enough light to navigate by. They cut through the neighborhood, crossed the Circle and took the path around the side of number 1 that ran along a fern garden and down some stone steps to the beach.

Charlotte slipped off her shoes as soon as they reached the sand, and he joined her, the shifting surface cool beneath his bare feet. He laid one of the blankets on the sand close to the water, and when she sat down, he arranged the other over her knees.

"Don't want you to be cold," he said.

"You think of everything."

"I do my best."

He popped the tops off two bottles of beer, handed one to Charlotte, then opened the bag of chips.

"You're amazing." She reached a hand in. "Oh my goodness. Salt." She took a swig of her beer. "This is fantastic."

Lincoln couldn't help laughing. "Anyone ever tell you you're a cowboy's dream girl?"

She smiled, and he was grateful for the moonlight that allowed him to see her expression. "Are you a cowboy?"

"No. We never had cattle on the Ridge—too steep up here. Most guys in Chance Creek would answer yes, though. If you're shopping for one, that's the place to go."

"I never thought about hooking up with a cowboy."

"What kind of man have you thought about hooking up with?"

When she looked at him, Lincoln's body tightened with desire. Had she thought about him?

He'd thought about her plenty today—especially after he'd turned in for the night.

She shrugged. "What about you?"

Deflecting the question. Fair enough, he supposed, although he'd already told her he was planning to make a move on her. He thought about his last girlfriend. What type had Katie been? Flaky as hell? That wasn't what he was looking for these days. "I guess I want someone who knows herself. Someone with staying power." He said the words lightly, but the truth of them went all the way down to his soul. "I plan to settle here at Elliott Ridge—for good. I want a woman who can commit to that, too. Who can commit to me that way."

She was silent. Had she just crossed him off her list of potential candidates? Was she afraid of commitment?

"You know yourself well," was all she said.

"I hope so. I'm thirty-two."

"I'm twenty-eight," she said. "And I thought I knew exactly what I wanted in life, but I was so wrong about all of it. Now I don't know what to think."

He had a lot of questions he wanted to ask her. He decided to start with a simple one. "Did you come here to get away from your memories of your family?"

Her face was a pale oval in the dim light as she shook her head. "To get away from my ex-boyfriend," she admitted. "It was… messy. I didn't break up with just him. I broke up with my whole life. My plans and dreams. Everything I'd been working for."

"Sounds rough." She hadn't mentioned a boyfriend before and Lincoln wondered what else he'd gotten wrong about her. Was there a chance she'd want to return to her prior relationship?

"It was rough," she said. "I was at the wrong place at the wrong time, and the wrong man made me both his girlfriend and his employee. Then it all went to hell." She lifted her hands. "I can't believe I wasted a minute on that relationship, let alone two years."

"Are you sure it's over?" He didn't want to ask the question, but he had to know.

"I'm positive." She sounded sure of that and Lincoln relaxed. "I need a new set of dreams, though."

"You've come to the perfect place for that. You can start over here on the Ridge. Do anything you want.

You don't even have to be a veterinarian if you don't want to be. Maybe you'd like working at a mill. Or running a hotel."

She thought that over. "I definitely want to be a veterinarian but not the kind of veterinarian I was before."

"What kind were you?" he asked softly.

Charlotte was quiet for so long, he thought she might not answer. Had her boyfriend owned a clinic and employed her to work in it?

"I was in charge of keeping about twenty thoroughbreds healthy enough to win their races. Or to make them able to race even when they weren't healthy enough. I'm not going to do that anymore." Charlotte's voice went flat, and he heard the hurt and anger she was trying not to show.

Lincoln lay back on the blanket and linked his fingers behind his head, knowing he'd just learned something important. Her ex-boyfriend had enough money to own racehorses and to employ her to work with them. And he was enough of a bastard to mistreat his animals.

"No one around here would make you do something like that. Anyone who did would have to answer to me. There's the Big Dipper," he added, keeping his tone even. He hadn't known Charlotte long, but the way she'd focused on his horses earlier, he could tell she loved them. He couldn't imagine her standing by and allowing an animal to be hurt. A man was supposed to protect the woman he loved, not ask her to ride roughshod over her values in the service of making him money.

How wealthy did you have to be to own twenty thoroughbreds? Suddenly the debt his family owed seemed like a crushing weight. Why would Charlotte want to be with him after experiencing that kind of luxury? He couldn't offer her thoroughbreds or a mansion or fancy vacations to Paris…

Lincoln took a steadying breath. He could offer her the Ridge, though. A home. A family who'd rally around her. Charlotte had left her boyfriend, wealthy or not. She was here—with him.

After a moment Charlotte lay back, too, and sighed. "I see it."

They pointed out constellations to each other for a while. When she shivered, Lincoln adjusted the second blanket to cover them both.

"Are you comfortable?" he asked. He reached an arm out. "Put your head on my shoulder. Don't worry; I won't push my luck." He waited and was rewarded when she shifted nearer and fit herself against him. Warmth flooded his body. God, she felt good there.

"My brothers and I slept outside all the time in the summer when we were kids." Lincoln struggled to keep his desire for her out of his voice.

"It must have been wonderful growing up here." She wriggled a little to get comfortable, and his blood heated. It was hard to keep from drawing her closer.

"It was."

"Why did everyone leave?"

He hated to even remember those days. "Price of

lumber fell. And kept falling. Everyone who lived here worked in the mill or to support those who did. Dad kept having to lay people off. He was having health issues, too. In the end we couldn't keep it all going."

There was a lot more to it than that, but he didn't want to talk about it tonight. Not with this beautiful woman snuggled up beside him.

"Are there ghosts here?" she asked.

Lincoln snapped out of the reverie he'd fallen into. "Ghosts?"

"Memories," she amended. "You lived here most of your life. It can be wonderful to go home, but sometimes it's tough, too. Like a butterfly trying to fit back into its cocoon."

"Sometimes it feels like that," he said and drew her in a little closer. "How'd you know?"

"It was like that when I spent time with my grandmother after I moved out. She was the one who raised me after my parents died, and she was great, but it felt like she wanted me to stay that little girl I'd been when I first moved in. All bright and shiny and innocent."

"You're not bright and shiny and innocent?"

"No." She nestled against him. "This is nice," she said.

Lincoln noticed she didn't elaborate on her answer. He decided to let it go for now. "It is nice," he agreed. He was dying to kiss her, but this was Charlotte's first day on the Ridge. He'd convinced her to come and look at the place—or Amanda had, anyway—and he'd convinced her to buy a house and stay here. He'd held her hand, and now he was lying beside her on the beach. Trying for more seemed like a good way to lose the ground he'd gained. He could be patient.

Even if it killed him.

CHARLOTTE HAD NO idea what time it was when they decided to pack it in. At some point she dozed off and woke to find herself still tucked against the length of Lincoln's body. More than once she thought about what she'd do if he tried to kiss her.

Let him, most likely.

Kiss him back.

She appreciated that he hadn't tried anything, though. As easy as it might have been to act on her feelings for him, it would have made the night less special. The togetherness she felt simply sharing a starry sky touched her on a soul level. Lincoln had been respectful of her in a way she doubted Ivan could even fathom.

Lincoln helped her to her feet, shook out the blankets and balled them under one arm with their beer bottles and the half-empty chip bag. When he took her hand, his fingers were warm around hers, and she was glad for the connection. Once more, they passed number 1 as quietly as they could and strolled back through town.

At her door Lincoln squeezed her hand and let go. "I hope you get some more sleep. Don't feel like you have to get up early in the morning. If you miss breakfast, just make yourself at home in the town hall kitchen when you're ready and whip up anything you like. I'll be at the mill."

"Thanks." She hesitated, not wanting the night to end and, if she was honest with herself, not wanting to try once more to sleep in her big, empty house. Every time she closed her eyes, she saw Ivan's expression the day she'd learned he'd torpedoed her attempt to escape. The smug satisfaction on his face. The cold glint in his eyes. Every rustle of the wind through the trees outside her window had left her tense with fear, despite what she'd told Lincoln earlier. What if Ivan came after her? What if he found her somehow?

Lincoln hesitated, too, as if he knew she wanted to ask him something. He was a gentleman, and he wasn't going to invite himself in. If she wanted his company— or his protection from the things that went bump in the night—she'd have to speak up.

Wouldn't it be foolish to invite one man in to protect her from another? Especially since there was no way Ivan could trace her here? What if she'd misjudged Lincoln, and he attacked her during the night?

Charlotte supposed if he was going to try something like that, he would already have done so. He'd proven himself to be an honorable man so far.

"Would you mind… sleeping here tonight? In one of the spare rooms," she finally asked. She wasn't inviting him into her bed, no matter how nice it had felt to cuddle with him on the beach. Much too soon for that.

"You sure you'll be comfortable with me in the

house?" He leaned against the doorframe and surveyed her.

"You're the lesser of two evils. The devil I know versus the devil I don't." When he raised an eyebrow, she added, "It's going to take a little time to get used to this place, okay? It's so… quiet."

"It is. Give me a minute." He slipped away and quickly returned with his things, but already Charlotte was second-guessing herself. She opened her mouth to say she'd changed her mind, but Lincoln beat her to it.

"I'm not reading anything into this," he assured her. "You're new to the Ridge. You're feeling a little skittish. People are like horses; they're meant to have a herd."

Tears pricked Charlotte's eyes at his understanding. Grateful for his kindness, she said, "That's it exactly." She took a deep breath and led him upstairs to one of the bedrooms she wasn't using. "You can stay in here."

He nodded, but before she left the room, he added, "You're safe, Charlotte, from whatever critters might be out there and from me. You know I'm interested, but we're going to take this at your pace. We've got all the time in the world. Get some sleep, okay?"

"Okay." Charlotte hesitated, then, propelled by a reasoning she couldn't quite explain, she lunged forward, went up on her toes and pressed a quick kiss to his jaw. "Good night," she called over her shoulder as she fled across the hall and shut her bedroom door hard. She leaned against it, her heart pounding.

What on earth had she done that for? She crossed the room, dropped onto her mattress and hugged a pillow to her chest. The man had just stated his willing-ness to go at her pace, and she'd kissed him. She was supposed to get her financial feet underneath her before she even looked at a man.

Maybe this is my pace.

The thought popped into her mind like a gopher popping out of its underground lair. The more she tried to deny it, the more stubbornly it persisted. She liked Lincoln. That was the truth of it. She liked the way he joked around with Amanda. The way he could be serious one moment, then laugh the next. The way he'd banded together with his brothers to reclaim the town they all so obviously cared about. When he'd spoken of bringing his parents home, her heart had squeezed. They were as important to him as her grandmother had been to her.

She'd thought she'd need months—maybe years—to get over the way her relationship with Ivan had gone so disastrously wrong, but now she realized she didn't want to take months or years to get on with her life. Ivan had wasted so much of her time already, first by fooling her about who he really was, then by making it impossible to leave once she learned the truth.

She was over Ivan. There wasn't any mourning to do, and she didn't need time to figure out who she wanted to be now that he was out of her life. What she wanted was right here in front of her. A home. A job. A community. The ability to support herself. A man she wanted and who wanted her, too—not because she filled a role in his moneymaking enterprise but because she was Charlotte.

She shook her head at her own certainty. She'd known Lincoln less than a day, not long enough to form any judgment about his character or what he did or didn't want. If she really thought he was the perfect man, and she didn't need any time to heal or grow or find herself before being with him, why didn't she walk across the hall right now and climb into Lincoln's bed?

When Charlotte found herself on her feet heading for the door, she let out a groan.

"You okay in there?" Lincoln called from his room.

God. He'd heard that? "No. I'm incorrigible."

"What?" His voice was closer now. He must be standing on the other side of her door. All she had to do was open it.

"Nothing. Get some sleep."

"How am I supposed to sleep when there's incorrigibleness happening in there?"

Charlotte snorted, then covered her mouth with her hand, hoping he hadn't heard that. "I'll settle down. Good night."

"Too bad. Night."

His footsteps padded back across the hall, and a moment later, his door shut. Charlotte sighed. She was sleeping in a strange house in the middle of a strange forest on a strange ridge in a state she'd never even visited before—and all she wanted was for the stranger sleeping not ten feet away to bust down her door and take her to bed.

This was madness.

But she wouldn't change a thing.

LINCOLN DIDN'T THINK he'd ever spent a more uncomfortable night, despite the foam mat he'd carried over from house number 35. He'd tossed and turned, alternating between the hope of getting a whole lot closer to Charlotte and the despair that maybe she'd change her mind and leave. He'd had infatuations before and knew how strong raw attraction could be, but he hadn't stayed awake all hours fantasizing about sleeping with Charlotte—he'd been strategizing about how to marry her before some other guy swept in and stole her out from under his nose.

Despite being up most of the night, Lincoln woke early. Old habits died hard, he thought as he turned over and got in another catnap. When he woke a second time, he still had plenty of time to stow away his gear for the day and take a shower before breakfast. He expected Charlotte to sleep in far longer than he had, but when he returned to his room, he heard her moving around in her bedroom, too. Before he was done dressing, she'd taken his place in the bathroom, and twenty minutes later, she appeared wearing jean shorts and a T-shirt, her hair still damp, just as he was heading downstairs.

"I desperately need to go shopping," she said, following him down the steps.

"I'll drive you to town later, and we can get a few things for your house, too. You need a new mattress and bed frame, at the very least. Maybe a dresser and some end tables?"

"Let's start with the bed," Charlotte said. "I want to put some thought into what the house will look like when it's renovated before I start furnishing it."

Lincoln accepted that, but he wondered if she was hedging her bets. Last night he thought they'd reached a good place when she'd kissed him, but maybe she was regretting all that. She seemed distant this morning. Uncertain around him. They stood in the front hall awkwardly.

He supposed he could understand her hesitation. If he wanted her to stay, he'd better get busy showing her all the reasons to fall in love with Elliott Ridge. Too bad he'd have to spend most of the day at the mill. It was rare he or his brothers took time off. They were scrambling to fulfill the contracts they had and to secure new ones.

"Ready to eat?"

She nodded but remained quiet on the way to the town hall. Breakfast was pancakes and sausages prepared by Gage. She perked up a little when Amanda arrived with Carter, however, and chatted along with everyone when the rest of Lincoln's brothers appeared for the meal. Afterward, Lincoln reluctantly dropped her off at number 37 with a promise to be back in a couple of hours. Amanda had loaned her a pad of paper and pen so she could jot down ideas about the renovation. He got to the mill by eight, but time at work dragged, worried as he was that left alone for too long, Charlotte might change her mind and want to leave Elliott Ridge.

During a break he tracked down the Petersons and gave them a call. Elaine Peterson answered, delighted to hear from him, and assured him they didn't need the horse figurine.

"Darla got over horses before we even left town," she said. "Next it was video games and then she got into tennis. She got a scholarship to TSU. If you sent that thing back to us, she'd just throw it out. Give it to someone who wants it."

"Will do."

"I'm so happy you and your brothers are back at the Ridge. If we hadn't put down roots here in Tennessee, I'd move there in a flash."

"If you change your mind, we've got lots of houses available," Lincoln told her.

After chatting a little more, they ended the call. Lincoln tapped the screen of his cell phone a few times and placed another one.

"Megan Lawrence speaking," Megan answered.

"Wondered if you could do me a favor," Lincoln said. "I know it's Sunday, but Charlotte's agreed to buy the house. She paid her dollar and signed the paperwork Nate copied from when we sold a house to Amanda. Could you help me find a notary who wouldn't mind working for an hour today?"

"I know just the person," Megan said. "Are the rest of those houses ready for me to list yet?" She spoke in a teasing tone, but he knew her question was serious.

"Any day now," he told her. "Let me talk to the others tonight and make a plan."

"Okay. I'll make a call and I'll get right back to you."

She was as good as her word, and soon Lincoln had an appointment in town with Don Reese, a notary. He got back to work, and at ten thirty, he left Gage in charge and came to drive Charlotte to Chance Creek.

She was more cheerful when she opened the door of number 37 and ushered him in. She'd found a tape measure somewhere and created a floor plan on the pad of paper.

"Looks like you made a good start," he said, dropping the horse figurine in her hand. "That's yours now. The Petersons don't want it back. Consider it a housewarming gift from them."

She held it up in her palm. "My first decoration! Seems fitting, doesn't it?"

"A horse for a horse veterinarian? Sure does." He was glad to see Charlotte in such a good mood.

"I think this house could be beautiful with a bit of work. I have so many ideas for it."

He warmed to her enthusiasm. "Then let's find you a bed. It's the most important piece of furniture in a house, right? I mean..." What did he mean? "You've got to sleep," he finished lamely when she raised an eyebrow.

"I guess so. I was thinking more about how this living room and kitchen could look if we knocked down the wall between them."

"Oh. Sure, kitchens and living rooms are important, too." He ran a hand through his hair, conscious he was being a little too obvious. He couldn't help it, though.

He wanted to get closer to Charlotte. Of course he had beds on his mind.

Charlotte smiled. "Kitchens and living rooms are important. You can't… *sleep*… all the time."

"I don't know about that. I think you can *sleep* an awful lot if you put your mind to it."

She heaved a long-suffering sigh. "Let's focus on the kitchen, shall we?"

"The kitchen can be fun, too."

"Lincoln."

"Charlotte?"

Her mouth twitched with a smile she wouldn't let break free. "Who's incorrigible now?" she asked softly.

"I'll be serious," he promised her. "Right after I do this." He moved close to her, hooked an arm around her waist and bent slowly, giving her time to pull back. Instead she leaned forward, her mouth meeting his halfway. Lincoln had meant to keep the kiss short and sweet, but the moment their lips met, that plan went out the window. He gathered her to him and took his time exploring the feel and taste of her.

When they pulled apart, she was flushed, and he was feeling a little hot and bothered himself.

"I've been thinking about doing that all morning," he said.

"Me, too," she admitted.

"You're still happy with your choice of house? No second thoughts?"

"None," Charlotte said quickly, then looked down, her cheeks flushing. "I mean about the house."

"Of course." Lincoln stood a little taller, though. She wasn't having second thoughts about him, either. It felt good to know their attraction was mutual. He doubted this small house held a candle to her ex-boyfriend's home, but Lincoln didn't believe the size of a home mattered all that much. It was what happened within its four walls. He'd do whatever he could to make sure good things happened here.

"I think this house suits you." He stole another kiss, loving the buzz of warmth and wanting that flooded his body every time they touched. "I hope you stay."

"I hope so, too." She wouldn't meet his gaze, and he decided he'd better lower the temperature a bit.

"Let's go find that bed."

They started at Thompson's Furniture, a small store with a limited selection of mattresses, bed frames, couches and other furnishings. Charlotte quickly picked out a wooden slatted frame but spent her time testing the mattresses, finally choosing a high-quality one.

They grabbed burgers for lunch and made it to their notary appointment on time. Don was a stickler for details and frowned when it came time to discuss the payment of the dollar and found out the money had already swapped hands.

"Normally there's an escrow process during the purchase of a house. The buyer transfers the payment to the notary, who doesn't forward it to the seller until the process is complete."

"It's just a dollar," Lincoln reminded him.

Don sighed and kept going. Finally, they were done.

"Clothes next?" Lincoln asked as they left the notary office. "A homeowner needs to keep up appearances."

Charlotte nodded happily. "Amanda told me about a store she likes. Should we meet up again in an hour?"

Lincoln's good spirits sagged. "You don't want me to come along?"

"Not really. I don't like an audience when I go clothes shopping," she added. "It makes me too self-conscious."

"All right," he conceded. "I'll run a couple of errands of my own and wait for you at Linda's Diner. Just ask directions at the store. They'll steer you right."

"Okay."

Lincoln dropped her off at Heloise's, which he'd heard was owned by Storm Hall now. Storm had married Zane Hall, whom Lincoln had known when they were kids, and lived with her husband and his extended family on a ranch outside town called Crescent Hall.

Lincoln remembered when the clothing store used to be called Mandy's Cowgirl Emporium, a dowdy establishment most of the Chance Creek women had avoided. Now it looked like the kind of updated boutique you'd find in a much larger city. He hoped Charlotte would find everything she needed there.

Meanwhile, he ducked into the feed store and the bank, then ambled down to the diner. He spotted Megan sitting at a table by the large front window as soon as he entered.

"Come join me," she called when she saw him, motioning him into the chair opposite her. "How did the signing go?"

"All done. That's two houses sold."

"And zero commission," Megan said. "I'm looking forward to selling a few of your houses for real."

He took a seat and, when a waitress came to greet him, ordered a cup of coffee.

"Do you want something to go with it?" the waitress asked.

"I've got a friend joining me later. I'll order a snack then."

The woman bustled off again.

"Who's joining you?" Megan asked. "Charlotte?"

Lincoln nodded. "She's shopping right now, but she's supposed to meet me here afterward." He watched as Megan picked at the muffin she was eating. "How are things with you?"

"They'll be better when I've got those listings," she admitted.

"Business is slow?"

"More than slow." She noticed what she was doing and wiped her hands on her napkin. "I sold Gage's house a couple of weeks ago, and Lainie knows that pretty soon I'll have the rest of the homes in Lucy's Corner to list, but she's constantly riding me about not having any new clients. Maybe she's right. Maybe I'm just no good at this."

"Seems like you sold Gage's house pretty quickly." He and the rest of his brothers had been surprised to find out Gage had owned one in town for years. He'd never lived in it, just rented it out.

"It was a nice house. Did you ever see it?"

"No." That rankled Lincoln. Why had Gage kept his purchase a secret all these years, and what had possessed him to buy a house in town in the first place? Apparently, he'd done so before they even left the Ridge, using the money he'd saved up for college to buy and renovate it before turning it into a rental.

"It wasn't fancy, but everything was fresh and well maintained. I gather he did all the renovations himself?"

"That's what I heard, too." Lincoln couldn't understand why Gage hadn't asked any of them to help, but in those days they'd all been short with each other as the economy tanked and they'd helped their parents try to keep the town afloat. Maybe Gage had simply wanted something of his own to work on. "Did he make a good profit?"

"A fair one, I'd say. He's smart." She looked away, color rising in her cheeks.

"He is." Lincoln felt for Megan. She so obviously liked Gage, and he was treating her shabbily. "Don't judge him too harshly for the way he's acting. I think he's worried we're going to let down our parents if we don't get the mill running at capacity again soon."

"Do you think that's why he dropped me?" Megan asked baldly. "I thought we started something together at Cindy Gladstone's wedding, but he's avoiding me now—which feels pretty awful." She made a face. "I should just move on and find someone else to pine over. I'm making a mess of my life."

"No, you're not, and I don't think you should give up on Gage yet. I saw how he looked at you at Cindy's wedding. Whatever is holding him back has nothing to do with you. He's probably worried we won't succeed, and we'll all have to leave again." Lincoln considered that. "Maybe I'm the fool thinking we'll stay."

It was Megan's turn to shake her head. "I don't think you're foolish. I think five years from now, you and your brothers are going to look like geniuses. That's a fabulous community you've got up there, and the way you're planning to diversify your workforce, you'll be better prepared to handle hiccups in the lumber market in the future."

Lincoln appreciated her vote of confidence.

"I should get going," Megan said. "Tell Charlotte I said hello."

"Tell her yourself. I bet she'd like to see a friendly face. She's at Heloise's."

Megan nodded. "I'll stop in and say hi."

CHARLOTTE WAS APPROACHING the counter to pay for her purchases at Heloise's when Megan came in and found her.

"Lincoln told me you'd be here," she said, looking with interest over the pile of clothing Charlotte handed to the sales associate. "Looks like you found a lot of good stuff."

"I did," Charlotte said happily. First, she'd ducked across the street and upgraded her phone and cell service since the burner phone Steven had given her wasn't going to cut it for normal use. Then she'd come back to Heloise's, where she'd picked out a starter wardrobe, a few fun extras, several pairs of shoes, including some flats and heels that were far more flattering than the thick-soled work shoes she'd worn since she'd run from Gasparyn Stables, and a pair of sturdy work boots she figured would come in handy, too. "This is the best women's clothing store I've ever been to. I didn't think I'd find half the things I needed, but I found them all."

"I'll take that as a compliment," the woman at the till said with a smile. She had blond hair that hung down to her waist and was dressed casually but neatly. "This is my store," she explained.

Megan made the introductions. "Storm Hall," she said, "this is Charlotte. She just got to town and she's staying up at Elliott Ridge. Charlotte, meet Storm."

The women shook hands over the counter. "Watch out. Chance Creek has a way of getting its hooks into you. If you meet a military man, be extra careful. They have a way of marrying women who breeze into town."

Megan laughed. "She's right. Maybe that's my problem—I grew up here. I should go somewhere else for a decade and come home. I'd be married in no time."

"I've already met a military man," Charlotte admitted.

"You're stuck now," Storm said. "Might as well go down the street to Caitlyn's place and buy your wedding dress."

"There can't be that many women marrying military

men in this town. Chance Creek isn't that big!"

"You'd be surprised. It's not just newcomers, either," Storm said to Megan. "Look at the Reed girls. All five of them married to military men and their family has lived in this town for generations."

"Their father is a general, and he ordered those men to marry them," Megan said. "My dad never served and he's gone now."

"Are you looking to get married?" Storm asked her. "I heard you and Gage Elliott were pretty cozy at Cindy Gladstone's wedding." She bit her lip. "Sorry, I probably shouldn't have said that."

"Oh, why shouldn't Storm know? I'm sure everyone knows," Megan grumbled.

"Does Gage know?" Storm asked curiously.

"He knows," Megan assured her.

"He knows you like him," Charlotte said, "but that doesn't necessarily mean he knows you want to marry him."

"Maybe you should tell him," Storm said.

"No!" Megan looked from one to the other. "I'm not telling him anything. I want the whole fairy-tale. He needs to ask me out, wine and dine me, take me somewhere romantic and get on his damn knee to propose. I deserve that!"

"You do," Charlotte assured her. "And if he doesn't do just that, I'll think less of him."

"I will, too," Storm said. "Be patient, Megan. He'll get there."

"He'd better pick up the pace." Megan pulled out

her phone and looked at it. "I'd better pick up the pace, too. I have to get back to work. Let's get together for coffee or something soon."

"I'd like that," Charlotte said. "I'd better meet Lincoln at the diner before he decides I've gotten lost."

CHAPTER 5

"**D**ID MEGAN FIND you?" Lincoln asked when Charlotte arrived. He stood up and helped push in her chair when she sat at his table, then asked the waitress to bring another round of coffee and a couple of banana-walnut muffins.

"She did. Thanks for sending her over. It was nice to see her again." They enjoyed their coffee and muffins as Lincoln told her what he knew about the people walking past the window.

"You really know everyone," she said when she'd finished her muffin.

"Not everyone, but most of them. It's hard not to in a town this size."

"Chance Creek is bigger than Elliott Ridge."

"It is, but not that much bigger. Drink up," he added. "I've got one more errand I'd like to run before we head home. Are you up for that?"

"Sure."

The bells over the diner's door jangled to announce a new customer, and a tall man with a hawk-like nose walked inside. He scanned the restaurant, noticed them and strode their way.

"Hell," Lincoln muttered.

"Who's that?" Charlotte asked.

"Blake Warrington, the man who wants our town. This should be fun." He stood up as the man approached. "Blake."

"Lincoln. You ready to sell yet?"

"No."

Warrington sighed. "You all keep dragging your feet, but it's not going to change how this ends." He nodded at Charlotte, who had stood up, as well. "Who's this?"

"Charlotte, meet Blake Warrington."

Charlotte nodded. "Nice to meet you," she said automatically, even though it really wasn't, and shook his hand when he offered it. His grip was uncomfortably firm.

"Charlotte just bought one of our houses," Lincoln said.

Warrington's jaw tightened. "Which is soon to be one of my houses. I hope the Elliotts explained I intend to annex their property," he said to her.

"They've explained everything," Charlotte said coolly. "Sounds like your expectations are going to be disappointed." She would not let this man intimidate her. He thought he was a tough customer, but she could already tell Ivan would give him a run for his money.

Warrington drew back. "I... don't think I'm the one who's going to be disappointed."

Charlotte shrugged and turned to Lincoln. "You said you had another errand before we return to the Ridge?"

"That's right. We'll see you around, Warrington."

"You can be sure of that." Warrington stalked back to the hostess station. Lincoln flagged down their waitress and settled the bill.

"Charming man," Charlotte said when they were outside on the sidewalk.

"Wish I'd never met him," Lincoln said.

"So what's this errand we're supposed to run?"

"Thought you might want to meet one of the local veterinarians. What do you say?"

Charlotte straightened in surprise. "I'd love to meet one of the local vets," she said eagerly. She needed to find a job as soon as possible, after all. She hadn't let herself think too hard about what would happen if there weren't any positions in town.

"We'll go there next." He led the way to his truck and drove her to the Chance Creek Pet Clinic and Shelter, a little outside of town. "I've known Bella Mortimer since grade school," Lincoln explained on the way. "She's a little older than me, but she was always friendly. I'm sure she'd be happy to chat."

When they arrived, Charlotte surveyed the large, modern facility. It looked prosperous and well cared for. She got out of the truck in time to meet up with a middle-aged woman who'd just exited the clinic, leading a frisky puppy on a leash.

Charlotte bent to let it lick her hand and gave it a

pat as Lincoln exchanged greetings with the woman.

"Janey used to work at the grocery store when I was a kid," he explained as he introduced them.

"I remember when you Elliott boys were babies. You were just as cute then as you are now," Janey said. "Nice to meet you, Charlotte. I'm sure I'll see you around."

"Nice to meet you, too." She struggled to keep from laughing at Lincoln's expression.

"I am not cute," he muttered when Janey was a safe distance away.

"Sure you are."

"I'm ruggedly handsome."

"Uh-huh. Keep telling yourself that."

She gave a little shriek when he swept her off her feet and cradled her in his arms as he covered the short distance to the front door. He set her on her feet again just outside it. "See? Rugged, not cute."

"Maybe rugged *and* cute," she allowed.

They were met at the front desk by a woman in her thirties with blond hair so light it was almost white. Her nametag read *Hannah Matheson*.

"Hi, Lincoln. I heard you were back," she exclaimed and came around the desk to give him a hug.

"I didn't know you worked here. And since when are you a Matheson? You were an Ashton last time I saw you."

"Married Jake the fall of the year you left. It was kind of sudden," she admitted with a smile. "Those Mathesons won't quit once they set their heart on you."

"Is Jake a military man?" Charlotte asked.

"No. He's a rancher. Why?"

"Just wondering."

"Glad to see you so happy," Lincoln said to Hannah.

"I am happy. I graduated from veterinarian school a couple of years ago, and Bella let me join her practice."

Charlotte's heart fell. It sounded like there were plenty of veterinarians to go around here. There wouldn't be any need for her. Still, when Lincoln explained their errand, Hannah asked them to wait and disappeared farther into the building. She came back with another woman, who smiled when she saw Lincoln. Her honey-blond hair was swept up in a messy bun. Her blue eyes matched her shirt. She wore jeans and a battered old pair of cowboy boots.

"I heard you were back in town," she cried. "It's good to see you, Lincoln."

"Good to see you, too," Lincoln said. "Charlotte, this is Bella Mortimer. Of course, she was Bella Chatham when I used to know her."

"I'm an old married lady now," the woman said, beaming. "Nice to meet you, Charlotte."

"Nice to meet you, too." All these new people were beginning to be overwhelming. Charlotte hoped she could keep them straight.

"Bella's husband isn't in the military, either," Hannah said.

"Is he supposed to be?" Bella asked, raising her eyebrows.

"I thought Charlotte might want to know." Hannah smiled.

"I was told earlier that newcomers to Chance Creek often marry men who've served," Charlotte rushed to explain, then wished she'd held her tongue when a smile tugged at the corner of Lincoln's mouth.

"That is true," Hannah said. "Happens a lot around here. I grew up here, though. So did Bella. We don't count. You're new to these parts, though. Might want to be careful."

"I guess so," Charlotte said. Was she blushing? She had a horrible feeling she might be.

Lincoln took pity on her and changed the subject. "Charlotte is a veterinarian. She's moving to Elliott Ridge and she's looking for work."

"Really?" Bella lit up. "We desperately need more vets in town. The three of us can't keep up."

"Three of you? Your brother is still in the business, too?" Lincoln asked as Charlotte perked up again, her hopes revived.

"That's right. Hannah and I care for pets, mostly," Bella said. "I'm a sucker for cats and dogs—and any animal, really. My brother, Craig, specializes in livestock. He's the one the ranchers call. Of course, they call me, too, constantly, because my brother is run off his feet. There's a fourth veterinarian in town. Old Chuck Fife. He's off on fishing trips half the time, though. He refuses to call himself retired, but he is. What's your specialty, Charlotte?"

"Horses, mostly," Charlotte said. "But I can handle

any kind of livestock."

"Awesome!" Hannah exclaimed, then bit her lip. "Sorry, but we're desperate around here for someone like that."

"Hannah's right," Bella said. "We could definitely use another livestock vet in town." She checked herself. "I mean, no pressure or anything."

"Don't listen to her," Hannah said. "Tons of pressure. Please save us! We'll find you a military man to marry."

"She's already found one," Lincoln said. "I mean…" He rubbed a hand over his head. "Hell, you know what I mean."

"Oh, we know what you mean," Bella said and rolled her eyes. "Don't scare her away before we put her to work. You should talk to my brother as soon as you can, Charlotte." Bella went behind the desk and tapped away at a computer. "He's pretty busy the next few days, but he's got some time Thursday morning. Is it okay if I give him your number?"

"Of course. Can't wait to meet him. In the meantime, would you show us around your place?" she asked.

"Sure. Come on back."

"I'll stay here," Hannah said. "Our receptionist is on a break."

Bella led the way, and Charlotte and Lincoln followed.

"This is the biggest clinic I've ever seen," Charlotte said.

"Well, we act as both an animal hospital and a no-kill shelter, so we need a lot of space. We work with a network of volunteer organizations to get our animals to good homes. Plus we have a spay-and-neuter program that's beginning to make inroads on the feral cat population in Chance Creek. Things were a little out of control when I started, but I think we're doing good work."

"It looks like it."

"We have a joint program with Chance Creek High where kids help us exercise the animals and habituate them to humans," Bella explained when they came upon three teenagers romping with several dogs in a grassy outside area. "That building has our surgery and recovery rooms." She pointed to it.

The tour lasted quite a while, and Bella answered all her questions patiently. Later, on the drive back to the Ridge, Charlotte couldn't stop marveling about Bella's facility. "How does she feed all those animals?" she asked Lincoln. "She must be a wizard at fundraising."

"Her husband is a billionaire," Lincoln said.

Charlotte turned to him in surprise.

"I'm not kidding," Lincoln said. "Evan Mortimer is an actual billionaire. They met on a reality TV show. I have to admit our trip to her clinic had two purposes. One was to introduce you to Bella. The other was to let her know—and her husband through her—what we're doing on the Ridge. Evan must have a lot of professional contacts. We want to diversify our income base, and I think entrepreneurs would be a good fit."

"Well, aren't you devious?" Charlotte asked. She'd

noticed the care Lincoln had taken during their visit to explain to Bella that he and his brothers were hoping to attract remote tech workers to the Ridge.

"I prefer to think of it as being enterprising."

As Lincoln drove, Charlotte decided it was time to face the music and pulled out her new phone. The man who'd sold it to her had helped her set it up, and she'd downloaded a few apps while she was in the range of the store's Wi-Fi. Unsurprisingly, she hadn't gotten any texts, but when she checked her email, there was one from Ivan.

Charlotte went cold, but she clicked to open it.

And immediately wished she hadn't.

I will find you, the email read. *You owe me, and you're going to pay.*

Charlotte swallowed. So much for him moving on.

There was an attachment labelled *Invoice*.

"Something wrong?" Lincoln glanced her way, then returned his attention to the road.

"No," she said absently. She braced herself and opened the attachment. The document contained a list of dates, descriptions and numbers. It went on for pages. Charlotte scrolled up and down until she finally understood. Ivan had documented every cent he'd ever spent on her, from the cost of her portion of their first dinner to the price of the toothpaste she'd purchased on his credit card two days before she left. There were items of clothing, movies and symphony tickets listed. He'd set a price for her rent and charged her for half of all their grocery bills. He'd listed her school loan payments, as well.

How long had it taken him to tally this up? Charlotte lowered the phone. Or had he been keeping a running total the whole time she'd been with him? Reminding himself daily of what she *owed* him. Of how much he could require of her.

She looked down at the phone again, scrolled to the end of the document and took in the final number. He hadn't deducted a single cent for the wages he should have paid her but never did. When she'd graduated and begun to work for him, she'd mustered the courage to ask what salary she'd earn. "Salary?" he'd said. "Forget a salary. Take this." He'd handed her a credit card that was linked to his account. "Buy whatever you like, whenever you like. Don't worry about the limit. You'll never reach it."

"Of course there's a limit," she'd told him. "What if I bought a yacht?"

"Baby, buy two yachts. Buy three." They'd been eating at an upscale restaurant, where he'd ordered a bottle of champagne and toasted her liberally. She'd thought he was reckless and romantic and that together they'd build a life and a racing dynasty to end all dynasties. She'd been so damn stupid.

Her hands shook as she pocketed her phone. Now what was she supposed to do? Did he really expect her to pay all that money back when he hadn't paid her a dime for her work? Could he take her to court?

Should she countersue him?

Would that only make him angrier?

Steven would know what to do.

"What's wrong?" Lincoln asked, glancing her way.

"It's nothing serious. Just something I need to take care of." She didn't want Lincoln or anyone else here to know what a fool she'd been. Bad enough her grandmother had passed away before Charlotte could correct her mistake. Shame heated her cheeks and carved a pit in her stomach every time she thought of how obvious it had been to everyone but her that she never should have been with Ivan. Grandma had strong feelings about "airing your dirty laundry in public," so Charlotte knew how much it must have pained her to phone Steven and request his help to save her.

Now Ivan was asserting his control over her again. The amount of money he'd demanded dwarfed her tiny savings, but she had a feeling it accurately represented the amount she'd charged on his credit card over the past few years. Of course, it was less than she should have earned if he'd simply paid her a salary, so she had no reason to feel guilty about what she'd done.

Still, the idea of facing Ivan in court terrified her.

She straightened her shoulders. If she had to go to court, she'd show everyone that letter, explain her story and trust that justice would be on her side. If not, she'd ask for time to pay off Ivan. Bella and Hannah had said they desperately needed another veterinarian in town. She'd live as frugally as possible until her debts were paid.

Or maybe she'd run all over again.

Lincoln glanced her way again. "Are you all right?

You look a little funny."

"Maybe I ate something that disagreed with me," she said faintly.

"We'll be home in a minute." He stepped on the gas. "Tell me if you're going to be sick."

She nodded. She just might. Ivan had lobbed a missile her way, and she had a feeling it wouldn't be the last one.

The minute she was alone, she'd call Steven and get his advice.

BY THE TIME they got to number 37, Charlotte's color had returned, and she felt well enough to offer to help Lincoln bring her new bed inside, but he called Nate instead. Together they moved the old mattress to the spare room, assembled the metal frame in Charlotte's bedroom and maneuvered the new mattress up the stairs and onto it.

"Did you buy any sheets and covers?" Lincoln asked when he ushered Charlotte in to see their handiwork.

She shook her head. "Totally forgot about it. I was too busy splurging on clothes." She placed her bags near the closet and sat on the bed, smoothing a hand over the new mattress, her head bowed.

"You can keep the ones you borrowed as long as you need them. Maybe you should make one of those mood board things before you go shopping for stuff for the house. This is going to be your dream home, right?"

When she didn't answer, Lincoln's gut tightened. Something was wrong, and he didn't think it was something she'd eaten. Charlotte had been fine until she'd pulled out her phone on the drive home. He'd bet his life she'd gotten some bad news, but she'd made it clear she didn't want to talk about it.

"My dream home. Right," Charlotte finally said. "Of course."

"It's a great house," Nate put in. "I should really grab one for myself before all the good ones are taken."

Charlotte nodded listlessly. "Sorry, I'm still feeling under the weather. I think I need to lie down."

"I'll head out then," Nate said. "See you two later." He clapped Lincoln on the shoulder and made for the door.

"Let me help you make up the bed," Lincoln offered. He grabbed the sheets, and when Charlotte stood, he began fitting one to the mattress. Charlotte moved to the other side. They got the bed made in short order, then Lincoln turned to go.

"Hope you feel better. I'll bring you dinner later, if you like. That way you don't have to go to the cafeteria."

"That would be great. Just knock on the door and I'll come grab it from you."

So much for eating with her, Lincoln thought wryly. Charlotte was making it very clear she wanted to be alone—and meant to spend the rest of the day that way.

"You sure you'll be all right while I'm gone?" He needed to get to the mill for the rest of the afternoon, but he hated to leave her when he didn't know what the problem was.

"I'll be fine. I'm going to take it easy. I'll look up design ideas. Make that mood board you were talking about."

He relaxed a little. She wouldn't spend time planning to fix up her house if she didn't mean to stay. He crossed the room but stopped in the doorway.

"How's your cell phone signal? Looks like you got a new phone."

"I did. I needed something better than the one I had." She named the service provider she'd chosen, and he winced.

"Let me guess. You didn't mention you were living up here on the Ridge?"

She shook her head. "Should I have?"

He nodded. "Give your phone a try."

She pulled it out and tapped on the screen. "What's your number?"

He told her and she tapped it in, then frowned. "I'm not getting any reception. No bars at all!"

"I'm not surprised. The Ridge is a dead zone for most carriers." Lincoln told her the name of the cell service provider he and his brothers used. "I should have warned you earlier. Next time we're in town, let's get you switched over. You need to be able to use your phone up here."

"Definitely." She didn't look happy about this latest development. Lincoln hurried to assure her she could still make calls while she was on the Ridge.

"Reception is somewhat better at the town hall. There's Wi-Fi coverage there, as well." He gave her the password. "Unfortunately, our Wi-Fi is pretty spotty, too, but we're getting an upgrade this fall."

"Good to know." She stared at her phone despondently.

"Are you sure you'll be okay while I'm gone?" He lingered a moment longer.

"Positive. I'm fine, really. Just need a rest."

She didn't look fine, and she wasn't meeting his gaze, but Lincoln decided not to push. She'd tell him what was wrong when she was ready.

"See you later."

"See you." As soon as he went out the door, Charlotte closed it behind him and locked it.

Yep. She definitely wanted to be left alone.

Lincoln texted Amanda, told her what had happened and asked her to check in on Charlotte if she could during the day. As he walked to the mill, he transferred the balance of the cost of her house from his personal account to the family one to which he and his brothers all had access. It was official. Charlotte was staying—he hoped.

Luckily, things went smoothly at the mill for the last few hours of the day. He'd braced himself for some awkwardness since Gage had taken the lead this morning, but Gage took a spot among the men without comment, and everyone got on with their work. They were fulfilling several orders at once, so there was plenty for everyone to do.

The only snag came when the board edger jammed, causing a bottleneck in their production line. Lincoln followed all the safety procedures, locked out the machine and unjammed its blades. He ignored the grumbling from some of the men; nothing could get him down today.

That good feeling came crashing down when he stopped by number 37 on his way home, however, and found Charlotte still wasn't feeling well. He'd hoped to spend the evening with her. Maybe sit on the beach again. Instead, she handed him the sleeping bag and foam mat he'd used the previous night.

"I think I need to be alone tonight," she said. "Sorry for being such a wet blanket, but I've got a headache now. Do you want to take the mattress I used last night, as well?"

"That's okay," he said quickly. No way in hell would he call Nate to help him carry that mattress back to his parents' house. Nate had helped him move it into the spare room earlier. Moving it again would be advertising that Charlotte had kicked him out. Next thing he knew, Hudson would be sniffing around. "Are you sure you don't want me to sleep here? I'll leave you alone to rest."

"Amanda kept me company this afternoon, which was nice, but now I'm feeling worse. I think I'll be better off alone."

"Okay," he said reluctantly and took the things she handed him. "I'll be right next door, though, so call me if you need anything. Meanwhile, I'll grab you some food."

Lincoln dumped his things in number 35 and

fetched Charlotte a tray from the cafeteria, which she accepted with only a few words of thanks before saying good-night.

"This isn't about the house, is it?" he asked and re-laxed a little when she quickly shook her head.

"Not at all. I'm happy to be here."

"I'm happy you're here, too."

When she'd shut the door, Lincoln stalked to his parents' place, grabbed a chair off the back deck, lugged it to his new front porch and sat there while he polished off the food he'd brought for himself. Afterward, he made another trip to his folks' place to replenish the ice in his cooler, snag a six-pack from the fridge and some snacks—in case Charlotte felt better later.

He had just made it back to number 35 when his phone chimed. He pulled it out of his pocket with alacrity, hoping it was Charlotte, but a different name came up on the screen.

"Hey, Lincoln, this is Lena Hughes. I don't know if you remember me. I used to be Lena Reed—from Two Willows," a female voice said when he answered. "I bumped into Bella Mortimer this afternoon, and she said you have a bunch of empty houses on Elliott Ridge and were looking for people to move there. Is that right?"

"That's right," Lincoln said. "And I do remember you. I talked to Cass at Carter's wedding." Lena and her four sisters had a wonderful ranch outside town. They'd had a wild upbringing, and he'd heard rumors about trouble in recent years, but according to Cass, Lena's oldest sister, things were better these days.

"I was sorry to miss that," Lena said. "One of our cows was sick, and I had to stay home, but I heard the ceremony went off without a hitch and everyone had a great time. Tell Carter congratulations."

"Will do. You're interested in our houses?"

"We had a family dinner tonight, and I told everyone what Bella said. Turns out Alice knows someone who's involved in a start-up. Have you heard that Alice works in costume design now?"

"I think Nate mentioned that." He'd seen Alice at the wedding but hadn't had the chance to say more than hello to her.

"She works on all the biggest movies, and she's got connections to everyone. Anyway, she met this woman at a premiere, Anne Thatcher, who makes video games, and the two of them hit it off. They've been online friends ever since. Now Anne is looking to relocate somewhere cheap because she's trying to stretch her angel investment money as far as it can go. She thinks she's got a project that's going to sell, but she needs a long runway before it can take off. Or something like that. I'm trying to quote what Alice told me."

"What's the product?"

"Hell if I know," Lena said cheerfully. "The minute she started talking about it, I tuned her out. Something super girly, I think."

Lincoln laughed. "Don't blame you. Do you have her number?"

"I'll send it to you. Alice says hi, by the way. She

says Dennis is right, but don't let it stop you. Stay the course, and you won't regret it in the end."

"She said… what?"

"Alice gets hunches sometimes, remember? They're rarely helpful, but they're pretty accurate. Listen, I've got to run."

She cut the call before Lincoln could ask any more questions.

Dennis was right? About what?

Lincoln's gut twisted. About Charlotte bringing trouble to the Ridge? Dennis had said something similar when Amanda arrived. Kept yammering on about a Trouble Summer or something.

Calamity Year.

The phrase came unbidden to his mind as he sat on his deck chair and popped open a beer.

Was more trouble coming?

He sure as hell hoped not.

SHE NEEDED TO know what was going on.

Charlotte paced her darkened bedroom, unable to keep still. It was nine thirty, and she was afraid to turn on her light, even though the sun had set a long time ago. She'd noticed Lincoln sitting on the front porch of the house next door earlier. Keeping watch or passing the time or whatever it was men did when they were thwarted. At one point he'd had a phone call, proving there really was a carrier that provided cell phone coverage on the Ridge. Her provider was useless. She hadn't been able to make a call or access the internet all day. Lincoln finally retreated inside, and a light came on in the bedroom across the way from hers. On the one hand, that was reassuring. If anything happened, all she needed to do was scream, and he'd come running.

On the other hand, it was a pain in the ass.

She'd meant to spend the afternoon doing research and coming up with a plan for how to fight back against Ivan, but first she hadn't been able to get on the internet—or even call Steven. Then, when she was about to try Lincoln's suggestion to go to the town hall, Amanda had shown up and refused to take Charlotte's hints that she wanted to be alone. She'd asked Charlotte about her plans for each room and come up with so many suggestions that soon they were brainstorming furniture and window coverings as well as kitchen cabinets and backsplashes. Since Charlotte's phone was hopeless, Amanda had used hers to create an online pin board for her, and together they'd filled it with images.

The afternoon had slipped away. By the time Amanda left, it was nearly dinner. The cafeteria would have been full of people, including Lincoln and his brothers. No way she could have made a private call from there. She'd stayed home, accepted the dinner tray Lincoln had brought her, and had been biding her time ever since. Now the settlement was quiet, and she could make her move.

As long as Lincoln didn't catch her.

She changed into dark clothing, slipped on the thick-soled shoes she used to wear to work and went downstairs. Opening the front door as quietly as she could, she edged outside without closing it fully, so she could return to the house with as little noise as possible. She didn't know if Lincoln could hear her from his bedroom in number 35, but she didn't want to take any chances. She could imagine his response if he learned she was being blackmailed by her thug ex-boyfriend. The Elliotts didn't need her trouble dropped in their laps. They had enough of their own.

Charlotte tiptoed down the porch steps and made it to the street as quietly as she could. Once there, she picked up the pace, traversing the dark roads until she drew close to the town hall. She sat on its steps, pulled up a web browser and was happy to find the internet worked here. It was far too late to call Steven, even though she had a couple of bars, so she emailed him instead, telling him how she'd found a new home. Then she forwarded Ivan's note to him, so he could read it for himself.

She moved on to haphazard searches for legal information. *Can my boyfriend sue me if I break up with him?* Before she got much further than that, her phone buzzed, making her jump.

It was Steven calling.

"Hello?" she whispered when she accepted the call. "Steven? What are you doing up so late?" It had to be past midnight on the East Coast.

"Couldn't sleep. You'll see how it is when you're my age. Got your email and figured you might want to talk."

Steven might not look the part of a hero, but this

past week he'd become one to Charlotte. She breathed a sigh of relief now that he was on the other end of the line. He already knew about her mistakes, so she could talk to him plainly.

"You saw Ivan's email. He sent me a bill for everything I ever charged on the credit card he gave me, plus rent and the student loan payments he covered. He wants me to pay him back for all of it—but he never paid me for the veterinarian work I did. He can't do that, can he?"

"Of course not. He's trying to intimidate you."

Relief swept through her. "That's what I thought." She hugged her arms across her chest. Now that the sun was down, it was a little chilly up here. "I don't think he knows where I am, or he'd be saying all this to my face. Can I just ignore him?"

"I think that's the best course. He'll have to sue you in court if he wants to try to collect," Steven said. "This is a bluff. He's trying to regain the power he lost when you left town. Trying to scare you into revealing where you are. Keep your head down for as long as you can."

"All right." When Steven put it like that, it all sounded so simple. "I have to admit, that email scared me."

"You should be scared. I wouldn't have had you crisscrossing the country and buying plane tickets in cash if I didn't think you were in danger." He was silent a moment. "Charlotte, if you ever think he's figured out where you are… leave. As fast as you can. Don't pack. Don't tell anyone where you're going. Just get out of there. Keep some cash on hand so you can use it to pay your way, just like you did before, all right?"

"All right," she said faintly. She couldn't believe she'd become some kind of fugitive.

"Ivan's crimes will catch up to him sooner or later," Steven assured her. "It's not your job to bring him to justice. It's your job to stay safe. Tell me about this place where you're staying."

Charlotte told him everything she knew, emphasizing the fact that Lincoln and his brothers were all military men and that there were temporary workers around, too.

"I should be safe here," she finished, trying to convince herself as much as Steven.

"Good," Steven said. "Keep me posted if you hear from Ivan again, though."

"Will do. Thanks, Steven."

"Any time."

As Charlotte pocketed the phone, she heard a small sound.

She stood up quickly, her breath catching in her throat. "Who's there?"

CHAPTER 6

B USTED.

"It's just me." Lincoln stepped out from the shadows, wishing now he'd approached Charlotte in a more direct way. He hadn't meant to scare her.

"Lincoln. What are you doing here?" Charlotte put a hand to heart. "Did you follow me?"

"No. Well… I followed you, but not the way you mean. I figured you were coming here to make a call or use the Wi-Fi. Problem is, I never told you about the bears."

"Bears?"

"And coyotes. Possibly wolves."

"Are you serious?"

He nodded. "I should have said something earlier. You know Elliott Ridge was empty for twelve years—except for Dennis. The local wildlife still thinks of this as their territory." He didn't ask her who Steven was, much as he wanted to. Charlotte looked thoroughly frightened and he couldn't blame her. He'd startled her when he approached.

"That doesn't give you an excuse to hide behind a bush and listen to my phone conversation."

"I didn't hide behind a bush," he explained patiently. "I just got here. Took a minute to put on some pants before I chased after you. I thought I was in for the night." When he saw she was still upset, he tried again. "I was trying to protect you."

"I don't need protecting!"

"Everybody needs protecting sometimes. Like I said, I just wanted to give you a heads-up." She was a jumpy one, wasn't she? Once again, Lincoln wondered what had happened before she came to Elliott Ridge.

Charlotte lifted her chin. "I don't want to be watched all the time, okay? If I stay here, I want to be my own woman. I want privacy. Is that too much to ask?"

"No, it's not." Lincoln took a steadying breath. It would be easy to escalate this if he took her attacks personally. He leaned on his military training and tried to defuse the situation instead. "Look, I scared you, and you're upset, but I didn't come after you to listen to your conversation or invade your privacy. I only wanted to make sure you got here safely—and made it back home safely, too. I can leave now, or I can wait until you're finished and walk you back. It's your choice." Their raised voices had probably scared off any nearby wildlife, anyway.

After a moment, Charlotte sighed. "Sorry," she said grudgingly. "I'm overreacting, aren't I? I couldn't get any cell reception at the house, and you said it was better up here. I needed to talk to a friend."

Lincoln winced, then reminded himself they'd just met, even if they had exchanged a few kisses. He couldn't blame Charlotte for wanting to talk to someone she'd known longer—even if it was a man.

"What?" she asked when he didn't say anything. "Is there something wrong with calling a friend?"

"No, but given that friend's name is Steven, I guess I'm wondering if I have competition." He knew he'd put his foot in it the moment the words came out of his mouth, but he couldn't help himself. He'd spent all evening thinking about a future with Charlotte, and he wanted to know if he was barking up the wrong tree.

She stalked past him. Lincoln bit back a curse and followed her. "Charlotte. Charlotte, hey—wait up." He had to jog a few steps to catch up and step in front of her.

She stopped short and folded her arms across her chest. "You don't get to ask me questions like that. I don't know you yet, Lincoln. Maybe I kissed you, and maybe I liked it, but I don't know if you're going to be an acquaintance, a friend, or... whatever. Right now you're just the guy who sold me a house." She cut around him and stalked off.

Lincoln jogged after her again. Stepped in front of her and made her stop. "If you want me to back off, all you have to do is tell me. I'm not the kind of guy who chases women who aren't interested. I don't play games. But I am human, Charlotte. I like you. I want to get to know you. I just don't want to make an ass out of myself if you're attached to someone else. It's that simple."

She planted her feet and faced him, beautiful in the starlight, her hair loose around her shoulders.

"Life is never that simple," she said, and his gut twisted. Did she like playing games and juggling multiple men for her amusement? As if she'd read his mind, she lifted her hands. "I don't play games, either, and the last thing I want is men competing for my attention. I'm a one-man woman, but I'm not interested in being pushed around—physically or mentally."

Lincoln stilled. "I will never do that," he said slowly and clearly. She had to know that about him right from the start.

Charlotte raised an eyebrow, as if she didn't believe him and that stung.

"Asking you if there's another man in your life isn't pushing you around," he said. "But," he added, forestalling her retort, "if I'd come here with the intention of listening to your phone calls because I thought I had the right to control who you talked to, that would cross a line."

"You're damn right about that." She eyed him. "You sure you didn't come here to do just that?"

"I'm positive. Like I said, I was worried some critter would cross your path and scare you right out of town before I could convince you to stay." He stood his ground. His mother had raised all of them to be gentlemen and nothing about his military service had changed that.

She considered what he'd said. Let out a sigh that said she was tired of arguing. "Steven is my lawyer," she said finally. "He's helping me sort out my grandmother's affairs. That's all. He's an old family friend, and he's been a big help to me."

Relief crashed through Lincoln, and he knew he was in deep trouble when it came to this woman. It wasn't a question of whether he'd fall for her; he'd fallen, hard.

"Got it. Old friends are worth their weight in gold. New friends can be pretty valuable, too. Any time you want to talk, just come and find me. I'll be happy to listen."

"Right. Sure. I'll spill my guts to you so you can turn around and use what you learn against me the next time you want something."

"What? No." Lincoln pulled back in surprise at her bitter words. "Who does that?"

"Men!"

"What kind of guys have you been hanging out with?"

She flinched, and her gaze dropped to the ground. She shrugged.

Some real assholes, he'd wager. And now she was tarring every man with the same brush.

"I'm not like that," he assured her. "Neither are my brothers." Not even Hudson.

"So you say."

"I'd like to think I'm one of the good guys," he said softly.

She rolled her eyes. "Now you sound like an ax

murderer again."

"I'm not an ax murderer." He thought he'd regained some ground, however. It was time to call it a night and try again in the morning, after she'd had some sleep. He hoped this Steven guy had given her the advice she needed.

"Let me walk you back and tuck you into bed," he said and almost groaned again. He'd been shooting for lighthearted, but it had come out suggestive instead.

"You don't miss a beat, do you?" Charlotte asked.

"Usually I'm better at this stuff," he said as they turned to go.

"Are you?"

"No," he admitted. "But I'm trying."

"Just walk me home," she said. "Before the bears get here."

CHARLOTTE WOKE TO the buzz of her new cell phone on the mattress beside her, far too early in the morning for comfort. She wished she'd set it to mute rather than vibrate, but since it had barely worked here at the house yesterday, she hadn't deemed it necessary. She fished around through the bedclothes for it and squinted at the screen.

It was a text from Amanda.

If you're up, meet me at the library.

Charlotte sat up, sleep forgotten. Why did Amanda want to see her so early? It was light out, but only because the sun came up at an unspeakable hour in the middle of the summer.

She supposed she'd better find out.

Charlotte tossed her covers aside and changed into shorts and a cute top, one of the purchases she'd made in town. Slipping her feet into a brand-new pair of sandals, she went downstairs, wondering if Lincoln would follow her again.

She felt bad now for the way she'd attacked him last night, but he'd startled her when he stepped out of the shadows near the town hall, and worse, she'd been afraid he'd overheard her conversation with Steven. She was here to start her life over, and she didn't want to drag all her ugly baggage along with her. Ivan needed to stay in her past.

After making her way through the deserted streets, she found Amanda in front of the town hall, wearing white shorts and a sweet peach-colored top, her hair in a ponytail.

"Want to help me pull off a trick?" she asked as Charlotte approached.

"What kind of trick?" The last thing Charlotte needed was to stir up more drama.

"A fun one," Amanda assured her. "Carter and his brothers play a game. It's basically Capture the Flag, but in their version, someone steals the flag off the pole on house number 1 and takes it to their base. Each brother has one in a different area of Elliott Ridge. Everyone else has to try and find it, and the first one who brings it back where it belongs wins."

Charlotte tried to make sense of what she was saying. "A game?" she repeated. She wasn't awake enough for this.

Amanda laughed. "That's right, a game. The Elliott boys are very competitive. They'll stand together against an outside threat, but among themselves it's a battle to the death. Last month Gage stole the flag and took it to his favorite beach. Hudson found it and swam it back, but then Carter wrestled it away from him. I managed to get it to the porch of number 1, so we won. I figured that means it's my turn to start the game." She shrugged. "Their dad is having his surgery today. They could use a distraction."

"Oh. Right." A new wave of shame washed through Charlotte. Lincoln had mentioned his father's upcoming surgery when they'd met, and she'd forgotten all about it. He'd probably been consumed with worry when he spotted her slipping out of her house last night and came after her to warn her about the bears. Charlotte sighed. Another mistake to add to the list. "If we steal the flag, where's our base?"

"I thought about that. Like I said, Gage's is on a beach you have to swim to. Hudson's base is up a huge tree. Carter's is a lookout near the top of the Ridge. I don't know where Lincoln's is."

"The graveyard," Charlotte said automatically. "Don't you think?" she added when Amanda's brows rose.

"I bet you're right," Amanda said slowly. "I wonder if Nate's is in the woodshop that used to be his grandfather's or if he has another special place?"

Charlotte didn't know about that.

"Anyway, I recently found my base."

"The library?" Charlotte guessed. After all, Amanda was the librarian.

"No—that's too obvious. I chose somewhere better. Here, I'll show you." She led the way around the side of the town hall and up the street to a plain white building behind it that was topped by a short steeple. "This is the chapel." She opened the door, and Charlotte went in. It was a clean, simple building, the door opening straight into a large room with rows of pews and tall windows. "I'm pretty sure the whole town could fit in here even when it was in its heyday. Carter said the last minister died in the eighties, and they haven't had one since. I guess religious people went to Chance Creek on Sundays after that."

"Makes sense. This is your base?"

"No." Amanda laughed. "Not the chapel. I finally got around to exploring it recently, though. That's when I found the rotunda."

"Rotunda?"

"That's what I call it. I'm not sure what its purpose is. Come and see." She walked the length of the hall to an unobtrusive door tucked near the vestry. Opening it, she beckoned Charlotte past her. The door led to a breezeway that connected to a small, round structure, tucked in the lee of the chapel and town hall. You couldn't see it from any road, Charlotte realized. "Go on in," Amanda told her.

Charlotte opened the rotunda's door and gasped. Inside, the small building was flooded with light. Large windows were set at intervals all the way around the walls. Beneath them, bench window seats circled a pine floor. The walls were pine, as well, making Charlotte feel as if she was in a tiny, wonderful cabin. Under each bench seat was open shelving.

"More books," Charlotte exclaimed.

"They're an interesting mixture of inspirational, crafting and art books, nature manuals and fiction." Amanda shrugged. "It's like the best librarian in the world curated the collection. Every time I come here, I pull one out and get sucked into reading for an hour."

"This would be a lovely place to sit and paint or knit or craft… or just read or chat," Charlotte said, turning in a slow circle to drink it all in. Each bench seat was topped with a thick, cloth-covered pad, with throw pillows scattered around to lean against. "You picked a wonderful base." She felt a stab of envy. Amanda had claimed two amazing spaces, the library and this one. But then, she'd come to Elliott Ridge first.

"I'll claim it as my base as far as the game goes, but I won't hog it all to myself. This is for all of us women."

"All of us?" There were only two of them so far. Three, counting the elusive Carolyn Snyder, whom she hadn't met yet. Yesterday, Amanda had told her Carolyn volunteered at the nearest hospital frequently, played bridge several times a week in Chance Creek and sang in a local choir there, too, among other activities.

"There'll be more soon. When we need to get away from the guys, we'll come here."

"You sure you don't mind sharing it?"

"Of course not. Besides, it's not really mine, is it? I figure if the two of us stake a claim to it, the guys will accept it as ours and keep their distance. I don't think they even remember it's here."

Charlotte looked around again. "We need to start a social calendar. We could do book club night, a craft night…"

"A wine and cheese night," Amanda suggested. "The sky is the limit." She went to one of the bench seats, crouched down and pulled a tote bag from the shelf. "Can you keep a secret?"

"Sure."

Amanda took out a ball of soft yellow yarn. "You can't tell anyone."

"Since when is yarn a crime?" Charlotte quipped. She touched it with her fingertip. It was as delicate as a cloud.

"Since I'm knitting a baby sweater and I'm not even pregnant yet."

"Are you and Carter trying for a baby?" Charlotte supposed it made sense. Amanda had to be in her late twenties, and she'd mentioned wanting kids.

"We're talking about it, and we both want to, but we haven't decided about the timing. It's like we're waiting for someone to give us permission." She chuckled. "It's kind of weird that you can have a baby any old time, isn't it? I mean, if everything works out. Shouldn't there be a test or something to pass first?"

"If there was, I'm sure you and Carter would ace it. And I think it's perfectly reasonable to knit for a baby you want, even if you're not pregnant yet."

Amanda pulled out a small, half-finished garment on tiny knitting needles to show her, and Charlotte exclaimed over the delicate work. "That's beautiful." She felt a pang she couldn't quite quantify. Did she want a baby?

Ivan hadn't been father material. Lincoln, however, was a different matter. She'd bet he'd be a wonderful father, given how gentle he'd been with her so far.

That made her think of their night on the beach, which made her think of the kiss she'd given him. Why had she been so awful to him last night? She hoped she hadn't scared him away.

"You want to join my knitting club? It's secret, remember."

"Of course I want to join your secret knitting club." Charlotte couldn't think of anything she'd rather do. It sounded so… safe. So normal. If only all her problems would disappear, and she could focus on happy activities like that.

"No men allowed in the rotunda. That's the rule," Amanda proclaimed.

"I can go along with that." Although given how much Amanda and Carter seemed to be in love with each other, she didn't believe for a minute the rule would last long.

"We'd better grab the flag before anyone else is around." She checked the time on her phone. "We've got fifteen minutes before Gage heads out for his daily swim. Let's go!"

They hurried back the way they'd come, through the chapel, down the hill, around the town hall and over to the big white house near the lake.

"Rule number one is everyone's lying," Amanda whispered. "That's what Carter told me, anyway."

"Okay." Charlotte wondered what they were lying about. Maybe whether or not they were the one who'd taken the flag?

"Rule number two is you can't hide the flag. You have to display it. Since the rotunda is tucked away, we can display it openly, and it will still be hard for anyone to spot it. We need to get the flag to the rotunda and then return to our houses before anyone knows we're gone. When it's time to start our day, we need to do everything exactly the way we normally would."

"I can do that." Charlotte quietly followed Amanda up the steps and helped her take the flag out of its holder. Now she knew how fiercely the Elliott brothers would play the game once they knew it was afoot, she understood that she and Amanda had one chance to surprise them. After today, they'd be prime suspects whenever the game was played.

They hurried to the rotunda, where there was a similar holder by the door.

"I'm guessing this one held holiday-themed banners back in the day," Amanda said. "Thank goodness it's here."

They stepped back to survey their handiwork. The men would have to come looking to see the flag, tucked away as it was.

"Can you get home without anyone seeing you?" Amanda asked as they retreated toward the Circle. "If they catch us out here, they'll ask questions."

"We'll say we decided to start a yoga practice. That'll send them running."

"Good idea." Amanda laughed. "See you at breakfast!"

Charlotte dropped her off at number 23, then cut through to her street, where she slipped her sandals off before padding the rest of the way barefoot. When she reached her house, she let herself in as quietly as she could. Only once she was in her bedroom on the second floor did she relax.

She'd done it, much to her surprise. No sign of Lincoln. Was he sleeping or up and getting ready for breakfast?

She'd better get ready, too, she thought ruefully. No time to go back to bed. Instead, she opted for a shower, hoping the hot water and some coffee later would be enough to get her through the day.

LINCOLN WAS JUST leaving his house, his hair damp from the shower, when a text came in. To his surprise, it was from Hudson.

Heard anything about Dad? No one else has. Mom isn't answering my texts.

Not yet, he texted back. *They're probably on their way to the hospital now.* His father wasn't due in surgery until noon Eastern Time but needed to arrive earlier to be prepped. Lincoln had called during a quiet moment yesterday to wish his father well, but his dad had gotten off the phone quickly. He wasn't one to dwell on medical matters. Lincoln knew his mother would call as soon as the surgery was over, around lunchtime here in Montana.

He'd made it halfway to the town hall when his phone buzzed again. It was Gage.

Flag's gone.

Excitement jolted through him. Who'd taken it this time? Last time Gage was the culprit. He'd brought it to his beach retreat, probably by kayak, and returned to number 1 before anyone noticed.

Lincoln's first instinct was to race to Hudson's favorite tree and stop by Nate's workshop on the way, killing two birds with one stone. If neither had taken it, Lincoln would be well on the way up the Ridge toward Carter's favorite lookout, where he'd hang the flag if he was the one who stole it.

He hesitated, though, made a decision and dashed for Charlotte's front porch instead. She answered his knock more quickly than expected. To his relief, she was already dressed.

"Flag's gone!" he blurted. "Come on. I'll explain as we go." He took her hand, tugged her out the door and shut it behind her. "Nate's workshop first." He set off at a run, pulling her along with him. He expected her to protest, especially after their argument last night, but she ran along with him gamely. Lincoln's estimation of her went up a notch, something he didn't know was possible until that moment.

"What flag?" she cried.

"Our family's flag."

"Who took it?"

"I don't know. That's the whole game."

"Game?"

"It's like Capture the Flag. Someone steals the El-liott flag from house number 1, and whoever finds it and gets it back there first wins."

"I like winning!" She was doing a good job keeping up with him despite wearing sandals. He should have told her to change her shoes.

"Good. Because I love winning."

They exchanged a grin, and any worry that remained after their disagreement the previous evening fell away. Lincoln tightened his grip on her hand and increased his speed. "It's not at Nate's workshop." They passed the rustic building with its sliding barn doors at a fast clip, and the ground began to slope up under their feet.

"This is… steep," Charlotte puffed. "Where are we going now?"

"Hudson's tree. It isn't far. You're doing great!" Ex-hilaration filled him. Lincoln knew many women wouldn't be amused by this game at all. Most would want to sit on the sidelines. Charlotte was throwing herself into it, no questions asked.

He swore as Carter and Amanda came into view, also running hand in hand. His brother waved as they raced past but didn't slow his steps. Amanda exchanged a smile with Charlotte. Had they come from Hudson's tree? Or was Carter the one who'd taken the flag? If so, he might have left it at his lookout.

If he hadn't, maybe Gage had taken it again, fooling them all.

"What's wrong?" Charlotte asked as he hesitated.

"If Carter took the flag, then it's at his lookout about three-quarters of the way up the Ridge. If he didn't take it, he and Amanda must have just been at Hudson's tree and the flag wasn't there. So do we think Carter took it or not?"

Charlotte shrugged. "You know him better than I do."

She was so damn pretty, even out of breath, pink-cheeked from the exercise. For one moment, Lincoln didn't care about the flag. He cared about being alone with Charlotte. Getting closer to her.

But he needed to stay focused. "Up or down?" he asked. "Use your woman's intuition."

Charlotte hesitated. Traced Carter and Amanda's course down the slope. "Down," she said after a moment.

"Down?" Lincoln knew they were taking a gamble. Carter very well could have taken the flag. "Down it is."

They raced together back the way they'd come, bursting out of the rows of houses onto the Circle and dashing straight across it. His brothers were gathering near the steps to number 1's porch.

"Gage doesn't have it," Nate gasped, slightly damp and very disheveled. "I saw everyone else racing for the Ridge, so I played the odds and went the other way. Kayaked all the way to his beach. It's not there."

"It's not in Hudson's tree," Carter said.

"It's not in Lincoln's graveyard," Gage said. "Just checked. Didn't see it at Nate's workshop, either."

"We were just there, too," Lincoln said. "No flag."

"Well, it's not at Carter's lookout," Hudson huffed. "I went all the way up the damn Ridge. I was sure it was him."

"That's everywhere," Lincoln said. "We've checked the beach, the tree, the lookout, the workshop, and I know it's not in the graveyard."

They stood in a ragged circle, breathing hard, Lincoln and his brothers eyeing each other.

"Did… Warrington take it?" Hudson finally asked.

Amanda laughed, then clapped a hand over her mouth.

Carter turned on her. "Did *you* take it?"

"Gotcha!" Amanda cried. "Charlotte and I took the flag this morning. Now you have to figure out where it is!"

"You're in on this?" Lincoln asked Charlotte. "Why didn't you say so?"

"Rule number 1: everyone's lying," Charlotte said giddily. "That's what Amanda told me."

"She's right." Gage laughed heartily, to Lincoln's surprise. He couldn't remember the last time he'd seen his brother do that.

"The kitchen," Hudson roared and took off running for the town hall. Carter, Nate and Gage took off after him, pushing and shoving as they ran. Gage tripped Carter, and the two of them went down hard in the dirt.

Hudson and Nate got into a shoving match in the town hall doorway.

Meanwhile, Lincoln grabbed Charlotte's hand. "I bet I know where it is." He raced toward the old chapel. If Amanda was using it as a private oasis, she might have chosen it as her base.

Charlotte ran along with him, but there was no flag in sight. "Shoot—*is* it in the kitchen?"

Charlotte shook her head. "You're warm," she said, then looked guilty.

Lincoln looked around. "Warm?" he repeated. Suddenly he straightened. "I know!"

As soon as he pulled open the chapel door, he could tell he'd guessed correctly from the way Charlotte was grinning. They ran through the chapel, out the little door and through the breezeway. When Lincoln spotted the flag waving beside the door to the rotunda, he gave a roar of triumph. "I knew it. Mom claimed it as her own back in the day. Said it was the one place we weren't allowed to bug her. I thought it was funny when I noticed Amanda was using the chapel to get away from us, too."

"I suppose you need a break once in a while when you have five sons," Charlotte said. "You still need to get that flag to your parents' place," she reminded him.

"You're right." And his brothers would know it wasn't in the kitchen by now. "We'll have to be fast!"

He took off, pulling her along with him, and in no time they reached the Circle again.

"They're coming!" Charlotte pointed toward the

town hall where his four brothers were spilling out of the doorway empty-handed. Amanda stood nearby, laughing.

Lincoln put his head down. "Run!"

They raced across the Circle, over the road and onto number 1's front yard. His brothers reached it at the same time.

"Get him!" Carter yelled, leaping toward him. Lincoln dodged him, shoved Hudson out of the way and slammed into Gage, knocking them both over. Charlotte, still holding his hand, fell, too, but quickly scrambled to her feet. She snatched the flag from Lincoln's hands and screamed when Nate caught her. He tried to take the flag, but she refused to let go, the two of them getting into a tug of war.

Regaining his feet at the same time Gage did, Lincoln saw Hudson lunge toward Charlotte. Lincoln ducked his shoulder and rammed his oldest brother into Hudson, whirled, grabbed Charlotte by the waist and lifted her off the ground, snatching the flag out of Nate's hands.

"Look out!" Charlotte screamed as he gave her the flag.

Too late.

Carter launched himself at them and knocked Lincoln off his feet, falling with him. Lincoln dropped Charlotte, who rolled several times and curled up in a ball. When Hudson went after the flag again, trying to rip it from her hands, she cried out in pain.

Hudson backpedaled quickly. "Shit. Are you okay?"

"Charlotte?" Lincoln elbowed Carter aside, got to his feet and rushed toward her. He dropped to his knees. "Charlotte? Where are you hurt?"

She thrust the flag into his hands. "Run!" she hissed, then sprang up to block Hudson and Nate from reaching him. "Lincoln, run!"

He ran. Carter was still on the ground. Hudson hadn't figured out what was happening yet. Gage had stopped and was shaking his head. In a flash Lincoln was up the steps. He slapped the palm of his hand on the front door.

"We won!"

"What? That's not fair," Hudson protested. "Charlotte took the flag. She can't help get it back."

"I'm the one who got it to the house," Lincoln said.

"Never thought this game could get any dirtier. I was wrong," Nate grumbled.

"Whose team are you on, anyway?" Carter asked Amanda. "I thought you were on mine. Now you're pairing up with Lincoln's girl?"

Lincoln looked to see how Charlotte would react to that designation. She was grinning. So was Amanda.

"Maybe there's a new team," Amanda said. "The women's team."

"You can make a women's team," Nate said. "But if you do, you can't be on Carter's team, too."

"It's supposed to be every man for himself." Hudson put his hands on his hips. "No fair some teams have two people on them."

"You're just mad you don't have a girl," Gage said.

"You don't, either."

Gage turned to Amanda and Charlotte. "What's it going to be? Are you on your men's teams, are you together, or are you each going to play on your own team next time?"

Charlotte glanced Lincoln's way with a questioning look that made him warm all over.

"Charlotte's on my team," he declared, knowing he was taking a chance but willing to risk it. "Right, Charlotte?" He came down the steps to take her hand.

"Do you mind?" Charlotte asked Amanda.

"No. Today was fun, but I'm Team Carter all the way," Amanda said, going up on tiptoe to kiss her husband. "I'm a newlywed, after all."

Carter kissed her back. "Don't you forget it."

"Team Lincoln it is," Charlotte said.

"That's settled, then. Time for breakfast," Gage said. "We're going to be late to work."

The others followed him, Hudson still grumbling and Nate wondering out loud how the addition of teams skewed the odds of winning. Lincoln waited until they were gone.

"Team Lincoln, huh?" he asked Charlotte, taking her other hand, too.

"Why not?" she said, smiling.

"I like the sound of that," he admitted. It felt natural to bend down and brush a kiss against her mouth. When she closed her eyes and let him, he let go of her hands, wrapped his arms around her and stepped in close. It felt good to hold her, his whole body waking up.

Charlotte reached her arms around his neck and pressed herself against him in a way that fired up all his senses. He'd hoped this would happen from the moment he'd spotted Charlotte at the airport, but he'd never dreamed they'd become a couple so fast.

He kissed her again, a hungry, satisfying kiss that went on and on. When they broke away from each other, he found it hard to catch his breath, and he wasn't sure what to say.

"Hungry?" he finally settled on.

"Very," she admitted.

"Charlotte." He didn't know how to put into words all the thoughts that were running through his mind as they turned toward the town hall.

"I know. We hardly know each other. We're rushing this. I keep telling myself to hold back."

"You do?" Did that mean she felt the way he did? Desperate to get close to him the way he was desperate to get close to her?

"Of course. I'm trying to make good decisions for once, and good decisions take time, but I like you," she said. "I just... do."

"I like you, too."

"But—"

Lincoln's phone buzzed, and he grabbed it from his pocket. It wasn't his mom. The name on the screen was familiar, but he couldn't place it. "I'll call them back," he said. This conversation was too important to interrupt.

Charlotte shook her head. "Take the call. I'll wait. I

mean it," she added. "I'm in no rush."

Reluctantly, he lifted his phone to his ear. "Hello?"

"Lincoln Elliott?" a woman's voice asked. "This is Anne Thatcher. Alice Sanders's friend?"

It took him a moment to realize she meant Lena's sister, Alice Reed, who was married now to Jack Sanders. "Right. Lena told me about you."

"She asked if she could give you my number, but I was in a hurry, so I made her give me yours. You've got houses for rent, right? Inexpensive ones?"

"Possibly," Lincoln said cautiously.

"Like I said, I'm in a hurry. I need a house with six bedrooms. I need a fast internet connection. My start-up just received angel investment funding, and we need to make it last until we're ready to ship our product. I'm looking for somewhere dirt cheap for us to live and work. Is that what you've got?"

Lincoln thought it over. There were one or two houses on the Ridge with that many bedrooms, but the goal was to sell the ones in Lucy's Corner, and none of them was that big. "You sure you don't want to buy? Our prices are low right now, and they'll go up over time."

"No," she said decisively. "This is a temporary situation—at least at first. If we meet our deadlines and our eventual sales goals, there's a chance we'll want to stay, but for now I'm concerned only with getting our first product out the door. We need proof of concept before we commit to anything."

"What's your product?"

"It's called Couture Campaign—a fashion game. I can't go into any more details before you sign an NDA."

Couture Campaign? Lena was right; that did sound girly. Lincoln pictured a group of fashionable women taking matters into their own hands and coding the game they always wished they had when they were teenagers. Given how desperately his family needed to attract more women to the Ridge, Anne and her friends sounded perfect. "Of course. I think I have something that might suit you, and I can offer you reasonable rent," he said. "But our internet won't be upgraded until September. There might be a workaround, though, if you can be flexible."

"What kind of workaround?"

"What if I can find you a workspace in town with fast internet for the rest of the summer—rent free? In return, you commit to staying through next June. You'll need time to move your operations here, anyway, right? It'll be only a couple of months and then the service out here will be upgraded."

She sighed. "That's not ideal, but I suppose I can fly in the day after tomorrow to check out the place. If you've got something worked out by then that covers our needs, I'll consider it."

"Day after tomorrow?"

"If everything's up to par, we'll move in next week."

"That's… fast." He needed to talk it over with his brothers. Charlotte was waiting for him expectantly, her brows raised.

"That's how I operate. See you on Wednesday."

"Wait—I'll need your flight details so I can come pick you up."

"No need. I'll rent a car so I can get the lay of the land. I will text my arrival time, though." Anne hung up.

"Who was that?" Charlotte asked him when he pocketed his phone.

"A new neighbor, I think. Let's go eat, and I'll fill you in."

Once they'd reached the town hall, stood in line and filled their plates, they took their seats with the rest of his brothers and Amanda at their usual table. He related his conversation with Anne as they ate breakfast.

"Good work," Nate said. "Six more women will liven up the place."

"They're coming here only temporarily," Hudson pointed out unnecessarily.

"How many women have *you* recruited to our town?" Lincoln shot back. Was his twin still out of shape that he hadn't won the game?

Hudson stood up so fast his chair scraped across the floor. "That's not my job, is it?"

"When are you going to do your job?" Lincoln said, surprised at his reaction. Hudson's face darkened. He dropped the dishes he'd just bent to pick up and stalked out of the cafeteria instead. The rest of them watched him go.

Nate shook his head. "What has gotten into him?"

"I don't know, but I'm over it." Lincoln turned to Gage. "We have to have logs. If he can't get it together, you'd better take that on."

"Working on it." Gage got up slowly, gathered Hudson's dishes as well as his own, returned them to the kitchen and followed his brother outside.

Lincoln met Charlotte's questioning gaze as he stood, too, and took a deep breath, struggling to let the tension seep out of his muscles. "Guess it's time for me to get to the mill. What will you do today?"

She stood, too. "I'm going to keep working on house plans, and Amanda and I are going to town later so I can buy a few things I forgot."

"I'll see you at lunch then."

"Looking forward to it."

When she leaned forward to meet his kiss, satisfaction filled him and he went to work with a light step despite his disagreement with Hudson. For once, the equipment worked without a hitch, and they were able to make progress toward the orders they were trying to fill, but as the morning went on, Lincoln found himself pulling his phone out of his pocket more frequently, checking the time and looking for messages from his mother he might somehow have missed.

His phone rang finally just as they were breaking for lunch, all the workers heading for the door to walk to the town hall. Instantly, Hudson, who'd kept his distance all morning, was by his side. "Is it Mom?"

"Yeah." Lincoln accepted the call. "Mom? Everything okay?"

"Dad's out of surgery and in the recovery room. The doctor says he did great."

The tears of relief in her voice hit him like a blow to the chest, and Lincoln suddenly realized how worried he'd been that something would go wrong. Hip surgery was routine, and he'd told himself everything would be fine, but ever since his father's heart problems started, he always feared the worst.

"I'm so glad." His voice was husky, and he cleared his throat. "When will you get to see him?"

Hudson nudged him. "Well?"

Lincoln gave his brother a thumbs-up. "He did great," he mouthed.

Hudson rubbed his jaw with his hand, then ran it over his face and through his hair as he turned away from Lincoln.

"Soon," his mother said. "Oh, Lincoln, I'm so relieved it's over. I told myself everything would be fine, but you know how I worry."

"I know, Mom. I was worried, too. I'm glad it's over. Want to talk to Hudson?"

Hudson glanced back at that, and Lincoln felt he'd been punched all over again. Hudson, who would rather die than betray a vulnerability, had tears in his eyes.

"Hey," Lincoln said, reaching to put a hand on his twin's shoulder. Hudson knocked it off, eyed him wildly for a moment, then stalked away again, like he had that morning, flinging open the door and slamming it shut behind him.

"Of course I want to talk to Hudson," his mother said.

Lincoln swallowed. "Um… sorry, Mom. He left before I could grab him. I'll tell him to call you when I see him at lunch."

There was a silence on the other end of the line. "Be good to him, Lincoln. He needs you, even if he won't admit it."

Despite the sorrow he'd just seen in Hudson's eyes, or maybe because of the strangeness of it, Lincoln's temper flared, and he fought to keep it under control. Why did everyone expect so much of him and let his twin off the hook? "Do you ever say things like that to Hudson?" he asked. "Do you tell *him* to be good to *me*? To make sure *I* don't get into trouble?"

His mother hesitated again. "No," she admitted. "You're not the one who needs watching. You never were."

He let out a disbelieving snort. "You seem sure of that."

"I am. I'm sorry, honey. I know it's unfair, but that's the way life is. Some people are given more responsibility than others, and you're one of them. But don't knock your brother. He'll come through when you really need him."

"Huh." Lincoln doubted that. When they were boys, he would have trusted Hudson with his life. Now he knew better. "Love you, Mom," he made himself say. "Say hi to Dad when you see him, and let us know when it's okay to call." He'd watch out for Hudson. He'd keep the mill running and get those loans paid off, too. His mother was right; he owed his parents that much.

"Will do. Love you, too."

CHARLOTTE WAS HAPPY to pull on her brand-new jogging outfit the following morning, one of the things she and Amanda had found while shopping together the previous day. She was happy, too, that Lincoln's father had come through his surgery with flying colors. Although he was uncomfortable now, the prognosis was that he'd soon be up and walking better than ever. Dinner the previous evening had been a festive affair, marred only by Hudson's absence. Apparently, he left straight after work and ate elsewhere. By the time she and Lincoln walked home, it had been getting late. Lincoln had left her at her door after a hot and heavy make-out session on the front porch that left her feeling like a teenager. She'd been very tempted to invite him inside, but in the end she hadn't. She was enjoying this slow courtship. It made her feel young again, like she'd erased all the years she'd wasted with Ivan and been wiped clean of the cynicism and bitterness he'd engendered in her.

She must have adjusted to her new surroundings, because she woke up at six feeling rested and ready for some exercise. Taking Steven's advice, she hadn't responded to Ivan's threatening email. He hadn't sent another, so she was beginning to hope that was the end of it. While in town with Amanda, she'd gone back to the phone store and made them help her switch providers. The boy behind the counter hadn't wanted to break her contract at first, but Amanda had asked to see the owner, who understood the problem the moment he found out where she and Charlotte lived. Now Charlotte could make phone calls whenever she wanted, no matter where she was.

A quick run would clean all the cobwebs from her brain and solidify her grasp of the layout of the community. She planned to make a circuit of the settlement, following the same path she'd taken with Lincoln on her first day in town. She'd mentioned to him last night she might start today with a jog if she woke early enough. He'd visibly struggled not to ask to come along but restrained himself and told her to have a good time.

"Take your phone, though," he'd added. "Just in case. And watch for bears. Make a bit of noise as you go so they know you're coming. They don't want to meet you any more than you want to meet them. They'll clear off if they hear you."

"I will," she assured him.

Outside, she warmed up a little by walking to the Circle, then broke into a jog, passed the town hall and turned toward the road that led up toward the mine. Soon she was breathing hard, since the hill was steep. When she finally reached the mine, her legs were wobbly.

From there she found Carter's lookout, where the vista that spread before her took her breath away. Up here, she could pretend she was the only one for miles.

She circled around a bit before she found the trail that led to the settlement. Hudson's tree was around here somewhere, wasn't it? Charlotte wasn't sure, but she followed a hunch, struck off the path and went looking for it. If she was going to play the game again, and she hoped she would, she needed to know where everything was.

Fifteen minutes later she stood at the base of an enormous tree with a wooden flagpole planted in the dirt nearby. This had to be it. She stared up at the branches that made a ladder to the sky. Did Hudson actually climb this behemoth? She'd loved clambering up trees when she was a girl, favoring a wide maple down the road from her grandmother's town house. She hadn't climbed anything in years, though.

"I don't have the flag, if that's what you're after," a voice said behind her.

Charlotte let out an unladylike shriek and spun to face the intruder.

Hudson.

He stared at her, his dark eyes sizing her up. He was so similar, yet so different from Lincoln. There was nothing flirtatious about him this morning. If anything, he looked… haunted.

"I wasn't after anything," she said quickly. "Just getting some exercise."

"Me, too." He was dressed in running pants and a black T-shirt. "I like to make sure everything is in its place before I start my day."

"I just like the sunshine and oxygen," she said warily. "I find if I run before breakfast, everything goes right, you know what I mean?"

After a moment he nodded. "Let's go, then." He gestured to a path she hadn't even noticed. She'd have to figure out how it connected to the other trails.

"You want to jog with me?" she asked in surprise.

"Why not?"

"Aren't you here to climb your tree?"

Hudson frowned, distant again. "You can climb it if you like."

"I don't think I'm up to that," she said truthfully, craning her neck to look up at the tree's crown.

"It's not tree-climbing time, anyway; it's jogging time. You coming or not?"

"After you." Charlotte wasn't sure why she was going for a jog with him, given his grumpiness, except she had a feeling if she didn't accept the invitation, she'd never get another one. Hudson reminded her of a temperamental stallion, as apt to buck you off as to let you ride. Still, her intuition told her Hudson could use company this morning. He'd been jumpy these past twenty-four hours and quick-tempered, and she could only suppose his father's surgery had something to do with it.

He set a quick pace that soon had her breathing hard again. As if knowing she'd already been to the top of the Ridge, he set off in the opposite direction, downhill toward the mill. They made a circuit of the log yard and the large, rectangular building, swung by the graveyard and headed for town.

When it became clear they weren't going to engage in any idle chitchat, Charlotte decided to take the bull by the horns and ask the obvious question. "What's with you and Lincoln?"

Hudson slowed a little. "What do you mean?"

"You're twins. Why aren't you close?"

"Who says we're not close?" He kept jogging.

"No one has to say it. It's obvious."

He slowed down until he was walking, his hands on his hips. "You ask a lot of questions."

"That's the only way I know how to get answers."

Hudson stopped short and faced her. "We're not close because I fucked up, okay? I thought I was doing him a favor, and I still think I was in my own way, but I should have handled things differently." He walked on.

Surprised, Charlotte trailed after him. Lincoln hadn't mentioned anything like that. "When did that happen?"

"Before we left the Ridge. I was kind of an ass back then. Air Force knocked some sense into me, I guess you could say. Lincoln just can't see it."

"Why don't you tell him you're sorry?"

He stopped again. "I shouldn't have to say it. He should know." Hudson stared down at her a moment, then sighed and took off. In a few strides, he set a pace fast enough to leave her sprinting after him. Soon she was too winded to speak at all. Whenever she drew near, Hudson went faster, until she had to admit defeat. He wasn't going to answer any more questions this morning.

Lincoln was sitting in the deck chair he'd placed on the front porch of number 35 when they rounded the corner, and he stood up slowly as they approached, waiting for them.

"Morning," he said when they arrived. Charlotte had the feeling he wasn't too pleased to see his brother.

She walked in a tight circle, fighting to regain her breath, then bent over and braced her hands on her knees. When she could speak, she said, "I met up with Hudson in the woods."

Lincoln nodded. "Doing better today?" he asked Hudson.

"I'm fine." Hudson didn't meet his gaze. "See you at breakfast," he said to Charlotte and jogged off.

"He caught me snooping around his tree," Charlotte told Lincoln. "I think he set that impossible pace to punish me." She was sweaty and her face felt flushed, her hair falling out of her ponytail. She thought about relaying the rest of their conversation but decided it would be better if Lincoln and Hudson worked things out between themselves in their own time.

"Did you climb it?"

"His tree? Are you kidding me? It's enormous. Hudson didn't climb it, either. I guess both of us wanted our feet on the ground this morning."

"Sensible," Lincoln said. "Half hour until breakfast." His gaze still tracked Hudson.

"I told you I wouldn't fall for him," she said.

He turned her way. "That's what you said. Hudson has a way of changing women's minds."

"He won't change mine," she assured him. "He's not you."

She moved toward her house, already anticipating her shower, but a moment later a pair of strong arms caught her around the waist. Lincoln turned her, lifted her straight off the ground, spun her in a circle and set her down, dropping a kiss on the top of her head.

"What was that for?" she asked, her heart beating fast as he pulled her into an embrace. She loved the feel of his arms around her and the solidity of his chest under her hands.

His voice rumbled low, and she felt it as much as heard it as she leaned against him. "For saying exactly the right thing."

CHAPTER 7

"AFTER WE RUN the Boston Marathon together, Charlotte and I can start training for some triathlons. Hell, maybe we'll find some dogs and try the Iditarod next," Hudson said a few hours later, following Lincoln into the mill office, where they were meeting with their brothers. They needed to discuss whether they were ready for Anne's visit the following day.

"For the last time, I didn't say you couldn't jog with my girlfriend," Lincoln said, taking a seat as the rest of his brothers filed in. Hudson had been trying to get a rise out of him for hours, and Lincoln was going to lose his cool if he didn't stop. "All I said was she bumped into you by accident this morning and jogged with you to be nice. Don't expect it to become a regular thing."

"Maybe it will become a regular thing. Maybe I'll move right into that spare bedroom you moved out of, set up some weights, and Charlotte and I can exercise together, too. You have to be fit if you want to do an Ironman." Hudson sat down across from him, and the others found seats as well.

"She's not interested in you." God, were they still in high school? Lincoln hadn't had a conversation like this in over a decade and didn't want to be having one now.

"You sure about that?"

"I'm positive."

"Can't be too careful. I think we've got chemistry. Hell, maybe I'll buy a ring and pop the question…" Hudson trailed off as silence descended around the conference table.

"You done making an ass out of yourself?" Gage asked him.

"Yep," Hudson said. He glanced uneasily at Lincoln, opened his mouth as if to say something, then shut it.

Had Hudson almost said, "Sorry?" Probably not, Lincoln decided, doing his best to tamp down his rising anger.

"Let's talk about the internet," Nate said loudly, turning the conversation to the real reason they'd gathered. "Carter? Any luck?"

Carter lifted his shoulders. "We can get the upgrade in August rather than September," he said, "but that's all the progress I've made."

"That's not good enough," Lincoln said, grateful to get down to business. He hated that Hudson brought out the worst in him these days. "Anne made it clear how important a strong connection is."

"Alice has offered part of her workshop at Two Willows free of charge as a temporary office," Carter countered. "It has a solid internet connection. I think that's the best we can do for now. How are the houses coming?"

"We'll have three of them cleaned up by tonight," Nate said.

"This whole community needs to shine when Anne gets here tomorrow," Carter said. "Look around today and fix anything that needs fixing. We've got one chance to convince her to move her business here."

"You know what we really need?" Hudson asked. "Old people."

The rest of them fell silent at this startling remark.

"What for?" Nate finally asked.

"To keep Mom and Dad company when they come back." Hudson shrugged, leaning back in his chair. "We should call up some of the old-timers. See if they want to buy the houses they used to rent, like Carolyn did."

"We need workers. People to contribute to the town's economy," Lincoln argued.

"Seems to me we need a mix of people," Hudson said.

"Hudson's right," Gage said. "Mom and Dad need people their age around."

"They're not exactly old," Carter countered.

"They're not young, either," Gage said. "Hudson, that's your new job. Start tracking down the people who used to live here and tell them our plans for the community. Maybe a few of them will want to return. Hell, maybe some of them will want a job."

"I'll get on it," Hudson said.

Lincoln wished he'd tackle his real job first, but he was smart enough not to say so.

"I DON'T KNOW why I'm nervous, but I am," Amanda said the next morning when Charlotte found her in the library. "There. Does the place look okay? Do programmers even care about libraries?"

"I'm sure Anne will love it. The real question is will she want to join our knitting club?" Charlotte teased her. Amanda wasn't the only one spurred to frantic activity after Lincoln had announced that a tech start-up was interested in moving to Elliott Ridge. Carter had spent most of yesterday on the phone with the Ridge's internet service provider. Hudson and Nate had spruced up three houses that each met Anne's requirement for the number of bedrooms. Lincoln had wondered aloud more than once why Anne couldn't rent two smaller houses, but the men had decided they'd better serve what she'd asked for.

"Women like to stick together," Hudson had said at dinner last night when they were discussing the matter.

"Like when they all go to the ladies' room at the same time," Nate had said.

Charlotte had exchanged a look with Amanda across the table. How young were these women? She couldn't imagine wanting to share a house with five adults at her age.

Still, she couldn't blame everyone for being excited. They were hoping that after a month or two, the women would each want to buy a house in Lucy's Corner.

"I hope they're nice." Charlotte was worried the influx of newcomers would change the dynamics on the

Ridge. She felt like she'd stepped out of the larger world, and now it was threatening to spill back in.

Speaking of the larger world, she realized she hadn't thought about Ivan in twenty-four hours. That was progress.

"I wonder if Dennis will accuse *them* of being part of his Calamity Year," Amanda said.

Charlotte straightened. "Did he call you *trouble*? That's what he said when he met me. He told Lincoln he'd regret bringing me here."

Amanda laughed. "He told Carter the same thing. Of course, he was right."

"What do you mean?" Carter looked perfectly happy.

"I was on the run when I came here. Didn't Lincoln tell you?" Amanda dusted another row of books.

"No." Charlotte couldn't imagine that. Amanda was the most normal-seeming woman she'd ever met.

"He probably didn't want to scare you. It's a long story," she added. "Suffice it to say my father stole an important painting and planned to sell it. I got caught in the middle of it all and escaped with the painting here to Elliott Ridge. I thought no one would ever find me here. I was wrong."

Charlotte's heart stilled. She was hoping Ivan would never track her down. "What happened?" She pushed a book in so that it lined up with all the other ones in its row and noticed her hand was shaking.

Amanda closed her eyes as if the memory still pained her. "My plan was to return it to its rightful owners before any damage was done. I stashed the painting in one of the old buildings by the mine."

"The ones that look like they're sinking into the ground?" Charlotte asked in surprise. "Lincoln said they aren't safe."

Amanda nodded, opening her eyes again. "They aren't, but it was just for a short time. I went back to get it as soon I figured out the logistics of returning it to the gallery it was stolen from. That's where my father found me. He had a gun."

Charlotte drew in a shocked breath. "How did he find you?"

"He asked around in town. People remember a stranger in a place as small as Chance Creek."

"Oh, my god." Suddenly chilled despite the warmth of the day, Charlotte hugged her arms across her chest. Ivan could ask around about her. He could find her, too. She should never have gone shopping in town or had coffee with Lincoln at Linda's Diner. She should have stayed hidden here on the Ridge.

"He hustled me all the way down to the highway before I managed to make a run for it. Luckily, the guys had figured out something was wrong and came looking for me. Carter… shot him."

"Amanda!" Charlotte was horrified. Amanda's new husband had killed her father?

"He didn't die," Amanda rushed to add. "Carter just stopped him from killing me. My dad shot me, too. Winged me, I should say." She touched her scalp. "I had to stay in the hospital overnight. It was a whole thing."

"I'm glad you're safe." Charlotte couldn't take all this in. A trace of nausea swirled inside her, making her want to sit down until it passed. Would Ivan try to shoot her if he traced her here? For the first time, she faced the possibility.

After all, she knew he had a gun.

"I'm glad, too, believe me."

"Where's your dad now?" Charlotte wasn't sure if it was okay to ask, but she felt compelled to know.

"He's being held in custody until trial," Amanda said. "He should serve time. He's out of my life, that's for sure. So is my sister. She helped him steal the painting."

Charlotte's heart went out to her. She could tell it hadn't been easy for Amanda to turn her back on her family.

"Now it's just me and my mom. And Carter and his brothers—and you." She smiled. "I'm starting over. Building a new family."

"I'm honored to be a part of it," Charlotte said truthfully. The ground didn't seem nearly as stable under her feet as it had before, however.

Toward the end of her time with Ivan, Charlotte had begun to realize not all his businesses were... legitimate. At first she'd thought those activities were simply unsavory rather than illegal. Maybe he placed some bets he wasn't supposed to place—things like that.

Over time she realized it went deeper than that. She began to suspect Ivan's racing activities were some kind of front. Men came to the house, but Ivan didn't introduce her to them. Conversations fell silent when she walked into a room. Once she saw a large stack of bills change hands when no one knew she was there. She'd slipped out as silently as she'd come in, reluctant to admit her boyfriend might be involved in something nefarious.

Charlotte didn't like to think of herself as stupid, but she'd been willfully blind to all of it for far longer than she liked to admit.

Amanda put the duster away and took a last look around. "I think I've done all I can for now. Let's see what everyone else is up to."

Charlotte did her best to push her uncomfortable thoughts away and focus on the present. "Where does Dennis live, anyway? I haven't seen him since my first day here."

"Supposedly he has a caretaker's cottage, but I've never seen it," Amanda said. "I think he's actually a wood sprite in disguise or something like that. He's never around when you look for him and always there when you don't expect him. We should probably keep on his good side with offerings of bread and ale."

"Does he eat meals with everyone?"

Amanda shook her head. "Not often. The man's a mystery."

"I guess so."

Charlotte followed her, and they found the men in the cafeteria. According to Lincoln, Anne had been adamant about renting a car when she landed at the airport and driving to the Ridge herself.

"Ready for this?" Charlotte asked him.

"Ready as I'll ever be. Wish Carter had managed to get those internet people out here sooner."

"Anne already knows the situation, and she's still flying in to see the place. I'm sure it will be fine."

"We'll see." He smoothed a hand over her back. "At least you're staying."

She nodded and leaned against him. His strength gave her courage, and she reminded herself that she was surrounded by military men here. Surely she was safe.

"Something wrong?" Lincoln asked, but before she could answer, Nate said, "Here she comes!"

They crowded around to look out the windows as a cherry-red sportscar pulled up in front of the town hall. A woman with ice-blond hair got out. She was dressed in wide-legged linen pants and a matching structured jacket, belted at the waist over a white shell. She was younger than Charlotte had imagined, in her late twenties at the outside, but the lift of her chin and the cold way she surveyed them gave her an imperious air.

"I could never pull off that outfit," Amanda murmured. "How is she not dirty already?"

"I don't know," Charlotte whispered back.

"Wow," Hudson said.

The woman drew a leather handbag over her shoulder, shut the car door and strode up the walk toward the town hall.

Charlotte stayed with Amanda, while the men headed for Anne. "She looks... nice," she ventured.

"I don't know," Amanda said. "Somehow I can't

imagine her playing the game."

"Or eating in the cafeteria." Charlotte was grateful she wasn't the only one with doubts.

"Or making love in a canoe."

Charlotte turned to her. "Have you done that?"

Amanda just smiled mysteriously.

"We're jumping to conclusions," Charlotte declared, filing that interesting tidbit away for a later conversation. "We should keep an open mind."

"I'll do my best," Amanda said.

LINCOLN REACHED ANNE just as another truck pulled up and Alice Sanders got out. She wore a flowy blouse over jeans, her dirty-blond hair twisted into a loose bun on top of her head. Lincoln remembered his mother commenting once that there was something fey about Alice, but later, after Alice's mother died, Lincoln's mom had had nothing but compassion for the Reed girls.

Today Alice seemed down to earth. She smiled broadly when she spotted Anne and went to fold her in a big hug.

"How are you doing, lady?" she asked. "Rocking the gaming world with that start-up of yours?"

"Trying to." When Anne smiled, she looked much more approachable. Younger, too. At first Lincoln had assumed she was nearly thirty, but now he thought she might be only twenty-five or twenty-six. That was young to be in charge of a start-up, wasn't it?

"Alice," he said as he neared them. "Good to see

you again."

"Good to see you, too, Lincoln." Alice gave him a hug, as well. "Anne, meet Lincoln Elliott—of the *Elliott Ridge* Elliotts," she added with a snobbish lilt, followed quickly by a mischievous smile.

"Honored to meet you." Anne went along with the joke, then sobered, as if remembering the dignity of her position. "Thank you for letting me come on such short notice," she said frostily.

"No problem," he said. "We're happy to have you. We're trying to build a community that has a diversified income base and is home to all kinds of movers and shakers."

Anne lifted her chin again and took in the forested slope of the Ridge, the houses tucked among the trees. "It's very remote, isn't it?"

Alice seemed to be biting back a smile at Anne's tone. "Come on, Anne, you have to admit it's lovely here."

"Still." Anne gave an expressive shrug.

"It's only forty-five minutes to town," Lincoln said firmly. "And when we hit capacity, we'll offer most amenities right here, including a general store, a bar and restaurant, and more." When he spotted Charlotte and Amanda approaching, he made the introductions. "Alice, Anne—this is Charlotte Holmes. She's a veterinarian, and she's just moved to town. This is Amanda, Carter's wife. You spoke to Carter on the phone."

When the women had exchanged greetings, Lincoln introduced his brothers next.

"Anne, you're leading a group of programmers?" Nate asked.

"Yes. I've been part of many creative teams and been lead programmer on several games," Anne said. She named two Lincoln hadn't heard of.

"When did you start working? When you were twelve?" Hudson asked. Nate elbowed him.

Anne ignored him. "I started my own company last fall," she went on, raising her voice. "Got some investors interested. Now I have to make my seed money last until I can launch our first product."

"Even in this day and age, women-led gaming companies don't get funded very often," Alice put in. "It's imperative that Anne succeed, not just for herself but for all the other women entering the industry. The creative life is always a struggle. Anne is pulling off something very unusual."

Lincoln noticed Anne didn't seem too happy with the praise. She'd pressed her lips together as if not wanting to be reminded of the pressure she was under.

"That sounds exciting," Charlotte said.

"It's exhausting," Anne said, then caught herself. "But invigorating. Nothing worth having is easy. I'm here to find a place where my team can work with little to no interruptions for the next fourteen months. We have very strict deadlines. Everything must be provided for my workers, and we must not be disturbed."

"For fourteen months?" Hudson said. "Gotta relax sometimes, don't you?"

"No," Anne snapped. "No relaxing. Not on a project like this."

Was it Lincoln's imagination, or was there something a little manic in Anne's tone? Fourteen months of constant work sounded like a grind. But if the women stayed here that long, they'd get so settled they would definitely want to stay.

"Anne is worried about meals," Alice put in, "since there aren't any restaurants nearby."

"We can provide meals," Carter said quickly. "For a fee, of course. We're already feeding our mill workers lunch and dinner. We have a cafeteria that can accommodate many more people."

A smile quirked Gage's mouth, and he exchanged a look with Amanda, who opened her mouth, then closed it without commenting. Did she object to more mouths to feed? Gage had tricked her into taking on the position of head chef when Amanda had arrived, but Lincoln thought she'd grown to like it. He figured they could work something out later if she protested.

"My programmers require quality food," Anne said.

"Our meals are excellent," Carter said, in full salesman mode.

Amanda sighed.

"Do you have a husband? Kids?" Hudson asked none too subtly.

"I don't have time for that." Anne looked him up and down and turned away.

Hudson's face fell, and Lincoln bit back a laugh. That set-down almost made up for all Hudson's teasing lately—but not quite.

"Let me show you around," he hurried to say before Hudson decided to lay on the charm regardless. "We'll start at the town hall and then look at the houses that meet your requirements." He moved to the front entrance, and everyone followed.

Anne frowned when she noticed the entourage they'd attracted. Lincoln stopped, sensing her discomfort. "All right, people. Carter and I will show Alice and Anne around. We'll meet here for lunch, okay?"

"Of course," Amanda said. "Charlotte, will you help me get the meal on? Gage, Nate, you're needed at the mill, right? Hudson—you, too?"

"I know when I've been given my marching orders," Hudson grumbled, heading off with his brothers. When everyone had dispersed, Lincoln led the way into the town hall.

"We were all excited to meet you," he said to Anne to smooth things over. She nodded curtly, and he figured he'd better get on with the tour.

"This is our library." He opened a door, gratified to see the large room looking so inviting now that Amanda had straightened it up. The tall windows let in lots of light. The window seats were lined with pillows, the shelves of books clean and orderly.

"No computers? That's unusual these days."

"We haven't gotten that far yet." Lincoln exchanged a glance with Carter. Did they plan to put computers in the library? "It's an informal system. I'm not sure it's worth the effort to bring our catalog online."

"Hm."

"The community's mailboxes are out here," Carter said, leading the way into the foyer. "And here's the cafeteria."

Anne poked her head in and nodded. "Adequate." She was all business again, no visible cracks in her facade, and he was beginning to think she was more bravado than businesswoman. He wished he could tell her there was nothing wrong in admitting you'd bitten off more than you could chew. It was when you pretended everything was under control—and it wasn't—that the problems started, as he could personally attest.

Lincoln stopped himself from saying any of that out loud. He had no idea if Anne was qualified, and he'd been far younger than she was now when the Army had trained him for war—and even younger when he'd made his own mistakes with the family business. Anne's decisions affected only her and a small number of programmers. She didn't have an entire town's livelihoods resting on her back, like he'd had when he'd pushed his father to take on those equipment loans. Besides, she was making a smart decision moving her group here to keep her costs down. There were few distractions on Elliott Ridge.

Outside, Lincoln took them by the buildings that had once housed the tiny hotel and restaurant and a general store. "The chapel is over there, but let me take you to see Elliott Lake before we go any farther."

"We've got kayaks, a canoe, barbecue pits for cookouts," Carter listed as they walked down the road, passed by house number 1 and came onto the beach.

"Of course, there's always swimming."

"My people won't have time for stuff like that."

"Ever?" Lincoln laughed, then sobered when Anne's frown deepened. "What about on weekends?" She couldn't mean for them to work for fourteen months straight.

"There's no such thing as weekends in a start-up." Anne sniffed. "Distracting," she announced, waving a hand at the view. "It's too pretty over here." She walked toward the road.

Too pretty? Behind her back, Lincoln raised his eyebrows at Carter. Carter shrugged.

"Let's go see the houses." He'd thought to show Anne to the top of the Ridge so she could take in the whole settlement at once, but now he decided against it.

They'd picked three homes outside Lucy's Corner to show Anne, since she was interested only in renting rather than buying. Houses 13, 62 and 75 all met her basic requirements, but they were very different from one another. House number 13 was straight out of a Gothic novel. Two stories high with a steep roof and dormer windows, it was one of the earliest structures built in the town and had once been a rooming house.

"Oh," Alice exclaimed when they walked in the front door. "Here's a kindred spirit for you, Anne."

Anne looked around the entryway. "What do you mean?"

"I mean the first mistress of this establishment was hell on wheels, just like you. That's what the house is telling me, anyway."

"I'm not hell on wheels," Anne protested. She shook her head, regaining her composure. "You and your premonitions. All this house is saying is it needs to be brought into the twenty-first century. What's the wiring like?"

Alice patted her shoulder. "Don't knock my premonitions. You *are* hell on wheels, sweetie, but that's why we like you."

"You've heard of Clara Marshall?" Lincoln asked Alice. He didn't think the Elliott Ridge ghost stories had made it down to Chance Creek. His mother had liked to collect information about the settlement's inhabitants, and she'd written about a lot of it, meaning to publish a book someday.

"No. The name suits her, though. A real harridan? Her vibes are all over this house."

"You got that right," Carter said. "In the late 1800s, Clara Marshall ruled the bachelors who stayed with her with an iron hand and had strict rules that covered just about everything. Legend has it if she caught a tenant smoking in his bedroom, she'd wait until the following day, and after he left to work at the mill, she'd pile up his possessions outside and set them on fire. Her catchphrase was, 'Better I burn your things than you burn the rest of us in our beds.'"

"Sounds fierce," Alice said.

"Sounds illegal," Anne said.

"Come see the rest of the place." Carter ushered the women through the house, with Lincoln bringing up the rear. There was a large living room and a smaller parlor, both with fireplaces. The kitchen was small but modernized. The formal dining room had seen better days, but there was a full bathroom and a laundry room as well as a bedroom with its own parlor to round out the first floor.

"That was Clara's room," Lincoln said. "She had private quarters."

"The wiring?" Anne asked again, an edge to her voice.

"The wiring was updated in the nineties," Carter said. "It will handle anything you can throw at it."

Anne sniffed, unimpressed.

Upstairs were five more bedrooms and two bathrooms.

"The tenants lived up here," Lincoln said. "I think there used to be another bedroom where the bathrooms are now. Someone renovated the place."

"What do you think?" Alice asked Anne.

Anne shrugged. "Adequate, I suppose."

There was that word again.

"Let's see some of the other places we want to show you," Carter said.

The other two houses were in the newer part of town, one a raised ranch built in the seventies and the other a boxy colonial built about twenty years earlier. Anne toured them wordlessly, although Alice kept up a running commentary about their layouts and the dated decor.

"Well?" Alice demanded when they were through. "Are you coming to live here or not, Anne?" She turned to Lincoln. "Have you told her about my workspace?"

"I haven't had the chance. I figured you'd tell her, anyway."

"I was waiting until she came in person." Alice turned to Anne. "While you're waiting for better internet here, I have a space you can use as an office at Two Willows. No one will bother you, and we'll set it up exactly to your specifications. You can join my family for lunch every day. We'd love the company."

"We don't take time for lunch," Anne protested. "And travel in and out of town will eat up an hour and a half a day."

"But think how cheap it will be," Alice said.

"We have a van you can use. You can hold meetings on the way there and back," Carter offered.

Lincoln bit back a protest. They'd had a van twelve years ago. His parents had left it behind when they moved to South Carolina. Had Dennis maintained it? They should check before making promises they couldn't keep.

"See? The universe wants you here, Anne. It believes in what you're doing, and it's sent us all to help you." Alice smiled. "Maybe you'll even find love."

Anne huffed out a disdainful breath. "Love? Why would I want that?"

"Everyone needs love," Alice said gently.

"I don't need love, but I do need a big house. A cheap one. What was the rent on number 13 again?"

Carter gave her a number so low Lincoln nearly choked. Had he forgotten how much money they needed? Carter met his gaze over Anne's head and mouthed the word *women*. He was right, Lincoln thought. They did need women, probably more than they needed cash.

"Of the three houses, this one has the best internet, such as it is for now, since it's the closest to the town hall. You'll still want to use Alice's workshop until we get the upgrade in August," Carter said.

Anne thought a moment. "Fine. I'll take it."

"I knew you'd say that," Alice crowed. "You're like Clara reincarnated. Welcome to Chance Creek, Anne. I'm so glad you're going to stay." She enveloped Anne in another big hug, but this time Anne allowed it almost cheerfully.

"Let's go sign some paperwork." Carter steered them toward the town hall. "We should make things official."

"Do you think you'll have to burn any of your people's belongings?" Alice linked her arm through Anne's.

"No one smokes anymore." Anne lifted her chin as if the idea was preposterous.

"Clara was dealing with a bunch of unruly men," Carter said. "I'm sure Anne's female employees will be much more dependable."

"Female employees?" Anne laughed. "I don't have any *female* employees."

"You don't?" Lincoln stopped. Carter stopped, too.

"That game you're making—Couture Campaign…" Carter trailed off.

"My customers might be women. That doesn't

mean my coders are. If they were, I wouldn't be here." When she noticed their blank looks, she laughed again. "Why do you think I'm coming to a backwater like this? Because they're *men*. If I don't lock them up in the woods, they'll never get anything done." Anne kept walking. "That's why Elliott Ridge is perfect—there aren't any women here."

Lincoln caught up with Alice, who was struggling to hide a smile. "Don't suppose you predicted this, too?"

"You didn't say you wanted women."

"But you guessed we did when we talked."

"I brought you *one*," she said innocently.

"And five men. If this keeps up, there's going to be a riot."

"I GUESS THAT didn't go as you expected," Charlotte said to Lincoln that evening as she helped him saddle Colonel. Thorn was ready to go. Lincoln had offered to take her for a ride after dinner, and she'd gladly accepted.

"Not exactly," Lincoln said grimly. "You could have knocked me over with a feather when she said her team was all male. Stupid of me to assume it would be women."

"You and your brothers have women on the brain, that's all." They led the horses out of the stable. "I'm sure you'll find some sooner or later."

"Maybe Gage is right. Maybe no woman in her right mind would move out here. Present company excepted, of course. And Amanda and Carolyn."

"Don't forget Anne. I think plenty of women would love it here."

"I hope you're right." Lincoln helped her into her saddle, climbed into his and led the way to a track that cut through the trees and circled the lake. Charlotte settled on her mount and found its swaying steps comforting.

"We won't go the whole way; that would take hours," Lincoln said. "The lake itself isn't too large, but the path follows the coastline for the most part, so it winds in and out."

"We should take a picnic sometime and make a day of it."

"Definitely."

He looked good on a horse, she decided. At ease but alert at the same time, his restless gaze scanning the trail, the woods and the lake. When she wondered what he looked like in uniform, a little zing of desire shot through her. Probably pretty hot.

A half hour later, Lincoln reined in. "This is as far as we should go tonight." He dismounted, and Charlotte followed suit. They let the horses graze as they went to sit on a fallen log. When Lincoln took her hand, Charlotte leaned against his shoulder and took in her surroundings. The sun was still far above the horizon, but the angle of the light had changed. Night was drawing in. She shivered involuntarily.

Lincoln looked down at her. "You cold?"

"No, just a little… tired. I didn't sleep well last night."

It was true enough. Her insomnia had returned with a vengeance. With the windows open to catch a breeze, she heard every noise small creatures and rustling leaves conjured up outside, and each time she'd wondered if Ivan or one of his men was creeping around looking for a way in. Too late she realized Lincoln might take what she said as an overture to invite himself back into her house.

"You know what I think about when I'm drifting off to sleep these nights?" he asked.

"What?" Did he think about her?

"What it would be like to have a wife."

Charlotte tried and failed to think of an answer. "A wife?" she repeated.

He glanced her way and laughed. "Don't worry, I'm not asking. Just never thought about it much until Carter got married. Now I think about it all the time."

"Really?" Did her voice sound normal? She sure hoped so. The most handsome man she'd ever met had taken her to a secluded lakeside vista and was talking about marriage. Another shiver traced up her spine, but this was a good one.

Lincoln nodded. "Carter and Amanda are a team. My parents are like that, too. Mom and Dad might bicker like any couple, but they always stand together against any outside threat. And they get things done. They divide up the work, consult each other—help each other." He trailed off. "They never go to bed alone," he added. "Marriage comes off as this stuffy institution, but it's actually kind of radical when you think about it."

"I think I know what you mean. It's this thing everybody does, but somehow you never think you'll be old enough—then suddenly you are." Charlotte wondered if she was saying too much but couldn't help continuing. "I've always wanted a partner. I want... a family." She surprised herself by voicing that. "I didn't let myself think about it when I was with my ex-boyfriend. He would have been an awful father," she admitted. "I should never have been with him."

"You're not with him now."

"Thank God."

Lincoln smiled.

"What?" She wanted to touch him when he smiled like that, but she kept her hands to herself.

"Can't help being glad you're not missing him."

"I'm not." She studied him. "What about you? Are you missing anyone? Are there old girlfriends I should be worried about?"

"No," he said firmly.

"Really? A guy like you hasn't left any broken hearts around?"

"I'm the one who got my heart broken." Lincoln made a face, as if regretting he'd said it. "Forget it. New topic."

"Absolutely not. You can't tease me like that. Who was she? What happened?" He sent her a dark look, and she fluttered her eyelashes back at him. "Spill it."

"Fine," he growled. "Only because it explains why Hudson and I... don't get along."

"I'm all ears. Hudson said it's his fault."

Lincoln frowned. "He said that?"

She nodded. "He said he was trying to do you a favor, and he thinks he did, but he also messed things up and should have handled it differently."

"He's never said any of that to me."

"I kind of asked him point blank," Charlotte admitted.

"Remind me to call you if I ever need to interrogate someone." Lincoln leaned back against the log and laced his hands together behind his neck. "It was when we were high school seniors. Things had already been rough around here for a while. We were all tense with each other, Hudson and me in particular. We had a history of falling for the same girl—and Hudson worked faster than I did."

"Sounds annoying."

"That's putting it mildly. I should have tried harder, but instead I pulled back. Let him have his pick and tried to choose girls I didn't think he'd go after."

"Girls you didn't really want to go after, either?" she suggested.

"Basically. That wasn't fair to anyone. Women aren't stupid."

"No, we're not," Charlotte agreed.

"I got dumped by more of the girls I didn't want to date than I got rejected by ones I did—who went for Hudson instead."

"That doesn't sound fun at all."

"I got a little desperate," Lincoln admitted. "Senior prom is a big deal in a small town. Some couples get engaged at prom. I'd barely dated at all that year, and things on the Ridge were beginning to fall apart. To block out all the chaos, I decided I'd fallen in love with Winona Shelton."

"Decided? Oh, no," Charlotte said.

"Oh, yes. Went to Thayer's Jewelers and bought the only ring in the place I could afford, this sad little thing no woman would want to wear. Asked Winona to the prom, and she said yes." He glanced her way. "Hudson had already asked Patricia Flynn. I never admitted to myself she was the one I really wanted to go with."

"And you proposed to Winona?" She couldn't even feel jealous since it was so obvious things hadn't gone well.

"Didn't get a chance to," Lincoln said. "The day before prom I came home to find Hudson screwing Winona—in my bed."

Charlotte gaped at him. "In your bed?"

"In my bed," Lincoln repeated. To her surprise, he grinned suddenly. "God, he was an ass. But I was, too, now that I think about it."

"What did you do?"

"Tossed the ring at her. Told her she'd made a big mistake. Told Hudson to join me outside and fight me like a man. Stormed out of there ready to beat the crap out of him."

"Did you?"

"Hell, yeah—that was one of our worst throw downs ever. Dad and Gage finally broke it up. Dad sent Hudson to stay with friends in town for a few days.

Mom drove Winona home. She was crying and begging me to take her back. She wanted that ring on her finger at prom. Needless to say I didn't take her back—or go to prom. Hudson didn't go, either, once Patricia heard what he'd done. It was a mess."

"Why did Hudson think he was doing you a favor?" Charlotte couldn't even imagine a scene like that. She had no siblings—no one to fight with. Maybe if she had, she'd have developed a backbone earlier in life.

Lincoln was quiet a moment. "Because I didn't love Winona any more than she loved me, but if we'd made it to prom, I would have proposed, and she would have said yes. We would have married."

"Maybe the two of you would have made a good life together."

"No, we wouldn't." He met her gaze. "Winona's on husband number three, and it isn't because she missed her chance with me. Turned out Hudson wasn't the only guy she slept with during the few weeks we were together."

"Oh, Lincoln. I'm sorry," Charlotte said.

"I'm not," Lincoln said. "Chalk it all up to life experience. I found out what I didn't want."

"And you didn't meet anyone during your time in the Army?"

"I had a couple of serious relationships. A few that were less so. I didn't meet the one."

"Have you been looking?"

"I'm looking now. Like I said, I want a wife. I want kids, too. All of it."

His direct gaze held her in place. Was that a warning in his eyes? Or a promise?

None of it mattered when he bent nearer and kissed her. Caught up in the taste and feel of him, the way her body buzzed with anticipation when she leaned into his touch, all thoughts of the future fled her mind. When he gathered her onto his lap, she went willingly, her arms wrapping around his shoulders. This kiss was different from the ones that had come before. Deeper. Hungrier. She couldn't get enough of him.

"Charlotte," he murmured against her neck some minutes later. "I want you."

"I want you, too."

He met her gaze again, asking a question.

"Yes," she said.

CHAPTER 8

LINCOLN'S PULSE DRUMMED harder as he drew Charlotte to her feet and led her away from the trail. It wasn't likely anyone would come along, but just in case, he took cover among the trees before sweeping her in his arms again and kissing her thoroughly.

She was soft and curvy, and he couldn't keep his hands off her. Lincoln wished he'd thought of bringing a blanket, but he hadn't, so he tugged his shirt up and over his head and laid it out on the ground before lowering Charlotte onto it.

"We could go back. Do this somewhere a lot more comfortable," he said, even though he figured it just might kill him if she agreed.

"I don't want to wait that long. Do you?" She pulled back to look at him.

"Hell, no. Just not sure you're the type of woman who likes messing around in the woods."

"I love messing around the woods. Shut up and kiss me."

She didn't have to ask him twice. One thing led to

another and soon he'd helped her off with her shirt and added it to the layer beneath them.

Then he lost track of everything when she reached behind her back, undid the clasp of her bra and tossed it away. It snagged on a nearby shrub and dangled there like a flag.

"Charlotte," he growled low in his throat, bending down to trace kisses over her breasts. She lay back, and sighed contentedly, the soft sound twisting him in knots with the desire to make her feel good. He teased and tasted her, caressing her with his kisses until she closed her eyes and moaned her satisfaction.

As Lincoln explored her body, he wondered if he'd really found the woman he could build a future with. She felt right in his arms, but he was afraid he was moving too fast. If he held on too tight, would she slip away? He couldn't stand the thought of losing her now that she'd come into his life.

He tugged at the button of her jeans, and she lifted her hips as he undid them and slipped them down. He waited for her to kick her boots off, then helped her untangle her legs. She tossed away the jeans too and laughed when they caught on a broken branch of a nearby pine tree. Lincoln claimed her mouth with another kiss, slid his hand into her panties, and Charlotte gasped.

He kept his touches gentle at first, but Charlotte seemed as desperate for him as he was for her.

When her fingers struggled with the waistband of his pants, he took over, getting them off in no time. She drew him on top of her and moaned with pleasure as he settled between her thighs.

"Should I be wearing a condom?" he asked. If so, they might have to stop and return home, after all. The thought of getting back on a horse sounded downright uncomfortable. He didn't want to wait another moment to be inside Charlotte, but he'd do whatever he had to.

She hesitated, then nodded.

"Might have one on me." He braced himself, reached for his jeans, pulled out his wallet, fished around and found one. It had been there awhile, but the wrapper was intact. He held it up to the fading light. "Hasn't expired."

"Thank goodness for small mercies."

He tore the wrapper, shifted and eased it on. Back between her legs, he paused. "You sure about this?" he asked, needing to know she wanted this as much as he did.

Charlotte slid her hands down his back. "Lincoln— please."

He pushed into her slowly, and she closed her eyes, her lips parting. As he buried himself inside her, Lincoln felt like he was exactly where he was supposed to be. Moving with her was exquisite torture. It was all he could do to keep his strokes slow and steady, building up the tension between them, giving Charlotte time to get used to the feel of him inside her. When she wrapped her legs around him, begging him with her body for more, he gladly obliged.

Bracing one forearm on the ground, he crushed her

to him with the other, their kisses hot and hard. Charlotte moved beneath him with the strength of his strokes, her hair fanned out around her, her breasts rounded beneath his chest.

She felt right in his arms.

He wanted a wife.

A family.

A future.

This felt like the beginning of a life that was more than just getting a job done. This felt like coming home in the best of ways. Like—

Charlotte cried out, arching back, her climax sweeping her away and any last vestiges of control he possessed dissolved, too.

His own release came fast and hard, pulsing through him, making him thrust into her even harder. His hand tangled in her hair as sensation overcame him. When at last it was over, he kept himself propped up on one arm, not wanting to crush Charlotte but wanting to feel her everywhere at the same time.

Charlotte clung to him, breathing hard.

Lincoln traced kisses over her mouth, her cheeks, down her neck to her breasts again.

"You are beautiful, you know that, Charlotte Holmes?"

She gave a little huff of laughter. "Hardly."

"You are." He couldn't stop kissing her, already feeling the stirrings of desire again, way too soon after he'd just been sated.

"You're pretty hot yourself." She buried her face in

his shoulder, as if embarrassed for saying so.

"Really?" The stirrings stiffened into something more.

"Lincoln."

They were still joined, which meant she could feel his interest.

"I don't have another condom." But he wanted to make love to her all over again.

"Then take me home and get one," she told him.

"You got it." He wanted all of Charlotte, over and over again. He wanted a lifetime of this. "Let's go."

CHARLOTTE THOUGHT THE ride home would take forever. You couldn't gallop on a trail that wound through the forest. By the time they reached the stable and cared for the horses, she was dying to get close to Lincoln again.

When they finally made it to house number 37, Lincoln locked the door behind them, took her hand and led her upstairs to the bathroom. He turned on the shower, stripped and waited for her to do the same. The warm water felt heavenly, and so did Lincoln's skin as they took turns washing each other. She ran her soapy hands over his shoulders, muscular arms and chest and then lower, relishing his six-pack abs and taut hips.

Lincoln turned her around and stood behind her, skimming his hands from her waist up to cup her breasts and caress them in circles.

Charlotte moaned and leaned back against him, feeling how ready he was for her again. She was ready, too, but there was no rush.

They had all night.

Lincoln's hands were quickly bringing her to a point of desperation, but two could play that game. She turned in his arms, sank to her knees and ran her hands up from his ankles over his calves, knees and thighs.

Lincoln groaned. "Charlotte." He gasped when she took him into her mouth, all his muscles straining.

Charlotte teased him and coaxed him almost to the breaking point, until he lifted her up, turned her around, braced her hands against the wall, used his knee to spread her legs—

And stopped a moment.

"Lincoln?"

"Forgot the condom. Hold on," he growled. He was gone before she could answer and came back in a flash, joining her under the warm water again. A moment later he fitted himself against her, nudged the core of her and slid inside.

"Lincoln," she breathed and was lost in a rush of sensation that threatened to overwhelm her. He felt so good inside her—like he was made to be hers. He moved slowly at first, the slide of him awakening every fiber of her being, building the tension within her until Charlotte didn't know if she could stand it anymore.

With one hand on her hip, the other cradling her breasts, he was everywhere, touching her, bringing her to a peak of desire that was driving her wild.

"Charlotte," he groaned into her ear. He was close, and so was she. The tile walls were cool beneath her hands, but Lincoln was stoking her to a fever pitch. When she came, wave after wave of release swept through her. She called out his name again as he joined her, each stroke of his body into hers pushing her over the edge again and again.

When it was over, Lincoln slid out of her, then cradled her in his arms as they both caught their breath.

Charlotte splayed her hands over his chest, wondering at the magnificence of him. She'd never felt like this with anyone before. She wished she could stay right here forever.

Lincoln cupped her face in his hands and kissed her so thoroughly she thought he might never stop.

"I want to spend the night with you," he said when he pulled away.

"I want that, too," she said.

When they crawled under the covers a short time later, Charlotte didn't bother with a T-shirt. She wanted Lincoln's skin against hers. As he gathered her into his arms, her breasts brushed his chest, the sensation sending ripples of desire through her again.

"I thought you said you were incorrigible, not insatiable," he said, kissing her neck as she wrapped a leg around his waist and pulled him close.

"I'm both," she said.

"YOU SURE YOU want to be a veterinarian? You could always work at the mill with me," Lincoln said the next morning as they approached the Chance Creek Pet Clinic. Charlotte was supposed to spend the day shadowing Bella's brother, Craig, to see whether work as a small-town veterinarian would suit her.

"That's a very tempting offer, but I think I'm going to pass." Charlotte's smile reached her eyes, and Lincoln's chest swelled. Was she thinking of the fun they'd had last night by the lake—and then at her house? He hadn't been able to get it out of his mind this morning.

"If you change your mind, just give me a call. I'll come get you and teach you how to repair an edger." He'd rather spend time with her than complete the list of tasks ahead of him. First thing this morning, Hudson had helped him load the back of his truck with a few of the old appliances they'd taken out of the houses in Lucy's Corner. As soon as he dropped off Charlotte, he needed to take them to the dump. Then it was back to the mill to try to keep the equipment running long enough to finish the order they were working on.

Last night had been something, though. He'd liked making love to Charlotte under the canopy of trees, with a backdrop of water lapping at the shore and birdsong in their ears. He'd liked making love to her in the shower—and in her bed—as well.

He didn't want to let her go for a minute, let alone an entire day.

When he pulled into the parking lot in front of the animal clinic, Bella was waiting for them along with her brother. Both came to greet them as soon as the truck stopped. Bella introduced her brother, and Lincoln and Charlotte shook Craig's hand. Lincoln was sure he'd crossed paths with Craig a few times during the years before he left Chance Creek, but Craig was so much older they'd never been in school together.

"I have a busy schedule today," Craig said to Charlotte. "Do you think you can keep up?"

"I'm used to long days," Charlotte said.

"Bella said you worked for a private operation taking care of racehorses."

"That's right. But I left that behind."

Craig nodded and refrained from asking any more questions. Too bad. Lincoln would have liked to hear some more answers. Charlotte was short on details about her former life, and he'd noticed she made a habit of turning the conversation to other topics any time the past came up.

"I might know some people who are interested in moving to the Ridge," Bella said to Lincoln. "Want to stay for a cup of coffee?"

He forgot all about Charlotte's shadowy history—and his list of chores. Finding inhabitants for the town trumped anything else he had on the schedule. "Sure thing. Charlotte, do you need anything else from the truck?"

"I've got everything."

"Just call me when you're ready to be picked up," Lincoln said. He bent and gave her a light kiss on the cheek. He knew he was going to spend his day thinking of her.

Her smile told him she'd be thinking of him, too. "Will do. See you later."

When they were gone, Bella led him inside, poured

him that cup of coffee she'd promised him and waved him into a seat in her office.

"I was talking to a friend of mine. She told me her niece, Veronica, is looking to move to the area and is looking for cheap housing. She went to school in Seattle and apparently is some kind of social media influencer or something like that. Anyway, she and a bunch of her school buddies want to move to a small town where their expenses will be low while they get their businesses off the ground." She shrugged. "I get the feeling they're starving-artist types just starting their careers, but they all work online, so they can go anywhere. I don't know if any will succeed with their businesses, but they're young and aspirational. I thought they might fit the bill."

"They might. Do you think they're looking to buy or rent?"

"I don't think they have much money, so they'll probably want to rent at first." Bella smiled. "They're a very artistic and energetic group. They produce a ton of social media content. I made the mistake of following some of them, and I've been inundated with notifications ever since. One of them is a lifestyle blogger. Another gives financial advice to people just out of college. A third is in interior design somehow. Don't ask me how she does that online. Another has her own virtual bookkeeping business, and a couple do website design. Sounds like those last three are the economic engine for the group. I get the feeling Veronica and her friends take on just about any job they can find to pay the bills, as long as they still have time to fool around with their real interests. They're the kind of people who are going to be broke until the day they're millionaires, if you know what I mean."

Lincoln wasn't sure he did. Bella must've seen that, because her smile widened. "Sooner or later one of them will hit it out of the park with one of their ventures," she explained. "But heaven only knows when that will be."

"How many are there?"

"Seven, as far as I know. I think they all want to cram into one house to save money, if that's okay. They might spread out over time if things go well financially."

Lincoln thought about it. He supposed it wouldn't hurt if they rented one house together. If they liked to put out social media content, maybe their posts about Elliott Ridge could attract other people.

"They're all women," Bella added innocently.

He straightened. That put a different spin on things. "All of them? Are you sure?" He didn't want to repeat the mistake they'd made about Anne's programmers.

"I'm sure."

"What makes you think that matters?" It did, but Bella shouldn't know that.

"A little bird told me there were far too many men and far too few women on the Ridge," she said with another smile. "Seven unattached women ought to liven things up a little."

Lincoln could only agree. "Do you have their information so I can call and set up a time for them to come and take a look?"

"How about we call them right now?"

BY ELEVEN, WHEN they were packing up the truck after attending to a steer suffering from bloat, Charlotte was ready to take back her earlier words. She had thought she worked hard at Gasparyn Stables, but she'd worked a lot harder this morning. At the stables there were always assistants to fetch and carry for her and help sedate an unruly horse. Working with Craig, there were just the two of them. She wondered how he coped when he was on his own.

When she asked, he laughed. "Sometimes the ranchers help me. Sometimes I have to get creative. You get used to it. What was it like to work in the racing world?" He shut the tailgate, and they climbed into their seats.

Charlotte wasn't sure how to answer that. She'd still been in veterinary school when she met Ivan, so at first she'd worked only weekends and evenings. In those days Peter Illych ruled the roost. Ivan and Peter had done a good job hiding the darker side of the job until she'd graduated.

"I loved caring for thoroughbreds," she said truthfully. "But I didn't realize until too late how prescribed a racehorse's life is. I thought I would coordinate with the trainers to maximize the horses' potential. It turned out that a lot of that maximizing had to do with chemicals. I didn't like that."

What she didn't say was how conflicted it had left her. She was Ivan's girlfriend and in the early days, he treated her like a princess, showering her with gifts and romantic gestures. After years of scrimping and saving to keep her school loans as low as possible, with him paying her way, she could breathe easy and experience some luxury. How could she complain about his methods, especially when it turned out they were the same ones most people used in the racing world?

"Now that I've seen the way you relate to animals," Craig said, "I can't imagine it would've been easy for you to go against your instincts when treating a horse."

"I suppose it must be like treating human athletes," Charlotte said. "Most of the time, when someone gets hurt, you fix the injury. But when it comes to athletes, human or otherwise, the main priority becomes getting them back on the field, whether or not that's best for them. It requires a type of care that isn't really care at all to my way of thinking."

"But you kept with it?" Craig asked. He turned on the truck, and its engine roared to life.

Charlotte nodded. "For longer than I want to admit. I'm here now, though." She didn't want to think about Ivan. He hadn't been in touch again after his threat, and she hoped that was the end of it.

Should she warn Craig not to say he knew her if someone came looking? She supposed that would help only if she told everyone else she'd met so far the same thing. Too many people already knew she was here, and every day she worked as a veterinarian, she'd make new acquaintances. That was the problem with small towns, wasn't it? Everybody knew everybody.

"Well, I think you've got a future working here, if that's what you're interested in." Craig broke into her thoughts.

Charlotte glowed at the praise and found it touched her more than she would've expected. Here was a benefit of small-town life. What you did mattered. Craig, Bella and Hannah all seemed grateful that she'd moved to town. All Ivan had cared about in the end was whether she followed his orders.

"Where to next?" she asked.

"I wish I could say it was lunchtime, but we have a call out to the Johnson place," Craig said. "Ed Johnson passed away a week ago, and his family from back east has been out trying to settle his affairs. Seems like he got weak toward the end, didn't tell anyone how much he was struggling and left a horse in bad shape. The neglect wasn't purposeful; he was simply too proud to ask for help when he needed it."

Charlotte felt like there was a message in there somewhere for her, but she pushed that thought away when her phone chimed. Lincoln was calling. She quickly answered.

"How's work?" Lincoln asked.

"Great so far."

"I'm still in town, if you can believe it. Ended up staying at Bella's for an hour, talking on the phone to some young women who are interested in moving to the Ridge. There was a backup at the dump. Then Amanda called and asked me to fetch a few things from the store for her. I was wondering if you and Craig want some lunch? I can pick it up and meet you wherever you are."

Charlotte relayed the offer to Craig and was cheered when he accepted. She told Lincoln the address they were headed to next, and he said he'd be there as soon as he could.

The drive took about half an hour, the road winding up into the hills. When they reached the Johnson place, Charlotte could see the neglect immediately. The clapboard house must've been white at one time, but now it was weathered to a silver gray. The trees crowded around it as if eager to reclaim the land that was once theirs. She had a feeling it was always damp in this hollow.

A man in his early thirties came to meet them.

"Hi there. I'm Eric Johnson. Ed was my great uncle. You must be the veterinarians."

"That's us," Craig said. "I'm Craig, and this is Charlotte. Where's this horse I've heard about?"

Eric led them to the barn, a dilapidated building that looked ready to fall over. "If we'd realized how bad things were, we would've come sooner."

"Your uncle Ed always was a stubborn old goat," Craig told him.

Although the interior of the barn was dark, Charlotte could make out a horse stall that looked like it had been hastily constructed about forty years ago and never fixed. Inside the stall was the sorriest horse she'd ever seen. When Craig caught sight of it, he let out a gusty sigh and murmured, "Hell, Ed, you should have called me. I'd have taken care of this fellow."

Ed, far from this earthly vale of tears, didn't answer, but Charlotte appreciated Craig's sentiment. He was a no-nonsense man with little time for emotional thinking, from what she'd seen so far, but he cared about the animals he served.

Craig approached the stall and crooned softly as he opened the door. To Charlotte's relief, the horse didn't try to bolt. It stood patiently and allowed him to stroke its neck.

"You've come to a pretty pass, haven't you?" he asked, handling it gently.

Tears pricked Charlotte's eyes now that she could see the animal more clearly. Its back was swayed and its coat mangy. There were signs of discharge from its eyes and nose.

"We've done what we could since we got here," Eric said. "I'm not much of a horse person."

"We'll take him off your hands and make sure he's taken care of," Craig said.

Charlotte bit back the protest that sprang to her lips. She knew what that meant. Ivan never allowed a horse to live past its usefulness, and this one was about as useless as they came. Her heart throbbed, but she kept her sentiments to herself, knowing how pointless it was to argue with a man who'd given up on an animal.

Eric stiffened. "Taken care of? What do you mean by that? You're not going to shoot him, are you?" He scratched the back of his head. "I've got two little girls I made the mistake of telling about Uncle Ed's horse. Now they're pretty invested, if you know what I mean."

"You want to take him home with you?" Charlotte blurted, a glimmer of hope inflating her chest.

Eric laughed. "To Boston? I don't think that's in the cards."

Of course not. Her hope evaporated again. The back of her throat ached with the unfairness of it all. Horses didn't ask to be brought into situations like this. They trusted their owners to take care of them. All too often those owners betrayed them.

"We won't put him down," Craig assured Eric, and Charlotte turned to him in surprise. "My sister, Bella, runs a no-kill shelter and takes in any kind of animal that needs a home. This old boy will get the best feed and treatment of its life and all the love and care he could want. If you leave an email address, I'm sure Bella would be happy to send photos when he's all fixed up."

Relief overwhelmed Charlotte, and suddenly she couldn't hold back the tears that pricked at her eyes. She'd been so sure she'd have to stand by and watch the old hack be put down, and she'd seen too many horses die already. She excused herself to step out of the barn, needing a moment to get her emotions under control.

A truck pulled up while she stood there with her back to the stables. She heard the engine shut down and a door slam.

"Charlotte?" Lincoln enveloped her in his arms and cradled her against his broad chest. "What happened?"

She shook her head, knowing if she tried to speak, she'd start to sob. She wiped her hand across her eyes as she heard the other men join them. How embarrassing could this get? If only they'd leave her alone for a minute, she could get a hold of herself.

"We found Ed Johnson's horse in bad shape," Craig explained to Lincoln. "It upset Charlotte."

Lincoln's arms tightened around her. "Are you okay?"

"I'm fine," she protested, her voice thick with un-shed tears. "I have a soft spot for horses, especially ones who have been mistreated. I just need a minute."

Craig nodded. "Take your time. Eric and I will load Admiral into the trailer."

"Admiral?" Charlotte had to laugh through her tears.

"That's right. Seems like Ed had a pretty high opinion of his horse, even if he let things go toward the end."

For some reason that brought another wave of emotion. Charlotte curled into Lincoln's arms, not wanting anyone to see her tears, but unable to stop them. She sent out a silent prayer for Ed Johnson, hoping he knew Admiral would be in good hands now. She was glad to know his neglect hadn't been malicious. So many men cared so little when it came to animals.

And people, for that matter.

"Why don't you and Lincoln eat your lunch. Take a break. I'll hang back and share mine with Eric," Craig said.

"There's a nice lookout in front of the house. You'll find a picnic table there," Eric offered.

"Does that work for you?" Lincoln asked Charlotte,

loosening the circle of his arms so he could see her face.

She scraped the remnants of her tears away and nodded, wishing helplessly that she hadn't had an audience for that emotional storm.

"It's okay to feel things," Lincoln murmured as Craig and Eric moved toward the stable. "In fact, it's healthy not to hold it all inside."

"Is that what they teach you in the Army?" she said wryly.

"No," he admitted with a chuckle. "Maybe they should."

Together they got the food from his truck, left Craig's portion on top of the hood and took the rest to the picnic table in front of Ed Johnson's ramshackle house. Eric was right; the view was nice here.

After several bites of the sandwich Lincoln brought her, Charlotte began to feel like herself again.

"Admiral must be in bad shape," Lincoln said, swallowing a bite. "I imagine you've seen all kinds of things in your work, but you're pretty shaken up."

She took a drink of water from the reusable bottle she'd brought with her. "I've seen much worse," she admitted. "It wasn't that. I thought we'd have to put him down." She blinked to clear her eyes when more tears gathered there. Where was all this sorrow coming from?

As if she didn't know.

"You must have had to do that a few times," Lincoln said carefully.

She nodded. "I... it's just..." She broke off, not

wanting to say what had happened the last time she'd faced an injured horse that couldn't be saved. Pain clogged her throat again, making it difficult to speak.

Lincoln didn't push her, simply waited until she'd brought her emotions under control. After a few minutes, Charlotte sighed. If she was going to be intimate with Lincoln, she'd have to tell him something about her past.

"My ex… wasn't a good guy," she said. "At least not when it came to horses." And people, she didn't add. "He viewed them as money-making machines. As long as they produced an income, he took care of them. When they stopped, he… disposed of them."

She meant to stop there, but Lincoln nodded and waited for her to go on. Somehow his silence gave her permission to tell him things she hadn't told anyone else. "There was this one horse—a really special one. Summer's Day. She'd been setting records in races all spring. Then she developed a stress fracture. She couldn't race on an injury like that, but my ex wouldn't hear of sidelining her while it healed. He demanded that she race again too soon. No matter what I said to him, he wouldn't change his mind. In the end, I had to treat her leg the best I could, give her something for the pain and let her go."

She buried her face in her hands as memories of that time came thick and fast, feeling just as ashamed now as when it happened that she'd been unable to stop Ivan.

"Just like I predicted, the next time she raced, she

reinjured it—badly. We brought her home, did everything we could, but the injury got worse instead of better. My ex was incensed. He blamed me, of course. When it was clear she wouldn't race again, he told me to put her out of her misery."

Lincoln didn't move except to cover her hand with his, letting her know he was here for her but that he wanted to hear the whole story.

"There are drugs for that procedure," she said, her voice wobbling with the pain of the memory. "He wouldn't let me use them."

Lincoln stilled.

"He... handed me his pistol. He's a very wealthy man, and he always carries one." Her voice was a whisper now. The memory had overtaken her. "He told me to do it quick." She shook her head. "I couldn't. There was no way—"

Lincoln moved to her, scooping her into his arms. "Of course not."

"He... he took the gun back. He wouldn't even let me turn away. He made me watch when he shot her." Charlotte buried her head against Lincoln's chest. She'd never cried about this before—

Why was she losing control now?

Lincoln held her, stroking her hair, murmuring to her like she was a child, and in the safety of his arms, she let her tears fall. She didn't tell him how loud the sound of the shot was. How she'd screamed. How Summer's Day had collapsed—

How her blood had flowed.

Charlotte had been covered in it.

"You're okay," Lincoln told her. "That's never going to happen again. I swear. I will never let that happen."

She'd told herself she'd never let it happen again, either. Then Ivan's prized racehorse, Forrester's Grand Rally, had gone lame. She'd sped up her attempt to leave, knowing she wouldn't survive another go-round with Ivan.

"It ought to be a crime to hurt a defenseless animal," Lincoln said. He was shaking, Charlotte realized. Incensed at what Ivan had done. Unlike Ivan, Lincoln had a moral compass. A love for all God's creatures. Respect for women.

There really were good men in the world.

"THAT'S THE THIRD time I've seen you on your phone in the past fifteen minutes," Carter complained, coming into the mill office. "Who are you talking to?"

Lincoln pushed the offending gadget into his pocket and stood from behind the worn old desk, trying to get his thoughts in order. It had been harder than he liked to admit to leave Charlotte with Craig after their lunch was over, but after she'd cried herself out and eaten more food, she'd calmed down and declared her desire to get back to work.

"I held that in a long time," she'd said when she was drying her eyes. "Guess it needed to come out."

He was glad he'd been there when it did, but Lincoln had to admit he was shaken by what she'd said.

What kind of sadistic creep shot a horse in front of his girlfriend?

And what else had he done?

"Some new tenants, hopefully," he answered Carter. "Bella connected me with them this morning, and I've been answering their questions ever since."

"That's good news. I don't suppose you want to find some more replacement workers while you're at it?"

"I thought you were working on that." Lincoln's thoughts were still so tangled up in the story Charlotte had told him he was having enough trouble handling the questions Veronica and her friends kept tossing his way.

"I got a lead on another contract that I'd like to follow up. Besides, you're the one who's going to work with them day in, day out." Carter stepped inside the office and shut the door against the din of the mill equipment. The noise dropped abruptly.

"Guess I could take that on," Lincoln said, looking up. "But you'd better not get too far ahead of yourself. We need to figure out our supply of logs."

"That's Hudson's thing. You need to talk to him about it."

"Me?" It used to be you couldn't get Hudson out of the woods, but every morning he showed up at the mill and joined the temporary workers producing lumber. "Why should I be the one to nag him? He doesn't even seem interested in logging anymore."

"Then talk to Gage," Carter said. "He helped run the logging operation last time."

"I already talked to him, remember? He said he was on it, but he's barely more enthusiastic than Hudson."

Lincoln's phone buzzed, and he drew it out of his pocket. It was another message from Veronica. She wanted to know how the night life was in town.

"Let's go find Hudson together," Carter said. "Maybe the two of us can get him to tell us what the problem is."

"Sure thing." Lincoln gratefully shoved his phone in his pocket again. He'd rather not explain how limited the night life was. Would a bunch of women from Seattle enjoy hanging out at the Dancing Boot?

They found Hudson in the mill and ushered him outside.

"What's all this?" he asked.

"This is us wondering when you're going to get us some new logs," Carter said. "We're going to have a serious workflow problem at some point if you don't."

Hudson rubbed the back of his head, took a pace or two away from them and turned back. For a moment Lincoln thought he might not answer. "Yeah, about that. Thing is, I can't do it all myself. Tried that once, remember? I need a crew."

Lincoln wasn't sure he'd ever heard his twin admit he needed help with anything. When they were teenagers, their dad used to send men after him when he'd disappear into the woods to take some trees down all on his own, safety be damned.

"How much help do you want?" Carter asked after a moment. He, too, must have been surprised by Hudson's admission.

Hudson looked off into the distance. Did a few internal calculations and rattled off several positions to fill. "Two or three people you hire need to be experienced climbers. That's crucial."

Lincoln exchanged a look with Carter. "Since when do you need climbers? You've always done that work yourself."

"You want a lot of logs, fast, right?" Hudson demanded. "Then I can't do it all myself. Besides, it's not like I'm asking to buy a bunch of brand-new equipment right before the price of lumber tanks."

Lincoln winced as the shot hit home. He knew damn well he was the cause of all their financial problems. He didn't need Hudson to rub his nose in it.

His first instinct was to retaliate, but he took a deep breath instead. His attitude toward Hudson had begun to change since Charlotte told him what his twin had said about why he'd slept with Winona. Now that he'd let go of his resentment, he'd noticed something had been bugging Hudson since they got home.

"You want me to do the hiring for you? You sure you don't want to find them yourself?" he asked evenly. They weren't kids anymore. He didn't need to take every barb Hudson shot his way personally.

"I've got enough to do." Hudson stalked away.

"I don't understand him," Carter said as they watched him go. "I know he wants to be here. And he loves logging. Always has. Why isn't he jumping at the chance to get back to it?"

"I don't know." Which made a pang of guilt twist low in Lincoln's gut. When they were kids, he'd known Hudson as well as he knew himself. He didn't often admit how much it hurt they lost that closeness. Maybe it was time to patch things up. "He was pretty damn worried about Dad the other day. Let's give him time to cool off," he said when Carter made a move to follow Hudson. "I'll keep talking to him and figure out what's wrong. Meanwhile, I'll work on hiring that crew for him."

"Fine. Guess I'll nail down that contract."

"Maybe we'll manage to make this work, after all."

"THIS IS THE best way to wake up in the morning," Lincoln said several weeks later, tracing a kiss over Charlotte's bare shoulder as they lay together in bed.

Still catching her breath from a rather vigorous round of lovemaking, Charlotte nodded. "I agree." They'd fallen into a rhythm of reaching for each other first thing in the morning and last thing at night. In between, she joined Craig for his daily rounds, then came home and worked on her house with Lincoln, who'd all but moved in.

She was grateful Lincoln hadn't pushed her too hard for more information about Ivan after the day they'd helped rescue Admiral. The last thing she wanted to do was recount all her bad decisions. What if Lincoln changed his mind about her and asked her to leave?

While Lincoln was a naturally early riser, worry about the lumber mill had been keeping him awake these past few weeks long after she fell asleep. He tended to slip into a quick catnap after they were together in the morning, so Charlotte took the opportunity to go for either a jog or a ride on one of his horses before work. These late July mornings were warm enough she often wished she had time for a swim, too.

She loved how quiet it was when almost everyone was still asleep. She'd found several trails that stayed close to the community, and she spotted something new almost every day.

On Tuesday and Thursday nights, Amanda had instituted knitting club. Carter had tried to follow them to the rotunda the first time, but Amanda shooed him away. Carolyn had her own knitting group in Chance Creek, but Megan had been thrilled to be invited. When the three of them were safely behind a closed door, Amanda brought out a bottle of wine and a few glasses, and they toasted each other before breaking out their projects. Amanda was still working on the baby sweater, although she reported no progress in getting pregnant. Charlotte had chosen a complicated pattern for a pair of mittens she could use in the winter. Megan was working on a beautiful scarf. She admitted she'd been knitting since she was a girl, and her skill put both of them to shame.

Lincoln had taken her to town one day to the used car dealership, where Charlotte picked out a red Chevy Silverado. It was nine years old, but the mileage was low, and it was big enough to haul anything she might want, including a horse trailer. She was relieved to have her own transportation for the first time in years, since she'd driven one of Ivan's vehicles the entire time she was with him. When she drove the Silverado off the lot, she'd felt like a teenager heading off for her first joyride. It made up for how much the purchase had drained her cash reserves. Even after she'd banked her first paycheck, her funds were noticeably low.

Nate had organized two cookouts down at the beach. There was an enormous wood-fired grill set up right on the sand, where all the men liked to stand around and take turns flipping the burgers and hot dogs. Charlotte liked the way the brothers talked and joked with each other and the way Amanda joined in. Lincoln told her his dad had always hosted Saturday cookouts, and she got the feeling he was happy to have the tradition reinstated.

On the Fourth of July, they all went to town to enjoy the parade, fair and fireworks.

All in all, she was settling in fine, Charlotte thought as Lincoln fell back to sleep and she showered and dressed. Still, a thread of unease wound itself through every day. On her morning rides, she caught herself looking over her shoulder in case Ivan had tracked her down. When she was making house calls with Craig, she dreaded questions new clients asked about her schooling and past work experience, wishing she could forget that time in her life. When she was with Lincoln and his brothers, or Amanda and Megan, she knew they accepted her, but somehow she still felt like an outsider looking in.

She was afraid Ivan hadn't finished with her yet.

Charlotte decided that today she'd shake off that unsettled feeling and act like her new life was permanent. After all, Amanda had lived here only a couple of months longer than she had, and she never questioned whether she belonged. Anne and her programmers were arriving this morning, Veronica and her friends were due next week, and tomorrow the first of the permanent mill workers Lincoln had hired was coming to town.

She settled into her ride, enjoying the quiet freshness of the morning, the birdsong, the strong sunlight awakening the world. She stretched her excursion a little too long, and by the time she turned back, she knew she'd miss breakfast. When she made it to the stable, she found Amanda and Megan talking outside.

She hurried through the process of unsaddling and feeding Thorn before joining them.

"What's going on?"

"I'm here to start taking photos of some of the houses that are ready to sell," Megan said. "I don't want to see my boss one more time without those listings."

"I wonder if any of the programmers moving in today will eventually buy a house here?" Charlotte said.

"Maybe," Amanda said, then frowned and shaded her eyes. "Who's that?" She pulled out her phone and checked the time. "It can't be them—it's too early." A large black truck pulled into the circle and followed it around to come to a stop in front of them. "Oh no, it's Blake Warrington. What does he want?"

"Awkward." Megan stepped back as if to hide behind them. "Blake hit on me at Cindy Gladstone's wedding in April. Didn't want to take no for an answer until Gage saved me. I've been avoiding the man ever since."

"That's when you and Gage hooked up!" Amanda said. "Carter told me."

"We didn't hook up," Megan said. "He just… kissed me. And he hasn't done anything since."

As Blake Warrington climbed out of his truck, Charlotte recognized him from Linda's Diner. He looked just as pleased with himself now as he did then.

"Ladies."

"Blake," Amanda said, crossing her arms. "What are you doing here?"

"Come to make sure you all are taking care of my future property."

"We're busy," Amanda said firmly. "Go away."

"Is Carter around? Or one of the other men?"

"No."

Charlotte knew darn well all the men had to be somewhere nearby, but she wasn't going to contradict her friend.

"Then you can give them a message. I'm still interested in buying this place, but I'm losing patience."

"Too bad."

"Just tell them." His gaze focused on Megan. "Ah. You."

"Me," Megan said, then blushed.

"If you'd played your cards right, you could have

made a commission on this deal. But you blew it. I hope you don't regret that mistake." He held her gaze a moment. "I could always give you a second chance, you know. I heard Gage hasn't come calling on you lately. You should be with a man who knows how to treat a woman right."

"Who would that be?" Megan asked, lifting her chin. "You didn't treat me very well at Cindy's wedding—or were you so drunk you don't even remember?"

He had the grace to look embarrassed. "I'll admit I wasn't my best that night. Personal matter. I apologize for any distress I caused you. It wasn't intentional."

Megan blinked. Amanda looked just as surprised. The man sounded almost earnest, as if he really cared what Megan thought of him. Charlotte looked to see Megan's response. Her friend was frowning, scanning Blake's face as if trying to make out his intentions.

"I hope you'll let me make it up to you soon," Blake went on.

When Megan didn't answer, he turned back to his truck and opened the door, but instead of climbing in, he surveyed the settlement and nodded. "This will make a terrific addition to my resort." He got in, shut the door and drove off.

"What does he mean, he wants to make it up to me?" Megan sputtered. "That man is... I don't even know what he is!"

"Sounds like he means to ask you out on a date," Amanda said. "For a second he was almost nice—and then he blew it again."

"I wouldn't date him if he was the last man on earth. *A terrific addition to my resort,*" she parroted. "He can shove his resort where the sun doesn't shine. I'd never do a real estate transaction for him, and I won't let him get his mitts on this town. I can't believe him."

"Don't let him rile you up," Amanda said and stopped. "Wait, now someone else is coming. That has to be Anne and her programmers."

Anne wasn't driving a rental sports car this time around. Instead, a large passenger van pulled into the Circle, followed by a moving van. Amanda took out her phone and tapped its screen quickly. A moment later, Lincoln and his brothers spilled out of the town hall and came to meet the newcomers.

By the time Charlotte, Amanda and Megan reached them, Anne was talking to the men, gesturing angrily. She was impeccably dressed again today in an outfit far more suitable for a boardroom than a small country town. A cluster of men in their twenties stood looking around them with a mixture of curiosity and concern.

Charlotte approached Lincoln. "What's happening?" she asked softly.

He leaned down to answer in an undertone. "Anne's unhappy that they already lost a day of work traveling here yesterday. She wants us to move their things into the house while she takes her workers to Two Willows and gets their new office set up. She needs to return that van to the rental company, too."

"I'd help, but I have to meet Craig. I'm running late."

"And the rest of us need to get to the mill. We're not a moving company." Lincoln dropped a kiss on the top of her head. "Anyway, don't worry about it. We'll sort this out."

"I'm sure you will."

"I have to get those photos done," Megan said. "I'll see you later."

Charlotte noticed she ignored Gage as she passed him, but he watched her walk away before turning his attention back to Carter's discussion with Anne.

When Charlotte started for her house to change, Amanda tagged along. "What do you think of our new neighbors?" she asked when they were out of earshot.

"I don't know. They seem nice enough, I guess." The programmers were talking among themselves, letting Anne sort out logistics with Carter. One of them had his phone out and was showing the others something on his screen.

"I'm sure we'll get to know them over time," Amanda agreed. "It's going to be different having more people around, though." She linked her arm through Charlotte's as they walked away together.

"In a good or bad way?"

"I'm not sure. I guess we'll have to wait and see."

Charlotte understood her hesitation. The newcomers would change things. With each passing week, if the Elliott men had their way, there would be more people coming to live here. She'd have to prepare for that.

As long as none of them asked too many questions about her past, she'd be fine, Charlotte decided.

"Do you think you'll adjust?" she asked Amanda.

"Of course," Amanda grumbled. "But I bet some-day I look back at these first few months as the good old days. It was special to come here and get my pick of houses."

"And Elliotts," Charlotte chimed in.

"Seems like you've been doing some picking, too," Amanda said good-naturedly. "Nate said Lincoln hasn't slept in their parents' house in weeks. Things must be pretty serious."

"I like Lincoln. A lot."

"I'm so happy for you both." Amanda detached herself after a block or so. "I'd better go back and see if Carter needs help."

"Good luck with the newcomers."

"Good luck with the cows."

Charlotte changed into her work clothes, grabbed a couple of granola bars and was nearly to her truck when her phone chimed. She checked it automatically but stopped in her tracks when she saw a new email from Ivan.

Reluctantly, she opened it.

I know where you are. You have 48 hours to come home, or I'll make sure all your new friends know exactly how you spent the past three years. You think your new boyfriend will stick around when he finds out you're a gold digger?

Come home, Charlotte. You're my gold digger. We'll forget all about your little trip West, I'll drop the lawsuit and we'll get back to our lives. Maybe take things to the next level? That's what you want, isn't it?

Lawsuit?

He'd attached a document. Charlotte tapped it with a shaking finger and discovered it was a legal one. Ivan was suing her for the money he claimed she owed him. She had 30 days to respond if she wanted the matter to be brought to court. Otherwise, a default judgement could be brought against her.

Fear and disgust left a bitter taste in her mouth. Once upon a time she'd wanted to marry Ivan, but not now. She wanted nothing to do with him, and she certainly didn't want to face him in court. She didn't think he'd win his case, but that barely mattered, because she knew he was capable of carrying out his threat to try to ruin her life here. Ivan was right: if he told Lincoln the story of their relationship, Lincoln might jump to the obvious conclusion. That she'd fallen in with Ivan because of his money. That she'd used an older man to further her ambitions and then run the moment she grew tired of him. That she'd racked up bills on Ivan's credit card and never paid him back. She'd look like a cheat and a…

Charlotte didn't even want to think the word.

The worst part was that in some ways it was true. Her parents' deaths and the student loans she'd accumulated had left her vulnerable to a wealthy older man. The things that stressed her out were mere inconveniences to him. Ivan liked to flash his money around. Letting him pay her way had been so seductive.

She wasn't a gold digger, though, and she didn't use her body to get what she wanted. When she'd moved in with Ivan, she'd honestly thought she was in love with him. If he'd proposed the first year they'd lived together, she would have accepted in a heartbeat. She'd been so blind to his faults back then.

Now she knew exactly what kind of man he was.

She had to stop him before he ruined everything.

She lifted her phone, determined to call Steven right away, but realized she was already running late. She'd make the call after she'd met Craig at their first appointment.

She had too much at stake here to wait a minute longer.

CHAPTER 9

"**N**O, I'M NOT bringing the mill workers to unload your truck," Carter said to Anne for the third time, looking to Lincoln like he might lose his temper in another minute. "We're on a deadline to get an order filled. Besides, you've got five men with you. Any more would just be in the way."

"Those aren't men. Those are programmers, and the last thing I need is one of them to jam a finger," Anne said. "We have deadlines, too. We should be working right now, not standing around."

"Hudson, Nate and I will head to the mill," Gage broke in. "You two stay and help our new arrivals settle in." He sounded reasonable, but his hands were spasming with obscene secret code words Lincoln hadn't seen since his teenage days.

Lincoln bit back a laugh and clapped him on the back. "Thanks. We'll be there as soon as we can."

When he, Nate and Hudson had gone, Lincoln stepped between Carter and Anne. "Let's get this show on the road. Hey—you," he called to the nearest programmer. "What's your name?"

The young man looked to Anne. "Uh... Gareth?"

"You tell me, man. It's your name," Lincoln joked, inwardly rolling his eyes. The kid was clearly out of his element here. He was five foot nine or ten, Lincoln estimated, with light brown hair and wire-rimmed glasses.

"Gareth," the young man repeated with a little more conviction. He stood with his hands jammed in his pockets, as if afraid if he took them out, some wild animal might race out of the woods and bite them off.

"Gareth, grab a partner. In fact, all of you partner up. We're going to unload this truck. While you're at it, why don't the rest of you introduce yourselves?"

"I'm Mark," said a tall man with dark skin and hair and an extremely deep voice.

"Nice to meet you, Mark. How about you team up with Gareth?"

"Will do." He stepped to Gareth's side.

"I'm Gregory." A redhead stepped forward. "That's Edwin. We can be a team." He pointed to a blond man who was built like a linebacker but stood with a slight hunch of his shoulders as if he was bent over a laptop even now.

"Glad to meet you both."

"I'm Troy. No one's left to be my partner, so I'll handle things myself." Troy was Gareth's height but a little stockier, with sandy brown hair.

Lincoln and Carter ushered the lot of them toward the moving van despite Anne's protests.

At the back of the moving van, which was already open, he had a moment of trepidation of his own. The vehicle was stacked to the roof with furniture and equipment.

"Is some of this going to town when you set up your office?"

Gareth shook his head. "That's a whole other truck."

Carter whistled under his breath.

"What's the holdup?" Anne said.

"You heard the lady," Lincoln said to the programmers. "Let's get going." He jumped up into the van, and Carter followed. Together, they started handing things down.

"I don't know where any of this goes, so you all will have to figure that out. Get Anne to show you."

He was afraid they wouldn't comply, but once he'd made the job clear, they got to it with more alacrity than he expected. Maybe they were simply shell-shocked from the change in their environments. If so, they'd settle in soon.

They were about a quarter of the way through the job when Carter straightened and pointed toward the Circle.

"Who's that?"

Lincoln watched a passenger van pull up the road, come around and park close by. Its doors opened, and women began to spill out. He and Carter weren't the only ones who stopped to watch. All the programmers, including Gregory and Edwin, who were struggling under the weight of a massive wooden desk, had stopped in their tracks.

"Who are they?" Mark asked.

"I think it's Bella's friends," Lincoln said slowly. "It has to be. They aren't due until next week, though."

One of them came striding toward them, a blonde with long, wavy hair. "Lincoln? Is that you?"

"Veronica?"

"That's me!" She bounded up to where he'd climbed down from the moving van and caught him in a surprise hug.

"You're... early."

"I know. Isn't it wonderful? We got so excited, we started packing our stuff and couldn't stop. When the van was full, we just drove off, and now we're here!" She flung her arms out to take in her surroundings.

"That's... great."

"I know it is. I'm so glad to meet you! Sasha, take a photo!" Veronica looped her arms around Lincoln's waist and squeezed hard. Another young woman took a photo with her phone. She moved like a dancer and had light brown hair that flowed past her waist.

"I'm posting," she said, tapping a few keys and smiling. "There. That was fabulous!"

"Wait," Lincoln protested, far too late. "What is going on?"

"We post constantly," Veronica explained. "Our followers expect updates at least every half hour."

"They prefer every ten minutes," Sasha said. "We've done studies." Looking around her, she pocketed her phone, did something twisty with her hair, looped it on top of her head and stabbed a pen through it.

The programmers watched with awe.

Hell, he was watching with awe. He'd been around the world, but he'd never seen anything quite like these two young women. They had so much… energy.

"There's so much to photograph here!" Veronica twirled around to take it all in, her blonde hair flying. She stretched out her arms and twirled again, while Sasha held out her phone and filmed. "Elliott Ridge is awesome!" she cried.

"I got all that," Sasha said. "Posting!" She tapped her phone with a flourish.

"I'm Gareth," Gareth said with quite a bit more certainty than the last time he'd given his name. He approached Sasha with his hand out, as if to shake. Sasha handed him her purse.

"I'm Sasha. That's Veronica." She pointed to the blonde. "That's Louise." She pointed to a young woman of medium height whose blonde hair hung in thick braids down her back. "That's Edie." She indicated a short girl who sported a towering dark bun. "That's Tania." Tania had a nose piercing, dramatic eyeliner and blue hair. "That's Elaine."

"Konnichiwa," Elaine said.

"Are you Japanese?" Troy asked in awe.

"My parents were. I was born in Wyoming," Elaine said.

"And that's Bettina," Sasha finished.

"Betty for short," Bettina said. Her light brown hair

was looped in braids across her head like a Swiss dairy maid. Tattoos covered her arms.

"We've got more bags in the van." Veronica spoke up, addressing Gareth. "Are you here to help us unpack?"

Gareth nodded vigorously.

"Oh, hell no!" Anne stormed up, eyes flashing. "You are not going to steal my programmers. Get your own."

"I just—"

"No," Anne boomed. "N. O. No! To everything you're about to ask," she added when Veronica opened her mouth again. "Gareth, Mark, back on task!" When she pointed to the truck, the programmers reluctantly returned to the work of emptying it. Gareth handed Sasha her purse. She blew him a kiss, and he flushed.

"Well. Okay," Veronica said, clapping her hands together. "Ladies, looks like we're on our own. Good thing we're goddesses, and we can do anything!" She whooped a battle cry and the other women whooped back at her in sync, a bloodcurdling sound that stopped everyone in their tracks all over again.

"Told you there'd be trouble," Dennis said, materializing at Lincoln's shoulder.

"Hell, Dennis." Lincoln took a steadying breath to try to calm his pulse. The old man had snuck up on him. "There's no trouble. Just people moving in. They'll be settled in no time."

"Doubt it." Dennis sidled off.

"Where's our house?" Veronica cried, emerging

from the van with a half-opened suitcase. Colorful items of clothing spilled out as she jumped to the ground.

"I'll take you there," Carter said. "Can you finish up here?" he asked Lincoln.

"Will do," Lincoln said.

Carter joined Veronica and pointed to one of the largest, oldest homes on Ridge. It didn't have the Gothic charm of the programmers' residence, but its stone facade and many windows gave it character of its own.

"Come on, goddesses!" Veronica led the way, the rest of the women following, laden down with baskets, bags, laundry hampers and the occasional piece of luggage. Carter leaned into the van, pulled out a suitcase and a cardboard box, and trailed after them.

"Is this Elliott Ridge?"

Lincoln wheeled around as a new voice reached his ears. He hadn't even noticed the dusty Ford truck drive up. A burly man with dark, close-cropped hair stood next to him.

"It is. Can I help you?"

"Cal Evers. I'm here for the mill job? I know I'm a few hours early…"

"Welcome." Lincoln shook his hand. So what if he was early? So what if the Ridge had descended into pandemonium?

He surveyed the chaos with satisfaction. Maybe he hadn't planned for it to look this way when he'd helped put the call out for people to join them. It didn't matter.

The Ridge was coming back to life.

"HE SAYS HE knows where you are, but he doesn't actually say where that is," Steven pointed out when Charlotte managed to call him. She'd sent Craig on ahead to their next appointment and told him she'd follow as soon as she could after she took care of a personal matter. After forwarding Ivan's message to Steven, she'd called him to ask his advice. "We will have to answer this court filing, though. I'll file a motion to dismiss."

"You think you can get the case shut down?" Her heart rose but for only a moment. Even if he did, that wouldn't be the end of it.

"Ivan could oppose the motion, but let's keep our fingers crossed. Only trouble is I'll have to disclose your address after I file. I'll ask the court for a protective order not to share your address with Ivan."

"What if they refuse?"

"We'll file a restraining order, too."

"I think that would only antagonize him."

Ivan didn't have to attack her physically to get revenge. He would take pleasure in torpedoing a family-run operation like Lincoln's lumber business. God help them all if he ever met Blake Warrington. Those two could throw enough money around to make the Elliotts' lives miserable—and hers along with them.

"I don't want him to ruin this life I'm building for myself," she went on. "You have to keep my whereabouts a secret if you can."

"Believe me, I'll try," Steven said. "Lie low. Send me copies of his emails and documents, and let me do my job. I doubt very sincerely that you'll have to travel back to Saratoga for that court case, and if you do, I'll be by your side all the way."

"Thanks, Steven."

Charlotte found it hard to concentrate on her work after that and was relieved when she pulled up to number 37 at the end of the day. She was too hungry to bother with more than a quick splash of water and a change of clothes before dinner. Knowing Lincoln would still be at the mill, she went straight to the town hall to see how Amanda was doing and find a snack.

On the way she met a swarm of pretty young women taking photographs on house number 1's front porch.

"Those are our newest town members," Carolyn Snyder said, coming from the direction of Elliott Lake wearing a bathing suit and straw hat, with a beach towel over one arm. "Quite a bunch, aren't they?" she added as she walked past. "See you at dinner."

"See you." Charlotte still hardly knew Carolyn, but she always found her to be friendly when they met. She kept going, but before she walked ten feet farther, she was swarmed by the young women.

"That's perfect," one of them cried as she held up her phone and took a photo of Charlotte walking. "Keep going. Smile!"

Charlotte stopped and crossed her arms in front of her face, warding off the photographic assault. "What are you doing?"

"Posting pics of all the townspeople we meet," the

young woman answered. "I'm Sasha, by the way. What's your name?"

"You can't post my photo!" Charlotte took a step forward and snatched the phone out of Sasha's hands.

"Hey!" Sasha lunged for it, but Charlotte held it high.

"You can't post my photo!"

"Why not?"

"I..." Against her better judgment, she decided to tell the truth. "I don't want my ex to know where I live."

Sasha rolled her eyes. "Drama." She spun the word out.

"It's not drama. It's serious. Listen to me." Charlotte took a deep breath as all the women crowded around. "My ex can't know where I am. Do you understand?" She looked from one to the other. "I'm not joking. I'm not making something up to call attention to myself, either. He can't know I'm here."

Sasha stopped trying to grab her phone. "Is he violent?"

"I... Maybe," Charlotte said reluctantly, wishing these women hadn't come to Elliott Ridge. "I love it here. I don't want to have to leave. He's pissed at me, and he'll do anything to ruin what I have if he can find me." She held out her free hand when the women started asking questions. "I don't want to talk about it. That part of my life is over. That means you can't ever post photos of me, and you can't ever post my name, either. That's all I'm asking."

"We're just trying to give Elliott Ridge some publicity," Sasha said sullenly.

"That's wonderful," Charlotte said and meant it. "Post away. Just leave me out of it. Can you do that?"

"Fine," Sasha said after a moment. "There are plenty of other things to post about." The others nodded.

"Thank you." Charlotte breathed a sigh of relief and handed Sasha her phone. "Can you delete those photos?"

Sasha tapped away and showed her the camera roll. No photos of Charlotte remained.

"Thanks again. See you at dinner," she said and hurried on, leaving the women murmuring behind her. As grateful as she was that they'd gone along with her request, she had a feeling she'd created a gulf between her and these new inhabitants of the Ridge.

She went to find Amanda, hoping for sympathy, but found her pacing the town hall's kitchen in agitation, and her heart sank. She wasn't the only one having a difficult day.

"I don't know how to cook for forty-one people," Amanda said as soon as she spotted Charlotte, pointing with dismay at a lasagna she'd just pulled from the oven. "I made four of these and rotated them on the upper and lower racks, but I still managed to burn one."

Charlotte came to see. "It doesn't look too bad," she said doubtfully. The lasagna in question was charred around the periphery but looked okay in the middle.

"I tried to cut it. It's burned to a crisp on the bottom," Amanda said. "It's inedible. Now what do I serve everyone?"

Charlotte looked around the kitchen. Amanda had made garlic bread and salad to go with the meal, so she moved to look in the cupboards and refrigerator. This was a problem she could solve. She was happy to be tucked away back here, far from the young women with their cell phones. She had a feeling it would take constant vigilance not to show up on their social media pages. "We can make more garlic bread. And here's another head of lettuce." She started pulling out all the salad vegetables she could find. "We can precut the pieces of lasagna to make sure everyone gets at least one," she added.

"The mill workers are going to revolt. No matter how much bread and salad we feed them, they love my lasagna and always want seconds."

"Maybe the influencers won't eat it. Because of the carbs," Charlotte hurried to clarify when Amanda frowned. "I bet they'll load up on salad. Hold on." She opened a few cupboards and pulled out a couple of cans of chickpeas triumphantly. "I can add these to it and dress it up a bit with a few more odds and ends. Make it a meal in itself. We'll call it the vegan option."

"I guess."

They both turned when the door to the kitchen opened and a man Charlotte didn't recognize stuck his head in. He was a large, burly man with close-cropped hair and a friendly smile.

"Hi," he said brightly. "Just checking when dinner is. Carter mentioned people tend to eat together here, but he didn't give me a time, and I don't want to be late."

Amanda's shoulders slumped. Charlotte could guess what she was thinking: another mouth to feed. "You probably won't want to come," Amanda said dispiritedly.

"Of course he will," Charlotte said quickly. "We've had a minor kitchen mishap," she explained to the stranger, "and Amanda's not used to that. She's a fabulous cook."

"I'm not a cook at all," Amanda said. "I'm just a person who knows how to cook a few things. Before I came here, the largest meal I ever made was for six people. Now I'm trying to feed more than forty."

The man let himself all the way into the kitchen.

"I cooked in camps up north in the oil patch for five years. In Canada."

"Like… summer camps?" Amanda asked, her forehead wrinkled in confusion.

The stranger laughed. "Hardly. In northern Canada, oil and gas extraction often happen in places so remote you have to fly in. Guys work two weeks on, two weeks off. While they're in camp, they're provided with housing, food, you name it. I was a cook in some of those places before I got into logging."

"Why did you switch careers?" Amanda asked. She made room for him as he came to inspect the lasagna.

"Better pay." He shrugged. "Kind of miss it sometimes, though."

"If you have ideas for how to salvage our meal, I'm

all ears. Charlotte is expanding the salad and making more garlic bread, but I don't think that's going to keep the mill workers happy. Everyone will be here in a few minutes. We eat at six," Amanda said. "I'm Amanda, by the way. That's Charlotte."

"I'm Cal. Calvin Evers. I think we can save some of this lasagna. Can I try?"

"Go ahead. Please."

Charlotte drained the chickpeas and chopped vegetables as Cal got to work skimming the top half of the burned lasagna out of the pan, leaving the charred bits behind. He placed what he salvaged in a new pan he fished out of a nearby cupboard, as if he already knew how the kitchen was laid out.

Amanda took the rest of the lasagnas out of the oven, set them aside and began slicing more Italian bread. Charlotte could hear voices in the cafeteria as people filed in. She divided the salad into two large serving bowls and grabbed bottles of dressing, arranging them all on the long table beneath the serving window in the cafeteria. The plates, silverware and napkins were already lined up there.

Amanda fired three more loaves of garlic bread into the oven to heat. Charlotte noticed Cal had cut up the salvaged portion of lasagna and was adding leftover mozzarella and ricotta cheese and a jar of sauce to it. "I'll just pop this in the oven, and we can serve it as seconds," he said. "Kind of like lasagna soup." He cut the other three lasagnas into small squares and covered them with aluminum foil.

"We'll hand out salad first," he said. "Make them come up for a second time to get bread and lasagna. By the time they come up a third time for lasagna soup and even more bread, they'll feel like they've gotten their money's worth."

"Sounds like a good plan," Charlotte said. She'd worried for a moment that Amanda might not like the way Cal was taking over, but Amanda seemed relieved. She couldn't blame her. Even twenty-six people was a lot to cook for on a regular basis. Forty-two verged into professional territory.

It worked out just as Cal said. Charlotte and Amanda directed everyone to eat their salads first. Even the men, who were hungry from a day's work, took a healthy serving, something they didn't always do if meat and potatoes were on offer right away. The women happily exclaimed over the salad. One of them, an attractive blonde, lingered at the window. "Are you new here, too?" she asked Cal. "I'm Veronica."

"I am new," Cal said. "I'm Cal. These two ladies have been here much longer, though."

"We met outside. I'm Charlotte. I've been here for a few weeks," Charlotte said.

"I'm Amanda. It's a few months for me," Amanda said. "I got here in April and married Carter Elliott in June."

"You found a husband here?" Veronica asked, perking up at the information.

"I did. Are you looking for one?" Amanda teased her.

"I am," Veronica said seriously. "Are you looking for a wife?" she asked Cal, who set a basket of garlic bread near the window.

"Uh... I guess?" he sputtered. "Hadn't thought about it much."

"Maybe you should think about it," Veronica said, took a slice of bread, dropped it on her plate and walked off.

"Maybe I should," Cal said, his gaze following her.

While everyone ate their first course, Charlotte, Amanda and Cal set out the rest of the bread and lasagna on platters on the buffet table outside the serving window.

They made everyone stay in line and behave in an orderly fashion as they came through a second time, serving them several slices of bread but only one piece of lasagna.

Charlotte heard some of the men grumbling, but when they put out the lasagna soup, as Cal called it, only a trickle of them came to get some. Everyone else was full and mellow enough to take their time.

"Why's Cal working in the kitchen?" Lincoln asked Charlotte when the meal was in progress and she and Amanda came out to join him and his brothers at their usual table.

She told him what had happened. "He took over like he'd been running the place all along. He just shooed us out of there to come and eat. Says he's got it all under control."

Lincoln looked alarmed. "He's supposed to be here

to work at the mill."

"Looks to me like he's here to cook," Gage said from the far end of the table. Charlotte thought she saw a glint of humor in his eyes.

"No way. You can't go poaching my men," Lincoln told Amanda.

"I didn't poach anyone. Charlotte told you—he came looking for work."

"Didn't you make her agree to do the cooking for a year?" Lincoln asked Gage.

"Not sure I said she couldn't have help." Gage shrugged and took another scoop of his lasagna soup.

"I can't cook two meals a day for forty-one people by myself," Amanda pointed out.

"Of course not," Carter said. "It wasn't fair to ask you to cook at all, anyway."

"Not when she's the town manager and librarian, too," Charlotte put in.

"I can't run the mill by myself, either." Lincoln tore a piece of bread in two and dipped it in red sauce. "I need Cal."

"Maybe we should leave it up to him to decide," Carter said.

"Are we going to keep eating together when the community gets even bigger?" Charlotte asked. "Is that how you did it when you were kids?"

"No," Lincoln said. "Back then the Ridge was full of families. People cooked at their own houses except on special celebrations when we all ate together."

"I guess we'll figure it out as we go," Carter said. "Is

that lasagna soup going to run out?" He craned his neck to look toward the kitchen.

"No," Amanda assured him. "There's plenty."

"CAN'T WE STAY right here?" Lincoln asked, wrapping an arm around Charlotte's waist when she moved to get out of bed the next morning. Summer was slipping by quickly. The sun was so bright he knew he'd struggle to go back to sleep, even though he'd been up past one the night before, his mind spinning.

"I have work. So do you. And I want my morning ride."

"I'll give you a morning ride," he growled into the side of her neck. "Another one, that is."

Charlotte pushed him away. "One is enough, and you know that's not what I mean."

"But you *could* mean it." He inched closer again.

He traced kisses down her neck to her shoulders, melting her resolve, and by the time they finished what he'd managed to start, it was too late to think of saddling any horses before breakfast.

"Sorry you won't get out on the trail," he said as they shared the shower.

"I suppose it's all right," she teased. "But I'm going to be late to work at this rate."

"You have plenty of time." But that wasn't exactly true. The kitchen in number 37 was still a shambles, so they had to rush over to the cafeteria for their breakfast. Twenty minutes later Charlotte shoved her plate away when she was only half done and wrapped a muffin in a paper napkin. "I'll eat this on the way. See you tonight." When she bent to kiss Lincoln's cheek, he caught her hand and held her there a moment longer.

"Drive carefully," he said. "Craig can wait five minutes."

"I'm not sure he can. We've got a busy day ahead of us."

A moment later she was gone.

Lincoln felt a pang as he watched her go. When Carter was wooing Amanda, there'd been hardly anyone on the Ridge. He'd ducked out of work all the time to fix her house and spend time with her. Meanwhile, he and Charlotte were always racing in different directions. They were making slow and steady progress on number 37, but he wished they could spend a full day together with no interruptions. At least they'd finished the renovations on both her bathrooms, had painted most of the rooms and were nearly ready to refinish the floors.

Meanwhile, he expected another new hire today and more tomorrow. No time for slacking off if he wanted the transition from temporary workers to permanent ones to go smoothly.

He was just finishing his own meal when Veronica, Sasha and the other women arrived in a flurry of loud exclamations, cell phones and laughter.

Gage, who'd just sat down with his plate of food, stood up again and slipped out a side door, carrying it with him.

Nate, already eating, chuckled.

Lincoln shoveled a last bite of food into his mouth and stood, too.

"What the hell are they doing?" Hudson asked, sitting back in his chair and craning his head.

Lincoln turned to find six of the women standing in a line, hands on their hips, while Veronica filmed them with her phone. The women broke into a cheerleading routine, their shouted words echoing off the high cafeteria ceiling.

"One, two, three, four! Where's the place we all adore? Elliott Ridge! Elliott Ridge! Go… Ridgebacks!

Nate winced. Even Hudson, genetically programmed to like everything women did, looked pained. "Ridgebacks? That doesn't make sense for an Elliott Ridge mascot. We don't have wild hogs here."

"We don't have any athletic teams, either," Lincoln pointed out.

"Do you have to act like children?" Anne got up from a table across the room and faced off with Veronica and her crew. "Don't you have any work to do?"

"This is our work," Sasha said, flipping her long hair over her shoulder, her mouth pursed in a pout. "We do our marketing as a team, creating interesting content that attracts a variety of people to our various businesses. We've decided to create a promotional campaign for Elliott Ridge to help Lincoln and his brothers attract new settlers to the town."

"That's ridiculous," Anne said. "We don't need any more settlers, and your nonsense won't attract anyone to the Ridge anyway. My team will be here in thirty seconds. I expect complete silence as long as we're present."

"This is a cafeteria, not a mausoleum," Louise spoke up, tugging on the end of one of a thick blonde braid. "We can talk all we want."

"Just... stay away from my team." Anne stalked off to take up a position by the door. The influencers trailed over to the serving window, where Carter was busy dishing out breakfast.

"Where's Cal?" Veronica asked, peering into the kitchen.

"He'll be here at lunch," Carter said.

"Did we agree to serve the newcomers breakfast?" Lincoln asked Nate, watching Carter fill Veronica's plate. Carter looked a little panicky, like there wasn't enough food to go around.

"I don't think so."

Traditionally, Lincoln and his brothers took turns cooking breakfast for each other, while the mill workers ate at the bunkhouse for the morning meal.

"Are Veronica and her friends paying us to cook for them? What about the permanent mill workers?" Nate asked suddenly. "Because we can't afford to feed everyone on our own dime."

Lincoln hadn't thought about that. They had served the temporary mill workers as part of their compensation, and Anne had already agreed to pay for the meals her programmers ate, but the influencers hadn't agreed to pay for anything, and neither had the permanent mill workers.

"I'd better help Carter sort this out."

He brought his empty plate to the serving window and leaned around the women gathered in front of it to pass it to Carter before he addressed them.

"Ladies, glad you could join us for your first week's welcome package of meals. On Sunday you can let us know if you want to continue on our eating plan or not and which meals you want to sign up for. We offer lunch and dinner and can start offering breakfast, if you're interested. We'll get you pricing for the different packages. You can let us know what you'd prefer. Would you like omelets or French toast this morning?" he asked Sasha, since Veronica had already been served.

"Omelets," Sasha said. "Plain toast is fine."

"Coming right up." He entered the kitchen. "Go eat," he said to Carter. "I got this."

"Thanks for saving me. I didn't know what to say when all these new people showed up. It didn't even occur to me they'd want breakfast, too."

"You're a newlywed. You've got other things on your mind." Lincoln pulled out a carton of eggs. "Do you think Amanda can shop today? We're running out of food."

"She already said she would. She and Cal are going to come up with a menu plan. She'll shop and help prep the meals, but he'll take over as chef from now on, I guess." He didn't look entirely happy about it, and Lincoln wondered if he disliked the idea of another man getting to spend so much time with his wife.

Lincoln wasn't happy to lose Cal, either. "Guess

that's another mill worker I need to find."

"Guess I should have learned to cook," Carter said darkly. "Then I could have spent my days with Amanda."

"Don't even think about it," Lincoln warned him. "We need you chasing contracts, not making soup. Any luck with that, by the way?"

"Got a few things in the works." Carter shrugged.

"I thought you had something sewn up the other day."

"I thought so, too, but it didn't pan out. Don't worry," he added. "There's more work where that came from. See you at the mill."

"See you."

Lincoln was whipping up breakfast for the ladies— and for Anne's programmers as they straggled in— when Cal appeared in the kitchen.

"Want me to take over?"

"Would you?" Lincoln asked gratefully. "I hate to lose you at the mill, but I'm no short-order cook. You'd better come have a talk with Carter and me, though. We need to work out another contract for you if you're going to take on kitchen duty."

"You bet. I'll handle clean up. You go ahead. I'll stop by the mill later. Sorry I won't be there to pitch in, like you expected."

"That's okay." Lincoln appreciated his offer to be chef—and dishwasher—now that he was faced with the prospect of doing it himself.

"Hi, Cal!" Veronica called.

"Hi, Veronica."

Lincoln left them and found Gage outside finishing his meal, perched on a stone wall near the entrance to the town hall.

"Enjoying yourself?" Lincoln asked.

"More than you are. That another one of your new hires?" He pointed to a truck that had pulled into the Circle and was slowly traversing it.

"Maybe." Lincoln felt like all he did these days was meet new people. On the one hand, these were folks who were motivated to be here and ready to settle in the town for the most part, unlike the crop of temporary workers who'd been so hard to manage in the early days. On the other hand, so many new faces all at once kept reminding him of bootcamp, when everything and everyone was unfamiliar, and he'd felt like the ground was constantly shifting beneath his feet. It had taken weeks before he felt anything like confidence back then, but the first time he'd been sure of himself—and sure of what he was supposed to do next—had been sweet. He looked forward to reaching that stage here.

He went to meet the stranger, waving at him to indicate where he could park, then stepped up to the open passenger window of the Dodge. "Are you Glenn Porter?" He recognized the burly man with short, graying hair from the photos he'd seen when he looked up Glenn online.

"That's me." Glenn hopped out, shook his hand vigorously, then froze as he glanced over Lincoln's shoulder. "What the hell is that?"

His abrupt change of tone made Lincoln spin around fast. He nearly groaned when he realized Veronica and her friends had spilled out of the town hall and were getting into a pyramid formation. As they erupted into another cheer, Sasha dutifully filming it, he bit back a sigh. He hadn't caught all the words, but Elliott Ridge had figured somewhere in the chant again. They were trying to help.

"Social media influencers. They're on a cheerleading kick today."

"Influencers? What're they doing here?"

"Saving money. Housing is cheap on Elliott Ridge compared to where they're from."

Glenn studied them. "Do they act like that all the time?"

"No," Lincoln said, although he had a feeling they might. "They work a lot, too. It's just that they're young," he added. "Excited to be in a new place."

"Huh."

Lincoln had a feeling Glenn was considering turning his Dodge around and driving away. "Let's get you settled in, and I'll take you to the mill," he hurried to say. "Did you have any thoughts about renting or buying one of our houses?" He'd mentioned both options to all the men he'd hired. Cal had rented one of the smaller cabins in the older part of town. He'd told Lincoln he wanted to get to know the place before he made any long-term decisions.

"Thinking about buying," Glenn said. "Or I was, anyway." He was still watching the influencers.

"We can set you up in a rental to get started," Lincoln assured him calmly. "We're getting a lot of interest in our houses for sale, so we'll have no problem filling them."

The old sales technique worked. Glenn straightened and focused on him. "Well, let's take a look at a few of those, too, just in case."

"This way," Lincoln said. "I'll show you the mill first and give our realtor a call. She can tour the houses with you. She's fantastic at her job."

She liked being a small-town livestock veterinarian, Charlotte thought as she pulled into the driveway of number 37 at the end of a workday later that week. She and Craig had a rhythm now. He was growing more cheerful by the minute as they caught up on a backlog of cases he'd been struggling to get to on his own.

"I really hope you mean to stay," he'd said as they'd packed up their things after their last appointment of the afternoon. "Don't think I could stand going back to the pace I was keeping when I was alone."

"I mean to stay," she told him. She was finding the work far more gratifying than she'd expected. It was varied and interesting, and she liked the people she met along the way. They were a far cry from the high-strung jockeys and stressed-out trainers she answered to in Saratoga. She and Craig had begun to split up for some of the work, now that she'd gotten familiar with the area, which meant that while they weren't quite doubling his former workload, they were getting close.

When she arrived home each night and cleaned herself up, she found a wonderful meal already cooked at the town hall. Dinners were lively affairs these days, even if she sometimes rolled her eyes at Veronica and her friends' more colorful antics. She followed their social media feeds obsessively to make sure she didn't feature in any of their posts. So far they'd kept their word and excluded her, which she appreciated more than she could say.

Now that she wasn't upset with them, she'd realized each of the women had a specialty they were pursuing, and it seemed like some of them were running several businesses at once—all remotely. They teased the programmers mercilessly when they got the chance. Each morning after breakfast, they waved and blew kisses at them as the men boarded the van Lincoln had brought out from storage and tuned up for them until Anne declared she was going to tint the windows. They'd created a welcome-home cheer that made the forest ring with their shouts when the van pulled in again at the end of the day. After the first couple of times, the mill workers complained they were being left out, so Sasha had made up a new cheer on the spot, and the women performed it every time the mill workers arrived at the cafeteria for dinner, too.

While the mill workers, both the temporary ones and permanent hires who were trickling in to take their places, were keenly interested in the sudden increase in women at lunch and dinner, Anne's programmers were doing a better job of romancing them, much to Anne's chagrin.

Veronica still flirted outrageously with Cal at every mealtime. Gareth trailed after Sasha whenever Anne's back was turned. Tall Mark and diminutive Edie could often be found in various corners talking earnestly. Redheaded Gregory showed his feelings for athletic, boisterous Tania by running his hands through his hair so often when she was around it stood on end. Troy, who did everything a little manically, must have been channeling his extra energy into studying Japanese, because whenever he saw Elaine, he began speaking it— very badly, if Elaine's alternately horrified and amused expressions were any indicator. Louise and Bettina held hands everywhere they went, and Charlotte was certain they were a couple, but she didn't think everyone had cottoned on to that yet. On the rare occasions they could be found apart, she'd seen various mill workers attempt to woo them.

The most startling couple by far, however, was line-backer Edwin—and Anne.

The tech start-up's fearless leader refused to acknowledge anything was happening between them. If Edwin tried to talk to her in public, she dressed him down in no uncertain terms, but on one of Charlotte's early mornings, she'd seen Edwin and Anne leave the stables just as she was approaching, and it wasn't difficult to guess what they'd snuck off there together to do.

Lincoln and his brothers really would have to lure more women to the Ridge, Charlotte thought as she let herself into her house and found him already there, pacing the living room, his phone pressed to his ear. With so much love blossoming between the young people, the mill workers were bound to feel restless.

"I know, Dad. I was there, remember?" Lincoln said, coming to a standstill by the front window. A floor sander stood in the corner, waiting for them to finally be ready to sand and refinish the floors. First they needed to move her clothes and what little furniture she had out of the house, but they'd both been so busy this week, they hadn't gotten to that yet. She knew it was frustrating Lincoln that their renovations were progressing so slowly, but Charlotte was more concerned with what Ivan might pull next. There'd been no word from Steven except to tell her he'd filed the motion to dismiss Ivan's claim against her and that he'd asked the judge to withhold her address in any discovery demands. Charlotte didn't know what she'd do if she had to return to Saratoga and face Ivan in court—or what else she'd tell Lincoln about him if she did. It was bad enough she'd spilled what happened to Summer's Day. Lincoln already had to be questioning her judgment.

"Dad—believe me, the last thing I want to do is take on more debt." Lincoln lowered his phone when he saw her. "Go ahead to dinner when you're ready. This might take a while."

Charlotte nodded, but he was already focused on his conversation again. "I've had to repair the edger every day this week. Once it conks out, we'll be at a standstill. If we're not sawing lumber, we won't make any money."

Charlotte left him to it, slipped upstairs to shower and found Lincoln still arguing with his father when she came down again. She waited a couple of minutes, checking emails and social media, then swore.

Lincoln held his phone away from his face. "Something wrong?"

"N-no," she stammered. "I'll meet you at the town hall like you said, okay?"

"I'll get there as soon as I can." He went back to his call.

Charlotte hurried outside and looked at her phone. As usual, Sasha had posted a slew of images over the course of the day. One of them featured Mark and Edie kissing passionately at the latest Saturday night beach cookout, with the hashtag #MarryingestTownInTheUSA. Clearly visible behind them was Charlotte, facing the camera directly. How had she missed that Sasha was taking the photo? And how had Sasha not noticed her in the background of it?

Furious, she stalked toward the influencer's house, determined to make Sasha take it down. Her name wasn't mentioned anywhere, but Ivan could be using facial recognition software.

She met Nate and Gage on her way.

"Where's Lincoln?" Nate asked cheerfully. She liked all Lincoln's brothers, but Nate was especially easygoing. He spent a lot of time in the little building they all referred to as their grandfather's workshop. Amanda had shown her the hutch Nate gave her as a wedding present, and Charlotte had been surprised to learn it wasn't an heirloom since the work was so fine.

"On the phone with your dad." She tried to keep her anger from her voice and must have managed it, because Gage chuckled.

"Let me guess. They're talking about the edger?"

She shrugged. "Something about the mill shutting down?"

Gage nodded. "I don't know how much longer Lincoln can keep repairing it. The blades keep jamming. We have to shut down the line every time it happens."

"He'd better keep doing his best. We can't afford a new one," Nate said. "Not until we pay for the equipment we already bought." He frowned. Charlotte thought that if easygoing Nate was worried about money, their situation must be bad. She'd known as much, but somehow it struck her more forcefully today. She was part of this community, which meant whatever happened to the Elliotts happened to her.

Charlotte opened her mouth to question them about it, but Nate pointed to the Circle. "What is going on over there?"

She followed his finger and noticed the programmers' van parked in front of their house, which meant they were home from Alice's workshop. Nearby, Veronica and her friends paced back and forth holding picket signs. Sasha held a megaphone and was shouting out the slogans they'd written. All of them were dressed in diaphanous outfits that hugged their bodies and flared at their feet, giving them the look of mermaids. They wore wigs of silver hair that reached almost to their knees.

"Programmers, programmers, let your hair down," Sasha shouted through her megaphone. "Don't let the wicked witch keep you trapped in your tower. Come out and have some fun! It's national *Hot Enough for Ya?* Day! Let's go for a swim!"

"Is she comparing the programmers to Rapunzel?" Charlotte asked Gage, her anger temporarily forgotten. "I mean, Anne's keeping them on a pretty tight leash, but they leave the Ridge every day."

"Beats the hell out of me."

"I want to know more about this *Hot Enough for Ya?* Day," Nate said, his serious expression relaxing into a grin. "Is there cake?"

Charlotte shrugged. "Seems like there ought to be ice cream at the very least."

"Fee fi fo fum, I smell the blood of a capitalist!" Sasha shouted.

"Guess we've moved on to 'Jack and the Beanstalk' now," Nate said.

"Open up your doors, Anne, or we'll cut this bean-stalk down!" Bettina hollered, confirming his guess.

A second-story window opened, and Anne leaned out. "Are you saying you're going to take an ax to my house? Because I'd be happy to call the sheriff and have you arrested!"

"Would you let the guys out for fifteen minutes? We just want to go for a swim before dinner!" Sasha said into her microphone.

"Hah! Not likely. We're in a meeting, so get going—

and stop bothering my men!"

"Why don't you eat this apple? It's probably not poisoned!" Sasha reached into a net grocery bag she was carrying, pulled one out and shook it at Anne.

"Are you threatening me?"

"I'm telling you I'm seriously pissed that you won't let my boyfriend come swimming with me for fifteen lousy minutes!"

Anne ducked when Sasha threw the apple at her, even though it struck the house about five feet away from where Anne peeped out. Sasha dumped a dozen or more apples from her bag onto the ground, and the other women dove for them and came up firing. Most bounced off the house harmlessly. One smacked against a window. Charlotte gasped, but the glass didn't break. Several more windows opened, and a few male heads appeared.

"What's going on?" Mark called down.

"They lost me on the apple thing," Gage said to Charlotte.

"Snow White, I think? Didn't the witch try to poison her with an apple?" Charlotte wasn't sure what that had to do with Anne and her programmers. "We'd better stop this, don't you think?"

"I guess—hell!"

Anne, who'd disappeared into the second-story room, reappeared with a bucket of water, which she dumped on Sasha's head. Sasha screamed, and her megaphone emitted a shrill squawk. The other women scattered.

"Are you crazy?" Sasha yelled up at Anne, dropping the megaphone and putting her hands on her head. "Do you know how much this wig costs? You can't get it WET!"

She trooped off, the other women trailing her, leaving behind the megaphone, the signs and a triumphant Anne.

"Come back," Gareth said half-heartedly from another window.

"Don't come back. Ever! Nobody breaches my Fortress of Solitude," Anne hollered.

But even as she said it, Mark disappeared from his window. There was some kind of scuffle inside the house. A moment later, the front door opened, and the programmers spilled out.

"Freedom!" Mark yelled, holding his fist in the air.

"To the lake!" Gregory cried as Anne burst out of the house behind them.

"Get back in here. We have five more minutes—"

But the influencers were back, led by a sodden Sasha, who now carried her ruined wig in her hand. "To the lake!" she screamed and dashed away. Her friends raced after her, and the programmers joined them in a bellowing horde all heading for house number 1 and the beach beyond it.

"For god's sake," Anne cried to Nate and Gage. "Why didn't you stop them?"

"They're adults. They can do what they want," Nate pointed out.

"That is the stupidest thing I ever heard."

"Told you the men needed a break," Edwin said, the last of the programmers to trail out of the house. He took Anne's hand, but she thrust it away and stalked after her team. Edwin sighed and followed.

Charlotte moved after them, but Gage stopped her. "Don't get involved. Let them sort it out themselves."

"Oh, I'm not getting involved," she assured him. "I just want to watch." She was curious what would happen next—and she still needed to tell off Sasha. "Aren't you coming?"

"I am," Nate said eagerly. "Do you think Anne's going to drown anyone? I bet she'll try."

"Gage?" Charlotte prompted.

"Oh, why the hell not." He followed Nate, who was already striding after the others.

"Charlotte, hold up!"

Charlotte turned to see Lincoln loping after them. "What's going on?" he asked when he fell in step by her side.

Charlotte filled him in as they walked. It was mayhem at the lake by the time they reached it. The beach was strewn with the programmers' jeans and T-shirts and the influencers' fairy-inspired dresses. Silver wigs dotted the sand like beached jellyfish.

"Are they skinny-dipping?" Charlotte bit back a smile. There was a lot of splashing and shrieking going on but not much swimming.

Lincoln scanned the sand and then the lake. "I think the girls are. Not so sure about the guys. Either they kept their briefs on, or they've been going commando all this time."

"I'm not sure I want to know."

Anne had reached the beach a few steps ahead of them and watched the chaos with her hands on her hips. "This is ridiculous. Total waste of time."

"They're just having a little fun," Edwin assured her. He stood a half step behind her, almost protectively, and Charlotte thought they made a good couple despite Anne's refusal to acknowledge they were together.

When a scream of real terror cut through his words, however, Charlotte froze. Sasha stood up and pointed at the woods across a stretch of water. "There's someone there! I saw him! A man!"

Charlotte sucked in a breath. The hairs on her neck prickled. Someone was in the woods? Watching them?

Who?

Could it be Ivan?

She remained frozen in place as Lincoln strode to the water's edge, his brothers on his heels. "Where?" he called out.

"He was filming us!" Sasha stood waist deep in the water, still pointing.

"Filming us?" Veronica waded over to stand next to her.

"What if he's from Flash House?" Edie gasped. "They're our rivals," she explained to Mark. "They hate us because we have actual jobs in addition to being content creators. They're just influencers, so they're really boring." She stumbled out of the water until she was thigh deep, then stopped and turned back, covering her body with her hands dramatically. "If they film us skinny-dipping, they'll definitely post photos."

She didn't seem too upset at the idea.

"I don't see anyone," Lincoln said, shading his eyes as he searched the far shore.

"I don't see anyone, either," Mark said, but since he was staring straight at Edie, Charlotte wasn't sure how he could.

"Well, I don't need anyone taking photos of *me*," Gareth said. Mark swore, and all the men splashed out of the water and pulled their jeans on over their soaking briefs.

"Let's go look," Lincoln said to Gage. The two men raced off on foot, sticking to the strip of beach between water and forest. Nate remained behind, still scanning the forest all around them, as if guarding everyone else from a possible attack.

"I bet it was Sean Sidwell." Sasha was still pointing.

"That wasn't Sean—if anyone, that was Timothy Towers," Veronica said, slowly making her way out of the water. "He was dark, not blond."

"Those were Sean Sidwell's shoulders," Sasha retorted, finally wading out, as well. "I'd know them anywhere."

"He had Timothy Towers's posture!"

"Why would either of those people be in our woods?" Charlotte challenged them as they pulled their costumes back on. The names they kept repeating sounded like Dickens characters, but she was in no mood to laugh. If someone was in the woods, Lincoln and Gage were racing toward danger.

Maybe racing toward Ivan.

The women took their time getting dressed, their complete lack of self-consciousness about their nudity frustrating Charlotte. How could they be so unconcerned—and so damn confident? She felt old and stodgy in comparison.

"Flash House are our rivals," Veronica said, echoing Edie, talking slowly as if Charlotte was a child. "They're the most self-centered, god-awful narcissists who constantly try to steal our sponsors."

"*They're* the narcissists? Really?" Anne asked her.

"Why? Did you think you were the only one?" Veronica retorted.

Charlotte breathed a sigh of relief when she spotted Lincoln jogging back, Gage trailing close behind him. "No one's there," Lincoln announced when he arrived.

"See?" Anne cried. "A lot of fuss about nothing!" She turned her back on the women and surveyed her ragtag group of men, then aimed a finger imperiously toward the settlement. "Home—now!" The programmers trundled off with shoulders slumped. When one or two cast backward looks at the pretty women they were leaving on the beach, Anne spurred them on with threats about curtailing their gaming time.

"There was definitely someone there," Veronica told Gage. Her costume was on, but it clung to her in such a revealing way she might as well still be nude. "It was Timothy from Flash House. Just wait. Tomorrow there will photos of us all over the internet."

"It was Sean," Sasha said. She was clothed, as well, but her wig sat on the sand, and she was wringing the water out of her hair. Charlotte wondered if all of it was her own. There was just so much of it.

"It was probably Dennis," Lincoln muttered to Charlotte when the influencers finally made their way off the beach. "I bet he got an eyeful and ran for the hills."

"Does Dennis own a phone? Sasha seemed pretty sure she saw someone filming them."

"Sasha's pretty sure she's the center of the universe," Gage said. "Come on, let's eat."

Charlotte nodded, but her stomach was tight with worry. What if it wasn't Flash House—or Dennis?

What if Ivan had discovered where she lived?

CHAPTER 10

"**D**O YOU THINK they really saw someone?" Hudson was asking Gage when Lincoln and Charlotte sat down at the table. Gage must have filled him in on what he'd missed.

Gage shrugged.

"Where are the programmers?" Lincoln asked. He'd noticed they hadn't showed up for dinner yet, but Anne was in the kitchen talking to Cal. The influencers had changed their clothes and were gathered at a table apart from the others, sending Anne disgruntled looks now and then.

"They're going back to Two Willows to do more work," Amanda said, arriving with a plate of food. "Anne's making Cal pack their dinners. She says they're behind and things are too chaotic around here."

"You don't think she's scared, do you?" Nate put in.

"What would she be afraid of?" Lincoln asked. "Even if there was someone in the woods, there's probably a logical explanation."

"Like what?" Hudson asked.

"Like they were out for a hike. There's a path around the lake. Why shouldn't someone hike it?"

"Never seen anyone other than us on it since I've been back," Hudson said.

"How often do you go out that way? We're working all the time. Maybe people use it constantly."

"Veronica and her friends think it was their rivals."

Lincoln noticed Charlotte gazing out the window absently. She'd taken Sasha aside on their way in, and the two women had spoken earnestly for a few minutes. When he'd asked Charlotte what it was about, she'd said she was pressing the young woman for details about the man she'd seen in the woods but that Sasha hadn't been able to give her any. "Charlotte? You okay?"

"What?" She blinked. Noticed them all looking at her. "I'm fine. Just... wondering who it was and what they wanted."

"It probably wasn't anyone," Lincoln said, worried the incident might scare Charlotte. He didn't want her souring on life on the Ridge just when things were going so well between them. "And if it was, it wasn't anyone who matters. You're safe here. You know that, right?"

"Of course." She pushed her plate away. She'd barely made a dent in the fettuccini Alfredo Cal had served today. "Did your call earlier go okay? How's your dad doing?"

"You talked to Dad? What did he say?" Hudson asked.

Lincoln drummed his fingers on the table, buying time. He'd had to repair the edger three separate times today, while the whole crew stood around waiting. The process was time consuming because each time he had to stop the line and lock out the machine to make sure it was safe to work on.

"He's doing okay. Frustrated that he's not a hundred percent recovered, of course, but it sounds like he's making progress. That wasn't the reason I called, though. I told him we need a new edger. He wasn't too happy about it. I got a lead on a used one for sale out of a mill that shut down recently. Thought that might make the pill go down easier, but it didn't."

"We can't take on any more debt," Nate said.

"If we don't, we might as well close the mill right now."

"Let's deal with this tomorrow—at the mill office," Carter said unexpectedly. He cocked his head in Amanda's direction and sent his brothers a meaningful glance. His message didn't require their secret language.

Amanda was fairly drooping.

"You okay?" Charlotte asked her.

"I'm fine." Amanda picked at her salad. "I just don't like the idea of a man in the woods…" She trailed off, shook her head and tried again. "My dad came for me like that, sneaking through the trees to get to me. I don't ever want to feel like that again—like I'm being hunted."

Charlotte pulled back, hugging her arms across her chest tightly. "You think that man was here to come after someone?"

"No one is coming after anyone," Lincoln said firmly. "Amanda's dad is in custody. We solved that problem, and we'll solve the problem with the edger, too. Come on. Everyone's acting like we're at a funeral, and we're not. We're just tired and hungry. Do you want me to get this warmed up?" he asked Charlotte, gesturing to her plate of noodles.

"I guess."

He stood and carried it to the counter where Cal was serving seconds to several mill workers. "Could you heat this up?" he asked when it was his turn. He served himself a second plate of dinner while he waited. When Charlotte's meal was ready, he brought it all back to the table, determined to turn the evening around.

"Did you get a chance to look at the link I sent you for those cabinets?" he asked Charlotte, sitting down and handing her the warmed-up food. "If you can get a general sense of what you want, it'll be easier when we go to pick them out."

"Not yet." Her expression didn't change. Lincoln felt a new twist of worry. Didn't women love choosing things for their houses?

"Better get on that. I know we've been going slowly, but we'll get those floors done soon. Then we'll pick up our pace, and before you know it, we'll be renovating the kitchen."

Charlotte sighed. "Slow is good right now," she said. "I want to get a few paychecks under my belt before I make any more purchases."

Nate flashed him a sign. *Cold feet?*

No, Lincoln flashed back. Charlotte wasn't getting

cold feet about living here. They'd spent every night together, and she went on and on about how much she was enjoying her new job.

"Are you worried about money?" he asked cautiously. This probably wasn't the place to talk about it, but he wanted to understand her sudden lack of interest.

She shrugged. "I think it's prudent to have more cash in the bank first."

"I could loan you a little."

Charlotte's head snapped up, her eyes wide. Nate frantically flashed a series of signs, something like *Quit now while you're still ahead.*

"I don't need a loan." Her voice was tight. "It's my house, my cabinets. I'll pay for them when I'm ready to."

She spoke quietly but firmly, establishing a rock-solid boundary with everyone at the table as her witnesses. He felt as awkward as a schoolboy getting dressed down by his mother—in front of all his friends.

"I know it's your house," Lincoln said slowly. "You bought it for a dollar, fair and square." He immediately regretted the edge that had crept into his voice, but he wasn't used to being chastised like that. He was a grown man. One who'd taken a leadership position in plenty of dangerous situations. Still, Charlotte didn't know he'd paid the rest of her house's market value into the family bank account. She didn't owe him anything, either, because if she'd known that was part of the bargain, she'd never have taken the house in the first place.

"What's that supposed to mean?" Charlotte stared at

him.

"Nothing." He took a bite of his food, barely tasting it as he chewed and swallowed.

Charlotte leaned forward. "No, answer me. Why did you say it that way—like I got away with something when I bought it?

Nate hurried to intervene, ever the peacemaker. "That's not what Lincoln is trying to say. He's disappointed, that's all."

Lincoln nearly choked as he swallowed another bite. He didn't know whether to thank Nate or punch him. He didn't need anyone to point out that Charlotte had hurt his delicate man feelings. Even if she had.

"Disappointed in what?" Charlotte still had that wary, half-angry look, like she'd been tricked and just found out.

Lincoln decided to take the bull by the horns. "Disappointed that it seems like renovating your house isn't a priority. Which means maybe you're having second thoughts about living here. I want you to stay, that's all. I'm kind of… invested in that." Literally and figuratively.

"Oh."

He'd made the right move. Her wariness subsided, and after a moment, she smiled a little. "I plan to stay, but I need to be careful with my money, that's all. I don't want to overspend, and I don't want to be beholden to anyone, either." She hesitated, then went on. "I made that mistake once before. I let my last boyfriend provide for me, and then suddenly he was controlling me. When I tried to break it off, he… made it difficult."

Lincoln swallowed down a rush of shame. He should have known her sudden thriftiness had nothing to do with him. Her ex sounded like a real bastard, shooting that horse in front of her—bossing her around.

Still, it bothered him that she wouldn't let him take care of her. As far as Lincoln was concerned, she was part of his family. You protected family whenever you could. Helped them in a pinch.

Amanda leaned forward. "Not all men would take advantage of you that way, Charlotte. When you're in a committed relationship, it's okay to help each other financially."

Charlotte was already shaking her head. "Not for me. Never again. I don't ever want a man to control whether I have a roof over my head, or food on the table, or clothes on my back."

Lincoln sat back in his chair. Charlotte had a deed that said she owned house number 37, and that deed would stand up in a court of law. That made him different from her previous boyfriend, didn't it? He might have contributed financially to her situation, but he'd done nothing to take away her independence.

"I don't think there's anything wrong with a man wanting to take care of his wife—or girlfriend," Hudson said. "Hell, that's what men are supposed to do."

"It's a nice idea," Charlotte said flatly. "But it doesn't work." She stood up. "Speaking of my house,

I'm going there now. Busy day tomorrow."

"Want some company?" Lincoln asked.

She hesitated. "I guess."

Relieved, Lincoln flashed a sign to his brothers—and Amanda, seeing as she'd learned their secret language, too—as they carried their dishes to the counter. *Keep quiet.* He knew they'd understand he meant that none of them better mention that he'd paid for the rest of house number 37. Charlotte might not stick around very long if she knew. Somehow he needed to establish that she could trust him—and then he'd tell her. Maybe they'd laugh about the newcomer deal someday.

Lincoln took Charlotte's hand and led the way outside. "You've convinced me," he said, trying to lighten the mood between them. "I swear to god I won't lend you money for those kitchen cabinets. Not even if you beg me."

Charlotte smiled. "You'd better not. And don't even think of buying me a porch swing."

"You want a porch swing?" He stopped and took her in his arms.

"I do," she admitted, coming into his embrace willingly, much to his satisfaction.

"I'd like to buy you a porch swing." He dropped a kiss on the top of her head, relishing the way she fit against him. "If you ever kick me out, I'll take it with me, though."

Charlotte laughed. "I guess I can agree to that." She snuggled against him and sighed. "This is my favorite part of the day. Coming home to you. I'm sorry I was prickly before. I guess I come with baggage."

Lincoln's heart warmed, erasing everything that had gone before. She wanted him. That would have to be enough for now.

"I don't mind your baggage," he told her. "You're my favorite part of the day, too."

THE FOLLOWING MONDAY, a text arrived from Steven while Charlotte was at work.

No court case. They don't have a leg to stand on and Ivan's lawyer pulled the case to avoid sanctions for a frivolous lawsuit. No need to come to Saratoga. Your address won't be disclosed, either.

Charlotte was so happy she nearly hugged the cow she and Craig were treating. Surely Ivan would give up now since even the court was taking her side. Sasha had taken down the photo that contained Charlotte's face as soon as she asked her, and when there were no more sightings of strangers in the woods, she decided Lincoln must have been right; it must have been Dennis the women had seen.

While she was relieved, the influencers seemed disappointed. Amanda had forwarded her a series of posts in which they'd recreated the skinny-dipping episode, with splashes of water conveniently covering parts of their naked bodies. Several more days passed in a blur of work and nights with Lincoln. She heard nothing from Ivan and was beginning to hope her nightmare was over.

Thursday evening, she stood at the base of her stairs watching Lincoln, Nate and Carter wrestle her mattress down. With one thing after another, she was still living in a practically empty, unfinished house, but that was about to change, and what few possessions she owned needed to be moved to number 35 while she and Lincoln refinished the floors of number 37.

When her phone chimed in her pocket with a notification, she drew it out absently, glanced at the screen and wished she hadn't. It was an email from Ivan.

You won this round, but I'll win the next. Come home, Charlotte.

Come home. This was her home, and she had no intention of leaving it. She shoved her phone in her pocket angrily, but Ivan's words replayed in her mind, and she found herself glancing over her shoulder, as if he might appear at her door.

She was relieved when Amanda arrived instead just as the men made it down the stairs and propped the mattress against the railing to take a break.

"Anne is driving me crazy," Amanda announced without preamble. She accepted one of the beers Lincoln went to fetch from the refrigerator, took a long drink and wiped her mouth with the back of her hand. "She wants us to package up breakfast every morning so her programmers can eat in the van on the way into town. She's mad that Veronica and her friends keep *talking* to them."

"Did she offer to pay more for the service?" Carter

asked.

"Of course not," Amanda huffed. "Just ordered boxed breakfasts for her workers like Cal and I were staff at a catering company."

"Maybe Cal should open a catering company," Nate said slowly. "He could hire some employees, and they could move to the Ridge."

"It's not a bad idea," Lincoln said. "That could supplement the salary we offered him."

"You're right, it's not a bad idea." Amanda looked around. "Charlotte, your floors are going to be gorgeous when they're done."

"I think so," Charlotte said, but her mind was still full of Ivan's threats.

"Everything out of the closets?" Lincoln asked her.

"Not yet." She hurried upstairs as the men set down their drinks, picked up the mattress and carried it outside. When she had an armful of clothing, she carefully made her way down again to bring it to number 35. She passed the men on the porch, heading back.

"Want help?" Lincoln asked.

"I've got it."

Come home, Ivan's voice said again in her mind.

She shrugged it off as she lugged the clothes into number 35. Maybe it was time to block Ivan. Up until now, she'd wanted to know if he was trying to reach her, but she dreaded looking at her email these days.

Charlotte hung her clothing in the closet of the nearest upstairs bedroom, the one Lincoln had slept in before he'd moved in with her. She had just made her way downstairs when her phone chimed again. Her heart sank until she realized it was a text, not an email notification. Steven was writing her.

Have you seen this?

He'd linked an article from the local Saratoga newspaper. Charlotte sat on the bottom step and clicked it.

Racehorse Missing, Presumed Stolen

She quickly read on.

Forrester's Grand Rally, two-time champion thoroughbred, has gone missing from Gasparyn Stables only weeks after being pulled from the Belmont Oaks last minute due to an injury. Sources suggest the theft could be linked to recent turnover among staff. Authorities aren't commenting on the ongoing investigation.

She scanned the short article twice, her throat tight. Who on earth had stolen Rally?

She shuddered to think of how Ivan would react, especially if he thought one of his employees was to blame. He prized loyalty above everything else. Besides, Rally was worth millions.

He'd already won the Kentucky Derby and the Preakness Stakes and had been on track for the Triple Crown before he'd injured his leg. That injury, coming hard on the heels of the one that had sidelined Summer's Day, had kicked off a vicious series of arguments between her and Ivan. She'd refused to follow his orders, all the while planning behind his back to leave, but he'd never quit demanding she fix things so Rally could run in the Belmont.

Now Rally was gone.

Even without that Triple Crown win, he could earn Ivan a fortune in stud fees. She thought about all the security cameras and precautions at the stables. Anyone entering the facility would have been filmed. She wondered why there hadn't been any arrests made already.

The line about *turnover among staff at the stables* made her pause. There had been a lot of new faces toward the end of her tenure there. Ivan was an irascible boss who'd never had qualms about firing people. She thought about Peter Illych's behavior on the day Ivan had told him his services were no longer needed. The way he'd sneered at her.

Good luck, he'd said.

Had he been nursing a grudge against Ivan all this time? Peter had worked for him for years before she'd come along. Knew everyone else Ivan had employed up until that time. Did he know the weaknesses of the security system? Or had someone else taken Rally? And where had they gone?

Charlotte pocketed her phone and hurried back to the others, wishing she could share the story with them and talk it over, but she was determined to keep this secret locked tight in her heart. No man wanted to hear about his girlfriend's shady ex-boyfriend. What kind of woman did she have to be to stay with a man like Ivan for so long?

"There she is," Lincoln said when she entered number 37 again. He came to wrap her in a hug.

"Here I am," she agreed. And here was where she planned to stay.

BY THE TIME everyone left, and he and Charlotte had settled into number 35, Lincoln was ready to call it a night, so when his phone buzzed, announcing a phone call, he nearly didn't answer it.

Almost too late he recognized the name. "Lincoln Elliott," he said quickly when he'd tapped the screen and lifted it to his ear.

"Hi, Lincoln. Ralph McInnis here. I'm handling the Grover Mill teardown. We talked about that edger you were interested in?"

"I'm still interested."

Ralph heaved a gusty sigh. "The thing is, it's not available anymore. Turns out the owner promised it to someone else and didn't bother to tell me."

Lincoln's heart sank. "You're kidding."

"Wish I was. He stiffed me on my salvage fee, too. Said he'd found the buyer, so I didn't earn it. Can you believe that?"

"No, I can't." And he couldn't believe the edger had slipped through his fingers. "You wouldn't happen to have a line on another one for sale, would you?"

"I'm afraid not. But I'll keep your number just in case I come across one."

"I'd appreciate that."

Lincoln hung up, shoved his phone in his pocket, and faced Charlotte, who was sitting on the bed they'd just set up. There wasn't anywhere else to sit, so he joined her.

"Bad news?" she asked.

He filled her in. "I don't know where I'll find another edger that cheap. It was really a good bargain. I shouldn't have hesitated once I'd convinced my father."

"You were busy," she pointed out.

"I was chicken." Lincoln couldn't believe he'd said that out loud, but it was true. He'd known they needed that machine, but when the moment came to buy it, he'd balked, not trusting his own judgment because his father and brothers didn't agree with it.

"Chicken?" She bumped his shoulder with her own. "I doubt that."

"I knew we had to spend that money, and I put it off." Frustration reared within him, and for one moment he wished he was back in the Army. He'd never second-guessed himself while serving because he hadn't had his family breathing down his neck, reminding him of how he'd gotten it wrong before.

Charlotte watched him expectantly, saying nothing until Lincoln heard himself spill the story. "The last time I pushed my dad to spend money, the whole business collapsed."

"That can't be right. I thought the price of lumber crashed and put your family out of business," she said softly.

"That happened, too, but we could have ridden out

that storm if we hadn't just taken on a huge loan to upgrade a bunch of our equipment. It was all my fault. I pushed and pushed Dad to get with the times. I told him all the other mills would leave us behind if we didn't update our machines. He kept saying we had to be prudent with our cash, but I wouldn't listen. Every time he turned around, there I was with my spreadsheets and proposals."

He couldn't stand the memory of it, how cocksure he'd been, as if a teenager knew more about running a mill than an experienced man like his father.

"It sounds like you were young and excited about building the family business."

"I was a stupid fuck who ruined everything." Lincoln stood up, unable to contain the anger—and shame—that coursed through him every time he thought about the way he'd hectored his father about spending that money. "It was my fault. I ruined everything."

"Lincoln," Charlotte chided him. "You were a kid. Your dad had run the mill for years. He wouldn't have invested in that equipment if he didn't think it was the right thing to do." She stood, too, coming to touch his arm.

"You don't understand." Lincoln ground out the words, shame burning through his body. "The mill was already struggling. And he was..." His throat clogged with a surge of anguish he'd managed to hold inside until now. "He was failing. His health had gone to shit." Watching his strong, vital father hollow out from overwork and the stress of watching the whole town slip away had been the worst experience of Lincoln's life. "He bought the equipment to keep me happy," he spit out. "I was that much of a prima donna. I kept saying if we didn't upgrade, we might as well shut the place down. He was afraid we'd all bail on him, so he gave in. You should have seen him the day they delivered all that equipment. We walked through the mill once it had been installed. I was so damn proud. So... triumphant." The word was sour in his mouth. "Two weeks later, the price of lumber crashed, and the layoffs started."

He turned away from her, remembering every moment of those days. "We'd watch them go from the front porch of house number 1. Day after day, family after family, packing up and driving away. The town emptying out. All our friends. All our parents' friends. Every last worker at that mill—gone."

His voice sounded like sandpaper over old, dried wood. "I did that. I killed our town."

"You did what you thought was right," Charlotte insisted.

"What I thought was right was dead wrong." He faced her, even though he didn't want to. She had to know how badly he'd screwed up, because he could do it again. "Then it was just us. My dad and my brothers and I. We tried to keep the mill alive ourselves, but of course we couldn't. And Dad... kept having episodes."

"Episodes?"

"He'd go gray." Lincoln's heart squeezed just remembering it. "He'd kind of fold over, like he couldn't breathe. He wouldn't go to the doctor. We could see he was going to have a heart attack someday."

His chest felt encased by iron and Lincoln fought to breathe, his voice becoming unsteady knowing he had to tell her the rest of it.

"Then there came this day—it was pouring rain, and we were racing to meet a deadline we didn't have a hope in hell of meeting. A hail-Mary pass supplying logs to another mill who still had contracts to fill. There was an accident with a logging truck." He tried to swallow past a lump that had grown in his throat, but couldn't. "Nate nearly got killed."

"Oh, Lincoln."

He rushed to say the rest of it, knowing he was close to letting his emotions overcome him, something he never did no matter what. Suddenly he was back there in the cold and wet, the rain coming down in sheets, the dusk closing in so they couldn't see anything. His father shouting orders. Hudson trying to maneuver the truck.

The sound of logs starting to fall.

"It was as close a call as you can get," he managed to say. "The shock must have done something to Dad's heart. After he made sure we were all okay, he just... bent over, his hands braced on his knees—and then he collapsed."

"Oh, my God. I'm so sorry." Charlotte's eyes filled with empathetic tears. "That must have been terrifying."

"I thought he was dead." Lincoln had never admitted that to himself. He'd stood paralyzed when his father had fallen, watching his brothers sprint to his aid. He'd thought he'd killed—

Lincoln swallowed again. "A minute later, Dad sat up. Scared the hell out of all of us. We thought he was down for the count. Hudson was calling an ambulance, but Dad grabbed the phone out of his hand. Said to stop being a bunch of crybabies and help him up." He shook his head. "Five minutes later he was back to work. He wouldn't listen no matter what we said. Wouldn't quit for the day or even take a break. Wouldn't even make a doctor's appointment to get checked out. We realized he wasn't going to slow down no matter how bad it got. That's why we joined up."

"Joined the military? Because of your dad's heart?"

"As long as we stayed on the Ridge, he would have kept trying to save the mill. He would have ended up dead one way or the other. So we left." Another wave of pain overwhelmed him. There was no way he could explain that morning around the kitchen table, he and his brothers telling their parents one by one that they were leaving the Ridge and wouldn't be back. "It was all my fault," he said again. "That's why I have to get it right this time."

"It wasn't your fault," Charlotte argued. "It was a sequence of events that went badly, that's all. Like you said, you're here now, and you're going to put everything right. There will be another edger for sale."

"What if there isn't? What if I let Dad down again?" His chest was so tight he wondered if he might be the one to have a heart attack this time.

Charlotte put her arms around him.

"You're not alone," she said. "I'm here. Your brothers are here. So are the mill workers, Veronica and her friends and Anne's programmers. Everyone wants Elliott Ridge to be a success."

"It has to be. I can't fail again." He pulled back and looked her in the eyes. "Do you understand? I couldn't face my father if I did—or anyone else. You have no idea what it feels like to screw up that badly."

She stilled. "Actually, I do," she said softly.

He gazed down at her in surprise. "You do?" He couldn't believe it.

Charlotte wriggled a little as if she wished she hadn't admitted it, but he waited her out and finally she let out a little sound that was half laugh, half despair. "I wasn't going to tell you this."

"I told you my secrets," he said gruffly. Now they were out, he wished he hadn't, but at the same time he was glad. The memories still hurt but somehow there was space around them, as if there was room now for the possibility of a different outcome in the future.

She pulled away from him and hugged her arms over her chest. "My last boyfriend was a real piece of work," she said helplessly. "You know some of what he did but not all. I don't want you to know." She covered her face and Lincoln moved close enough that he could run his hands up and down her upper arms, wanting to reassure her. When she looked up again, he was stunned to see tears in her eyes. "I like you, Lincoln. A lot. But you won't like me when you find out who I was."

He drew back to study her again. "Yes, I will." Nothing she could say would change the way he felt about her.

"No, you won't." She stepped back, too. Tried to pull out of his arms. "I don't like myself."

"It can't be that bad." He took her hands and didn't let her shake him off.

"It feels that bad," she said quietly.

He waited, knowing how hard it was to let down your guard when you'd held it up for so long.

"You have to understand he was charming at first. So... grown up and sophisticated. I was in awe of him when we met. I couldn't believe he even noticed me let alone asked me out. I was in my last year of veterinary school, waiting tables at a local restaurant. He was... in his forties." She looked down, color rising in her cheeks. "He came from a very wealthy Eastern European family. He ran businesses I didn't understand—and he had a stable full of horses. Very, very expensive ones."

Lincoln tried to keep his breathing even. He'd known her ex was rich, but the idea of some hardened businessman preying on his Charlotte made him want to hurt someone.

"I don't know if he ever actually liked me or if he just needed a new veterinarian." She looked up at him. "I still don't know why he wanted to replace the old one."

"The old veterinarian or girlfriend?"

She smiled at that. "The old veterinarian, although I imagine there was an old girlfriend, too. I just don't know who she was. He lured me in by offering me work on the weekends that paid better and was far more appropriate to my upcoming career than my waitressing job. He never hired me officially—just slipped me a few hundred-dollar bills every week. By the time I graduated I'd moved in with him. He dismissed his private veterinarian and installed me in his place." She broke free of Lincoln and paced around the room. "A few months later, things began to go south."

Lincoln waited for her to gather her thoughts. He wanted to wrap her in his arms again, but she was lost in the past, and he wanted to hear what she had to say.

"At first he let me do things my way, and I treated those horses the way they deserved to be cared for, but pretty quickly he began to step in and dictate what I could and couldn't do. While I'd worked part-time under his previous veterinarian, I'd begun to have an inkling what went on behind the scenes of the racing world. I promised myself it would be different if I was in charge, but as soon as I was, my boyfriend insisted I give his horses performance enhancers. We were still in our honeymoon phase, and I wanted to please him. I knew we were cheating, but I thought that was the extent of the crime. It seemed like everyone else was doing it." She shook her head. "That's how I justified it. Over time I saw firsthand what those chemicals did to the animals. What they allowed the owners to do to them."

"The drugs hurt the horses?"

She nodded slowly. "The drugs weren't good for

them, that's for sure. They allowed the horses to race when they were injured so badly they shouldn't have been running at all. The way my ex treated those horses—it was criminal. And now I was involved. Of course, it was only a matter of time before the excitement wore off and I saw him for who he really was. Gradually, he began to take me for granted. He still took me to restaurants and galas but as arm candy, not because he cared. He stopped suggesting what I should do with the horses and started demanding. Began to raise his voice when he didn't immediately get his way…" She trailed off, hugging herself as if she was cold. "Once I stopped being in awe of him, I started noticing things that didn't seem right. These men came to the house now and then. I don't know what language they were speaking, but the way they stopped talking when I came into the room—it made me uncomfortable."

Lincoln straightened. "You think your ex was involved in something shady?"

She nodded again. "I never found out what it was, but I realized over time he kept a lot of cash in the house. I don't think it was drugs, because he didn't use them and I never saw anyone else take them, either. I don't know what it was."

"Money laundering," Lincoln suggested. "Arms smuggling. Human trafficking. Could have been anything."

Charlotte paled. "I was never any part of that."

He closed the distance between them. "Of course

you weren't. He was using you to dope his horses. He didn't need you to do anything else." When she pulled back like he'd slapped her, Lincoln cursed himself for being so blunt. "I mean your ex knew how to find people to do his dirty work. He didn't need you to multitask."

"That doesn't make me feel any better."

"You have nothing to feel bad about. He's the one who lured you in, then put you in a position to compromise your morals."

"But I'm the one who compromised them." Charlotte lifted her hands and pressed them to her cheeks. "I... went along with it. Helped a horse run a little faster here. Helped another one overcome its pain there. By the time I knew what a monster he was, it was too late."

"What do you mean?"

"He'd gotten control of me. He... didn't pay me. Not with money. Instead, he gave me a credit card and said I could buy whatever I liked. It sounds generous, but it wasn't."

"He could track every penny you spent, and I bet you didn't spend as much as you should have earned."

She shook her head. "He was having me watched all the time, too." Charlotte's voice was thready, and there were tears in her eyes. "The first time I tried to get away, I did everything you're supposed to do when you're leaving a controlling relationship. I found a little apartment. Got a different job. I never breathed a word of it to him or anyone he knew."

Lincoln had a feeling he knew where this was going. Her boyfriend was a powerful man. He wouldn't stand for that.

"He found out. The night before I planned to leave, he came home early with a huge bouquet of flowers. He had his chef prepare a wonderful meal. When we were done eating, he toasted me with champagne. What could I do? I drank it. I don't remember anything else until I woke up the following morning. I found my phone to check the time and discovered an email from my new employer saying he regretfully had to rescind the job offer he'd made. Then I got a call from my new landlord. She was in tears. I'd found a little apartment in this beautiful old house that was split into six residences. Overnight, the house had burned down."

Lincoln took it all in. Charlotte's ex was far more than a two-bit thug.

"I told myself it had to be a coincidence. Ivan couldn't have had me fired, let alone burn down a house, except Ivan could do all sorts of things. I was too terrified to try to leave him again."

Lincoln took her in his arms and held her tightly. "You got away." She was here now, after all.

She took a deep breath but allowed him to hold her. "My grandmother died," she said. "Ivan couldn't keep me away from her funeral. How would that look? After all, he was an important man in town. Her lawyer found me there and told me he could help." She looked up at Lincoln. "It was all very cloak and dagger. He explained my ex was monitoring my phone, and he had one of his associates take it and create a diversion. Meanwhile, Steven slipped me cash and a passport and sent me on my way. I flew back and forth across the country several times before I landed in Chance Creek."

"Thank god for Steven," Lincoln said without any irony. He recognized the name. That's who Charlotte had been talking to on her phone her second night on the Ridge.

A smile tugged at one corner of her mouth. "Yes. Thank god for Steven." Then her smile fled and tears filled her eyes, but she raised her gaze to his. "I understand if you want me to leave."

"Leave?" Lincoln's pulse jumped. "Why would I want you to leave?"

She stared at him. "I just told you my ex was a dangerous criminal and that I doped his horses so he could win races."

"You know I served twelve years in the Special Forces, right?" he asked her drily. When she nodded, he went on. "You think we spent all that time handing out cupcakes? Charlotte, I know how the world works. I've seen a thing or two." She kept watching him warily and his heart fell. He wished they could skip all this and go straight to bed, but he could tell she blamed herself for everything she'd been a part of, even though she'd done nothing wrong. "Guys like your ex—they're a dime a dozen, and they all operate in the same way." When her expression didn't change, he tried again. "Bad guys manipulate good guys. They know what levers to push. How to convince and how to threaten. They break all the rules good guys live by. You stayed true to your values, Charlotte, so you were no match for your ex. I bet he made you feel like shit every time you tried to say no."

"He was an expert at that," she admitted. "I'd think I was trying to do the right thing, and he'd convince me it was all wrong or worse—selfish and ungrateful. I'd walk away from our conversations not knowing up from down, let alone right from wrong. But I should have been able to stay true to myself even if he was a good talker."

"You're human," Lincoln told her. "And he had twenty years on you. Sounds like he spent a lifetime in the business of manipulating people. You didn't stand a chance."

"But I… hate myself," Charlotte blurted, shocking Lincoln to silence. She pressed her lips together, but he could tell it was the truth—and he bet it ate her alive when she was alone. God, he understood exactly how she felt, which made it that much worse to know how she was suffering.

"I just… hate everything I've done," she went on, her voice thick with unshed tears. She pushed out of his arms again. "I don't even know why I did it. That's the worst of it, you know? I was a good person once. I wanted to do good things, but when I was with him, I became someone else. Now I don't know who I am."

"I know who you are." Lincoln came to stand next to her. "You are a wonderful woman who cares deeply for the people and animals around her."

"But I let everyone down. I let myself down. My grandmother died while I was with Ivan."

Lincoln drew her into his arms. "You couldn't have known who your ex was when you met him. You couldn't have predicted what he'd do."

"You couldn't have known the price of lumber would crash, either," she pointed out shakily. Lincoln stiffened, then relaxed again as the truth of it sank in. She was right; he couldn't.

"Guess we both had a difficult lesson to learn," he said, savoring the feeling of her pressed close to him. "We need to look more carefully before we leap."

She laughed suddenly.

"What?" Lincoln asked, looking down at her in concern.

"I didn't learn that lesson, did I?" She shook her head at his confusion. "I met you at the airport, you invited me here and I took another flying leap."

"I guess I didn't learn it, either, then. This time it worked out, though, so I don't regret leaping." Lincoln bent down and kissed her.

She sighed. "Honestly? I don't regret it, either. Are you sure you don't think I'm a horrible person?"

"Do you think I'm one?" He countered.

"No," she said. "I think you're wonderful."

"And I think the sun rises and sets because of you."

WHEN CHARLOTTE WOKE up the next morning, she rolled over, grabbed her phone off the floor, looked at its screen and groaned to see she'd woken up nearly an hour before her alarm was due to go off. Sunlight shone through the curtainless windows of house 35. After a minute or two of trying, she knew she wouldn't get back to sleep. Instead she got up as quietly as she could and slipped into her clothes. At least she could get an extralong ride since she hadn't gotten one yesterday.

Lincoln was sleeping so soundly he didn't even turn over when she got out of bed. Last night's conversation seemed to have freed him from a burden he'd been carrying for a long time. Charlotte was grateful she'd found the questions to get him talking about what was going on in his head.

She felt lighter, too, as she made her way downstairs and out the front door. She'd been so sure Lincoln would look down on her if he knew the truth about her relationship with Ivan. In the end he'd surprised her, and in talking about it, she'd felt able to let go of some of her shame. Maybe Lincoln was right; maybe Ivan had simply outmatched her. She was older now. Wiser. She wouldn't make the same mistakes again.

As Charlotte cut through the empty streets, she spotted Sasha slipping into the house she shared with her friends near the town hall. Where had she been so early in the morning? Charlotte stifled a laugh when she saw Gareth opening the front door of Anne's boarding house and sneaking inside, as well. The two of them must have been together. If Anne ever caught them, there'd be hell to pay.

A wave of contentment washed over her. Birds were singing overhead, and the air was fresh, although it was warm already. Gage wouldn't be up for another half hour. Hudson wouldn't be jogging for an hour or so. Now that Sasha and Gareth were safely in their homes, she had the whole place to herself.

She wandered in the direction of the stable, so lost in thought as she approached the corral that flanked it that it was only when she rested her arms on the top rail she noticed something out of place. Colonel, Thorn and Eagle were gathered in a knot on the far side, their eyes rolling, whickering now and then. Closer to her an unfamiliar stallion snorted at her intrusion.

Charlotte stilled.

Not unfamiliar. She knew that horse.

What was Rally doing here?

She gripped the top rail, her fingers digging into the wood. Rally had been stolen from Gasparyn Stables. Now he was here on Elliott Ridge.

It didn't make any sense.

Rally nickered and took a step toward her. When she saw he still had a slight limp, her stomach sank. She'd assumed when she'd left Ivan would hire another veterinarian right away. Had his new hire botched Rally's care?

If so, Rally might never race again.

Stunned, Charlotte could barely credit the evidence in front of her eyes. That mistake could cost Ivan a lot of cash. Had he arranged for Rally to be stolen so he could collect the insurance money?

No, Charlotte thought, staring at the horse who was stretching its neck over the rails, looking for a scratch behind the ears. Not for the insurance money. Not yet, anyway. If he'd wanted that, Ivan would have arranged for Rally to disappear for good.

He was framing her.

The earth tilted beneath Charlotte's feet, and she held on to the corral fence with both hands as Rally nudged her with his nose. If anyone found him here, they'd think she'd stolen him, and she'd go to jail. That's what Ivan wanted—to punish her.

Charlotte fought to make sense of it. She had no idea how he'd gotten Rally into this corral, but she had no doubt Ivan was behind this. He'd probably called the sheriff already, who'd be on his way to catch her with his stolen horse. And Rally was on Elliott property. Did that mean Lincoln and his brothers could be charged as accessories to the theft? They could lose their contracts—

They could lose their town.

Horror gripped her. For an awful moment she thought she might be sick. She had to get Rally away from here.

She had to leave Elliott Ridge.

That's what Steven had said: if she thought Ivan knew where she was, she had to leave. She'd left cash in her bank account for just such a possibility. Before Ivan could bring the sheriff to witness this "crime," she needed to run far enough that no one would ever find her.

But somehow she couldn't move. Her breath was coming in gasps, and she thought if she let go of the corral fence, she might collapse to the ground. She didn't want to leave the Ridge. Didn't want to leave Lincoln. Not when everything was going so well. This was the home she'd always craved. Lincoln was the man she wanted to spend her life with.

But if she stayed, he could lose everything he loved.

Charlotte stared into Rally's liquid eyes. How had Ivan found her? More to the point, how had he gotten Rally into this corral? There was no way someone could drive up Elliott Way without waking up everyone in house number 1. Could someone have walked the horse onto the Ridge and cut through the woods to muffle the sound of its hooves?

Was that what had woken her so early?

Maybe she was still asleep, Charlotte thought desperately. Maybe she was still in bed with Lincoln lying next to her. Maybe she would wake up in a minute, and this would all be a dream.

Charlotte squeezed her eyes shut. Took a deep breath. Opened them again.

Rally stepped closer. He gave a little whinny. Nudged her. Did he recognize her? She had worked with him often enough.

Was the person who brought him here watching them now?

Charlotte drew in a quick breath, but as she scanned her surroundings, she felt sure she was alone. She had time—but not much. Someone would wake up soon. The sheriff would arrive. She had to move Rally, now.

She couldn't ask Lincoln for help. If she did, he'd

think they could deal with the situation logically. He'd call the sheriff, explain what had happened and expect justice to prevail.

That wasn't how things worked when Ivan was involved. She couldn't use normal channels to fix this mess. She had to outsmart him at his own game.

She took another steadying breath and quickly considered her options. As long as no one looked out their window, she had a chance of getting Rally out of here unseen. After all, she'd been saddling up a horse and riding it early most mornings for the past week, so the sound of her leading Rally away wouldn't cause any alarm.

She glanced around again, made sure she was alone, then unhooked the gate, grabbed Rally's lead and directed him out the corral, fastening the gate behind them.

She needed somewhere to stash the thoroughbred. Food for him. And a way to transport him far away as soon as she got the chance.

Charlotte thought of the clearing at the mine. Amanda had hidden her stolen painting up there in the abandoned buildings. Could she tether a horse there for the day out of sight of the rest of the community?

She didn't let herself think it through. Rally already wore a bridle. Grateful no one lived directly behind the stables, she walked Rally slowly to the outskirts of the community before picking up the pace a little as the ground grew steeper under her feet. She made a wide loop past the northern side of town until they reached the road that led to the mine.

When they finally arrived at the clearing, she breathed a sigh of relief. Charlotte examined the area, found a spot beneath some trees where she could leave Rally tied up and spotted a water tap near one of the buildings. She raced to test it. Turning it gingerly, she was relieved to find it still worked. It took long minutes to find an old metal bucket that was still watertight. She let the water flow for a while before filling the bucket and left it within Rally's reach. She hated leaving the horse here, but there was nothing for it. She would have to return as soon as possible after she found a better situation for him.

"I'll bring food for you before the day is over and get you out of here," she told him, smoothing his sleek neck. "I have to go now before anyone notices I'm gone, but I swear I'll be back."

She had to get a trailer. And figure out where to take Rally.

Time was ticking along, though, and soon Elliott Ridge's inhabitants would be awake. Charlotte found the track she'd taken with Lincoln on their tour but made a large detour around Hudson's tree. She cut through the streets to her house and slipped inside as quietly as she could.

She heard Lincoln moving around upstairs and the shower running. Relieved, she hurried to the bedroom. She managed to change into a clean outfit and was making the bed when he came out, a towel wrapped around his waist.

"There you are," he said and drew her into a damp embrace. "I woke up, and you were gone."

"It's such a beautiful morning, I had to ride," she told him.

"I was afraid maybe I scared you off," he said, kissing the top of her head.

"Never," she said, her mind still working away at the problem she'd hidden at the mine.

Suddenly she remembered Admiral, the sad, old horse she and Craig had rescued from Ed Johnson's place a week ago. He was housed at Bella's facility now, eating, exercising and healing from his neglect.

Maybe she knew a way to get a trailer here, after all.

CHAPTER 11

"LINCOLN—WAIT UP," CARTER called out as Lincoln crossed the Circle toward the town hall later that day. It was nearly dinnertime, and Charlotte hadn't arrived home yet. Lincoln assumed she and Craig had been kept late at an appointment, but he was wondering if this was how life would be from now on, both of them always busy with work and responsibilities, with little time to spend together. He and his brothers had left the mill an hour early to wrestle the old washer and dryer out of number 37, because they'd decided to replace the linoleum while they were doing the floors. He'd managed to do the upstairs but still needed to run the sander over the downstairs rooms tonight. At least he'd get to sleep with Charlotte later, if nothing else.

"What's going on?" he asked when his brother caught up.

"Landed a contract today—a big one. You're going to have to hire more men." Carter launched into a description of the lumber they'd need to produce, while

Lincoln listened with growing excitement. This was a big deal.

There was a problem, though.

"I got a call last night. That edger I wanted to buy isn't available anymore. We're going to have to find another one, and it'll probably cost more money. I doubt I can find another bargain like that."

"We need logs coming in, too," Carter said as Gage, Nate and Hudson joined them. "Hudson, what's the hold up on that?"

"I told you I need help," Hudson said.

"I've forwarded you a dozen applications so far," Lincoln said. "Have you talked to any of those people?"

"They're no good. You need to find some better ones."

"Are you kidding me?" Lincoln drew up short, his frustration flaring. "One of them was a guy with twenty years of experience as a climber. How much better can you get?"

"He's too old."

"He's forty," Lincoln contradicted. "In his prime."

Hudson shrugged. "He didn't fit the bill. None of them did. Try again."

Lincoln stared at him. "There has to be one quali-fied candidate in that pile. You're stonewalling."

"Why the hell would I do that?" Hudson faced off with him.

"I don't know. You tell me." Lincoln didn't back down.

"You know what? I don't need this shit." Hudson

walked away, muttering to himself. The others watched him go.

"I'm forwarding those candidates to you," Lincoln told Gage. He'd had enough. Hudson had been putting them off for weeks now and obviously wasn't going to do the job he was supposed to do. "You can hire the crew."

"What about Hudson?" Gage asked.

"I'm not wasting any more of my time on him. The job's yours now," Lincoln said. "Pick the crew you need and get started."

"We'll need more climbers, then. I'm not taking that on."

"I got another application this morning. Looks solid. I'll forward it to you. And that forty-year-old was perfectly acceptable."

Gage's attention snapped to something behind Lincoln, however. "Here comes trouble," he said. Lincoln and the others turned to see what he meant.

A sheriff's department cruiser was coming up Elliott Way. It traversed the Circle and came to a stop near the town hall.

"Here we go again," Carter muttered as the four of them went to meet it. When they'd first come back to the Ridge, some of the temporary mill workers had made it a habit to get into trouble in town on their days off. The sheriff had visited far more often than was comfortable.

"Sheriff. What can I do for you?" Carter asked as a large man in a uniform got out of the vehicle.

"Looking for something," the sheriff said. Cab Johnson was a bear of a man with a barrel chest, and judging by his expression, he'd had a rough day. "Man came in this morning and said he lost his horse. Know anything about that?"

"Lost his horse?" Lincoln repeated. It was the last thing he'd expected Cab to say.

"We have three horses in our corral, and they all belong to us," Carter said.

"What about the rest of you? Seen anything suspicious?" Cab asked the others.

Gage and Nate both shook their heads.

"What kind of horse are you looking for?" Nate asked.

"A thoroughbred, if you can believe it." A vein pulsed at Cab's temple, and Lincoln wondered what had happened before he got here.

"I think someone would have noticed one of those." Nate grinned at the thought of it. "Was there a race nearby?"

"Nope. Just an out-of-towner who thinks his expensive racehorse is stashed on your ranch but won't say how or why it might have gotten here."

"A racehorse?" Gage turned to Lincoln, who knew where his thoughts had gone. Charlotte used to work with racehorses. Did this have something to do with her?

Lincoln swiftly signed, *Don't talk*, knowing his brothers would get the gist of what he meant. No need to bring up Charlotte until the sheriff asked directly about her. Besides, she was at work, and there were no racehorses on the Ridge.

"Mind if I look around?" Cab asked tiredly.

"Not at all," Lincoln said. His stomach growled. So much for dinner.

"I'll be as quick as I can," Cab assured him. "I know I'm keeping you from your evening meal. Believe me, it's been a hell of a day at the department, or I'd have come a lot sooner, and we'd all be home by now. That guy came in first thing this morning, before most people are even out of their beds, but it wasn't early enough. We'd already had a pileup on the highway outside town. Had to attend to that first. Four people went to the hospital, one of them in critical condition. A child." The muscles around Cab's jaw tightened, and Lincoln saw what a toll that had taken on the sheriff, who had children of his own. "Soon as we got that cleared up, we got a call about a domestic dispute at one of the ranches on the edge of the county. Man threatening to shoot his cheating girlfriend. Took hours to talk him into surrendering, but we managed it. Meanwhile our new friend camped out at the department, bothering my staff and demanding his case take precedence over everything else. I about had him taken to the hospital for a psych evaluation."

"Sounds like a real pain in the ass," Lincoln said.

"Got that right." Cab tipped his hat back and wiped his forehead. "Hot today, too."

"Go ahead and look around," Gage said. "Don't think you'll find any thoroughbreds tucked away here, though."

"I don't expect I will, either." He walked away, looked in the stables and barn and made a cursory lap around the community. Lincoln and his brothers waited for him near the town hall. Eventually Hudson wandered out again to see what they were up to, and Carter filled him in on what he'd missed.

"Missing thoroughbred, huh?" Hudson asked, then broke off and raised his chin. "What's Charlotte doing with that trailer?"

Lincoln looked to see her truck trundling up the road with a horse trailer hitched to it.

"Maybe she found the thoroughbred," Nate said with a laugh. "What do you think, Sheriff?" he added as Cab appeared again. "Maybe that horse you were looking for is being delivered right now."

Lincoln's stomach sank. There was no reason for Charlotte to be driving a trailer—not even if she had found a horse running around loose. "If she found a missing horse, Bella and Craig would have picked it up and taken it to the shelter. They wouldn't have made Charlotte bring it here."

Nate shrugged. "Just a theory," he said as they all drifted toward the Circle.

Charlotte parked behind the sheriff's cruiser and got out, eyeing the vehicle askance. "What's happening?" she asked cautiously, coming to join them. "Is someone hurt?"

"Sheriff's out here looking for a lost thoroughbred," Hudson answered. "Have you seen one?"

"A thoroughbred?" she repeated faintly. When a faint flush swept up her cheeks, Lincoln's concerns turned into full-fledged worry.

"One was reported missing this morning. The owner thinks it might be here," Cab said. "You wouldn't happen to have one tucked away in your trailer, would you?" He jabbed a thumb at it. "Mind if I take a look?"

"Oh. I…" She looked at the trailer and bit her lip. "It's just…"

"Just a quick look," Cab assured Charlotte. "That's all right, isn't it?"

"Of course… but I should explain…"

Lincoln's heart beat hard. She didn't have a thoroughbred in that trailer, did she? Had she made up that whole sob story about her ex-boyfriend the other night? Was *she* the shady one?

He remembered Dennis's reaction when she arrived at the Ridge.

Trouble.

Was Dennis right?

Cab ambled to the back of the rig. "Come open this door, would you?" he called.

Lincoln held his breath as Charlotte slowly followed and stepped up to open the tailgate. She threw Lincoln a pleading look over her shoulder, and his heart stopped.

Hell.

"I was going to tell you… really…"

Tell him what? That he'd fallen in love with a horse thief? That the woman he craved was seconds away from a jail sentence? The thought of losing Charlotte, just when he'd found her—no, the thought that she'd never really been his at all. She'd been playing with him. Or—

"Take your time," Cab said in a tone that suggested Charlotte had better hurry up.

She nodded helplessly, opened the tailgate and stepped into the trailer. Lincoln could hear her crooning to the horse inside, calming the animal before turning him around, leading him out into the daylight and down the ramp.

All the men sucked in their breath.

"What the hell?" Nate asked.

Hudson let out a laugh, long and loud. "That... is not a thoroughbred."

"No, it is not," Cab said. He lifted a hand and rubbed the back of his neck.

"That is the saddest excuse for a horse I have ever seen," Carter announced. "Charlotte, what are you doing with it?"

"This is Admiral," Charlotte said defensively. "And I bought him. He's sensitive, so I'd be grateful if you stopped making fun of him."

"I am never going to stop making fun of him," Hudson said.

"I'm sorry to waste your time, folks," Cab said. "I'll get out of here and let you all get your dinner."

"Hope you find that horse," Lincoln said, still awash in relief. He couldn't believe he'd doubted her. Why would he think Charlotte—his Charlotte—would steal a thoroughbred?

Because life had been so good lately, he'd been sure disaster was around the corner?

"You bought Admiral?" he asked her as the sheriff's cruiser disappeared toward the highway. "I thought you wanted a horse you could ride."

"I do, but…"

When a shout cut through the rest of what she meant to say, they all turned to see what was going on. A disgruntled, dark-haired man came storming up the road from the direction of the mill.

"It's a damn good thing I'm leaving next week," he roared as he crossed the Circle, "because the way things are run around here, I wouldn't be staying anyhow!"

"Mick? What's wrong?" Lincoln hurried to meet him, his brothers following. Mick Harney was one of the first temporary workers they'd hired. He'd been a big help during his time at the mill. Normally, he kept calm when others were losing their cool, but today he looked like thunder.

"You know what's wrong! Stop and start, stop and start, all day long. I've unjammed that edger a dozen times since you left. We're just about done with our goal for the day, and we all stayed late to finish it, but it's stuck again! How the hell are we supposed to go on like this? You've known for weeks it needs to be replaced, yet here we are holding it together with chewing gum and packing tape. I'm sick of it! I told the men you'd either come and fix it for good, or we all better walk away now. The whole lot of us!"

Lincoln exchanged a panicked glance with the others. "You can't walk!"

"I'm not going back there today, I'll tell you that much. I've had it." He kept going toward the town hall.

This was bad. They needed to do something—fast. Lincoln looked at Charlotte, but whatever questions he wanted to ask her would have to wait. "Go have dinner," he told her. "I'll catch up with you tonight."

"Of course. Go fix the edger."

Lincoln hated to leave her. Someday he'd have the time to ask her everything he wanted to know. But first he had to save his family's business.

CHARLOTTE WATCHED THE men leave, relief making her almost dizzy. This was her chance to fetch Rally and get him off the Ridge before Lincoln and the others returned, but she'd have to move swiftly, or they'd catch her in the act.

"Why'd you buy that broken-down horse?"

"Oh!" Charlotte jumped when Sasha spoke up directly behind her. How long had she been standing there? Charlotte turned to find that most of the other influencers had trailed out of their house and were coming to look at Admiral, too. "I… like him, and I want him to have a good home, that's all. I'm a sucker for horses."

"Can we ride him?" Edie asked.

"Who would want to? You'd probably get fleas," Veronica said.

"He'd make a good backdrop for content," Sasha said, tossing her long hair. "Let's get our cowboy stuff and take some videos."

"No!" Charlotte bit her lip. She hadn't meant to say it so sharply. "He's old and tired, and his owner wasn't able to care for him for months. He needs to be left alone until he's recovered."

"We won't touch him," Veronica said. "He'll just be in the background, that's all."

"I really wish you wouldn't." She was losing precious time arguing with them. She needed to move Admiral into one of the stalls and leave so she could get Rally.

"You aren't the boss of us," Sasha said.

"I'm the boss of Admiral."

"That's hardly something to brag about," Veronica said. "Really, Charlotte, we're not going to hurt your horse. I promise. You can be in the content, too."

"She doesn't want to be in the content," Sasha reminded her. "She's too good for that, and now she thinks her horse is, too."

"I bet Admiral would love to be a star," Edie said. "We'll make him go viral. Just wait," she said to Charlotte.

"I don't want him to go viral!" Why couldn't these women take no for an answer?

"I told you," Sasha said. "She probably doesn't want us here on the Ridge at all."

"That's not true. What I want is for my horse to get his rest tonight so he can get better. Can't you understand that?" To Charlotte's horror, tears pricked her eyes. The old horse had already endured a ride in the trailer when by all rights he shouldn't have had to do that again. Now she was going to leave him, possibly forever, so she could get Rally away from the Ridge. She needed to know Admiral wasn't going to be harassed to death when she was gone.

Gone. Charlotte's heart ached at the thought of it. Would she ever be able to come back? She hadn't even said a proper goodbye to Lincoln.

She didn't want to say goodbye. Didn't want to leave.

This was her home.

Not anymore, she told herself firmly. Ivan had followed her. She couldn't allow him to ruin things for everyone.

Veronica pulled back. "Hey, no worries. We'll do it another time. No need to get upset."

"But…" Sasha began.

Veronica shook her head. "It's dinnertime, anyway. You all go grab us a table before all the good ones are taken. I want to be able to see Cal while he works."

"On it!" Edie saluted and led the way, the other women following her.

"Thank you," Charlotte said to Veronica quietly when they had set off.

"Are you okay?" Veronica asked her.

"No," Charlotte said. "But I will be. First things first. Admiral needs his rest, and I need to get this trailer back to Bella Mortimer. She needs it tomorrow."

"Drive carefully. You seem upset."

"I'm not upset," Charlotte lied. "Just… tired. I will

drive carefully." She forced herself to smile and waved as Veronica walked away, then hurried to lead Admiral to his stall, made him as comfortable as she could and climbed back into her truck. She drove slowly out to the highway, hoping Veronica would repeat what she'd told her to anyone who asked where she'd gone. A half mile down the road, she pulled onto the shoulder and parked.

As she hiked up the Ridge through the woods, she remembered what Lincoln had said about the wild animals that frequented the area. She hoped there weren't any bears around today. Picking up her pace, she figured she was making so much noise she'd probably scare off any within a mile of her, but it seemed to take forever to reach the top of the Ridge and even more time to bushwhack around until she finally stumbled into the clearing near the mine.

Thank God Rally was still where she'd left him. He nickered at her when she approached and let her scratch behind his ears, but soon he was moving his head from side to side, searching to see if she'd brought anything to eat.

Charlotte untied his lead. "I've got a full feed bag for you in the trailer. Come on, Rally. It's time for us to leave."

"AM I THE only one who thinks Charlotte might have stolen a racehorse?" Hudson asked as they jogged to the mill.

"You're the only one who thinks there *is* a missing

racehorse," Nate said. "Sounds like Cab's dealing with a man with a screw loose."

"Seems like a hell of a coincidence he's missing a racehorse just weeks after a veterinarian who specializes in them shows up in town," Hudson said.

"So where's the thoroughbred?" Carter asked. "Have you seen one running around the Ridge? Because I haven't."

"I haven't either," Lincoln said, although he'd been suppressing similar concerns since he'd left Charlotte behind. It did seem like an improbable coincidence, even if the horse in her trailer had turned out to be Admiral.

"Let's focus on the real problem," Carter said, pointing to the mill as they approached it. "We can't let those men walk."

"I've got this," Lincoln said. "I'll fix the edger and order a new one—tonight—no matter what it takes." He grasped the handle of the mill's front door and swore. He could feel the hum of the machinery inside from here—a hum that shouldn't exist. The whole line should be off if there were repairs to be made to the edger. He yanked the door open and dashed inside, followed quickly by his brothers.

He cut through the mill to where the edger stood, a long, low piece of machinery that sucked rough-cut boards in, sawed them into usable planks and spit them out the other side.

The machine had been shut off with one rough board on its way in and a finished plank most of the way out. It must have gotten jammed three-quarters of the way through, because a group of men huddled around the saw. One of the youngest temporary workers—Scott Henshell—stood on top of the machine, a pry bar in his hands. Lincoln swore at the sight of him, then swore again when he noticed the front and rear guards were up.

"What the hell are you doing?" he yelled.

"Just a second. Almost got it, boss!" The young man jabbed the pry bar into the machine to clear debris from the blades.

"Get down!" Lincoln shoved between the men. "Are you crazy? This edger isn't locked out!" If it turned on, it could pull Scott into those blades in an instant. There were reasons for safety protocols—life or death ones.

"There!" Scott called. "Got it." He jumped down with a triumphant holler and handed the pry bar to Lincoln. "I should get a promotion for that. Didn't even have to shut down the line. Let 'er rip!" he shouted to another worker.

"Stop!" Lincoln shouted—too late. Another young man—Dan Yates—flipped the switch. The machine bucked to life with a screech that told Lincoln lumber scraps were caught in its blades. It yanked the rough board into its maw—and simultaneously spat out the edged one.

With the guard up, the board shot straight across the roller belt, over the rail that should have turned it toward the next piece of equipment and into the group of bystanders on the far side. They shouted and dove out of the way but not fast enough. Sid Newport toppled like a felled tree.

"Stop the line!" Lincoln shouted. Someone hit the emergency button, and the whole production line went dead. Lincoln sprinted to the fallen man and bent to see how badly he was hurt.

"Call 911," he called over his shoulder.

"On it," Nate said.

"I've got the emergency kit." Hudson appeared by his side.

"Sid? You with us?" Lincoln asked the man, but it was clear he wasn't. Lincoln pressed his fingers to the side of Sid's neck and felt a thready pulse. He nodded to Hudson. "He's alive." Barely. The bump rising on the side of his head looked bad.

"Everybody out," he heard Gage shout and was thankful his brothers were here to help. He didn't know what to do except keep Sid still until the paramedics arrived.

"This is my fault," he said to Hudson.

"No, it's not."

Lincoln didn't answer him, but he knew it was. Why the hell hadn't he bought a replacement edger weeks ago, no matter what anyone else in his family had said? He'd known this one couldn't be fixed. Hell, the thing was forty years old if it was a day, like the rest of the equipment had been before he'd talked his father into that loan.

It seemed like hours passed before they heard the

wail of sirens. When the paramedics rushed in, they took Lincoln's place and got to work stabilizing Sid. Hudson took him by the arm and led him out the back of the building. The broken-down hulks of the equipment graveyard stood nearby, but no one was in sight.

"You okay?" Hudson asked.

Lincoln tried to swallow but found he couldn't. In fact, he was finding it hard to breathe.

"Lincoln?"

Sid could have been killed. That board had to have been going a hundred miles an hour. He could still die.

"Lincoln. Come on, man. Hell." Hudson peered at his face. "Shit, you're white as a ghost. Lincoln, breathe. You gotta breathe."

He tried to, but the air caught in his lungs and held there. Spots formed in front of his eyes, and the edges of his vision pulsed, then grew dark. It was his fault that damned edger kept breaking down. His fault he hadn't replaced it. His fault Sid could be dead.

"Sid's going to be fine. He's halfway to the hospital by now. Think of something else, Lincoln. Think of Charlotte."

Lincoln tried to blink back the spots but couldn't. The air still wouldn't fill his lungs. He tried to do as Hudson said. Tried to form the word *Charlotte*, but no sound came out of his mouth. The ground under his feet was tilting.

"Whoa. Come on. Get a grip, Lincoln. You can do this."

"My fault…" Lincoln managed.

"Fuck that. It wasn't your fault. Blame whoever de-cided to fix that edger without locking it out. You've been right all this time; we need a new one."

Lincoln still couldn't catch his breath. The air whis-tled in his lungs when he tried to fill them. He kept seeing Scott up on that machine. Dan flipping the switch. As bad as it had been, it could have been so much worse.

No. Not worse—Sid could still die of that head wound.

"My... fault," Lincoln gasped. He should have been there. He'd been worming his way out of work for weeks, spending time with Charlotte, fixing her house, greeting newcomers. Not doing his damn job.

Hudson gripped Lincoln's shoulders in his fingers. "Listen to me," he said. "Snap out of it. Sid isn't dead. You didn't cause this." He stared at Lincoln. Must have seen his words weren't working. "Lincoln, focus. What do you see?"

"See?" he panted.

"What do you see—not in your head. What do you see right here around us. Name three things." He gave Lincoln a little shake.

"I... You," Lincoln said, confused. "I... see you. The mill." The words came out in gasps of air he couldn't afford to lose.

"Good. One more."

"Machines." There were broken-down machines everywhere, but that reminded him of the broken edger and the grind of the mill line, the log going through the sawblades. Shooting out the other side.

"Two things you feel," Hudson said and shook him again. "What do you feel?"

Was Hudson losing his mind? Lincoln rubbed his damp hands against the rough cotton of his pants. "Fabric. Sweat."

"One thing you smell."

Lincoln decided this game wasn't so odd because everything had gone off the rails today. Nothing was how it was supposed to be. A stolen racehorse. Charlotte buying Admiral. Men working on machinery without following any of the rules. "Sawdust," Lincoln said.

"You breathing okay?" Hudson asked.

Lincoln took a breath and found that it made it to the bottom of his lungs. He could breathe. He nodded in relief.

"Good." Hudson let go and stepped back. "Don't make any sudden moves. Get your balance back." He watched Lincoln suck in deep gulps of air. "It's going to be okay."

Lincoln shook his head. He didn't believe that. "What the fuck just happened?" He wasn't sure what he meant by the question, but his brother seemed to understand.

"You glitched out. Your reality became unbearable, so your body stopped working." When Lincoln didn't respond, he added, "That was a panic attack."

Lincoln pulled back. "Panic attack? I've never had one of those." The accusation angered him. He'd been in the Special Forces for twelve years. He'd seen some stuff.

He'd never been overwhelmed by it.

"It's different when you think it's your fault, isn't it?"

Guilt flooded Lincoln all over again. He braced himself for the overwhelming feeling to come back, but his breathing remained steady.

Too bad. If he passed out, he wouldn't have to live with himself.

"Listen, that ambulance got here fast. Sid's getting the help he needs, and everything is going to be fine," Hudson said again.

"Is it?"

"Yes." Hudson took a deep breath. "Look, there's something else I've been meaning to say since we got home. About Winona. What happened in senior year."

Senior year? Lincoln waved that off. "Ancient history." There was enough going on right now.

"I have to say it." Hudson stood his ground. "I was wrong. I shouldn't have done that to you. I told myself I was saving you from making a big mistake—I knew Winona was sleeping around, and I saw you going into Thayer's. I knew you were going to propose to her at prom. That didn't give me the right to do what I did."

"You saved me from making an ass out of myself," Lincoln said. "From ruining my life." His mind was still on the accident, but Hudson's apology was distracting him. He could barely take in what his brother was saying, it was so out of character for him to talk this way.

"But that's not why I really did it. Or why I stole any of your girls." Remorse twisted Hudson's features. "You were such a fucking saint back then. Always doing the right thing. The steady one—the one everyone depended on. Remember what Mom said whenever we left the house? 'Be careful, Lincoln. Make sure Hudson gets home okay,'" he parroted in a singsong voice. "She never told me to make sure you got home. She knew who the responsible one was—and who was bound to screw up."

Lincoln stared at his brother. He'd had no idea Hudson felt that way. "You're the one everyone wanted to hang out with."

"Sure—kids our age. Grown-ups thought I was dumb as a stump."

"That's not true."

"I know it's not." Hudson paced away and came back. "But it was mostly true. I could fell trees like a pro. That's all I was good at—and we were losing the mill." His voice cracked, and suddenly Lincoln understood. By the time they'd left the Ridge, Hudson must have wondered if he'd ever shine at anything again.

"But it turned out you were an ace fighter pilot, too," he pointed out.

"Yeah." Hudson blew out a breath. "Yeah," he said again. He shook his head. "None of that makes what I did right. I'm… sorry."

Lincoln found it hard to answer him in a steady voice. "Thanks." They stood there awkwardly until

Hudson cleared his throat.

"Tonight you'll call around and find a new edger. It's all going to get easier from here on out, you'll see."

"Lincoln! Hudson!" a woman screamed. They both turned to see Veronica racing toward them. "Your parents' house! It's on fire!"

IT HAD BEEN hard enough to get up this damn ridge on her own without a path. Getting Rally back down it was a whole different matter. He was miffed that Charlotte hadn't brought any food and not at all impressed by the terrain she was trying to get him to traverse. Rally was used to groomed tracks and flat paddocks, not steep, forested hillsides covered with brambles wherever there was a break in the trees. Worse, his limp was growing more pronounced.

At least the loamy forest floor muffled the sound of Rally's hooves. Charlotte decided slow and steady was a lot better than trying to go fast and then having Rally balk altogether. The last thing she wanted was to lame him by rushing him out of here.

"Charlotte. There you are."

Charlotte shrieked when Ivan stepped out from behind a tree and pointed a gun at her with a very steady hand.

"Ivan!"

"Missed me?" He moved closer. "How thoughtful of you to bring me my horse."

She blinked, trying to understand how he could be here. Ivan in the woods of a small Montana ghost town didn't compute.

"How did you find me?" she asked faintly, keeping her gaze on that weapon. Would he really shoot her if she kept going?

She had a feeling he was capable of it.

"You didn't make it easy, I'll give you that," he said, taking a step closer. "Disappeared right off the face of the earth, didn't you? But you slipped up once, and that's all it took. I know the best people, Charlotte. Your face couldn't appear in any online photo without me finding out. I couldn't believe you were spending time with a bunch of silly women in a ghost town. Then I discovered the Elliotts owned this place, with four unmarried sons about to inherit the whole thing. Suddenly it made sense. My Charlotte likes a wealthy man."

That damn photograph. She'd been right to be angry when Sasha posted it, but how dare Ivan imply she'd picked this place because she thought she could trick a man into paying her way? She opened her mouth to explain that the Elliotts were in debt, then changed her mind. He was baiting her, like usual. Ivan wanted her off balance and on the defensive so he could use his tricks to manipulate her.

She was done with that.

"So you sent someone to spy on me that very day?" Had it been one of his cronies in the woods filming the influencers and programmers skinny-dipping in Elliott Lake?

He chuckled. "I'm good, but I'm not that good. It

took a little time to set up this trap."

So it had been Dennis, after all. Or a random hiker.

"How did you get Rally into the corral? He doesn't even like you—and I didn't hear a thing." Maybe if she kept talking, he wouldn't put a bullet in her head.

Ivan frowned. "Rally likes me. All animals like me. But no—I wasn't the one who slipped him into your corral. I have people for that. Felt pads and hoof boots," he added, answering her question. "Muffles the sound considerably."

"None of that explains how you found me today." No animals liked Ivan. They saw right through his act, even if she hadn't. Was the man really that oblivious to his own character?

Maybe he was.

"You're right; it doesn't. I should have been here first thing this morning with the sheriff to arrest your ass and have you locked away for years, but the sheriff didn't seem to think your crimes were sufficient to take priority. He may find it difficult to get re-elected when his term expires."

"Leave the sheriff alone. He was doing his job."

"Not very well. You slipped through my fingers, and you might have gotten away with it if I didn't have all your movements under surveillance. As soon as we saw you with that trailer, I knew we had you."

She cursed herself for not having made a better plan. "Why do any of this? You don't love me. You can have any woman you want in Saratoga. You don't think much of my skill as a veterinarian, either—you never listened to me about your horses' care."

"No one leaves me," Ivan said succinctly. "Not until I tell them to go."

"Then tell me to go," Charlotte said. "And then walk away yourself—before all this gets out of hand."

For one moment she thought she'd reached him, but then a strange smile stretched the corners of his mouth. "No. I don't think I'll make it that easy. I saw you, you know."

"Saw me… what?"

"Saw you with him. With Lincoln Elliott. Going to bed with him last night. Getting up with him this morning."

"Saw me going to bed…" She trailed off. "How? Were you watching us through our windows?" Anger rushed through her veins, but so did disgust. He'd spied on her… when she was with Lincoln? They'd slept on the second floor.

"If you don't want people watching, get some curtains." Ivan's voice flattened, like he'd lost interest in all of it. "Time to call the sheriff again. Maybe this time he'll be interested to learn that not only are you a horse thief, but you're an arsonist, too. Setting your boyfriend's parents' house on fire. What kind of a reprobate does that?"

Charlotte's heart squeezed as the breath whooshed out of her lungs.

"What are you talking about?"

"It hasn't rained much in these parts this summer. Everything is so dry. I wonder if the blaze will spread?"

"You set fire to house number 1?" He couldn't have picked a better way to get back at Lincoln if it was true.

And if people believed she'd done it… Charlotte couldn't bear to follow the thought to its conclusion. The Elliotts would hate her. Lincoln would turn his back and leave her behind.

"You sent the sheriff here earlier—everyone will know it was you," she stuttered through chattering teeth.

"But you left so much evidence at the scene," Ivan said and tsked at her. "So careless, Charlotte. Should have stayed with me. I would have taken care of you."

"You're a bastard."

"That's right, let it out, but don't go too far," he warned her. "I'm the only one who's going to give a damn about you after this. You'll be dying to see me after a year or two in prison. Begging me to take you home."

She gaped at him. Is that what he thought? He could frame her for a crime she didn't commit, threaten to kill her, have her put in jail—and then she'd beg to come back to him?

Was he insane?

She took in the triumphant glint in his eyes and the satisfied set of his jaw.

Yes. He was insane.

And he was pointing that gun at her head.

CHAPTER 12

B Y THE TIME Lincoln reached the Circle, his parents' house was fully ablaze, despite the ragged bucket brigade the influencers and programmers had cobbled together. Amanda was with them, as was Cal. Lincoln raced across the green and joined them, knowing it was already too late.

"Charlotte," Amanda yelled at him.

"What about Charlotte?"

"We think she's in there!"

Cold fear slid down his spine as Lincoln rushed toward the house.

"Lincoln!" Hudson caught him just as he reached the flames. "You can't go in there. You'll burn alive."

"Charlotte's in there!" Lincoln pointed at sandals he recognized as hers strewn on the ground outside the house. Had she seen the fire, kicked them off in the yard before entering? It didn't make sense, but—

"Get back!" Sasha screamed. "Everyone back!"

Lincoln snapped around to look at her. Followed her pointing finger. Part of the roof was sagging, about to collapse. Hudson dragged him backward, even as Lincoln strained against his grip. If Charlotte was in there…

An explosion hit him and slammed him to the ground.

Half a second later, Lincoln spat out dirt as he pushed himself up, his ears ringing. Hudson, flat in the grass beside him, staggered to his feet, as dazed as he was.

"Lincoln. Hudson." Nate came running to help them up, his voice a distorted blur of sound. Gage and Carter arrived a moment later.

"Hell," Hudson said. Lincoln turned around to see the wreckage of his parents' house. Part of it still stood, but the rest lay in burning splinters.

"Oil tank," Gage said. "The fire must have reached the basement."

A second later, firefighters rushed past, pulling hoses. Lincoln hadn't even heard sirens. His hearing was still muted as he fell back with his brothers. He felt a curious dissociation from the scene in front of him, as if he'd been given some drug that left him perfectly numb. There was a smoldering house, a number of people milling around it. Firetrucks.

"Where's Charlotte?" Carter asked suddenly.

Reality came whooshing in with a snap that left his mind reeling.

Charlotte.

She was under that burning mess.

And she wasn't coming back.

"HERE'S HOW IT'S going to go," Ivan said. "You're going to lead the way down this hill, making sure you don't harm one hair on that horse's head. He's still worth a lot of money, even after you botched his care. You're going to pay for that, too, you know. He would have won the Triple Crown if it wasn't for your incompetence."

Rally, as if knowing Ivan was talking about him, danced a little, pulling at his lead. Charlotte considered releasing him, but the thoroughbred could hurt himself racing down this hill, and she had no doubt Ivan would shoot her.

She didn't bother to refute Ivan's lies. Instead she kept a tight grip on Rally's lead and began walking. Ivan wouldn't do anything to an animal worth so much money. She was safest right beside him.

"Don't try anything. This thing's loaded." Ivan walked behind her, the gun trained on her back.

She'd never doubted that. "Watch it. Rally doesn't like people right behind him."

"What Rally likes doesn't matter, does it?" Ivan stepped closer to her and tapped the barrel of the pistol against the back of her head. "Control him and do what I say, got it?" He kept tapping the pistol against her skull. There'd be a bruise if she got out of this alive.

"Got it."

She kept walking, but Ivan stayed right behind her, tapping the gun against her skull, brushing up against Rally's haunch now and then. The horse whinnied and sidestepped once or twice, and Charlotte struggled to keep him calm.

"Ivan, you're scaring Rally. Back off."

"Shut up! You don't get to call the shots." Ivan grabbed her arm, stepped between her and Rally, tugged her back and jammed the pistol against her forehead. "I'm the boss. I call the shots. It's time you remembered that." Rally shied away again.

Charlotte stared up at Ivan. Had she really ever let this man take her to bed? The thought was repugnant. Ivan's eyes narrowed as if she'd said that out loud, and he pulled back, bumping into Rally's haunch again. Rally danced away, and Charlotte clutched the lead hard, stumbling forward, which pushed Ivan into Rally a second time. The horse reared and yanked the lead right out of her hand.

"Rally!"

"What the fuck?" Ivan lurched back.

"Watch out!" Charlotte screamed just as Rally's hooves came down, sending him sprawling to the ground. The horse reared again, whirled and raced away.

Ivan moaned but stayed prone. Charlotte hesitated only a moment, then took off after the horse. She expected the thud of a bullet in her spine any moment as she careened downhill, but it didn't come, so she kept going, darting among the trees and leaping over fallen branches. She twisted her ankle and cried out, but raced on, moaning with pain.

Rally didn't head for the highway. Instead he found the trail that led to the settlement. Charlotte was heaving for air by the time she burst out of the trees and found herself behind the old cabins that were among the first homes to be built on the Ridge. She spotted Rally racing toward the Circle, fought to regain her breath and hobbled after him, relieved he hadn't injured himself further on the way down.

She was out in the open here, but she did her best to duck among the houses rather than take a straight line. She had no idea if Ivan was following her, but she knew she couldn't take any chances. The hatred she'd seen in his eyes had cut through any doubts that remained about his capability to kill her. When the Circle came in sight, she nearly sobbed with relief.

She was going to make it.

The sight in front of her slowed her steps, however. House number 1 was a smoldering wreck, flames and smoke billowing out of its fallen walls. Firefighters battled the blaze while Lincoln stood with his brothers watching, their sagging figures telling her everything she needed to know.

There was Anne and the programmers. Veronica and the influencers, too, all standing dazed and silent, not a single one filming the scene.

Charlotte swallowed hard, pushed forward and finally reached the edge of the Circle.

"Lincoln," she croaked, cleared her throat and tried again. "Lincoln," she cried. She was almost there.

He turned. "Charlotte?" He seemed frozen in place, his voice unbelieving.

She took another few stumbling steps toward him.

A sound cracked out behind her. Something simultaneously ice cold and burning hot tore through her shoulder, shocked the breath out of her and sent her forward into the grass.

Ivan.

He'd caught up to her.

She was going to die.

"Lincoln." When she breathed out the word, her lungs couldn't find a way to breathe back in. All too soon, the world went dark.

"CHARLOTTE!" LINCOLN YELLED as she crashed to the ground only a dozen yards ahead of him. How had she gotten there? Where had that shot come from? And was that a thoroughbred racing away?

"Get down! Everybody—down!" Gage shouted.

No one listened. The firefighters scattered, leaving their hoses on the ground. Anne and the programmers ran for the town hall. Veronica and the influencers raced around the wreckage of house number 1 toward the lake. The only real cover was a couple of vehicles parked along the Circle. Lincoln ran to them, along with his brothers.

He wasn't armed, and by the looks of things, neither was Hudson or Nate. Carter drew a Glock from the concealed shoulder holster he'd worn most days since Amanda's father had tracked her down and attacked her on the Ridge. Gage was armed, too.

"I'm calling for help," Nate said, his phone to his ear.

"Give me that," Lincoln said to Carter. "I have to

get to Charlotte."

"You go out there and you'll be a sitting duck," Gage growled at him.

"There's one of them." Hudson pointed. Lincoln caught a glimpse of a man before he ducked behind a tree beside one of the houses on the far side of the Circle.

"Shit, there's another," Nate said, pointing. That one was farther away, a few houses down.

"They're trying to get to Charlotte," Gage said. He took a shot but missed the second man, who ducked behind the house he was closest to.

"I have to get her first," Lincoln said. "Carter!"

"Take this."

Lincoln looked up to find Dennis beside him, dressed in his usual dingy work clothes, white hair mussed and sticking out in all directions. The caretaker placed a pistol in his hand, the weight of it a relief.

"Get those bastards," Dennis said. "Mucking up my forest." To Lincoln's surprise, he handed another weapon to Hudson. He didn't have time to wonder if Dennis had an arsenal stashed somewhere on the Ridge. He had to save Charlotte. It had been such a relief to see her after he thought she'd been trapped in the wreckage of his childhood home. He couldn't lose her now.

"I'm going out there," Lincoln told them.

"We've got you covered," Nate said.

With his brothers arrayed behind the vehicles, weapons ready, Lincoln knew it was now or never. He'd still be an easy target, but he didn't care.

"There's a third one," Hudson said. "Look!"

That was Charlotte's ex-boyfriend. Lincoln was sure he was right, although he couldn't have said why. The man was middle-aged. Even from here Lincoln could tell he was well dressed. He didn't skulk behind trees like the others. He strode toward Charlotte like he owned her.

"Get that bastard," Hudson said. "I've got your back."

Gratitude rushed through Lincoln. There was no one he trusted more than his brothers in a situation like this. He took a deep breath—

And ran.

Zigzagging across the grassy circle, Lincoln picked up speed as one bullet and then another—and another—zinged past him and kicked up clods of dirt and grass. He heard shouts behind him, his brothers pointing out targets to each other. Ahead, the three strangers shouted orders. The older man's voice rang out over the rest.

"If you don't kill him, I'll kill you. Charlotte is mine!"

Ivan. It had to be him.

He couldn't let the bastard win. He lowered his head and ran for all he was worth, dropping down to his knees beside Charlotte when he reached her.

Someone yelled and collapsed a hundred feet ahead of him. One of Ivan's men. The shots coming from behind him—from his brothers—came thick and fast, giving him the time he needed to pick her up in his arms and get back to his feet.

"Lincoln, duck!" Veronica yelled from near the smoldering remains of his family's home. Lincoln lurched to the right and a bullet zipped past, no doubt aimed at where he'd been a second earlier. He shifted Charlotte over his shoulder, turned and got off a clumsy shot that took out the man who'd tried to end his life. That was two of them. Were there more, or was Ivan the only one left?

"I got you covered, get back!" Suddenly Hudson was by his side, taking shot after shot at a shadow lurking near one of the closest houses. Lincoln broke into a run toward the vehicles. Each step felt like an eternity before he gained safety behind them. He lowered Charlotte carefully to the ground and felt for a pulse at her neck. It was there but unsteady. He searched for the bullet that had caused the blossom of blood to spread over her chest and shoulder. Found it much too close to her heart for comfort.

"We have to get her to a hospital," he said. "Now."

"Get in." Nate tossed him a set of keys as Gage took another shot across the Circle.

"I'll drive." Hudson had made it back and grabbed the keys from his hand as Lincoln bent to pick up Charlotte. He carried her with him into the passenger seat of Nate's truck as Hudson took the driver's side.

"Drive fast. He'll try to shoot out the wheels."

"I won't let him." Hudson started the engine, spun the steering wheel and, instead of traversing the Circle, made a U-turn. He punched the accelerator to the floor, and the truck's tires squealed before lurching forward. A spate of gunshot shattered the side windows. Lincoln swore, trying to cover as much of Charlotte as he could with his own body. Reflexively, he pulled his pistol from his waistband, took aim at Ivan, who was racing toward them, and pulled the trigger. The man's body buckled and crashed to the ground.

"Go!" He didn't need to stick around to find out Ivan's fate. If he hadn't finished the job, his brothers would guard him until the sheriff came back.

He was pretty sure he'd finished the job, though.

He flicked on the Glock's safety. Set it down and gathered the woman he loved to his chest. She was breathing, but she'd lost a lot of blood.

"Hurry."

Hudson nodded tightly but kept his eyes on the road. He swung them onto the highway.

Three sheriff's cruisers shot past them and turned toward the Ridge. Lincoln breathed a sigh of relief. If there were any more men hiding in the woods, his brothers would have help finding them.

"How's she doing?" Hudson asked.

"Still alive—for now."

"GET... OFF," CHARLOTTE groaned, trying to get free of the crushing weight on her shoulder. Was Rally... sitting on her?

Rally.

Dim memories fluttered in her mind even as pain

washed over her and that crushing feeling persisted. The mine. Rally. Trying to get down the hill to the trailer.

Men talking.

Ivan.

Fear shot through her. Charlotte opened her eyes, then shut them again with a groan, defeated by the bright light that flooded them.

"Charlotte?" A deep male voice sounded at her side. "Are you awake?"

She groaned again, incapable of forming words. Where was she, and why did her shoulder ache like she'd been split open and sewn back together?

She opened one eye a sliver. "Who...?" was all she managed to get out.

A shape came into view and coalesced into Lincoln's familiar face. "You *are* awake." A hand took hers and squeezed it, sending warmth and love through her despite the pain. If Lincoln was here, she was safe. Charlotte closed her eyes—

And slept.

SHE DIDN'T KNOW how long it was before she woke again, but she had a feeling it was morning when she opened her eyes and was able to keep them that way. As before, Lincoln was close by her side. This time she could read the worry in the lines of his face.

"Honey?"

"Lincoln," she said. "Where am I?" At least that was what she was trying to say. It came out a slur of vowels.

"You're in the hospital, but you're doing great."

"The hospital?" Again, the words were much clearer in her head than when she spoke.

Lincoln looked away for a long moment. She waited, her confusion growing. "Lincoln?"

That came out correctly, although her voice was thin and ragged.

He let out a rough sound. When he turned back, his gaze was bleak, his eyes red-rimmed. "Thought I'd lost you."

Lost her?

The events of the day came back with a rush.

"Ivan," she breathed. Where was he? He'd been armed…

"Dead." Lincoln bit out the word. "It's all over. He can't come after you anymore."

Charlotte lay back, her heart pounding. Ivan was dead? She could barely take it in, but she remembered the way he'd spoken to her on the Ridge and the shot that had sliced through her flesh.

She looked down and saw bandages wrapping her left shoulder.

"You're going to be fine," Lincoln assured her. "It will take some time, but you should be as good as new when you've recovered."

Ivan had shot her. He'd tried to kill her. Rally had given her a head start, but it nearly hadn't been enough.

"Rally?" She surged up and cried out as pain flooded her shoulder.

"Rally's fine, too." Lincoln squeezed her hand. "Don't try to move. You've got to heal."

"Where is he?" It was her fault he'd had to traipse up and down the Ridge. Ivan had brought him there to try to frame her.

She sucked in a breath. Had he succeeded?

"Rally's safe. Bella's got him for now."

"The sheriff. He'll think I stole him." Panic filled her voice. Ivan could win from beyond the grave if she was arrested and tried for the theft.

"The sheriff knows you didn't steal that horse," Lincoln assured her. "Cab Johnson has been around the block a few times, honey. He knows a shady character when he sees one. Ivan tripped all his alarm bells the minute he met the man. He put out some calls after he left yesterday afternoon. You were right; Ivan was involved in some unlawful stuff."

Just as she'd thought. Shame washed over Charlotte as she stared at the hospital room ceiling and a tear leaked from one eye. She'd led a killer straight to the Ridge. The enormity of it shook her to her core.

"I should never have come to Elliott Ridge," she said as more tears followed.

Lincoln stilled. "What do you mean?"

"I brought trouble, just like Dennis said, and it wasn't fair to any of you."

Lincoln's shoulders lowered. "I'm glad you came to Elliott Ridge," he said. "I'm glad my brothers and I were there to help when it got bad."

She could have been killed. More tears welled up, but they were ones of gratitude. "He burned down your house. What if he'd killed you?" she asked. "What would I have done then? Or if he'd shot one of your brothers? I couldn't have stood myself."

"The day I met you was the best day of my life." Lincoln's words cut through her rising hysteria. Charlotte swallowed.

"How can you say that?" Her coming had nearly destroyed them all. If Ivan had gotten away, he would have spent the rest of his life trying to wipe Elliott Ridge off the map.

"Because it was. Because since then, I've known the reason I was put on this earth—to be with you. Charlotte, you are my life."

She couldn't take in what she was hearing. After everything that had happened—after Ivan had shot at his family, had burned down his parents' house—could he really feel that way?

"Why?" she asked.

"Why what?" Lincoln's brow furrowed. He smoothed a strand of hair back from her face.

"Why don't you hate me?"

Lincoln stared at her. "For what?"

"For being stupid. For being with a man like that. For bringing my problems here—to your home."

"You're not stupid. You're human. Humans make mistakes, Charlotte. That's pretty much the definition of us—creatures that screw up and learn and screw up and learn some more. That's how life works."

"But my mistakes were so bad."

He shook his head. "Not nearly as bad as mine," he said with a rueful laugh. "God, Charlotte, first I pushed too hard to get my way at the mill and then I didn't push hard enough. That nearly got someone killed last night." His voice roughened, and Charlotte was shocked to see emotion nearly get the better of him.

"What do you mean?"

She listened as he explained about the jammed edger and Sid's accident.

"Is he okay?" Charlotte asked.

"Thankfully, yes," Lincoln said. "But he could have died." When he stared across the room for a moment, she could see he was in his own private hell.

"That wasn't your fault," she said. "You told everyone again and again you needed to replace that piece of equipment. I heard you. You would have done it weeks ago, but you felt you needed your family's approval. You and your brothers—and your father, too—need to work out what part of the company each of you is responsible for and what decisions you're allowed to make unilaterally."

"You're right. We've been sloppy," Lincoln said. "It's time to run our business like a business. Charlotte." He hesitated, then bent closer to brush a kiss over her mouth. "I love you. You know that, right?"

The sudden change of topic startled her, as did his words, but as they sank in, she realized she did know that. He'd been saying it with his actions from the day he'd met her, in a way Ivan had never done.

From the first, he'd anticipated her needs and rushed to supply them. He'd listened to what she had to say. He'd made sure she was never alone when she didn't want to be—but let her be alone when she did.

He'd been there—for her.

"I love you, too," she breathed, tears sliding down her cheeks.

He kissed her again, then held her hand. She could read the desire in his eyes and knew he wanted to do so much more but was afraid to hurt her.

She couldn't seem to stop crying.

"It's okay," he murmured. "Let it out."

She did. She cried for the fear she'd been holding inside these past few weeks. For all her regrets and lost dreams. She mourned her grandmother's passing and the knowledge that she was alone on this earth—alone except for Lincoln. And his four brothers. And Amanda. And Anne and her programmers and Veronica and her influencers. And a whole potential town of friends.

Her tears came thick and fast as her sorrow began to shift to gratitude. She'd lost so much, but she'd gained so much more.

Through it all, Lincoln held her hand and now and then gently wiped the tears from her cheeks. "It's okay," he said again and again. "I'm right here."

She cried even more because of that. Lincoln was here—after everything.

He loved her.

"I'm always going to be here for you," Lincoln promised her, stroking her hair.

As she slipped into unconsciousness again, Charlotte vowed she'd always be there for him, too.

CHAPTER 13

"I STILL CAN'T believe it's gone," Lincoln said to Hudson as they paused their morning jog to stand in front of the bare foundation where their parents' home once stood. Three weeks had passed since Ivan had shot Charlotte. She was mending well, but bad dreams often woke her at night, so she often slept in. Lincoln was struggling to sleep as well, but staying in bed didn't seem to help, so they'd swapped habits. Now he was the one who went for a run or ride after their mornings together while she settled in for more shut-eye.

Nearly losing Charlotte had brought to the surface tough memories of his own—things he'd seen and experienced during his service he'd never sufficiently processed. He'd taken to joining Hudson on his morning jogs. The exercise settled his mind—and sometimes they even talked. It was almost like the old days.

"I keep waking up expecting it to be back somehow," Hudson confessed. "That house was as solid as they come. It was the basis for... everything."

Lincoln knew what he meant. All their best child-hood memories took place there.

"Charlotte's lawyer thinks we can get some money from Ivan's estate if we file a claim. I'm not sure, though. Sounds like he's implicated in at least one other arson. Who knows how many other people will go after his cash." He shrugged. "Even if we don't get much, we'll build it back, just as it was."

"Not exactly like it was," Hudson countered. Lincoln turned to him.

"What do you mean?"

"Mom's been sending me ideas. Improvements, she calls them. This is her chance to fix all the things that bothered her about the place over the years."

"That house was perfect," Lincoln said. He didn't want it to be different.

"Except for the lack of a dishwasher," Hudson pointed out.

"Well, yeah, that kind of sucked," Lincoln had to admit.

"And the washer and dryer being in the basement, so Mom had to lug all the laundry up and down the stairs."

Lincoln supposed that wasn't entirely practical.

"And the way the dining room was just a foot too narrow so the people on the far side of the table couldn't get out without everyone standing up."

"So Mom's designing new house plans?"

"Something like that. It'll be the same but better," Hudson said.

"That isn't going to be cheap," Lincoln said.

"No, it isn't."

Lincoln knew they'd make it work, though. Somehow. The fire had thrown another obstacle in their path, but that only served to make them all that much more determined to reach their goal. Even Gage wasn't talking about selling the town anymore. They'd known Warrington would come sniffing around trying to use the fire to his advantage, but Gage had taken the bull by the horns and gone to see him first, telling him in no uncertain terms to stay off their part of the Ridge.

Women, Hudson signed in their secret twin language.

Women, Lincoln agreed and turned to jog on.

Anticipation tugged at Lincoln when house number 37 came into view. Hudson, Nate and Gage had all chosen homes in Lucy's Corner to camp out in now that House number 1 was gone. They'd lost clothing and personal belongings in the fire and were each starting fresh, but they were used to traveling light, and none of them complained.

Lincoln was simply grateful all the people he loved were alive. Returning to Elliott Ridge for the first time in twelve years in April had been sweet. Returning to this house after Charlotte got out of the hospital was far sweeter. His service had taught him that life was fragile, but now each day seemed made of gossamer and thistledown. Something as permanent as his childhood home was gone—but something new had taken its place in his heart. Lincoln knew that from now on, wherever Charlotte was would be his real home.

Charlotte was still sleeping when he slipped inside the house, so Lincoln showered and drove to town, humming along with the radio. Rose Johnson, the sheriff's wife, had agreed to open her jewelry store early for him so he wouldn't be late to work. These days they were racing to catch up at the mill, but with the brand-new edger they'd purchased, their output had nearly doubled. Carter was busy finding more contracts and had taken over hiring the rest of the workers while Lincoln had been distracted by caring for Charlotte. Now she was on the mend, Lincoln worked as many hours as he could stand at the mill, knowing how important it was to keep morale high as they transitioned from the last of the temporary workers to permanent ones. The best news yet was that Megan had sold houses in Lucy's Corner to two of those new workers, and the proceeds would pay off the loan they'd taken out for the edger. Megan was pleased with the small commissions she'd earned and eager to sell more, so she was frequently on the Ridge. She visited Charlotte every time, bringing gossip from town and helping with chores around the house so that Charlotte didn't do too much.

Everyone was pitching in to make the community work, except Dennis, who seemed to have gone missing. Lincoln had gone looking for him several days after the shootout because he wanted to thank the caretaker for the loan of his pistol. Without it, he wasn't sure Charlotte would be alive.

"Haven't seen him since," Hudson said when Lincoln questioned his brothers about the man's whereabouts a few days after the fire.

"I think he's sulking," Gage said.

"About what?"

"He's not sulking; he's… examining his life choices," Nate said.

Lincoln had sighed impatiently. "You want to explain that?"

"When the shooting started, he saw Veronica's crew head for the lake and went after them. He tried to give Veronica one of those pistols of his—for their protection. They had no idea who Dennis was, of course," Nate said. "They figured he was one of the bad guys."

Lincoln could picture it.

"They ran off screaming," Nate went on. "Most of them dove straight into the lake and swam away. I guess Veronica ran back toward the shooting. What did Dennis expect? The man skulks around like he's a backwoods serial killer and then bursts out one day waving a gun at them? Of course they're going to freak out."

"Veronica saved my life," Lincoln said, "so I guess that means I should be doubly thankful for Dennis."

"The whole thing hurt his feelings," Nate said. "He's been gone ever since."

"He'll turn up sooner or later." Hudson had clapped Lincoln on the back. "Let's get to work."

Dennis still hadn't shown up, but Lincoln figured he would when the time was right. His thanks would have to wait until then. He'd caught Charlotte and Amanda leaving picnic baskets full of food and beer around the periphery of the settlement for Dennis and hoped the man understood how grateful they all were for his help. Meanwhile, he needed a ring.

He parked on the street and entered the little storefront. As Rose waited for him behind the counter, he threaded his way through the display cases to get to her.

"Lincoln Elliott, it's good to see you. Cab told me all about what happened on the Ridge. You've had some bad luck up there. I'm glad you're safe." She came to give him a hug. "Come and take a look at what I pulled out for you." She already had several trays of rings laid out on the counter.

"How the hell do I choose one?" Lincoln asked, taken aback by the array. He'd pictured a circle with a diamond on top, like a child's drawing, he realized now. He'd never paid much attention to women's jewelry before.

He pushed down memories of the last time he'd bought an engagement ring, when he'd slunk into the store with a pit in his stomach and asked to see the cheapest ring they had. He'd known he was doing the wrong thing back then.

This time was different. Proposing to Charlotte was absolutely right.

"Is she casual or sophisticated?" Rose asked.

"A little of both." Charlotte worked hard as a veterinarian and dressed the part, but she had a kind of natural grace.

"Ornate or clean lines?"

"Clean lines."

"Subtle or bold?"

"Bold." Charlotte knew what she wanted and what she believed in.

Rose picked out five rings and put the rest to the side. Relief filled Lincoln. He could see at a glance that any of them might suit, but one in particular drew his gaze, a bold swoop of five diamonds that increased in size.

"That one." He pointed to it.

"Couldn't have done better myself." Rose picked it up and held it a moment, shutting her eyes. "You're right; that's the one. You and your bride are going to be very happy."

Lincoln's chest swelled. He'd heard stories about Rose's predictions and the way they seemed to come true. In any case, he liked that he had her goodwill. "You think she'll say yes?"

"Of course she'll say yes." Rose gave an exasperated sigh. "How could anyone say no to a handsome man like you? It would be like saying no to the prince in a fairy tale."

"I don't know about that." But his heart warmed to think Rose thought of him in such a positive light.

She smiled at him and patted his hand. "Lincoln, you deserve happiness. I'm sure Charlotte does, too. I'll box this up for you. Bring it back to be sized when she's proved me right."

"Will do." Lincoln paid for the ring and tucked the little velvet box in his pocket. Back in his truck, he found himself humming along to the radio as he drove home. He had a feeling this was a new habit that would last now he'd found Charlotte. He was… happy.

The shower was running when he made it back to number 37. Lincoln was able to climb the stairs, pocket the ring and be ready to face Charlotte when she came out of the bathroom a minute later, one towel wrapped around her torso, another around her hair.

"Got a minute?" he asked.

"For you? Of course. You know I don't start work again until next week." She bent at the waist and gave her hair a final, vigorous rub with the towel.

"Good." Lincoln took the opportunity to drop to one knee. When Charlotte straightened, she gasped.

"Lincoln?" She clutched the towel to her chest.

"Charlotte—will you marry me?"

CHARLOTTE STARED AT the man kneeling in front of her, trying to comprehend what was happening. Lincoln was asking her to marry him?

And he had a ring and everything?

He held a little black-velvet box in his hand and was waiting for her to answer his question.

But she wasn't wearing anything. She wasn't ready for this. Wasn't she supposed to see it coming and get her hair and nails done and—

"Charlotte?" Lincoln prompted.

She nearly laughed at her own confusion. What did hair and nails and outfits matter at a time like this? Lincoln was on one knee. He had proposed to her. He was offering her everything—his heart, his love, his home. Well, *her* home, she supposed. But *his* town. Elliott Ridge and everything in it.

"I…" She couldn't seem to get the words out. She'd thought this might happen… hoped it might… someday. When she'd proved herself worthy of it. When she'd stopped making so many damn mistakes—

"Charlotte?" Lincoln scanned her face, alarm dawning over his handsome features.

"Yes!" She blurted out the word before she lost her chance, suddenly terrified he'd change his mind and take it all back. "Yes, I'll marry you."

He surged to his feet and caught her in his arms, and when he bent to kiss her, she went up on tiptoe to meet him.

"Thought you might say no for a minute," he admitted when they finally broke apart.

"I couldn't remember how to say anything!"

"You'll really marry me?" He picked her up and carried her to their bed, placing her on top of the covers carefully. She pulled him down on top of her.

"Of course I will. You're all I want in life."

"You're all I want, too."

"Forever." She cupped his face as he fit his body carefully to hers, avoiding any pressure on her hurt shoulder. "Promise me, Lincoln. We'll be together always."

"I promise." He bent to kiss her again. Charlotte let everything else slip away as the man she loved most in the world proved to her how much he loved her.

This was the man she'd always wanted to share her life with, a man who understood her vision for the future and matched it with his own. Lincoln was everything she'd hoped for, even during the years when she'd settled for so much less.

All her dreams were coming true. "Yes," she said again.

Lincoln laughed. "Yes, what?"

"Yes, I'll marry you. I'm going to say that every day of our lives, because I'm going to choose this every single day. I will never take this for granted, Lincoln."

"Neither will I." And he gathered her close again.

"ARE YOU SURE you've got it?" Charlotte said. She placed a screw to a predrilled guide hole and steadied the electric screwdriver.

"I've got it for now," Lincoln said as he held the cabinet they were installing in place against the laundry room wall. The thing was heavier than it looked, but he'd hold it in place as long as necessary. Charlotte was working as quickly as she could to screw in each fastener with the electric screwdriver, but she was a novice when it came to renovations, and this was taking some time.

It was the end of August, and Charlotte's shoulder had gotten steadily better. Lincoln's brothers had stepped in to relieve him of most of his hours at the mill the past few weeks so he could help take care of her and work on the house's renovation, but today they were both going back to work. They'd gotten up early to get this job done before they left.

With the floors refinished, the bathrooms and the bedrooms done, fresh tile laid in the laundry and a new washer and dryer installed, putting up the cabinets was that last job they needed to finish before they could tackle the kitchen renovation.

"There," she proclaimed. "You can let go."

"Are you sure all the screws are in tight?"

"Positive."

He tentatively let go and grunted his approval of her handiwork when the cabinet held. "Looks solid enough."

When she jumped down from the step stool she'd been perched on, Lincoln took her in his arms. "Of course it is. We did it together." She surveyed all they'd accomplished.

"Do you like the way the room turned out?" He kissed the side of her neck appreciatively. He liked working with Charlotte. She was calm and steady. Always read the directions and sorted the hardware before they started a project. He teased her for being so methodical, but he had to admit things went far more smoothly when she did.

"I love it. I've never been a fan of laundry, but I've never had my own beautiful laundry room to do it in." She ran a hand over the smooth countertop.

He gathered the rest of the tools as she screwed in the handles on the cabinet doors. When everything was tidied away, they took one last look at the room.

"We make a good team," Charlotte said, leaning

against him.

"You got that right." Soon they'd make it official. Their wedding was coming up fast, which meant they needed to start working on the kitchen right away. He wanted everything completed before they tied the knot. Somehow it was important that they start the rest of their life together in a real home.

His hands slid to her hips, and he bent to kiss her as she wrapped her arms around his neck. Every time she came to him willingly, Lincoln's heart melted a little. It was gratifying that she wanted to be with him as much as he wanted her.

When he lifted her on top of the countertop they'd built over the washer and dryer as a surface to fold their clothes on, she squeaked in surprise. "Don't break it."

"We're not going to break it. We built this thing to last." He leaned into her, and she wrapped her legs around his waist. Lincoln undid a button of her shirt and drew kisses over the rise of her breasts.

"We have to get to work," she reminded him.

"We will." He undid another button and nudged a bra strap off her shoulder. Kissing circles around her exposed breast, he teased her nipple until she moaned.

"Lincoln."

"We have all the time we need."

She laughed, low and throaty. "We can be fast, can't we?"

They'd discovered a hundred ways to be together in the past few weeks, taking it slow and luxuriously after her stay in the hospital, then fast and hard in the quick breaks they took between doing projects on the house once her shoulder had mended.

"We can be fast. If that's what you want."

He wasn't sure who moved first, but after a flurry of unbuttoning and shucking off extraneous clothing, Charlotte was naked in his arms, his jeans were pooled around his ankles, her legs were wrapped around him again and he was lifting her off the countertop and sliding into her, carrying her weight as they came together, each of them moaning with the heaven of it.

"Don't drop me," Charlotte said into his ear, clinging to him for dear life as he began to move with her, his hands firm on her bottom, lifting and cradling her.

"I won't drop you," he growled and caught her mouth with his own, showing her exactly how he felt as he plunged into her.

There were no more words after that—only Charlotte's cries and his own guttural sounds as he swiftly brought her over the edge. Her orgasm brought his, and he bucked against her, moving one hand to the countertop to keep them upright, cradling her with the other to keep from banging her against it.

Charlotte was laughing by the time they were done.

"What's so funny?" he demanded.

"You're amazing. You can do it anywhere, and you make me see stars every time."

"You sure you didn't bump your head?" He pretended to inspect it.

"Lincoln."

"You make me see stars, too." He set her on the

counter and kissed her all over so she knew he was serious. "I want this to be our life."

"Having sex in the laundry room?"

"Wanting each other like this. Working together. Laughing together. There's going to be times when it isn't easy. Life has ups and downs."

"I know." She kissed the corner of his mouth. "I'm willing to work hard for our marriage. I know it won't always be sunshine and roses, but we've got something worth fighting for."

"I agree." He wrapped his arms around her, loving the feel of her resting against his chest. "I will always fight for you."

"I'll always fight for us."

CHARLOTTE WAS STILL glowing from their morning bout of lovemaking when she arrived—five minutes late—again—for work at the clinic, where she and Craig met before morning rounds.

"Have you heard how Rally is doing?" Bella asked her.

Charlotte nodded. "He's doing great."

After Ivan's death, his solicitor had appointed a Saratoga local to supervise Gasparyn Stables while he searched for Ivan's closest living relative. Ivan didn't seem to have any family in the country, and it seemed likely that his property and horses would be sold and the proceeds distributed to his kin in Albania.

Meanwhile, the new supervisor turned out to be remarkably willing to update Charlotte about the horses she'd once tended. After Rally was shipped back to New York, she'd told him all about the horse's previous injury and the care he needed to regain his health. The supervisor assured her he'd follow her advice, which had relieved her of some of her worry.

"I wish I could open a home for racehorses past their prime," she said wistfully, thinking Rally could use a place like that someday.

Bella perked up. "That's an amazing idea!"

"Bella," her brother warned. "You have enough animals. What's Evan going to say?"

"He's going to ask what I need to make it happen, and then we'll get to work."

"She's right," Craig said ruefully when Bella wandered off to help a client who'd arrived with a rabbit in a cage. "That's exactly what he'll do. I hope you don't regret saying that out loud." When Charlotte laughed, he shook his head. "You don't know Bella. You're going to be running the Chance Creek Home for Retired Racehorses within the month. You'll see. You won't have time to work with me anymore."

"I'm not going to stop working with you. I like this job too much. If Bella does create a home for racehorses, I'll just stop by and spoil them all from time to time."

Craig kept grumbling, but Charlotte's heart was singing as they climbed into his truck and drove to their first appointment. She loved her work.

She loved her life.

Three months ago, she'd been sure her life was over,

but it turned out it had only just begun.

When her phone buzzed in her pocket, she pulled it out, thinking it would be a message from the clinic, adding an appointment to their already full day. Instead it was from Veronica.

Check it out, she wrote. There was a link.

Charlotte clicked it to find the influencers had created a virtual campaign to raise funds to rebuild house number 1, a "home of great historical significance in the Marryingest Town in the USA."

Charlotte laughed.

"What's so funny?" Craig asked.

"Veronica and her friends seem to think you can declare something to be true—and then it will magically become so."

"What are they manifesting?" His mouth quirked at her surprise. "What? You think a country bumpkin like me hasn't heard of manifesting?"

"I didn't think you'd believe in it, at the very least." She told him about the influencers' campaign.

"That's a great idea. I hope they manifest a lot of money for the Elliotts."

Charlotte spotted the "funds raised" part of the site and gasped.

"What now?" Craig asked, turning a corner but sending a worried glance her way.

"People have already pledged thirty thousand dollars!"

"How long have they been running that thing?"

She looked. "Five hours." Her voice sounded funny

to her ears, and her eyes filled with tears. "People are helping. People who don't even know the Elliotts."

"That's what people do when you let them."

It was true. When you surrounded yourself with the right people, they were there for you. Charlotte still couldn't believe her luck at finding a community like that just by landing at the Chance Creek airport.

"You okay?" Craig asked a few minutes later when Charlotte was still dabbing her eyes.

She nodded. "I'm crying because it's all so good."

CHAPTER 14

"**L**OGGING," LINCOLN SAID when his brothers arrived at the mill conference room and took their seats just before noon. He figured he didn't have to expand on his statement and knew he was right when Nate, Carter and Gage nodded. Hudson didn't respond.

"I went through those applications," Gage said. "Interviewed a bunch of people. I've got most of the positions filled for September."

Lincoln turned to Hudson. "What's it going to be? Are you going to work with the loggers or stay at the mill?"

For one split second Hudson's features twisted with pain, but a moment later, he'd mastered himself, his expression unreadable. "I'll stay at the mill."

"You want to tell us why?"

"No." Hudson folded his arms over his chest. Even though Lincoln tried to wait him out, he kept quiet.

"Guess it's up to you," Lincoln said to Gage.

At least the changeover from temporary mill workers to full-time ones was complete. Most of the new men had settled in the bunkhouse for now, a few had taken on rental houses and two were working through the escrow process to buy homes in the subdivision. Megan was working hard to persuade more of them to buy houses.

"I can help with the logging. Work is work, right?" Nate said.

There was a pause. They all knew Nate's heart wasn't in the mill or the logging operation, but he had never been a slacker.

"You've been busy in Grandpa's workshop in the evenings. Are you building something new?" Lincoln finally asked to break the silence.

"Yep. Don't bother asking me what, though. That's a surprise. Word on the street is there's a wedding coming up."

Lincoln suppressed a smile. "You don't say."

"Seems like we're finally getting somewhere," Carter said. "We've got contracts for the mill, we're getting the logging operation up and running, we're selling some houses. I heard from Sid today. He's making a full recovery. Soon he's going to be able to move on to his next position in North Dakota."

"That's good to hear. Even Veronica and Anne seem to be getting along better these days," Nate said.

"We'll see how long that lasts," Lincoln hedged, but Nate was right. Veronica had changed tactics. She and her crew had begun to produce content that promoted the game Anne's crew was coding, along with the programmers themselves. The programmers, meanwhile, must have been slipping beta versions of the game to the influencers, because lately there'd been posts showing the women in various haute couture outfits in locations he recognized from around the Ridge, playing the game on their phones with shrieks of excitement.

Since they were promoting Elliott Ridge along with Anne's game and their own endeavors, word was getting out about the place and Carter had told them he'd begun to field calls from people wanting to know if they could come check it out. As soon as the wedding was over, they were planning to host open houses during which people could tour the community, view the homes available for sale and speak with Lincoln and his brothers about job opportunities.

"Wouldn't be surprised if there were more weddings coming our way," Nate said. "Veronica and Cal seem pretty tight these days, and her friends and the programmers are inseparable."

"Anne would never allow her programmers to marry," Hudson said darkly. Lincoln knew he was frustrated that he'd made no progress with any of the women himself.

"That's not our problem," Carter said. "For once our problems seem under control."

"Don't get too complacent," Gage warned him. "There's a lot that could go wrong between now and next June."

"After all, it's a Calamity Year," Nate intoned.

Lincoln shook his head and stood up. "I'm pretty

sure it'll be smooth sailing from here on in."

"I'm not so sure," Carter said, standing as well. "We might have handled Ivan Gasparyn, but Blake Warrington is still sniffing around."

"At least he hasn't tried to kill anyone," Nate said.

"Yet," Gage said darkly. "Warrington's no saint."

"He's no outlaw, either," Lincoln said, refusing to let anyone rain on his parade. With Charlotte by his side, he could handle anything.

"A FEW MORE steps," Nate directed. "A couple more, keep going... there."

Charlotte stopped walking. Lincoln, following close behind, bumped into her but managed to keep his hands covering her eyes.

"What's the big surprise?" she asked, laughing. The men had corralled her near the town hall and insisted she see Nate's wedding present. Lincoln had already seen it because he'd helped carry it into their house.

"Three, two, one... ta-da!" Lincoln said and removed his hands from her eyes. Charlotte found herself standing in their renovated dining room area. In front of her was a beautiful long farm-style table and chair set that went perfectly with their new decor.

"Oh my goodness. It's beautiful," Charlotte exclaimed, taking it in. "You made this?" she asked Nate.

"That's right."

"I can't believe it. You're an artist." She ran a hand over the solid wood. It was built to last generations, and she could picture her future family seated around it.

They'd make so many happy memories here.

"I'm no artist," Nate said.

"Tell him," Charlotte prompted Lincoln.

"You are an artist. You should be doing this for a living."

Nate just shrugged and pulled out his phone. "There's no money in it. I have to get going."

"Thank you," Charlotte said. "I mean it, Nate—I love what you made for us."

He shrugged again and slipped away, uncomfortable with the praise, Charlotte thought.

She checked her phone, too. "Unfortunately I have to run as well. It's knitting club time. Sure you don't want to come?"

"I'm sure." Lincoln dropped a kiss on her nose. "See you later."

"Definitely." She touched the back of a chair. "This is really becoming a home," she said.

"Yes, it is."

Ten minutes later Charlotte was on her way to meet Amanda at the chapel when her phone rang. She was pleased to see Steven's name on the screen. She'd filled him in on everything that had happened when she'd come home from the hospital. While he'd been relieved to know Ivan couldn't come after her again, he'd been upset that the man had found her in the first place.

"Steven," Charlotte said when she answered the call. "How are you?"

"I'm great. I got your wedding invitation. Congratulations!"

"I understand it's probably too far for you to come."

"Are you kidding? Wouldn't miss it for the world. My wife and I will be proud to share your special day."

"It never would have happened if not for you," Charlotte said. "You're my guardian angel, you know that?"

"No one's ever called me that before," Steven said gruffly. She thought he was touched.

"It's true. I never would have gotten away from Ivan without your help, and if I hadn't come to Montana, I'd never have met the love of my life."

"You sound happy," Steven said.

"I am."

"Can't wait to see you walk down that aisle. By the way, check your bank account. I deposited your inheritance this morning. It should show up soon."

"Thank you." A twinge of pain cut through the joy she'd been feeling all day. She didn't want her grandmother's money; she wanted her grandmother to be here to share in her happiness.

"Your grandmother would be very proud of you, Charlotte, and she'd be thrilled to know you've found a worthy partner."

"I miss her."

"I know."

When she was finished with the call, Charlotte checked her bank account and found it had swelled significantly. Lincoln had been pitching in to pay for renovations to the house despite her protests, but she knew the Elliotts needed all the money they could get to pay their debts. Now she could help.

Amanda was waiting for her at the door to the chapel. "Want to see my decoy project?" Amanda asked.

"Decoy project?" They'd put up a sign on the bulletin board in the town hall foyer announcing knitting club was happening this evening. They'd decided to keep one night a week just for hanging out with Megan but to get together a second time with anyone else interested in knitting.

"I can't very well knit a baby sweater when you know any influencers who join us are going to take photographs." She pulled out skeins of blue yarn. "I'm going to make a scarf instead."

"Still no luck with getting pregnant?" Charlotte asked.

"Not yet," Amanda answered cheerfully. "Which means we get to keep trying."

"I guess that's true. Look! Veronica is coming," Charlotte said.

Charlotte had figured Sasha would join them, but she was a little surprised to see Veronica.

"Looks like she brought friends." A line of women came into view. To Charlotte's surprise, all the influencers were joining them.

"And there's Carolyn," Amanda said.

The older woman approached cheerfully, a large canvas bag over her shoulder.

"Can't get enough knitting time," she said in explanation. "I try to donate at least ten throw blankets to the hospital charity bazaar every year."

"That's a lot," Charlotte said.

Carolyn waved that off and kept going.

"Oops, I think Gareth is lost," Amanda said.

"Maybe he just wants to stay close to Sasha." It was no secret now those two were dating. "There's Mark, too. And Gregory." It looked like all the programmers were coming.

"There's Anne," Amanda said in awe. "And she doesn't even look angry."

"It looks like she has something with her." Charlotte turned to Amanda. "Do you think she's come to knit, too?"

"She seems a lot more relaxed now she doesn't have to drive her programmers into town every day to work." Their internet provider had finally upgraded service to the Ridge, and everyone was happier now they had a snappy connection to the online world.

"I think we'd better set up in the chapel," Amanda said. "We won't all fit in the rotunda."

"The rotunda is for women only, anyway," Charlotte said in an undertone. "We can save it for *our* nights."

"Sounds good."

Megan joined them a moment later. "You'll never guess who called me today."

"Gage?" Charlotte asked hopefully.

Megan shook her head. "Blake Warrington. He asked me out on a date. Can you believe that?"

"What did you say?" Amanda asked.

"I turned him down, of course. He just laughed and said he'll try again next week." Megan rolled her eyes. "How are all these people going to fit in the rotunda?"

Charlotte explained their new plan, and they got to work. Amanda greeted each person as they arrived, and Charlotte ushered them into the chapel. It turned out the pews weren't stuck in place, so she and Megan moved several to form a circle, shifting the podium to one side.

Charlotte hoped they weren't being sacrilegious, but she thought gathering to knit was close to a holy experience. Besides, there hadn't been a service here in years.

"Have you knitted before?" she asked Mark as he helped her shift a pew.

He shook his head. "Edie says it's like coding with yarn. Sounds easy enough."

Charlotte bit back a smile and went to transfer the refreshments she and Amanda had brought from the rotunda to the chapel. She set them up on a side table. The influencers had brought a variety of balls of yarn and knitting needles with them. They passed them out to the men and helped cast on stitches. Amanda walked among them, helping.

Charlotte took her seat and drew out her own project, a gossamer shawl with difficult directions. She let the murmur of voices swirl around her as she got to work. She'd always found knitting to be soothing, but now she considered it from Mark's point of view. She was coding a piece of clothing.

That was new.

"Have you found a wedding dress?" Sasha asked her, drawing near. She'd been photographing the proceedings until Amanda gently took her phone out of her hands and placed her knitting in them.

"I have. I'm going for my fitting tomorrow."

"Can I come? I'd love to see it!"

"I want to come!" Veronica said.

"Me, too," Edie said. All the other women chimed in, as well.

"I don't know if you'll all fit into the bridal shop!" She'd found her gown at Caitlyn Warren's store in town.

"We need photos. After all, this is the Marryingest Town in the USA. It's our brand," Veronica said. "We have to document everything about your wedding."

"How can it be the Marryingest Town when ours will be only the second wedding?" Charlotte protested.

"Fake it till you make it," Veronica said with a smile.

WHEN LINCOLN LET himself into house number 37 at the end of the day, he'd expected to find Charlotte waiting for him, ready to go to dinner. Instead the first floor was empty.

"Charlotte?" he called.

"Up here!"

He took the stairs to the second floor, but she wasn't in the bedroom changing.

"Charlotte?" he asked again.

"In here."

Her voice led him to the bathroom, where he found

the door partially open. Pushing it wider, he spotted Charlotte in the refinished claw-foot tub, surrounded by bubbles.

"Join me," she said. "I'm letting it all sink in."

"Letting what sink in?"

"Get in here and I'll tell you." She fluttered her eyelashes at him coyly.

Lincoln didn't waste time questioning this new, flirtatious fiancée he'd come home to. He stripped down and climbed into the tub with her, groaning in pleasure as the water eased his sore muscles.

They relaxed at opposite ends of the tub, their legs tangled together. Charlotte reached over the side and handed him a glass.

"Champagne? Are we celebrating?"

She shook her head. "Not celebrating. Honoring… my grandmother, Steven, you, your family…"

He took a sip and sputtered. "This isn't champagne."

"I didn't have any kicking around," she said with a laugh. "It's sparkling water, but at least it has bubbles. I'm doing my best."

He took another sip. It was flavored with some kind of berries and wasn't terrible… for sparkling water.

"I think you need to start at the beginning. What's going on?"

"Steven called today to say congratulations—and to let me know he'd deposited my inheritance in my bank account. It got me thinking about how much has changed in such a short time. I lost the last member of my family this year, but I've also gained a whole new family. I lost my job—and got a new, much better one. I gained the courage to leave a bad relationship—and now I'm marrying the man I love." She toasted him with her glass and took a sip. "So I'm letting it all sink in." She smiled at him. "I know what I'm going to do with my inheritance."

"Oh yeah? What?"

"Buy this house. For real. For exactly what it's worth." She put a hand up to stop him as he sat up, protests spilling from his lips. "You lured me in with a free house—an almost-free house. And it worked—here I am making a life on Elliott Ridge. This is my home now. But I'm going to lose it if your family can't pay its debts. You can't just give houses away."

Guilt swept over Lincoln that he hadn't been wholly truthful about selling the house for a dollar. It must have shown, because Charlotte sat up straight, too.

"What?" she demanded. "What aren't you telling me?"

"I already bought it," he admitted, unwilling to lie to the woman he was going to marry. He braced himself for her reaction.

"What do you mean?"

"I paid the market rate for this house to my family. I'm the one who sold it to you for a dollar."

"Lincoln Elliott!" A parade of emotions passed over her face. "You did that... for me? Before you even knew me?"

"I knew the minute I saw you that you were the one

for me," he said simply. "I can't explain it. It's supposed to be a family thing, actually. All the Elliott men know they've found the woman they're going to marry the minute they lay eyes on them. I always thought it was a cheesy story, but the day we met at the airport, I knew it was true."

"That's…" She trailed off. "I don't even know what to say."

"Say you love me as much as I love you."

"You know I do." Her expression clouded. "But I still want to help your family."

He shook his head. "You are helping, just by being here. You're showing people this is a community that's worth taking a chance on. You're bringing a valuable service to everyone in Chance Creek. Now you have a nest egg, so your life here is that much more secured."

"*We* have a nest egg," she corrected him. "We're either in this together or we aren't."

"We are definitely in this together." He leaned forward and kissed her, gathering her to his end of the tub so she rested in his arms. The water sloshed around and settled again.

"Do you have any more secrets I should know about?" Charlotte asked when they finally broke their kiss.

He was about to say no when he realized he did. "So… remember that day Amanda yelled at Hudson and you didn't know what was going on?" he began.

Charlotte nodded, tracing a hand over his shoulder and arm, distracting him. He struggled to keep his thoughts in line.

"My brothers and I have a secret language."

Charlotte stopped. "Secret language?"

"Secret sign language. And Hudson and I have one, too, that's just for us."

She closed her eyes. "Of course you do."

CHAPTER 15

"I'VE WAITED DECADES for one of my children to get married, and now this is the second wedding in a matter of months!" Lincoln's mother exclaimed. She straightened Lincoln's tie and brushed a fleck of dust off his shoulder. With the wreckage of house number 1 cleared away and the new foundation going in, they'd decided to hold the wedding in the backyard of number 37. They were using the bedrooms as a staging area to get ready for the ceremony.

"Well, this is the Marryingest Town in the USA," Lincoln said. Charlotte had told him about Veronica's designation and showed him some of the posts the influencers were making on that theme lately. There were lots of photos of the women in matching bridesmaids' dresses pretending to catch bouquets. Sometimes one of them wore a wedding gown with her back to the camera, coyly faded out in the distance as the rest of the women hammed it up in the foreground.

"That isn't even English. And it's not true, either," his mother protested.

"Seems like our resident publicity team is determined to make it true," Lincoln said.

"Has Carter said anything about Amanda?"

"Like what?"

"Like am I going to be a grandmother soon?" His mother stepped back and looked him over.

"I haven't heard anything."

She tutted. "Well, you can't say we didn't set you boys a good example."

"Mom."

"Are *you* going to have children?"

"I hope so." He and Charlotte had talked about it and decided to wait a year to give themselves time to settle into their relationship first. He wouldn't tell his mother that right this moment, though. No need to disappoint her before the wedding even took place. A year would pass swiftly with all the work they still needed to do. He hoped that before it was over, his parents would come home to Elliott Ridge themselves. "You heard the Davises are moving back to town, right? One of their grown kids is coming, too, and bringing the grandchildren." They'd lived on the Ridge right until the end, when the mill failed and everyone had to leave. Hudson had contacted them along with many of the other families who'd lived in town during its heyday, and they were the first to decide to return.

"I did hear that." His mother smiled happily. "They'll be a credit to the town, I'm sure."

A credit to the town. Lincoln hadn't heard that turn of phrase in years, and it brought back memories of how things used to be. How they'd all been so proud to belong to the Ridge.

He felt that way again.

"And I heard talk of a catering business," his mother added. "I poked my nose into the kitchen earlier. Cal Evers sure looks like he knows his way around a kitchen. He's preparing quite a feast for the reception."

"So far the catering idea is just talk, but I wouldn't be surprised if it turns into more," Lincoln said.

"I'll go find my seat. Your father wants a word with you." With one last hug and kiss, his mother slipped out of the room. A moment later his father came in. He was walking confidently, and Lincoln thought he looked better than he had in years. The first few weeks of rehab after his hip replacement had been difficult, but lately his father's progress had advanced by leaps and bounds.

"Heard you wanted a word with me," he said.

Lincoln laughed. His mother always worked hard to make sure the men in her family communicated with each other. "Well, what do you think?" he asked. "Will I do the family proud?" He held his hands wide and let his father get a look at him.

"You always do the family proud," his father said gruffly. "All you boys do."

Lincoln let his hands drop to his sides. His father had never said anything like that to him before. All his levity gone in a heartbeat, Lincoln cleared his throat. "That's not true. I know I caused our family to break up. I made us leave the Ridge. Now I—"

"*You* made us leave? I'd like to know how." His father stared at him in astonishment, and Lincoln stared back.

"I told you to buy that new equipment just before the market crashed. If you hadn't taken that loan, we wouldn't have gotten into the fix we did."

His father waved that all away. "That loan was just the tip of the iceberg of our problems, and you were a kid back then. You think I listened to you?"

"Didn't you?"

"I let you feel your oats," his father said. "I let you practice having an opinion. That's what I did." He studied Lincoln. "You blamed yourself all this time?"

"Of course I did." Lincoln studied him in return, feeling like he was seeing his father for the first time. "I took my job seriously, even if I was only twenty. I researched everything I could find about how to improve our mill. I wanted us to shine. Instead we crashed and burned."

"Because the economy tanked, the price of lumber fell, a bunch of banks made a bunch of loans to a bunch of people who couldn't pay them off. Handed out credit left and right and then tried to reel it all in when the tide turned. Sank themselves with their own greed and took us all down with them! The crash didn't have anything to do with you or me."

"I thought you blamed me all this time."

His father stilled, suddenly looking every year of his age. "If you did, then I'm the one who let you down." He studied Lincoln's face. "Carter said something like that at his wedding. He thought if he hadn't agreed to leave the Ridge and join the military, none of the rest of you would have gone. He thought he'd disappointed me—or worse. But he wasn't to blame for what happened, and neither are you. I was angry back then—at the world. At our competitors. Hell, at myself for judging conditions wrong. I was angry at you and your brothers for forcing me to confront the fact we had lost the battle. That doesn't mean…" His words trailed off. Lincoln understood he couldn't finish the sentence, but what he didn't say echoed between them. *That doesn't mean you weren't right.*

He found it hard to swallow suddenly and turned to the mirror, fussing with the tie his mother had just straightened.

His father laid a heavy hand on his shoulder. "You've done good. You and Carter have our mill churning out lumber at a solid pace."

"We're not back to how it was."

"Not yet, but you will be. I can see you lot are determined to make this work." His father squeezed his shoulder. "I'd better find your mother. Think you can make it to the altar on your own?"

Lincoln laughed, but the sound was shaky. "Yeah, I got this."

"I know you do."

"YOUR HOUSE TURNED out so well," Megan said as Amanda helped Charlotte with her veil. "It's all so pretty."

"I think so, too," Bella chimed in. She handed Charlotte a glass of water. "Remember to hydrate."

"Thank you. I can't believe it's finally done." It had been a scramble to complete the kitchen in time, and the stove had arrived only two days ago, but now it was installed, and the whole house shone brand-new.

"Even Admiral looks spiffy today," Megan went on. "He's a completely different horse from the first time I saw him."

"He's come a long way," Charlotte agreed.

"He's the town mascot," Amanda said. "Veronica and her friends are making him famous. Did you know he has his own social media account?"

"I follow it," Megan said with a smile.

"I think he likes Elliott Ridge," Charlotte said.

"What's not to like?" Megan looked around the bedroom, pausing when she noticed the little horse figurine on Charlotte's dresser. "That's so cute. Did you have it when you were a girl?"

"I found it here in the house, actually. The day I picked it out." She smiled at the memory. "It's kind of a talisman now, since Rally helped me escape from Ivan."

"What a coincidence," Amanda said, pinning the veil to Charlotte's hair. "I found a bear statuette in my house the day I picked it out—and if a bear hadn't startled my father when he tried to shoot me, I might not be here today."

"That's creepy," Megan said. "But I still wish I lived on Elliott Ridge. You two get to see each other all the time. There's always something going on up here. I follow Veronica and her friends online," she admitted.

"When I'm sitting alone in my house after work, there's post after post of everyone having fun."

"I know," Bella chimed in. "I'm jealous, too."

"That's not real," Charlotte told them. "I mean, it is lots of fun up here, but every minute isn't a party, the way those women make it out to be."

"But this is the Marryingest Town in the USA," Megan said wistfully.

"That's right," Bella said.

Amanda groaned. "If Veronica and the others keep posting that, we'll be overrun with single women."

"Isn't that what Carter wants?" Charlotte asked. "Lincoln told me they need women to lure in more men."

"I bet more will come," Bella said.

"They have to," Amanda said tartly. "That's part of the Calamity Year narrative, right? Women flocking to Elliott Ridge from all over the country, bringing problems and marrying the locals. At least, that's what Dennis says."

"Have you seen him lately?" Charlotte asked her. She hadn't seen him in weeks. Not since Ivan had shot her.

"No." Amanda shook her head. "It'll be a shame if he misses the wedding."

"Want me to go look for him?" Megan asked. "He knows *I'm* not trouble."

"Speaking of trouble, how are things between you and Gage?" Amanda asked.

"Okay, I guess. We're talking to each other, at least,

but he's still holding back. I confronted him once about why he hasn't asked me out again, and he told me he didn't want to jinx it."

"Jinx what?"

"He didn't clarify, but I think he meant all this. Bringing the Ridge back to life. Like, if he dated me, his family would lose the mill and the town. Guess he thinks I'm bad luck." When she looked at her hands, Charlotte's heart squeezed for her. Megan obviously cared the world for Gage. What was he playing at keeping her hanging like this?

"You're not bad luck," Amanda said. "If Gage is holding back, it's because he doesn't trust himself—not you. He didn't want to return to the Ridge in the first place. He's so scared of losing it again, he can't let himself enjoy being here."

"Maybe." Megan didn't seem convinced, though. Charlotte thought there was more to it than that, too. It seemed to her Gage was afraid to be happy. A lot of people thought if they reached for what they wanted, fate would step in and slap their hand away from the prize. They thought it was better not to love at all than love and lose, to turn an old adage on its head.

"He'd better watch out," Megan said. "Blake Warrington is being awfully persistent. He's sent me flowers twice and keeps asking me out. I keep turning him down." She sighed. "I'll find Dennis."

"Thanks. Dennis saved my life in a way," Charlotte said. "Lincoln told me he gave him the weapon he needed to protect me from Ivan. I want to thank him."

"I'll help you find him, Megan," Bella said, and they left. Charlotte faced Amanda.

"How do I look?"

"Stunning. I'm so glad you're marrying into the Elliott family. I never had such a good friend before."

"Me, neither."

"The two of us really are trouble, aren't we?"

"We *were* trouble. Now we're going to just be a couple of old, boring, married ladies."

There was a snort behind them, and they turned to find Dennis in the doorway. "You don't know the half of being old," he told them. He was dressed in a clean, pressed suit, leaving Charlotte so surprised she didn't know what to say.

Megan slipped back into the room after him, Bella on her heels. "I found Dennis right outside, lurking in the bushes," Megan said.

"I don't lurk," he said.

"You always lurk," Amanda said. "But that's okay. It suits you." A corner of her mouth twisted, and Charlotte had to bite her lip not to laugh.

When Dennis scowled at them both, Charlotte rushed to assuage his hurt feelings.

"Where have you been, Dennis? Where do you go when you disappear like that?"

"Been here the whole time." He shrugged.

"No, you haven't. I've been searching for you for a month!" she exclaimed.

"Not looking in the right places."

"That's why I'm asking where the right places are."

Dennis shrugged again. "Here and there. Where there's work needs doing."

Charlotte realized she wasn't going to get anywhere with this line of questioning. The picnic baskets she and Amanda had left for him always turned up empty several days later. She hoped he'd enjoyed the treats. "I'm so glad you reappeared," she said truthfully.

"Don't see why."

"Because I wanted to thank you!" She crossed the room and took his hands. Dennis eyed her suspiciously, but she didn't let go.

"Thank me?" Her gesture seemed to confuse the old man. "For what?"

"For saving my life."

"Humph. I didn't do anything."

"You gave Lincoln that pistol. If you hadn't, who knows how many people might be injured—or dead?" She leaned up on tiptoe and kissed his cheek. "Thank you, Dennis. I'll never forget what you did."

He grumbled but didn't pull away.

"Dennis walked me down the aisle," Amanda told her. "My father couldn't, since he was in jail—and I didn't want him there."

"I don't have anyone to walk me down the aisle, either," Charlotte said. "Dennis, would you do me the honor, too? Then I wouldn't have to walk alone."

He grumbled some more, but in the end, that's what they did. After Megan checked that all the guests and the men in the wedding party had assembled in the backyard for the ceremony, she, Bella and Amanda went down the stairs first, resplendent in their sage green bridesmaids' gowns, and positioned themselves near the back door. One by one, they exited down the steps and onto the lawn, making their way down the aisle between the rows of chairs.

Last, Dennis walked with Charlotte, lending her a surprisingly strong arm to lean on. It pained her to know none of her family were there to fill the seats on the bride's side of the aisle, but Steven was there with his wife, smiling broadly, and Veronica and her influencers and Anne and her programmers filled in the rest of the rows. They all cheered her on as she made her way past. Though there were unfamiliar faces on Lincoln's side there were many others familiar to her, and she couldn't stay melancholy long when she took in the joy and friendship reflected in their expressions. She was still new to Elliott Ridge and Chance Creek County, but she had already made a home here. She was surrounded by people who wished her well.

And the most important person in her life stood waiting at the end of the aisle, smiling.

Love shining in his eyes.

WHEN LINCOLN TOOK his place near the flower-covered archway that stood in for an altar and looked back at the crowd of friends and family gathered to celebrate this day with him, he felt like he was looking at their progress personified. Their numbers had swelled in the past few months. The twenty temporary mill workers had increased to thirty-five permanent ones.

Anne and her programmers and Veronica and her influencers made an island of fresh-faced city folk among the more weathered visages of the country people he'd grown up with.

"They're coming," Hudson warned him. He added with a gesture of his hand, *You've got this*, in their private language.

Lincoln watched Megan step carefully down the back steps from the house and approach the aisle between the rows of seats in her pretty sage green dress. She was followed by Bella and then Amanda, who smiled broadly at him as she approached.

But when Charlotte stepped out of the house, everyone else faded away. She was radiant in a gown fit for a princess. With its tailored bodice and floating layers of poufy fabric—tulle? his brain supplied from somewhere deep in the recesses of his memory—she seemed to float down the aisle toward him, her gaze never leaving his. He almost felt like he was drawing her toward him by the sheer magnetism of his desire. He would never get enough of this woman, he decided right then and there. He had to be the luckiest man in the world to have won a partner as smart and beautiful and kind and—

"Hits you right in the gut, doesn't it?" Carter murmured.

"Yeah." Lincoln told himself he'd spend his life creating a whole world for Charlotte. He'd build up the mill. Attract more settlers. Make every decision as carefully as he could.

And once in a while, he'd take a wild leap of faith, trusting that it would go this well again.

When Dennis placed her hand in his, it was all Lincoln could do not to kiss her on the spot.

"Dearly Beloved," Reverend Halpern began.

This is what happiness is, Lincoln thought. And they were just getting started.

CHARLOTTE WAS TREMBLING when she took Lincoln's hand and faced the reverend, but it was with pure joy, not fear.

She'd never dreamed a world like this one would invite her to be a part of it. She had a whole family now. Good friends. More acquaintances than she could shake a stick at.

A knitting club.

She wanted to laugh for the wonder of it all, but she kept her expression solemn, afraid that people wouldn't understand. Lincoln squeezed her fingers lightly, as if reading her thoughts. There would be plenty of time for laughter later. Among other things.

As she spoke her vows, all Charlotte could do was tell Lincoln with her eyes how happy she was to be saying them. She knew how hard he was working to build a community on Elliott Ridge—and knew he was doing it at least partly for her.

More couples would find their way to each other here in the future. She was sure of it, even without Dennis's premonition or the influencers' online campaign. This was a vibrant, growing place people would be drawn to. There were still hurdles to overcome, but there were so many people to help overcome them.

She glanced at Lincoln's brothers and saw her own determination to get it done echoed in their eyes. Stripped of their bantering and bickering, she saw them for who they were: men dedicated to repairing the community they loved.

They were good men, she thought, her throat tightening. And Amanda, Megan and Bella were good women, the kind she'd always wanted for friends.

She wasn't alone anymore. Would never need to be so again in the future if she didn't want to be. No one would treat her the way Ivan had. Not here.

She'd found love. Friendship. Work. Community.

And a man to share it all with.

"You may now kiss the bride," Reverend Halpern said.

Lincoln turned her to face him. Charlotte went up on her toes, her heart full to bursting as they kissed. The cheers of her new friends rang in her ears as she clung to Lincoln.

"Hello, Mrs. Elliott," Lincoln whispered in her ear.

"Hello, Mr. Elliott." Charlotte leaned against him, so happy in his arms.

She'd finally found her home.

And she meant to stay right here.

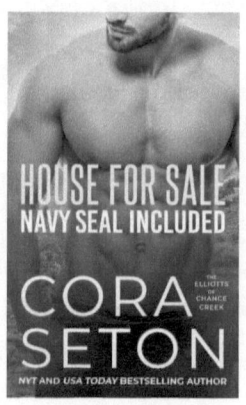

Read on for an excerpt of
House for Sale Navy SEAL Included.

Last Year

"YOU CAN'T SELL Elliott Ridge," Carter Elliott sputtered into his phone. "Dad—that's our home." He stood in the middle of his quarters at Naval Base Coronado, where his SEAL team was stationed. During the past twelve years, his missions had pushed him to his mental and physical limits, but the pain that lanced through him now was unlike anything he'd known before. His family had owned Elliott Ridge in Montana for generations. Carter still had nightmares about the day he'd left it. He'd sworn he'd get back there somehow. Planned to make things right so his whole family could return.

"Couldn't have been much of a home considering how fast you ran from it," his father countered gruffly. Carter's parents lived in South Carolina now, driven there by his father's ailments. His dad would be pacing their condo's small, modern living room, a caged tiger fretting against his constraints. "I seem to remember you cast the final vote to leave, but all five of you boys couldn't wait to get out of there. Now you're spread around the world playing superheroes. What do you care if I sell the Ridge?"

Guilt surged through Carter, and his fingers gripped his phone hard. "You know I cast that vote to save your life. I couldn't stay there and watch you kill yourself."

"You boys made a mountain out of a molehill."

"No, Dad. It was the other way around. You were trying to make a molehill out of a mountain. Trying to pretend the six of us could run a mill and logging business it took dozens of men to operate. I did what I had to do, just like my brothers. You're still alive, so it was worth it."

"Meanwhile you've spent the past twelve years trying to get *yourself* killed," his father said. "Doesn't matter what happens to the Ridge anyway. None of you are ever coming back."

"Like hell I'm not." Carter surprised himself with his vehemence, given that until this moment he'd had no immediate plans to leave the SEALs. He'd never figured out how to fix what he'd done. Didn't even know where to start when it came to reclaiming the little town where he'd grown up. Now it seemed like he'd run out of time.

He refused to believe that, though. Carter thought fast. This couldn't be the way things ended. The Ridge gone, his family scattered to the four winds. "Look, my current term of service expires next year. I haven't extended it yet. I can be back at the Ridge next April. You can wait that long, can't you?" He didn't give himself time to think over the implications of his words. He'd be turning his back on a career he'd invested his entire adult life in. Walking away—again.

"Why would you do something like that?"

"So I can bring the place back to what it should be." Wasn't that what his father wanted? It was what he wanted, career or no career. Elliotts belonged in Montana. They belonged at the Ridge.

"Can't be done," his father said. "The Ridge emptied out for a reason."

"Because the price of lumber crashed along with everything else. No one was building houses. Things are different now." This defeatist attitude wasn't like his dad at all. Had something happened he didn't know about? "Are you having heart problems again?"

"I'm fit as a fiddle."

Thank god. "Except that hip of yours," he pointed out to cover his relief.

"After the surgery it'll be good as new."

So why was he set on selling the Ridge now?

"Thing is." His father hesitated. "I got a good offer."

"For the property?" Carter's stomach knotted, and he sat down on the edge of his bed. He hadn't expected things had progressed that far. Who could afford to buy an entire town?

"That's right."

"You really want to sell, Dad?" He couldn't fathom it. Carter hadn't been back there since he left, but the Ridge still anchored his world. He knew every inch of the place.

Loved it.

There was a long silence. "No one said anything about *wanting* to sell."

Relief flooded Carter all over again. His father wasn't committed to selling yet, which meant this phone call was more of a fishing expedition than an announcement of his intentions. Well, Carter supposed he'd been hooked. Hell, now that he'd considered going home, he couldn't wait to be reeled in.

"Then let me give it a go."

"You won't get your brothers back to Montana."

"Yes, I will. Lincoln and Hudson miss the Ridge. Nate, too." They talked about it from time to time, swapping reminiscences when their mother roped them into family video chats.

"What about Gage?"

"Haven't talked to him lately." He neglected to say he rarely did. There were things between them that hadn't been right since they left Montana.

"He's a stubborn one."

"And you aren't?" Carter asked.

"Maybe I am. Maybe you are, too," his father said. "But stubborn won't pay our debts."

"How bad are they?" He turned and paced the other way. His father had upgraded the mill equipment right before the crash. If he hadn't, they might have been able to ride out the years where it was almost impossible to sell lumber.

"There's the monthly payment and then there's the balloon payment to close out the loan we got to buy all that equipment. The balloon payment is due two years from now." His father named the sums, and Carter whistled. He did some calculating in his head. It was June now, and it took time to separate from the Navy, but if he could get home to the Ridge by next April, that would give him just over a year to get the mill up and running and earn enough to make that large final payment. "If you can't pay off that loan, I'll have to sell," his father continued. "I just liquidated the last property we own in town. That'll cover the payments and taxes and so on until you get there next spring, but that's it. The rest is on you."

Carter swallowed. There it was: the bottom line. The real reason for this phone call. Without more town properties to sell, his dad couldn't hold on to the Ridge by himself. He needed Carter and his brothers to get the mill running again in order to keep up with the payments.

That meant Carter would have to scare up buyers for their lumber. He'd need sources for logs once they ran out of the surplus they'd left behind. He'd need to get their own logging operation up and running again. He'd need to find dozens of men to sign on and do the work. His mind ticked through the steps. This wasn't going to be easy.

"If I'm going to take this on, I want more than just your promise not to sell," he said, realizing he was giving up a secure career for a very risky proposition.

"Oh yeah? What else do you want?" his father challenged him.

"The day we pay off those debts, I want you to sign over the Ridge to the five of us. If I'm going to throw heart and soul into the place, I need to know I can stay there—for the rest of my life. There'll always be a place there for you and Mom, of course."

He waited for his father's answer. He'd never bargained with him before, man to man. When he'd left home, he was barely eighteen. The baby of the family.

"Deal," his father said. "The whole point of the Ridge is to pass it down. But no one gets a piece of it unless they help. You tell your brothers that. If they don't show up next spring and stay long enough to pay off that loan, don't bother showing up at all."

Carter heard the steel in his voice and knew his father meant it. He hadn't forgiven them for walking away last time, even if they'd done it to save his life.

He swallowed the words he wished he could say. The apology he could never seem to choke out. "Will do, Dad. What about that offer you got, though? You might not get another one if you pass it up. What if we fail?"

"That offer isn't going anywhere. I'll get your mother to write up something for you to sign. We'll make this official. Better call your brothers," his father said. "You've got your work cut out for you."

When he hung up, Carter lowered his phone and wondered what had just happened. Whose idea was it for him to leave the Navy and resurrect Elliott Ridge—his or his father's?

Somehow he wasn't sure anymore.

Carter decided it didn't matter. It was his vote that had shut down Elliott Ridge twelve years ago. It was his job to bring it back to life. It was the best kind of mission, after all. One that required strategic planning, careful consideration, tactical maneuvers and determination. For once, no one would be shooting at him while he worked, either.

Could he pull it off?

His father was right; it wouldn't be easy. He lifted his phone again. Called his brother Nate, the best listener of the bunch. He'd help figure out the best way to approach the others.

"Carter? What's up?"

Carter took a deep breath. "You ready to go home?"

This Year

"DAD? I'M HOME." Amanda Stakewell entered her ground-floor apartment, kicked off her high heels and breathed a sigh of relief. It was only nine o'clock in the evening, two full hours earlier than she'd told her father to expect her. She'd been prepared to find him parked in front of the television or fixing himself a snack, but although the lights were on throughout her apartment, the television was off and the visible rooms empty. Amanda locked the door behind her, hesitated, then checked to make sure the bolt had engaged.

Maybe he'd decided to do some painting. Usually, he did so only while she was at work. He'd told her the light was better during the day and he could paint for only an hour or two at a time, since his back gave him trouble. Strange to think of her father as old enough to have ailments like that.

He'd definitely changed in the eleven years he'd been away. His hair was streaked with gray now. He was thinner, too. Amanda remembered a man who'd loved a good dinner more than anything, but these days he picked at his meals and swallowed vitamins several times a day.

"Dad?" she called again. She switched off the lights in the kitchen and headed down the hall to where the bedrooms were tucked away. "I'm back early. Want to watch something?"

The night hadn't been a success. She'd joined the other women in her office to celebrate her boss's twentieth year with Biddington Foods, but all anyone wanted to talk about was the rising cost of living in Los Angeles. One of her coworkers, a smug sixty-year-old who owned a bungalow in Los Feliz, grilled her on how much she'd saved since she'd come to work five years ago. Amanda was proud she'd put anything aside, but Gwen had tsked at her. "You'll never even own a condo at that rate."

Didn't she know it.

Every year prices rose while her salary stayed pitiful-ly low, and Amanda had begun to feel a sense of rising panic every time she consulted a real estate website. When she'd first come to LA, she'd amused herself attending open houses in desirable neighborhoods, dreaming of the day when she'd take possession of her first home. In those fantasies she always had a hand-some husband—and a pregnancy bump. She wanted a family. A partner. She wanted to be making progress in her life.

Somehow she never seemed to get anywhere.

When Gwen switched to grilling her about her love life, Amanda decided she'd had enough. She'd said her good-nights and come home instead.

At least her father was here now, she told herself as she passed her bedroom, always neat with her bed made and decorative pillows in pretty array. He'd resurfaced in her life several months ago, swearing he wanted to start over and be the dad she'd always deserved. Ever since, she'd been putting him up on the sofa bed in the small "bonus" room she'd been using for her office. She braced herself to face the chaos she knew she'd meet when she got to his door. He had a habit of tossing covers and clothes on the floor, as if waiting for some-one else to come and clean up after him. Lately, Amanda had stopped doing so. He was a grown man, after all, and a guest stopped being a guest after they'd been living with you for months. When the mess bothered her too much, she simply closed the door.

Right now his door was open, giving a full view inside, and Amanda stopped short when she noticed his sofa bed was tidied away and the top of his tiny dresser was bare.

"Dad?"

His portable easel was disassembled, and several canvases were propped against the hide-a-bed. Her father's suitcases sat on the floor beside them. One was closed tight. The other lay open, full of clothing and the notebooks he was always filling with sketches and ideas. Amanda moved into the room. He was ready to leave, by the looks of things. There was his shaving kit and toiletries bag. There were all the clothes she'd washed and folded just yesterday.

There was—

What was that?

Amanda bent down to see. An unframed canvas was rolled up and tucked among his clothes in the open suitcase. As she drew it out, she could see it had been previously stretched on a frame but removed for transport, something well within her father's capabilities.

She gingerly picked it up, unrolled it and gasped.

Amanda knew that painting.

She'd seen it at the Warden Gallery only two weeks ago with her father. It was part of a traveling exhibit featuring famous works by Deloitte, but at the time, Amanda wouldn't have cared if it featured finger paintings by local kindergarteners. When she was viewing art with her father, she could pretend he'd never disappeared from her life at all. He was so engaged then, so talkative, his sly humor resurfacing, the way it had when she was a girl.

Afternoon in Sunshine and Shadow was one of many of Leonard Deloitte's paintings featured in the exhibition. A small canvas among larger, showier ones, it was considered one of his best. It had to be worth millions.

Why was it here in her father's luggage?

Amanda closed her eyes. She knew exactly why it was here. They'd been down this road before, and her entire family had paid for it dearly.

She replaced the canvas carefully before picking up the top sketchbook from the pile she'd moved.

Page after page of studies confirmed her suspicions. Her father had been planning this for months. Years, maybe. When had he found out this painting would be part of a traveling exhibit? How many museums had he visited along the way to study it as it moved across the continent from city to city?

More to the point—when had he decided to come back into her life? Before or after he decided to steal a masterpiece?

Pain spiked through her again. Amanda knew the answer to that question, too. Which meant every moment she'd savored with her father had been just another lie.

She thought again of their trip to the exhibit. Her father had excused himself at one point, needing to visit the men's room, and now that she thought about it, he'd been gone awhile, but that wasn't out of the ordinary.

She'd figured some other work of art had caught his attention on his way back to meet her. Her father could stand lost in contemplation of a painting for hours if no one was there to herd him onward.

Had he made the switch then?

No. That would be impossible. The place had been full of people.

Maybe he'd taken a page from his old partner, Buck Bronson, and found a connection who worked at the gallery. Maybe someone had met him at the back door after-hours, taken his forgery and switched it for the original when no one else was around. Her father could have gone back to fetch the real masterpiece any day when she was at work.

It didn't matter how he'd done it.

Afternoon in Sunshine and Shadow sat here in his bag, and her father was ready to run.

He was ready to leave her without saying goodbye.

Again.

Her throat ached with the betrayal she felt. How could she have been such a dupe? What kind of father used his daughter as cover when he was plotting a crime?

Where was he now? Was he meeting with some new criminal friends? Or a go-between who'd turn over the painting to a rich benefactor who wanted to build a private collection? Last time Buck had been the one with all the connections. Could her father really pull off a transaction like this all on his own?

Amanda texted him.

Dad? Where are you?

The answer came almost immediately. *Where are you?*

Home.

There was a long pause. Amanda stared at the tiny screen, willing him to offer her an explanation. Something that would stop the sting of shame that filled her, knowing he'd treat her like this, when she'd been so happy to welcome him back into her life.

Get out of there. Now!

Amanda wasn't sure what she'd expected him to say, but it wasn't this.

Why?

Buck's coming! Amanda, leave right now!

Buck? Amanda stood up fast. Buck Bronson knew where she lived?

Amanda told herself to get a grip. Why wouldn't he? Buck had served for years with the Dallas police, and his friends always seemed to have his back no matter what he did. He used to brag he knew cops all over the country. If he wanted her address, he could get it—even in LA. If he was out of jail already, he could be anywhere.

There was no time to ask for details. She grabbed the canvas, raced to her bedroom, wrapped it in a T-shirt and shoved it in her gym bag. She threw her purse over her shoulder and checked her phone again. More messages from her father.

GET OUT OF THERE! Now, Amanda!

Buck knows everything!

He's been tracking us!

He's on his way!

Did her father mean Buck knew he'd stolen a masterpiece? Was he coming to exact revenge for what happened last time?

He'd want the painting for himself.

Her heart pounding, Amanda turned to leave and heard a sound at her front door. Cold fear gripped her. Buck was already here. He was breaking into her apartment. She spun around, looking for another way out.

Her bedroom window was low and wide, already open to let in a spring breeze. She popped its screen, threw a leg up and over the sill, hopped outside and thrashed her way through the decorative bushes to reach the sidewalk. The concrete was cool under her bare feet in the gathering dark. The parking lot quiet.

Amanda ran.

Her footsteps sounded loud in the quiet of the night. Gravel sharp against the tender skin of her soles, she picked up speed.

Buck had been tracking them? For how long? How much did he know about her?

Did he know the make of her car? Her license plate number?

Had he hacked her phone?

Nearly stumbling, Amanda bobbled the small gadget she still held in her hand, caught it and threw it into a garbage can as she raced past.

When she finally reached her Toyota, she used the key to manually unlock it, not wanting to call attention to herself by pressing the button on her fob and activating the lights. She got in as quickly as possible, locked the door and started the engine. She kept her headlights off, hoping she could sneak past the building without Buck noticing her progress through a window.

She had a pair of runners in her gym bag. As soon as she was safely away, she'd pull over and put them on, but there wasn't time for that now.

She had to get out of here.

There was no sign of Buck as she drove past the entrance to the building. No sign of anything amiss at all. Amanda pressed the gas pedal and sped away. Was Buck rummaging through their things even now? Did he know she'd taken the painting with her?

She should have left it behind. Should have never let her dad back into her life in the first place.

Should have known he hadn't come back to make amends.

By now he'd be long gone. Ian Stakewell wasn't the kind of man who stuck around when things got hard.

She needed to disappear, too.

Buck Bronson was a killer. He hated her family. She'd been safe while he was in prison, but now she needed to get out of town, fast.

After she returned the painting.

Amanda slowed for a moment, then pressed the accelerator again.

She wasn't like her father. She had a moral compass. There was no way she was allowing this beautiful piece of art to fall into the wrong hands. Besides, if she returned it, her father wouldn't be a criminal anymore. No harm, no foul. He could disappear again, and Buck would lose interest.

She would have her life back.

Such as it was.

Amanda shook the wayward thought from her head, pulled into the parking lot of the Warden Gallery, slowed to a stop and realized she hadn't thought this through. It was well past closing time, and no doubt the gallery was wired with alarms. Cameras were probably recording her right now. She couldn't just march up the steps and leave a masterpiece outside the door to be discovered in the morning.

In fact, she couldn't return it herself at any time. There'd be too many questions she didn't want to answer.

She couldn't afford to wait for daylight, either. If Buck was tracking her, she had to make use of her head start.

All her bravado gone, Amanda started the car again, gripping the steering wheel tightly as she accelerated out of the parking lot. She swung onto Highway 15 and headed toward Las Vegas, as good a town as any from which to disappear.

She'd have to ditch her car. Pay cash for a flight out of town. Find somewhere to hide.

Who did you call for help when you couldn't call the police?

Maybe no one, Amanda thought. She was on her own.

But she had her credit card. She could go anywhere. As long as it wasn't home.

End of Excerpt

The Elliotts of Chance Creek Series:

House for Sale Navy SEAL Included
House for Sale Soldier Included
House for Sale Airman Included
House for Sale Marine Included
House for Sale Ranger Included

The Cowboys of Chance Creek Series:

The Cowboy Inherits a Bride (Volume 0)
The Cowboy's E-Mail Order Bride (Volume 1)
The Cowboy Wins a Bride (Volume 2)
The Cowboy Imports a Bride (Volume 3)
The Cowgirl Ropes a Billionaire (Volume 4)
The Sheriff Catches a Bride (Volume 5)
The Cowboy Lassos a Bride (Volume 6)
The Cowboy Rescues a Bride (Volume 7)
The Cowboy Earns a Bride (Volume 8)
The Cowboy's Christmas Bride (Volume 9)

The Heroes of Chance Creek Series:

The Navy SEAL's E-Mail Order Bride (Volume 1)
The Soldier's E-Mail Order Bride (Volume 2)
The Marine's E-Mail Order Bride (Volume 3)
The Navy SEAL's Christmas Bride (Volume 4)
The Airman's E-Mail Order Bride (Volume 5)
The Navy SEAL's Second Chance Bride
(Volume 6)

The SEALs of Chance Creek Series:

A SEAL's Oath

A SEAL's Vow

A SEAL's Pledge

A SEAL's Consent

A SEAL's Purpose

A SEAL's Resolve

A SEAL's Devotion

A SEAL's Desire

A SEAL's Struggle

A SEAL's Triumph

The Brides of Chance Creek Series:

Issued to the Bride One Navy SEAL
Issued to the Bride One Airman
Issued to the Bride One Sniper
Issued to the Bride One Marine

Issued to the Bride One Soldier

Issued to the Bride One Sergeant for Christmas

The Turners v. Coopers Series:

The Cowboy's Secret Bride (Volume 1)

The Cowboy's Outlaw Bride (Volume 2)

The Cowboy's Hidden Bride (Volume 3)

The Cowboy's Stolen Bride (Volume 4)

The Cowboy's Forbidden Bride (Volume 5)

About the Author

With over one-and-a-half million books sold, NYT and USA Today bestselling author Cora Seton has created a world readers love in Chance Creek, Montana. She has over forty novels and novellas currently set in her fictional town, with many more in the works. Like her characters, Cora loves cowboys, military heroes, country life, gardening, jogging, binge-watching Jane Austen movies, keeping up with the latest technology and indulging in old-fashioned pursuits. She lives on beautiful Vancouver Island with her husband and cat. Visit **www.coraseton.com** to read about new releases, contests and other cool events!

Facebook:

facebook.com/coraseton

www.ingramcontent.com/pod-product-compliance
Lightning Source LLC
Chambersburg PA
CBHW060242030726
47493CB00025B/1547